KILLER
STORY

ALSO BY MATT WITTEN

The Necklace

The Jacob Burns Mystery Series
The Killing Bee
Strange Bedfellows
Grand Delusion
Breakfast at Madeline's

KILLER STORY

MATT WITTEN

OCEANVIEW (((PUBLISHING
SARASOTA, FLORIDA

ISBN 978-1-60809-524-7

Published in the United States of America by Oceanview Publishing

Sarasota, Florida

www.oceanviewpub.com

10 9 8 7 6 5 4 3 2 1

PRINTED IN THE UNITED STATES OF AMERICA

For journalists everywhere

KILLER
STORY

PROLOGUE

I LIKE TO *think of you the way you were the summer night we first met, before you became the most loved and hated teenage girl in America. Long before the Murder of the Century changed both our lives forever.*

Your mom didn't want you taking an Uber, so I picked you up at the airport with my "Olivia Anderson" sign. Your big blue eyes lit up when you saw me. You were pudgy then, and so earnest! In the vertical lines creasing your forehead whenever you asked a question, in the slight quavering at the end of your sentences, I always felt you were searching for something, some truth just out of your reach. As if life confused you.

Of course it did—you were fourteen!

We put your purple suitcases plastered with Taylor Swift stickers in the back of the UCLA van, and I drove you to campus. I asked, "So what would you like to work on at journalism boot camp?"

You answered, "I want to write an article about what to do when you find a wounded bird or animal."

When I think of you, that's the girl I remember.

Before you changed.

I was a college senior then, majoring in journalism and working as a camp counselor to pay the bills. I tried to treat all the kids the same, but let's face it, you were my favorite. During morning workshops, you would sit in the front row with those wide open eyes tracking my every move. After class, you'd follow me to the cafeteria like a puppy, asking heartfelt questions along the way.

Then came that day in mid-August. We were walking from the cafeteria back to class. "Whether you write for the Washington Post *or your high school newspaper," I was saying, "you're an ambassador for the truth. It's a sacred duty."*

As we cut through the sculpture garden, you gazed up at me and asked, "So what kind of like, career, does a journalist have?"

I couldn't help smiling at how serious you looked. "Well, I'm only twenty-one. I don't really know yet."

Then I gave you a longer answer. "Most people start at a small-town paper for a year or two. Then you go to a bigger city, and hopefully one day you go on to a major market. My dream is to be an investigative crime reporter for the New York Times."

You clapped your hand to your mouth. "Oh my God, Petra, I can totally see you on CNN."

I smiled again. "Me too." As we walked up the steps to the classroom building, I launched into The Talk. "Of course, most reporters never make it to the Times. *The business is crazy now, with so many newspapers laying people off." I always felt it was my responsibility to warn campers about the obstacles they'd face. It was a fine line, because I didn't want to discourage you guys too much either.*

With you, I didn't have to worry. You said, "Basically, I want to do good in the world, and also be famous."

I laughed. Your eyes grew round with embarrassment. "Did that sound dumb?"

"No, it's perfect. It's what we all want."

You brightened up, and then your phone rang. "I should get that. It's my stepdad," you said apologetically. You had told me about him;

he was the consul general from Sweden. Into the phone you said, "Hi, Dad."

I was about to head inside, but then you said, "Is she okay?"

You started taking quick, shallow breaths. By the time you got off the phone, your whole body was shaking. I took you in my arms and held you, your tears landing on my shoulders.

You could barely get words out, but I finally understood that your mom had been walking across the street and a hit-and-run driver crashed into her. I got the van and took you to the airport so you could catch a red-eye back to Boston. You made it to the hospital just in time to see your mom die.

I understood all too well how you felt.

One morning ten years before, when I was eight, I had begged my Tata—my father—to take me to MacArthur Park, down the street. He finally gave in. Just as we came to the domino tables and the hopscotch area, a man whose face I couldn't see rode by in a black car and put a gun out the window. He must have been on drugs, and he started shooting all around. One bullet hit Tata in the heart.

The police didn't work that hard to find the killer. At least that's how it seemed to me and Mama. They said random killings like this, "thrill killings," were hard to solve. And with us not having a lot of money and living in East LA, they didn't feel like they had to make a big deal out of it.

The day of your mom's funeral, I told you about Tata on the phone, and how I wrote a Letter to the Editor of the Los Angeles Times *two weeks after he was killed. I got the idea because Tata used to write for a newspaper back in Sarajevo, and in LA we would sit at the table reading the paper together, talking about the stories and the five "W" questions and making up funny headlines. They published my letter and it got a lot of publicity, this eight-year-old kid writing about her dad's murder, so the police started coming around again. They questioned everybody in the neighborhood. They even arrested some drug dealers to get them to talk.*

In the end, they didn't catch my Tata's killer. But I never forgot how people all over the city read my Letter to the Editor, and it changed how the police acted. That's when I decided to become a newspaper reporter.

After we talked, you wrote a Letter to the Editor of the Boston Globe *asking any witnesses to please come forward. But the police never found your mom's killer either. We began texting each other just about every night, all the way through high school graduation. Sometimes I felt like your big sister, other times like your mom. When you got accepted to Harvard, I was the first person you called.*

September of your freshman year was an exciting time for both of us. I had just started a new job as a reporter in Oxford, Mississippi, and I'd met the guy who I was pretty sure was the love of my life. His name was Jonah, and he was a cute, curly haired guy with a grant from the National Science Foundation who was doing his post-doc at UMiss. He enjoyed hearing me talk about my work, and he was by far the best dancer of any computer nerd I'd ever met. On Saturday night of Labor Day weekend, we were in bed together after a perfect jambalaya dinner he'd made and some even more perfect sex. I was about to fall asleep when I picked up my phone and saw a group email you'd sent out promoting "my first YouTube video ever! Check it out!"

I was surprised. You'd never told me you were making a video. I put in my earbuds, clicked on the "Greetings from Hahvahd University" link—and there you were. As the video loaded and the little wheel went round and round, I saw the still shot of you perched on the edge of your dorm room bed, next to a blue ceramic lamp. There was a window behind you with ivy-covered brick buildings in the background. It was so great to see you at your dream school. God, you looked so mature! Kind of tough looking, with an attitude in the set of your jaw. You were eighteen now, a young woman. One look at your red scoop-neck top was enough to tell me you weren't that pudgy kid from boot camp anymore.

The wheel quit spinning. Your eyes hardened, showing a look I'd never seen from you before. Then you spoke.

"Hi, my name's Olivia—and no, not stripping for you. Sorry, guys, get your webgasms elsewhere. This is my very first missive from inside the hallowed halls of Hah-vahd, and let me tell you: this place is a fucking cesspool of professors puking forth nonstop crap about white people destroying the world. And the students! Call somebody a him or a her instead of a them, and it's like you drowned their kitten. Tell people you're a Christian, and fuck, you're worse than a serial killer!"

I watched the next six minutes of your video, hoping it would all turn out to be some bizarre joke. But it got worse. When you started in about how we needed to "protect America forever" because "illegals are invading our country and committing thousands of unsolved crimes," I stabbed the stop button.

What the hell?!

In all your midnight texts, you never expressed any views like these.

You knew I was an immigrant: I came here from Sarajevo with my parents when I was three, escaping civil war. I tried to figure out what to say to you. Finally I texted, Just saw your video. I had no idea you felt this way about immigrants.

You texted right back, I don't mean you, Petra, just the illegals! :)

Great, so reassuring. I slipped out of bed so I wouldn't wake up Jonah, poured a glass of wine, and composed the longest text I ever sent. I told you I had been an "illegal" too, and I still remembered sitting in the back of a police car with Mama crying and Tata trying to comfort her. Luckily, instead of getting deported, we were granted asylum.

You sent back a one-sentence text: I'M SORRY, PETRA, I KNEW WE'D DISAGREE ABOUT THIS 😃 😃

I texted, WHEN DID YOU START FEELING THIS WAY?

You texted back, I'VE BEEN DOING A LOT OF READING AND THINKING. THERE'S SO MANY THINGS THE MAINSTREAM MEDIA DOESN'T TELL YOU

Mainstream media? I texted I THOUGHT YOU WANTED TO BE A PART OF THAT!

DON'T BE MAD AT ME, PETRA! I LOVE YOU! ♥ ♥ ♥ ♥ ♥

Then it got worse. As the months passed, you put out new videos where you attacked not just immigrants but "radical feminists," "gay activists," and "baby killing atheists" that "want to destroy our way of life."

I was bewildered. How did you suddenly morph into this wild extremist? Or were you always this full of hate, and somehow I didn't see it?

I sent you more texts. You took longer to respond, and your texts grew more distant. Meanwhile your videos caught fire. On Insta you announced you'd reached ten thousand viewers . . . thirty thousand . . . eighty thousand . . .

Then, in January, came the worst video of all, titled "Who Raped Who?" I forced myself to watch because all my co-workers at the Oxford Eagle *were talking about it.*

You sat on the edge of your bed as usual, wearing a pink camisole cut even lower than the shirt you wore for your first video. The big ceramic lamp still sat next to your bed, but your lighting was less harsh now, more professional looking.

"Hey, everybody!" you said. "Major shout-out to all the three hundred thousand people *watching my videos. Thank you so much!" You toasted us with a bottle of Budweiser. "But don't send me a fucking dick pic, okay? Your dicks are fucking gross."*

I thought that was pretty funny. But then you put the beer down and got serious. "If you spent any time at all online this week, you know

that Harvard football stud Danny Madsen, the kind of guy feminists and cancel culture Nazis love to hate, has been accused of horrible shit. Rape. Well, here's the deal: my boyfriend Brandon and I hang out with Danny. That's Danny on the left."

You held up a photo of you with the two guys. Brandon had his arm around you. Handsome, a football player too judging by his thick neck, but with dark sensitive eyes. I instinctively liked him. His other arm was around Danny, a big guy with ears that stuck out and a buzz cut. I stared at his wide face, imagining him as a predator.

You said, "I love Danny. He's a sweetheart. And now some pathetic freshman girl tells lies, ruining his life—and she gets to stay anonymous." You gave an angry laugh, then your face grew hard. "But not anymore. 'Cause I'm gonna tell you her name: Sarah Fain. And nobody raped her. She's a slut. Pro tip: she has a tattoo on her right ass cheek that says 'Fuck 'em' and a tattoo on her left ass cheek that says 'Fuck me.'"

I felt sick. How could you do this to a girl that your friend probably raped?

I hit STOP, *and I gave up on watching your videos. I quit texting you. I didn't know what I could say that would be remotely polite.*

Basically I abandoned you.

I kept reading about you, though. When your viewership made it into the millions, the "lamestream media" noticed. You got a new nickname, "Olive Oil." You said immigrants were "riddled with dangerous contagious diseases," and it trended on Twitter for three days. My liberal friends despised you, but you became a darling to the alt-right and their allies all over the country. I remembered you saying, "I want to do good in the world, and also be famous." Well, one out of two, I thought.

But I wondered where the girl I'd known had gone. I wondered if I would ever get to meet her again.

Then, one morning in April as I was walking toward a coffee shop before work, I checked my phone. There was a headline: "YouTube Celeb Murdered."

Underneath it was a picture of you.

I walked headfirst into the door of the coffee shop and fell down. I sat there on the sidewalk unable to move as the world swirled all around me.

Livvy, you were so young. Just a kid. With so much time ahead of you to find your true path.

I felt so guilty. I was the big sister you had confided in for years. Then suddenly you were a college freshman. God knows that's a bewildering time. Instead of arguing and turning away, I should have tried harder to find out what was really going on in your life.

Maybe if I'd listened to you better, I would have learned what kind of trouble you were in and helped you get out of it. Before you ended up dead.

But I did nothing. So now you were gone forever.

I had no idea that one day I would do everything I could to solve your murder, and it would make me just as famous—and infamous— as you were.

PART ONE
THE STORY OF A LIFETIME

CHAPTER ONE

TWO YEARS LATER, I was sitting in my white-walled cubicle at the *Boston Clarion* when I got a text from Dave Rollins, my managing editor. CAN I SEE YOU FOR A SEC, it read.

I smiled. Dave must want to congratulate me in person for my story on last night's City Council meeting. It already had twelve hundred hits, no doubt thanks to my headline: "*Tempers and Candles Flare at City Council.*" In truth, the meeting had been about as exciting as your average OkCupid date. But an elderly gray-haired lady from Southie lit a candle to dramatize her complaint about how there weren't enough streetlights, and I jazzed that up.

BE RIGHT IN, I texted back.

And then I thought, *I should give Dave my pitch. Now!*

I was doing well at the *Clarion*. Dave liked me. I finally had some professional stability, thank God.

If he said yes, I would get a chance to do the biggest story of my life. The story I'd been wanting to do ever since Livvy died.

* * *

The past two years had not been easy. First the *Oxford Eagle* laid me off, along with three other young writers. Last hired, first fired.

So I found a job at the *Bozeman Daily Chronicle* in Montana. That's where I was when Livvy was killed. But then they laid off five writers, including me.

I landed a job at an internet news startup in Seattle with big dreams. I thought they were really onto something. They folded a few months later.

I got back on the merry-go-round. I wasn't the young star fresh out of UCLA anymore, and the job market had gotten even worse, so it wasn't easy to find a new gig. In college I had done some cool investigative journalism, but recently I'd been covering local news, from zoning board meetings to cats getting stuck in trees. I'd never gotten a shot at any of the stories I craved—the big, impactful crime stories. So my clips were good, but not brilliant. Not "undeniable," to use the jargon. I sent out application after application, hundreds of them, and the months piled up.

Like I'd done after college, I wrote freelance for internet sites— pieces like "*Is Swiping Left Swiping Your Soul?*" and "*21 Reasons to Buy New Underwear.*" It was fun, but the pay was virtually nothing. So I worked at Starbucks, making coffee for successful young women who paid while looking at their phones and barely noticed me. Mama wanted me to go back to school and become a teacher. "You need a job where you're *siguran*," she kept telling me. *Secure.* I started stress-eating pastries and my weight shot back up.

Sometimes I thought Mama was right. Even before this most recent run of bad luck, my life had been way too full of news week-lies that folded and internet gigs where they never got around to paying me.

The only good news in all my job disasters was that Jonah stuck with me, from Oxford to Bozeman to Seattle. His grant from the National Science Foundation enabled him to work from anywhere.

"All I need is my laptop," he would say, fluttering his arms like wings. "I can go where the wind blows." Then, when his grant ran out, he got a job at a cybersecurity startup in Seattle.

But our constant moves started to frustrate him, and he began making noises about settling down somewhere and putting down roots. When he turned thirty, he hinted that he felt ready for kids. We jokingly invented names for them: Jedediah for a boy, Jededette for a girl. I so wanted to have kids with Jonah. He would be the world's sweetest dad! But I wanted to establish my career first.

I was afraid that Jonah would decide being with a journalist was just too much chaos, and if I had to move again, he wouldn't come with me.

But I stubbornly stuck to my dream. When I woke up at three in the morning, panicked about our relationship and ever finding a newspaper job again, I imagined the stories I would write one day. Inevitably my mind would turn to one thing.

Livvy's murder. After two years, her killer still hadn't been brought to justice.

I would get out of bed, turn on my computer, and study the stories about the police investigation. I watched Livvy's final video over and over, the one she was making the night she died. I kept thinking there might be a clue there that the police had missed.

I had first seen Livvy's video the week after her death, when CNN got a copy. The video showed Livvy barefoot in tight jeans, wearing a purple T-shirt with gold letters that read, "I Don't Give a Fuck." On TV the final word was blurred out.

On her bedside table was the big ceramic lamp. Next to it sat a metal nail file with a sharp pointed end. This nail file had a mystery attached: when the police arrived at Livvy's room the next day, it had somehow disappeared.

Livvy began her video with: "Holy shit. Tomorrow is spring break already, can you believe it? And another thing I can't believe: I just hit five million viewers."

She gave a loud squeak on a kazoo. Then she said, "But the weirdest thing is, all you guys are watching... and tonight's video is gonna be like, super fucking personal. There's something that's really messing me up."

She blinked, like she was holding back tears. I had never seen Livvy be vulnerable in any of her videos before. "I don't know how to tell you guys this—"

There was the sound of somebody knocking on her door. Livvy said, "Fuck." She stood up and for some reason pulled up the window shade, even though it was night. Did she want people to be able to see into the room, because she had a premonition of danger? But then why did she turn her camera off, which is what she did next?

I didn't know. Because that "Fuck" was the last word Livvy would ever say to anyone—except her killer.

The next day, the janitor noticed her door was slightly ajar even though it was spring break and she had presumably gone home. So he entered the room. Livvy lay on her bed, legs splayed, blood pooling from a crack in her skull.

At first, most people believed Livvy's murder was a political act. The only disagreement was the details: Fox News speculated some angry, deranged liberal went over the edge, while MSNBC surmised the killer was one of the crazy alt-righters and white supremacist types that Livvy consorted with.

The other prime suspect was Livvy's boyfriend, Brandon, a freshman linebacker reputed to be the best football player to attend Harvard in decades. As the old saying goes, "It's always the boyfriend." And the murder did seem like a crime of passion. Livvy had been smashed in the head, so hard her skull cracked, by one blow from the heavy ceramic base of her bedside lamp. Not exactly a carefully planned act.

Personally, my money was on Danny, the alleged rapist. I didn't know what his motive would be, but he was the one guy in Livvy's life who had demonstrated a violent streak.

But then the Cambridge homicide detectives learned about Livvy's secret affair with a Harvard sociology professor named William Reynolds. Reynolds was thirty, a rising academic star who had published two widely acclaimed books about people creating new identities on the internet. He and Livvy were an odd couple, not only because of the age difference, but also because his politics were pretty far left.

The evidence against Reynolds quickly mounted. Livvy's blood spotted his brown leather jacket. His fingerprints matched the prints on the murder weapon, the ceramic lamp. There was also a fraught email exchange between him and Livvy from seven a.m. on the day of the murder.

Livvy: *"You were such a dick last night!"*

Reynolds: *"What do you expect? You stood me up again."*

Livvy: *"We can't keep seeing each other. It's fucking insane."*

On the night she was killed, Livvy began recording her video at 10:58. At 10:59 somebody knocked on her door, presumably her killer. Most of the other students had already left for spring break, and no one heard any screaming fights or saw anything through Livvy's window. But Reynolds admitted he went to her room that night—though he claimed it wasn't until eleven thirty.

The police questioned him, before he got smart and asked for a lawyer. The entire country eventually got to see the interrogation video during the nationally televised trial. It showed Reynolds, looking every bit the Harvard professor with his high forehead and navy-blue chamois shirt from L.L. Bean, sitting across from Hope

O'Keefe, a thin-lipped, short-haired homicide detective in her mid-fifties.

"Olivia and I talked on the phone the morning before she was killed, and we made up," Reynolds said, his eyes appealing for sympathy. But Detective O'Keefe just sat watching him like he was a lab animal. He squirmed in his plastic chair. "I knew it was reckless, being a professor and going to her dorm room. But I'd had a couple drinks. The dorm would be mostly empty, and she was going away for a week, so I thought it would be romantic to surprise her."

Basically he was drunk and horny. And, I believed, so angry at Livvy for breaking up with him that he stormed into her room and ended up killing her.

In the video, he claimed Livvy's door was unlocked. So he went in—and found her body. He felt her neck to see if she was still alive, which was how her blood got on his jacket.

"How'd your fingerprints get on the murder weapon?" O'Keefe asked in a flat tone.

Reynolds shook his head, acting bewildered. "I must have picked up the lamp. Maybe it was on top of her. I don't remember—I was in shock. Then I panicked. Olivia wasn't in any of my classes, so technically our relationship wasn't against the Code of Conduct. But if people found out, I'd never get tenure. It might end my career. And . . ."

"And what?" O'Keefe prompted.

"I was afraid I'd be suspected of hurting her. So I backed out of her room and ran."

I was positive his defense was bullshit and he was guilty. Six months after Livvy's death, he was put on trial. On TV, they called it "The Murder of the Century." The whole world was sure the "Killer Professor" would be convicted.

The jury found him not guilty on all counts.

Everybody was shocked. Livvy's older brother Eric, a business student at Boston University, jumped over the railing from the spectators' gallery and practically strangled Reynolds before three court officers pulled him off.

It seemed obvious why the jurors had acquitted Reynolds: They were from the "People's Republic of Cambridge," where socialists are more common than Republicans. They loathed Olivia. They didn't want to put a liberal professor in prison for killing her.

For me, the professor's acquittal triggered bitter memories of Tata's killer going unpunished. I ranted to Jonah and anyone else who would listen about the world's injustices. I kept seeing that arrogant fuck in the gray suit who had killed Livvy smiling when the verdict was read. Like Eric, I wanted to physically rip him apart.

Late at night in the Seattle apartment where Jonah and I lived, I would dream of going to Boston and investigating on my own. What if I could find additional evidence against Reynolds? The Constitution says you can't try somebody twice for the same crime, but there are ways around that. Since Livvy's stepfather was a foreign diplomat, her murder was a federal crime. The FBI could arrest Reynolds for killing an "internationally protected person."

I would write a story about the murder and make sure the whole world knew there was a way to still get justice for Livvy. Like I'd done with my Letter to the Editor when I was eight, I would use the power of the press to force the police to act.

Livvy would finally get to rest in peace, like my Tata and Livvy's mom never did.

Of course, this was all a dream. I couldn't fly out to Boston on spec, with no place to live, no real job, and zero money saved up.

But then it happened. I found out the managing editor of the *Boston Clarion* had grown up in Bozeman, so when they had an opening, I sent him my best clips from there. I still expected to get rejected; after all, he probably received a thousand applications. And I hadn't exactly set the world on fire so far, getting laid off from small-town newspapers.

But I guess Dave was feeling nostalgic about his hometown, because I got the interview.

And the job.

And now here I was, in Boston.

Finally ready to pitch the story I'd been obsessed about for two years.

*   *   *

As I got ready to go back to Dave's office, my heart started racing. I did a quick check in my compact: lipstick perfect, shoulder-length hair riding down just right. My new silk blouse looked good too. I'd bought it two weeks before in a fit of retail therapy when my last City Council story—"Water Use Makes Splash at City Council"—only got eight hundred hits total.

I stood up from my desk, and my phone buzzed: Jonah.

One of the best things about getting hired at the *Clarion* was that Boston had a lot of high tech, especially in Jonah's primary field, computational biology. He got a job he was excited about right away, working for a biogenetics startup. Their new machine learning model for analyzing genetic tests was showing major commercial potential.

I thought about not answering the phone since I didn't want to keep my boss waiting. But I hit the green button and said, "Morning, peach blossom." I'd given Jonah that nickname when we were walking through an orchard near Oxford and I decided he was as sweet and gorgeous as a peach blossom.

"Hey, sprite, how's it going?" He gave me that nickname because . . . well, I was never quite sure why, but it always made me smile inside. I heard street noises and figured Jonah was biking to the We-Work on Charles Street, where his startup was based for now. I pictured him riding along in his sexy biker shorts.

"I just hit twelve hundred"—I refreshed the website—"no, make that thirteen."

"Whoa!"

"I bet I hit seven thousand by tonight."

"Maybe now's the time to ask old Dave for a weekend off."

"I'm going way stronger than that." I punched the air. "I'm gonna pitch him the Olivia story today."

"Hot damn," Jonah said. "You sure you're ready?"

"Born ready, baby," I said, dialing up the bravado even further. "This story is my *destiny.*"

There was a brief pause and a car honk, then he said, "Okay, destiny's child—break a leg. You're gonna do great."

Thank you, Jonah. "Love you, babe," I said.

"I love you more," he said.

"Impossible."

I turned off the phone and drew a deep breath. Then I stepped out into the fluorescent hallway, heading up the row of cubicles toward Dave's office. The last cubicle belonged to Natalie Blair. It was the one closest to the boss; no doubt that was why she'd made sure to get it.

Natalie was holding court to three other reporters when I walked up. Chuck, a sixty-year-old sports columnist, was saying to her, "Thirty thousand hits? Holy shit!"

My face tightened with jealousy. Stephanie from the Living section asked, "So who's your unnamed source?"

"A little birdie," Natalie answered, and everybody laughed. I was willing to bet there was no source. At UCLA they taught us to despise that kind of "reporting."

Though it had certainly worked for Natalie, a blonde Princeton grad with more pairs of shoes than I had underwear and an air of self-assurance from growing up with money. Her mother was a corporate lawyer and her father was a golf buddy of Dave's who was the editor-in-chief at *Travel + Leisure*. Natalie got hired a month after me, but Dave immediately put her on the crime desk—the beat I was dying for.

Natalie and I were friendly at first, hanging out in each other's cubicles and sharing chocolate éclairs. Then four months ago, I got a lead on a cool story: an international crime ring was smuggling contraband rare butterflies into Boston Harbor. I never told anyone about it, but I wrote notes in a legal pad on my desk. I planned to spend a few days researching and getting all of my ducks, or butterflies, in a row. Then I would go in and pitch Dave.

But before I got a chance, Natalie went in and pitched him the exact same story.

She ended up winning all kinds of attention for her three-part series, "Winged Obsession," and becoming the new star reporter. I was positive she'd seen my notes and stolen my story. But when I confronted her, she denied it. "I have my own sources," she said huffily, acting offended. But she refused to reveal who they were. I decided Natalie was probably lying and couldn't be trusted, and I gradually put an end to our snack breaks.

She looked up from her admirers as I walked by and said, overflowing with condescension, "Hey, Petch, cute little piece this morning."

I pasted a smile on my face and kept walking. I hated being called "Petch," and I'd told her that more than once. But she always either forgot or pretended to forget.

Feeling her eyes on my back, I put an extra strut in my step as I headed up the hall to Dave's office. Let Natalie be jealous for once about me having a private confab with the boss. My story about Livvy would be so big, everybody would forget that damn butterfly story.

As I stood outside Dave's door, I paused. Natalie had messed with my composure, and I needed to center myself again.

I had something exciting to offer Dave. Through a combination of grit and luck, I had just gotten a new lead on Livvy's murder, from her brother Eric. It wasn't a hundred percent solid, but it was a great place to start. It could take the investigation into Livvy's murder in a whole new direction.

Even though the story was burning a hole in my heart, I had thought about not pitching Dave until I nailed down my lead. But with the second anniversary of the Killer Professor's murder trial coming up, I was pretty sure Dave would assign somebody to write a story on it; and unless I moved fast, that somebody would be Natalie.

I knocked on Dave's door. "Come in," his voice said.

I opened the door and gave him my most brilliant smile. "Hi, Dave."

He smiled back, though he seemed a bit preoccupied. Dave was a smart editor and a solid, no-nonsense boss, whose one quirk was that he hated the word "some" in a news story. Once I learned to cut all my somes before turning in copy, Dave and I got along well.

But he'd been stressed lately, probably due to his recent divorce. He had a habit of tugging on his right earlobe when he felt uncertain, and the earlobe had gotten a lot of action the last couple months. He was on the chubby side and always said he would start going to the gym, but he never did, staying late at the office most nights. His hair was gray with a big bald spot on the crown. "Hi,

Petra," he said, pointing to the one other comfortable chair in the room. "Sit down."

As I sat, he stood and came behind me to shut the door. *Huh?* Dave never did that during our meetings. My throat went dry. Was something bad about to happen?

No, don't be paranoid. This was just my PTSD from getting fired—laid off—all those times. Only last week Dave had told me how much he liked my School Board story. Yesterday, we spent five minutes in the snack room chatting about the Red Sox.

I waited as he sat down again behind his shiny metal desk. His office had three computers but not a single scrap of paper, except a manila folder with a document peeping out of it. He also had a *New Yorker* and an *Editor & Publisher* with a cover story titled, "The Podcast Boom: What It Means for You."

I said brightly, "You going to the game tonight?"

Dave looked me in the eye, and the edges of his lips turned downward. As I tried to figure out what his expression meant, he said, "Petra, I have some bad news."

Bad news?

My heart started pounding. *It can't be that. He probably wants me to cover some stupid meeting on Saturday night or something, and he feels guilty about it—*

"I'm afraid we're gonna have to lay you off."

CHAPTER TWO

I FELT MY mouth open wide, and then I couldn't feel anything at all. It was like I'd left my body. All I could do was watch Dave's lips move around and try to understand what the sounds coming from them meant.

"This isn't about your performance. You're doing a good job, it's just the nature of the business. The publisher ordered me to lay off fifteen percent of the staff to cut costs."

I was incapable of speech, so he kept going. "I'll give you an excellent recommendation. Anything I can do for you, I'll do."

I'm such an idiot. Why didn't I see this coming?! I always prided myself on being able to read people, but I'd been blind.

And then came the inevitable: *Did I do something wrong? Is Natalie getting fired too? I bet not.*

"I'm sure things will work out for you," Dave was saying now. *Yeah, easy for you, you're not the one with the monster stink on you from getting fired all the time.* Shit, three times in a row now, not even counting Seattle. Soon I'd be unhirable.

As he talked on, I thought, *Maybe I'm already unhirable.* Editors would take one look at my resume and think, *What's the matter with this girl, why does she keep getting fired everywhere?* My body went rigid, my nails biting into my palms under the desk. *What if this is the last newspaper job I ever get, and I can never find justice for Livvy or do any of the other things I've always dreamed of?*

I'd been so sure I was safe here. True, the *Clarion* was Boston's number two paper, but it filled such a good niche: a flashy easy-to-read tabloid, unlike the far more sober *Boston Globe.* I had one of the only serious, newsy beats on the paper.

Which was my downfall, as I now learned. "Abernathy decided we can't cover local government nearly as much anymore," Dave said. Colin Abernathy was our publisher, a white-haired mogul from Scotland who had bought the paper last year. "Nobody reads the articles."

I finally found my voice, even if it sounded kind of squeaky. "I'd be happy to move to a different beat," I said, relieved I wasn't crying. In Oxford my tears had been humiliating. In Bozeman I was so shook, and so desperate to hang onto a little self-respect and *not* cry, I barely said ten words the entire meeting.

But this time I decided to fight for my job. So what if it was hopeless, what choice did I have? My life was at stake. I leaned forward, putting my forearms on Dave's desk. "I'd be a big asset on the crime beat. I can show you pieces I wrote in both Montana and Mississippi that—"

"We already have the crime beat covered."

I stifled a scream. "Sure, Natalie does the day-to-day stuff. But we can go deeper." I started pitching for all I was worth. "I was gonna come see you today. I have an incredible story—"

"Petra, this isn't my decision." Dave picked up the manila folder from his desk. That document poking out of it must be corporate paperwork. "We'll give you two weeks' severance and—"

I tried to sound confident, but my squeakiness betrayed me. "What if I told you I have a major lead on the murder of the century? *Olivia Anderson.*"

Dave's hand with the folder stopped in midair. Then he gave his head a little shake. "Honestly, Petra, I'd say you were full of crap."

I deepened my voice. "I was Livvy's counselor at summer camp when her mom died. We became like sisters. That gave me an entry to one of the key players, and I spoke to him last week." This was true; last Thursday night I had encountered Eric at a bar in Cambridge. "He was drunk"—also true, he was blitzed—"and he told me a secret he's never told the police. A secret that will turn everyone's perceptions of this case totally upside down."

Okay, so this last part was, well . . . an exaggeration. Eric did tell me he had a secret like that. But he hadn't revealed exactly what his secret was yet, so I couldn't be sure it would have this kind of impact.

No way I was admitting that to Dave, though. I gazed straight into his eyes, trying to appear as sincere and trustworthy as possible.

His eyes narrowed. "So what's this big secret?"

I shook my head. "I can't disclose that right now. For one thing, if you do lay me off, I'm pursuing this story on my own. I have contacts at the *Times* and the *New Yorker*. I'll sell it there."

I couldn't believe that all these flat-out lies were coming out of my mouth. Dave sat there eyeing me. I hoped he was thinking how bad he'd look if he laid me off and I turned around and sold a huge Boston-based story to the *Times*. It hit me maybe his recent stress wasn't just about his divorce; he was probably scared of getting laid off himself. In his fifties, after spending his whole life in a now-dying business, what kind of job could *he* get? His two teenage kids would need money for college.

But when he spoke, his voice was cold. "I'd need to know a hell of a lot more before I—"

"You'll get more," I said quickly. "Give me two weeks. We're talking kick-ass five-part series—"

"Yeah, problem with that is, nobody reads long-form anymore."

That stumped me. Dave held up the folder again and my heart sank. "I wish I could help you, but—"

Suddenly I got an inspiration. I like to think it was Livvy's spirit guiding me. I picked up the copy of *Editor & Publisher,* with its cover story on the podcast boom, and waved it at Dave. "I was thinking a podcast," I said.

Dave hesitated and I took advantage, plunging onward fast and nervous. "Olive Oil's murder is perfect for that. We'd bring in a whole new revenue stream for the newspaper. Look at the *Cincinnati Enquirer*—they were about to go bankrupt, but then they do a podcast about an unsolved murder and get *one million listeners.* Not only was it totally advertising-supported, it was also credited with increasing print sales by twenty-seven thousand." I was pulling these numbers out of my ass, but hopefully by the time Dave double-checked them, if he did, he would already have said yes. "It was such a success they launched a second season about another cold case, and the paper's financial situation totally turned around."

I stopped for breath. Dave's lips were tight and doubtful. I fired one more shot, hoping I wasn't getting too personal. "Dave, I bet I'm not the only person here who's worried about getting laid off."

He folded his arms. Maybe I *had* gotten too personal, but I couldn't turn back now. I leaned forward even closer to Dave. "This will help both of us."

At last he spoke. "We've tried the podcast thing before. For every one that works there's a thousand that fail."

I'm acting too desperate, I thought. I stood up, holding my chin high. "Fine, I'll take it to the *Times.* And the *Globe,* of course," I added for good measure.

I headed for the door, praying he'd call me back. But he didn't say a word. I reached for the knob and opened the door. *Oh God, I am so screwed—*

"Who do you figure killed her?" Dave said. "It was the professor, right?"

Yes!

Somehow I managed to play it cool. I turned. "Listen to my podcast and find out."

He was still holding up the folder, but at least he wasn't shoving it toward me anymore. "Do you even know how to do a podcast?"

"Yeah, I did one in Seattle." *Like hell I did. But if I watch a lot of YouTube videos, I must be able to figure it out.*

"Podcasts aren't cheap."

I had no idea how much they cost. "You can do one for virtually nothing. You don't even need a recording studio. We can record in a walk-in closet and get decent sound."

Dave bit his lip. "This big lead of yours, you really think you can spin something good out of it?"

"No doubt." I stepped back toward him. "Two weeks. That's all I ask. Take it out of my severance pay."

Finally he gave me the glimmer of a smile. A shock wave of hope electrified me as he set his folder back down. "All right, Kovach. Two weeks."

"You won't regret it," I said, trying not to gasp with relief.

Dave tugged at his right earlobe. "I already do."

I threw him a confident grin.

*   *   *

Moments later, with an easy stride and radiating self-assurance, I left Dave's office. I sauntered past Cubicle Row, where Natalie watched me with threaded eyebrows raised. I went straight to the bathroom.

When I got there, I stood in front of the toilet, ready to throw up. Instead I hyperventilated so badly I almost passed out. I had to sit down.

As I put my hand to my chest, I thought, *I have never lied so much in my entire life.*

I finally caught my breath. *Focus.* How could I pry that big secret out of Eric? That was my only hope to turn this around in just two weeks.

I sat there replaying my strange Thursday night with him in my head. Maybe that would give me a clue about how best to approach him.

If I didn't figure this out, Livvy would lose her shot at justice, and I would lose my career.

CHAPTER THREE

LAST THURSDAY NIGHT, I had been sitting in a corner booth at a place called the Parting Glass. It was an Irish pub in North Cambridge, packed with a boisterous mix of locals and college students starting their weekends early. But I was off by myself eating a burger and writing up a Cambridge City Council story. I've always worked well surrounded by noise, and I wanted to get my story finished and off my plate before I went home to Jonah. I liked not being distracted by work when we were together.

I was just about ready to hit send when I happened to glance up and see a guy drinking Guinness at the bar. He looked strangely familiar, like an actor I'd seen on TV. He was handsome, with thick sand-colored hair and even features, but I sensed a sadness in the droop of his jaw.

Suddenly I recognized him. *Holy crap, that's Livvy's brother.* I had been planning to contact him now that I was in Boston.

No doubt he was sick of strangers accosting him. But even though we'd never met, I didn't feel like a stranger. I walked up to him. I remembered that Eric was eight years older than Livvy, which would put him at twenty-nine now, but he looked mid-thirties. His shoulders slumped, and my feeling he harbored a deep sadness was magnified.

But maybe he was just half-wasted. This didn't seem like his first Guinness of the night. I waited until he looked up and said, "Hi. You're Eric Anderson, aren't you?"

He eyed me warily. "Guilty as charged."

"I knew your sister. I was her counselor at journalism camp."

A smile dimpled his cheeks, making him look much younger. "Petra something, right?"

I smiled in return, gratified Livvy had talked about me to her family. "Petra Kovach."

"Nice to meet you." He got to his feet and reached out his hand. "Livvy really liked you."

We shook. "I liked her very much. She was always so full of enthusiasm and ideas."

He nodded somberly. "When our mom died, you were a big comfort to her."

My throat caught. "Thank you. I feel bad I didn't go to her funeral. I was in Los Angeles, but . . ." Really, what I felt bad about was that I hadn't been there for Livvy during her final months.

"No worries." Eric called to the bartender, a brunette with pink streaks, "Hey, Katrina, two more Guinnesses." He turned back to me with a flirtatious smile. "You look like a Guinness kind of girl."

I wasn't eager to do a whole flirting-in-a-pickup-bar thing. But I wasn't about to leave, either. What if Eric could help me launch my investigation? We shared my booth, me nursing my Guinness while Eric guzzled his. "Livvy said you two were really close," I began. It never hurts to butter up a potential source. Also, it was true. Livvy looked up to Eric.

He gazed at the far wall with unfocused eyes, and I sensed him reliving his bittersweet past. His fingers rimmed the glass of beer. "When our father left us and took off for France—our birth father, I mean—Livvy was only three. From then on, I always felt like her dad, not just a big brother." He looked back at me. "'Course, when Livvy was seven, my mom married Viktor, and he took over the dad role."

"Yeah, Livvy said he was a good guy."

Suddenly it was like an emotional switch turned off inside Eric. His lips twisted and the quiet sincerity disappeared from his eyes. "Viktor's super," Eric said, but he didn't sound like he meant it. "Couldn't ask for a better stepdad." Then he lifted his Guinness and threw out a drunken laugh. "Drink up! To Livvy!"

Hunh. Why did Eric lose it when I asked about his stepfather? I did some probing, asking questions about him, but Eric started babbling about how God drinks Guinness.

So I switched gears and asked about Livvy's YouTube videos. Maybe Eric had insights into the strange puzzle of Livvy's conversion into a hate-filled fanatic. I tried all kinds of openers, like "Were you surprised by all those things Livvy said?" "When did Livvy get so into politics?" and "Was she always that extreme?"

But no matter how I asked, Eric deflected, moving our conversation back to booze. "That girl was a pro. She could drink me under the table," he said, slurring his words and hoisting his glass again to Livvy's memory.

We clinked glasses. I was a little surprised that Eric used to drink with his teenage sister who was so much younger than he was, but maybe their Swedish stepfather raised them with different social mores. Then Eric took my hand. "You're really great. I can see why my sister loved you."

Okay, so now the flirting was getting a little too much. I've never enjoyed hanging out with drunk people, they're too silly. I like a glass of wine sometimes, but I'm not into getting out-of-control wasted. I definitely wanted to talk to Eric when he was sober, but now it was time to go. "Thank you," I said, withdrawing my hand. "I should take off. I have to get to work early tomorrow."

But before I was able to stand up, he said, "I could tell you some major mind-blowing shit about Livvy's murder."

I blinked. My body tingled. If Eric was trying to hold me here, he had succeeded. "What kind of major mind-blowing shit?"

His slurring got more pronounced. "Like shit nobody knows but me and my stepdad. The cops don't even know."

My pulse quickened. "What is it?"

"Major serious, mind-blowing shit."

He leaned forward in the booth, inviting more questions. His eyes held a challenge, like I was supposed to ask something and I needed to figure out what.

Major serious, mind-blowing shit?

My mind went to: *Does he think the professor didn't kill her after all?*

That seemed impossible. Eric had been beyond furious, just like me, when the jury found Professor Reynolds not guilty.

But now, sitting in the booth with Eric, the intensity in every muscle of his face sent an electric charge through me. There was some fraught message he was trying to communicate. I waited for him to go on, but he just stared into my eyes.

I asked, "Do you still think Professor Reynolds killed her?"

Eric's eyes widened slightly and he gave a crooked smile, as if to say: *Got it in one try.* But he still didn't speak, just tipped back his Guinness.

My body grew hot. I couldn't believe he was hinting at this. "You don't think he killed her anymore?"

"Life is fucking weird, dude," Eric said.

"Then who did kill her?"

He took another drink and looked away.

I spent the next twenty minutes flirting and begging without getting any more out of him.

I gave him my phone number. But he never called, and by now it had been a week already. He gave me his number too, but when I tried it some lady answered in Chinese. Either he screwed up his number because he was drunk, or he gave me the wrong one on purpose.

But so what? If Eric thought a dumb little trick like that would stop me, he was about to learn otherwise.

I had been so positive that Professor Reynolds was the killer. It still seemed like the most likely scenario. But on the other hand, from the TV interviews I'd seen, Eric was a smart guy. And he certainly had more inside information than I did. So if he had doubts . . .

Sitting in the bathroom at the *Clarion* and revisiting that scene with Eric in my head, I thought: *What a podcast that would be, if I could give people a credible alternate theory of the murder! I'd get a million listeners, easy!*

As I got up and splashed water on my face, I pictured myself getting interviewed on CNN, just like Livvy had imagined. Then I eyed myself in the mirror. *Cut the self-centered crap,* I told myself. *This isn't about me. It's about Livvy and catching her killer, whether it's Reynolds or somebody else.*

I closed my eyes and pictured Livvy. Not the YouTube star she turned into, but the fourteen-year-old girl with innocent blue eyes so open and full of life. She kept a notepad covered with kitten stickers in her purse, in case she got a sudden idea she just *had* to write down.

I owed it to Livvy to get this story right.

I went back to my cubicle to research Eric some more, hunting for a new angle to come at him with the next time I saw him. I needed to get him talking—fast, or else I'd forever lose my chance to try and solve Livvy's murder. But before I could get down to work, my phone pinged with a text from Jonah: How'd it go with the boss?

Oh God, what should I say? How would Jonah react when he learned I almost got fired yet again—and probably would be fired for real in two weeks.

I decided I'd tell him tonight in person—that would be easier. Maybe. For now, I went with a half-truth: I GOT THE STORY!

Moments later, his text came back: NICE! I'LL COOK DINNER AND WE'LL CELEBRATE 🍷💚🔪 !!

Upset though I was, I couldn't help smiling at the eggplant, which if you don't know, symbolizes a . . . well, a penis. In response, I sent him a scissors emoji.

Then my phone buzzed: Mama calling. I shut my eyes. Telling her would be torture too. Mama would say, "It'll be okay, *moj mišić.*" My little mouse. "God will take care of you." But I knew Mama. As soon as she got off the phone, she would sit on her worn blue sofa and start crying with worry about her poor daughter—*fired again.* I felt so much weight on me to make her happy, after everything she'd been through in her life. I let the call go to voicemail, googled "Eric Anderson," and started clicking.

The first site I hit was more about Livvy than Eric. It showed the famous crime scene photo of her sprawled in bed, her purple "I Don't Give a Fuck" T-shirt smeared with blood. As always when I came across that photo, I stared not at Livvy but at her bedside table. At the thing that wasn't there: the sharp-pointed metal nail file that had been visible in her final video, but was missing from the murder scene.

The detectives had speculated that Livvy fought back with the file, stabbing her attacker and drawing blood; and he took it with him so the cops wouldn't find his blood on it. But maybe some of his blood dripped off during the assault. So the CSIs tested the spatter on Livvy's clothes and sheets. Unfortunately, all of the blood belonged to her.

I pictured Livvy fighting for her life and tried to imagine the man she was stabbing. But where I had once seen William Reynolds, all I could see now was a faceless antagonist.

It hit me that the police never mentioned finding a stab wound or scar on Reynolds' body. No doubt if they had found one, they would have brought it up at trial.

I exited the site and clicked on a BuzzFeed feature with a photo of Livvy and Eric together. *"Olivia Anderson chased fame with a lush body and a stiletto tongue,"* the piece began. *"A blogger in Arizona nicknamed her 'Olive Oil' and she tweeted, 'Just don't call me Extra Virgin.' The nickname stuck.*

"Olive Oil's fame hopscotched even higher in January, when she dropped 'Who Raped Who?' and became the world's most controversial college girl. After her death she morphed into a legend, a prophet, a fiery goddess who died way too young."

I frowned at my screen. Skimming the article, I found nothing that would help explain Livvy's metamorphosis into a virulent extremist. The writer had totally missed her essence: a mixed-up girl who missed her mother. The whole piece was pretty silly—"empty calories," my old journalism prof would have said.

But I had to admit it was entertaining, written in a nice, easy style. The kind of flashy, underreported stuff Natalie specialized in. That thought was followed of course by: *Is my stuff as breezy as this?*

I thrust the negativity aside and went back to work, trying to imagine what Eric's "mind-blowing" secret might be that "nobody knows but me and my stepdad."

Maybe he knew something about the "super fucking personal" video Livvy started recording right before she was killed. Everyone assumed her video was going to be about her relationship with Professor Reynolds. But what if it was actually going to be about somebody else—somebody connected to her murder?

Or maybe Eric was just a delusional drunk, imagining things. I didn't know much about Eric except Livvy loved him. After their mom died, she hated when he went back to Boston University and left her alone with their stepfather to mourn. I KNOW I'M BEING WEIRD, BUT I FEEL LIKE MY BRO IS ABANDONING ME, she texted me.

But other than that, Livvy didn't talk about Eric much. I needed to figure out the magic "Open Sesame" that would get him to reveal all. I googled images of him. In several photos something seemed off: Only half his mouth was smiling, or his eyes were too wide, like they were held open with toothpicks. Jonah liked to tease me for believing I could figure people out at a glance, but I considered that one of my best journalistic skills. And what I saw in Eric was pain and desperation.

Or was I just projecting my own mood onto him?

No, he had gone through hell, losing his mom and then his sister—

"That guy's hot," a woman said, and I looked up, startled. Natalie stood at the opening of my cubicle, checking out Eric's photos. "Personal or professional?"

"Yes," I said, quickly closing out of the internet window. No way I wanted Natalie up in my business, not after that episode with the contraband butterflies.

"So what did Dave want?" she asked brightly.

I looked up into her greenish eyes. She must have smelled blood when I went back to Dave's office. Maybe she suspected I was about to get fired. Natalie was always one step ahead of the office politics.

Well, now *I* was a step ahead. "He assigned me a story."

She blinked. "Really. Something juicy?"

"Can't talk about it." I gathered up my laptop and purse. "Gotta run."

"Mysterious." She smirked. "What is it, a neighborhood planning board meeting?"

"See ya later," I said, throwing as much haughtiness as possible into those three words. I strode out of my cubicle, heading for who knows where, leaving Natalie to ponder the mystery.

* * *

Walking down the hallway toward the elevators, I realized exactly what I should do: call my old college pal Mateo Navarro. Mateo was an immigrant, too, from another public school in East LA. We were co-editors of the student newspaper, the *Daily Bruin*, or as Mateo called it, the *Daily Ruin*. We would haunt the corridors 'til midnight to get the paper out in time.

After a year working in the real world of journalism, Mateo turned sensible and went to law school. Now he was an associate at a big firm on Boylston Street, living with a guy who was also a lawyer. One of the perks of moving to Boston was reconnecting with Mateo.

He was always super busy, but this time I got lucky and he answered immediately. "Hey, girl, s'up?"

"You wanna do lunch, like right now? I need to talk to you about something."

There was a pause, then: "You know I love you, sweetie, but I was planning to eat in. I'm swamped."

"No worries. It's only like the most important thing ever."

This was how I used to cajole Mateo into helping me at the *Daily Bruin*. And it still worked. Thirty minutes later, we were eating falafel in a Lebanese restaurant that looked out onto Copley Plaza. Old men were playing cards and dominos in one corner, just like in MacArthur Park back in East LA.

In his fitted suit, light blue tie, and high-top haircut, Mateo was the most stylish guy there. Also the handsomest, with lively blue eyes, a tan face, and even, white teeth. But now his forehead was lined in a frown. I had just laid out what happened this morning, and he shook his head.

"Damn, am I glad I didn't follow my dreams," he said. "That's a fool's game."

"Thanks for the encouragement. I need you to help me."

"Have you ever even done a podcast?"

"No, but how hard can it be?" I said petulantly.

Mateo said, "I can't believe after two years of ragging on the professor, now you think maybe he's innocent." I shifted in my chair. I felt weird about it too. "Petra, this whole thing is thinner than water. That boy Eric was just spouting nonsense. Using his sister to try and get laid."

"I can't think that way. This lead is all I got."

"Then you better spend the next two weeks polishing your resume."

The falafel spices stirred in my stomach. "I need to do this story!" I pounded the table with my fist, then felt tears come into my eyes. "I loved Livvy. I owe it to her to try and get justice. And I've wanted to do stories like this ever since I was eight and my dad was killed!"

Mateo gave a groan. Then he threw up his hands in mock surrender—a gesture I remembered from long ago. "Okay, *chiquita loca, cálmese.* What can I do for you?"

I grabbed his hand. "Thanks, Mateo, you're the best."

"What the hell, it beats sitting in my office doing corporate law bullshit."

"I need some brilliant ideas for how to get Eric to talk."

"Have sex with him."

"Besides that."

I told Mateo everything I'd learned about Eric. His only public social media account was Twitter, so I showed Mateo that. "But his tweets are all innocuous. Nothing about Livvy's murder. Mostly he tweets about food."

Mateo put down his falafel. "You're thinking too hard."

"What do you mean?"

"You've been through so much crap the last two years, you don't trust your instincts anymore. You already know the best way to get through to him. It's how you got through to me just now."

I frowned, not getting it. Mateo said, "Tell him about your dad. Connect his pain to yours."

I bit my lip. Using my personal tragedy in this way seemed creepy. Or cheesy.

But it was true. I related to Eric all too well. Like him, my life had been forever scarred by unfathomable violence. When I looked out at the domino players in the Plaza, I could still hear the twenty-year-old gunshots.

"You're right," I said to Mateo. "I'll tell Eric my whole damn sob story."

"Excellent. Between that and your soulful brown eyes, he won't stand a chance. So how will you get hold of him?"

"According to LinkedIn, he's a junior investment banker at a venture capital firm called Populus. They're on Tremont. I was thinking of just going over there, but—"

"You're afraid he won't talk openly at work."

I nodded. "I tried People Finder, but they don't have his phone number."

Mateo scrolled down Eric's Twitter feed. "How about this tweet from last week: *Best clam chowder in Boston: the Thursday lunch special at the Red Dolphin.*"

I got his point: today was Thursday again. "I saw that. But I doubt he goes there every Thursday."

Mateo scrolled down further. "He did tweet about it two Thursdays in a row."

I blinked at him. Then I checked the time: twelve thirty-nine. I jumped up from my chair.

"Take the T," Mateo said. "It'll be quicker."

I hugged him. "Love you, Mateo."

"Love you too."

As I hurried out, he called after me, "And people here pronounce it 'chowda.'"

I ran down to the Copley T station, and for once the subway gods were on my side: the T was right there waiting. We made it to the Haymarket station just before one. I ran up the steps, rushed two blocks to the Red Dolphin, and looked in the window. Neon red dolphins were painted on the walls. And there was Eric, standing in line at the counter!

This setup was perfect, so much better than meeting in some stuffy office—especially if he had beer with his chowder. I tried to quiet my pulse and act casual. I got the strongest feeling that finding him here was a lucky omen.

Eric would lead me to Livvy's killer.

I opened the restaurant door and walked toward Eric and my destiny. I smoothed my hair, stepped up to the counter behind him, and got ready. *Don't fuck this up.*

CHAPTER FOUR

ERIC FINISHED ORDERING his chowder, then turned around. "Oh hey," I said, arranging my face into a surprised smile. "Fancy seeing you here."

He frowned, then recognized me and put on the charm. He was even better looking sober, his eyes sharper. "Whassup, girl reporter?" he said, then added, embarrassed, "I was gonna call you."

I cheerfully waved that aside. "No worries. How's the clam chowda? My friend told me it's fire."

"No doubt. Order the large size, you won't regret it."

I was full with falafel, but I wasn't about to go against Eric's advice. A couple minutes later we were sharing a back booth and reminiscing about great chowders we had known. The Red Dolphin chowder was darn good, in fact; too bad I had to force it down.

Eric was beerless but still chatty. "I'll tell you the secret ingredient these guys use: salt pork." He leaned his body toward me over the table. I had once written a listicle about the *"10 Signs a Guy is Flirting With You,"* and this was one. I leaned toward him, mirroring him—another thing I'd written about. He tilted his head and his eyes shone; he was definitely into it.

From chowder, we moved on to the weather—and the Red Sox, of course. I said, "I'd feel a lot better if Barnes could get his fastball over the plate once in a while."

Eric whistled, impressed. "Damn, the girl knows her baseball."

Actually, that one line about Barnes was pretty much the only baseball thing I knew. Jonah had taught it to me so I'd have something to say at the office when guys bonded about the Sox. Now I wriggled back to a simpler topic, so my ignorance wouldn't be unmasked. "This chowda fucking kills, dude. And it's cheap. I'm coming here every Thursday from now on."

"That's what *I* do."

I acted surprised. "For real?"

"Yup. And the same bar every Thursday night. My philosophy is . . ." He leaned forward again, turning what he said next into a come-on line. "If you find something good, stick with it."

I said teasingly, "How boring." Then I touched his arm, flirting for all I was worth. I felt a little like a jerk, but I was doing this for Eric's sister, and if I helped nail her killer, Eric would be grateful. "Just kidding. I think it's sweet that you have like, rituals."

He pretended to pout. "Sweet? I'm going for tough and sexy."

I smiled. The old jazz classic "Summertime" played over the restaurant speakers, and I debated within myself whether now was the time to kick it up a notch. I decided yes. Maybe I was pushing it, but with my deadline I had no choice. I needed to move fast. My eyes opened wider and I gave him an earnest look. "After all you've been through, it probably feels good to have a little stability in your life. Like whatever crap happens, you know you've got that pint of Guinness waiting for you."

Eric nodded, looking touched. But he kept it light. "True dat. You can always count on Dr. Guinness."

"No doubt."

As I smiled at him and contemplated my next line, he checked his watch. "Shit, I need to get back."

No, we're just getting started. I batted my eyes, the old tried and true. "It's great to see you again."

"We should hang out some time," he said.

How do I do this without turning it into a date?

"I'd say this weekend," he continued, "but I'm going out of town tomorrow."

"For how long?" *God, I must sound so aggressive.*

"A couple weeks."

My heart sank. *I only have two weeks to save my job!*

"Long time," I said brightly, trying not to let my agony show.

"Yeah, I'm meeting with some startups in California. You wanna give me your number again?"

"I do."

"I promise I'll call you this time, when I get back." He looked into my eyes, a little shyly. He *would* call me this time, I felt sure.

But: *a couple weeks.*

As I put my number into his phone, and he put his into mine, I thought: *fuck, it's now or never.* We'd only had thirty minutes together, but the vibe felt strong. I wouldn't have a better chance 'til it was too late. Our booth felt romantic in its own quirky way, with dolphins and ocean waves gallivanting all around us on the table and walls. Lowering my voice and trying to ignore my thumping heart, I leaned in even closer. "It's so weird I ran into you twice in one week."

"Destiny, baby," he said, smiling. Crows' feet formed around his eyes—the smile was real.

"But you know, what if it is? Destiny, I mean." I moved my hand closer to his. "Eric, you're such a charming guy. But I feel a sadness inside you."

He looked affected but played it off. "Well, it's called being human, huh?"

"You know why I connected so deeply with Livvy? And with you." I paused. "I lost someone I loved when I was a child." My chest grew tight. For now, at least, I wouldn't have to act. "My father. He was killed in a drive-by shooting. They never caught the guy."

Eric blinked. "I'm sorry."

"I couldn't talk about it for years. It was too painful." My eyes welled up. "The only reason he was in the park that day was to take care of me. I made him go there. So I always felt it was my fault."

Eric nodded and rubbed his eyes—a sympathetic reaction to my tears. "Eric, I feel like you need to tell your truth. That's the only way you'll ever escape from the trauma of your sister's murder."

I'm not just hustling him, I realized. If he opened up about his feelings and his dark secrets, it would help him. Maybe he wouldn't drink so much. He could move on with his life.

The truth shall set you free. Yeah, it's a cliché, but it's also something I and every reporter I know believe. It's at the core of our beings.

Eric fingered the sides of his water glass. Then he gazed into my eyes. His own eyes looked so open and vulnerable. "Maybe you're right," he said, almost whispering. "And maybe you're the person who can help me open up."

"I know," I said softly, though my mind was shouting, *Yes!* "And maybe I can help you find out what really happened to Livvy."

Eric nodded slowly, then said, "So what did you do, read my tweet?"

Oh shit. I tried to look bewildered. "What do you mean?"

"You knew I'd be here. You're stalking me."

"No, of course not—"

"Babe, you're not the first—or the best. You fuckers have been trying to game me for two years."

He stood up. I said desperately, "Eric, I care about Livvy."

"Yeah, you all do."

"But I'm different!"

He shook his head and started out of the restaurant. I felt my dreams leaving with him.

"Eric!" I called out. "You need help. Just talking to your stepdad is not enough!"

I was just trying anything I could. But once again, I like to think Livvy's spirit was guiding me. Eric turned. The people in the other booths watched as he came back toward me. "What's that about my stepfather?" he snapped.

"Last week. You said nobody knows the secret but you and your stepdad."

Something dark and heavy landed on Eric's face. "I never said that about him. And there is no secret."

Then he stalked out of the restaurant.

He was lying. *There's a secret, all right—and his stepfather knows it.*

I needed to get hold of the stepdad. Right now, before Eric got to him first.

CHAPTER FIVE

THE INTERNET QUICKLY revealed that Eric and Livvy's stepfather, Viktor Anderson, was still the Swedish consul general. People Finder didn't have his phone number. But the consulate was on Beacon Street, only half a mile from the Red Dolphin.

I jumped up and ran all the way there. Luckily I wasn't wearing heels. When I got to the consulate, I stopped and caught my breath. It was in a large, red brick building with an investment company on one side and a yoga studio on the other.

I opened the heavy wooden door and approached the front desk. Framed paintings of sun-dappled Swedish forests and lakes decorated the walls. No one was in the lobby besides the receptionist, an icily attractive woman in her forties with perfect ombre highlights and a Max Mara dress. She gave me a cool professional smile and asked, "May I help you?"

I smiled back, putting everything I had into it. "Yes, thank you. I'd like to speak with Consul Anderson."

"Appointment?"

I smiled again. "I'm just hoping for a moment of his time."

The receptionist's eyes flickered. "Hungry look, worn-out shoes, I'm guessing reporter."

I hesitated, trying to formulate a reply. But just then Viktor Anderson himself appeared from the back hallway. I recognized his strong chin and the medium-length silver hair framing his distinguished-looking, fifty-five-year-old face.

"Consul Anderson," I said brightly, wondering if I should have said "Mr." instead of "Consul." "May I have a quick word?"

The receptionist said, "I'm afraid Mr. Anderson is busy right now."

But Viktor gave me a look—or more accurately, he gave my breasts a look. *Yuck.* With a slight Swedish accent, he said, "How can I help you?"

The receptionist interrupted with distaste, "She's a reporter."

I forced another smile. "You make that sound so *awful.*" Then I stepped toward Viktor. "I'm Petra Kovach. I met your stepdaughter at UCLA. She probably mentioned me."

Viktor rubbed his chin. "I don't recall. So let me guess: you have some new conspiracy theory about her death."

I managed to keep my voice loose. "I wouldn't say that, no."

"Then what would you say?"

How to play this? "Sir," I began, "I understand you're in possession of..." I paused, then said portentously, *"Key information,* regarding what happened."

"What is this key information?"

Good question. I wondered if Eric had contacted him about me yet, but got the feeling the answer was no. I cocked my head knowingly. "It's a secret you're aware of that may be more important than you realize. It might unlock the whole mystery."

Viktor looked at me. "You think so?"

"Yes, I do," I said, thinking, *Hey, maybe this is working!*

But then he turned without a word and started back to his office.

What a dick. Raising my voice, I fired a wild shot. "I'd like your perspective on this secret before I share it with our readers."

He turned back and eyed me again, like I was a lowly worm. I stood tall, drawing my shoulders back. "Mr. Anderson, if you refuse to talk about this, it won't look good for you."

He blinked. I couldn't believe I was acting so ballsy, issuing vague threats to this powerful man. Maybe I was channeling Livvy. A thrill went through me.

Then Viktor nodded his head and said, "I will say one thing for you: nice tits."

I stared at him, too outraged to speak, then took my notepad out of my purse and wrote down his comment. "Thanks for the quote," I said. "It will sum you up perfectly."

With that I stalked out the door. From the corner of my eye, I could see Viktor and the receptionist gaping at me.

*   *   *

My face-off with Viktor was invigorating. But outside a cold autumn wind started up and my adrenaline wore off. I hadn't gotten the secret out of Viktor, or even confirmed that he knew it. I wrapped my jacket around me and wandered back down Beacon Street and into Boston Commons, not sure what to do next.

My phone pinged with a text from Mateo: HOW'D IT GO, NANCY DREW? I didn't answer. Then it pinged again with a text from Jonah: P, SALMON OR CHICKEN FOR DINNER? L, J.

I wanted to respond, *Who gives a fuck? My life is falling apart!* Instead I texted, SALMON, THANKS! L, P.

I sat down on a bench and watched leaves fall from the trees. Several ducks waddled up to me, hoping for handouts. "Hey, duckies," I said. "You got any hot leads for me? I'll buy you a loaf of bread."

A man with light blond hair sat next to me. I didn't think any-thing of it; there were no unoccupied benches nearby where he could have sat instead.

But then he put his arm around me. He was short, but with fore-arm muscles like Popeye's. I opened my mouth to scream.

His fingers pressed hard into my neck, right under the jawline, sending agonizing pain all the way down into my legs. He must be hitting some vital nerve. My scream died in my throat. It was broad daylight with so many people around. But they must have thought we were lovers, arm in arm.

This man could kill me and walk away and nobody would notice.

CHAPTER SIX

THE MAN WITH the Popeye muscles dug his fingers into me even harder, until I saw red dots in front of my eyes. Leaning into my ear, he whispered, in a foreign accent, "Don't fuck with the Andersons."

Then he smiled at me, stood up, and walked away down the footpath.

I was too overwhelmed to do anything except rub my neck. A young woman rolled a baby carriage past me. A couple of ducks returned, eyeing me quizzically.

That accent, I guessed, was Swedish. And he was walking toward the consulate. *He works for Viktor. Viktor ordered him to assault me.*

Fury blazed up inside me, burning away the pain. Did they really think they could scare me off with this shit? I was from East LA. I'd seen my father killed. *Fuck these people.*

And then I thought, *The secret is real. I'm on the right track.* That thug's attack—so soon after I met Viktor—meant he knew the secret and it terrified him!

I pumped my fist. I'd get to the bottom of this. Eric could be wrong, or lying, and somebody else besides his stepfather knew the secret too. Like one of Livvy's friends, or her boyfriend, Brandon.

Or Professor Reynolds.

My pulse sped up. After all this time, Reynolds might finally be ready to talk—especially if he was innocent, and especially to a friendly, pretty young woman who seemed nonthreatening, at first. Sitting on the bench, I pulled out my phone and searched for his contact info.

Reynolds wasn't actually a professor anymore. After his acquittal, furious Olive Oil fans and alt-right protesters constantly interrupted his classes and shouted him down. Someone fired shots through his apartment window, then somebody broke into his office and smeared feces everywhere. The Harvard administration wasn't eager to spend money on extra security for their outcast professor. He stuck it out for a semester but then resigned.

I clicked on a lot of different sites without discovering what he did for a living now, or if he was still in Boston. But I did track down an email address on a two-year-old website asking for contributions to his legal defense fund.

So I composed an email. *"Dear Professor Reynolds,"* I began—no, not a prof anymore— *"Dear Mr. Reynolds"*—no, he has a PhD, kiss his ass a little— *"Dear Dr. Reynolds, I am a reporter from the Boston Clarion, and I believe you may have been done a great wrong. I would like to discuss it with you as soon as possible. Best regards, Petra Kovach."*

I looked at what I'd written and debated changing it to something stronger like, *"I have a lead indicating you're innocent."* But that wasn't strictly speaking true, and I'd already done enough deceiving and exaggerating for one day.

But then, as my finger hovered above the SEND button, I gave myself a mental shake. *You're trying to find out once and for all who killed Livvy. Forget your little-girl scruples.*

I deleted what I'd written and replaced it with, *"I have discovered stunning new evidence that may prove you're innocent. It could remove the dark cloud that still lingers over you. Please contact me ASAP."*

Perfect. I hit SEND.

With that done, it was time to chase down Livvy's football-playing boyfriend, Brandon Allen. He was probably closer to her than anyone except her family. Whatever secrets were out there, there was a good chance he knew them.

Brandon had been a freshman when Livvy was murdered and he was still at Harvard, a senior now. The experts ranked him as one of the top college linebackers in the country, which was surprising because Harvard was barely Division 1. ESPN projected him as a first-round pick in the upcoming NFL draft.

As the ducks finally gave up and wobbled away, I searched the internet for a lead on Brandon. The *Deep Crimson Love* fan blog said that the football team, the Harvard Crimson, was practicing this afternoon at four. I could still make it if I hurried. I jogged to the Park Street Station and headed for the Red Line platform.

The T took a long time to arrive, though. As I waited, a grizzled-looking man who could have been anywhere from forty to seventy, with bloodshot eyes and a booze-scratched voice, twanged an out-of-tune guitar and sang a sad song about a tambourine man on a weary jingle-jangle morning. He forgot some words and had to repeat a verse. A battered guitar case lay open in front of him with a couple dollars' worth of change. I wondered what had brought the guy to this state. *He's an ex–newspaper reporter,* I decided.

The T finally came, and fifteen minutes later spilled me out onto Harvard Square. I hurried past college students and across the Charles River to the practice field at the Harvard University Athletics Complex. About fifty fans, mainly teenage girls with too much makeup trying to look older, were watching the practice through a tall metal fence. I took up a post alongside them.

At midfield, thirty or so players, supervised by coaches in sweatpants, rammed their bodies over and over again into heavy, plastic-covered slabs that started out vertical but bent and gave way each time they were attacked. The players wore shoulder pads but no helmets, so I was able to spot Brandon Allen. Even from this distance, I recognized his light brown hair and jutting chin.

I don't like football any more than baseball; I've never totally gotten the point of watching sports. But I couldn't help being impressed by the viciousness of the players' repeated onslaughts against the plastic slabs. The guy who bashed them hardest was Brandon. He would start out semi-kneeling, then leap up and drive his slab into the ground like it was a sworn enemy trying to massacre his whole family.

I already knew from photos that Brandon was a good-looking guy whose deep, thoughtful, dark eyes didn't fit my image of a dumb football player. I'd never had time for the jocks back in high school; I assumed they were shallow even though I didn't know any of them well. Now, seeing Brandon in person, I tried to reconcile the softness I'd detected in his eyes with his violent assaults on the slabs.

A wrinkly-faced octogenarian wearing a white bun stepped up to the fence a few feet away. After a few moments, she turned toward me. "I love watching these boys. They make me feel like a chippy again," she said with a laugh.

Watching them alongside her, a lonesome wind blew through me. "They make me feel old. I can't believe it's six years since I was in college."

"Honey, you look like a teenager."

I smiled. "Thank you." As Brandon smashed into his slab again, I thought about how I might get him to talk.

"You've got your eye on Brandon, don't you?" the elderly woman asked.

I nodded, not sure I wanted to encourage more conversation.

"Cute, huh?" she said. "Like Paul McCartney but with muscles. Look at those hands. You know what they say about big hands."

I couldn't help laughing. "I've heard that too."

She clucked her tongue sympathetically. "That boy's been through hell, his girlfriend getting murdered and all. You just want to take him and give him a big hug." Her face broke into an impish grin. "And a couple other things too."

"You're terrible," I said, and she chuckled. Maybe a superfan like her would have helpful information. "Is there any way to talk to these guys?"

"Good luck. Hon, every girl in Boston wants *his* babies—he's gonna be rich. I bet he's one of the first ten players that get drafted."

I realized one of the other guys bashing the slabs looked familiar too. He was taller than Brandon but not as muscular, with close-cropped hair, big ears, and eyes set wide apart. "Who's the tall guy?" I asked.

"That's Danny Madsen."

Right—Brandon and Livvy's friend. The accused rapist Livvy advocated for in her "Who Raped Who?" video.

The elderly woman read my thoughts. "Danny didn't do it, you know. He never hurt that Sarah Fain girl. Olivia was one hundred percent right about that."

"What makes you so sure?"

"I can tell. He gave me his autograph and signed it, 'Love, Danny.'"

Suddenly a piercing whistle sounded. One of the coaches called out so loud we could all hear it. "Okay, hit the showers, guys!"

As the players ran off the field, I noticed Brandon and Danny heading toward each other, between two tackling dummies. There wasn't room enough for both of them, but neither one was willing to turn sideways and let the other pass. They gave each other macho stares and ended up banging pretty hard into each other's shoulders. Then they walked on without looking at each other.

Odd. I remembered the photo of Brandon, Danny, and Livvy, arm in arm. "I thought Brandon and Danny were friends," I said to the elderly woman. "That's what Olivia said in her video."

"These boys are very competitive."

But it sure looked to me like there was more than just competitive spirit dividing Brandon and Danny. They had a beef with each other. *About what?* I wondered.

After the players disappeared into the locker room, I went to the front steps of the gym so I could be there when they came out. My new friend and ten or fifteen giggling teenagers joined me.

Half an hour later, the players finally began to exit the gym. They looked even younger in street clothes. The teenage girls pressed forward for autographs, but I hung back.

Brandon came out at last, flanked by a campus security cop and a red-faced coach whose belly hung out over his sweatshirt. I made my move, elbowing my way to the front of all the girls rushing toward him. "Brandon, can I talk to you—"

The campus cop got in my way. "Step back, please."

I went around him. Brandon was walking swiftly to a campus security car that had just driven up; evidently he got extra protection. "Brandon, my name is—"

From behind me, the cop grabbed my elbow. "*Step back.*"

But I twisted out of his grip. Brandon was only ten feet away. Raising my voice, I played my best card. "I'm Petra Kovach. I was a friend of Livvy's."

Brandon turned to me, eyes widening. He had recognized my name; Livvy must have mentioned me. But then the cop grabbed my arm, wrenching it, and the red-faced coach got hold of my other arm.

"You understand English? Get your ass out of here," the coach snapped.

"I'm a reporter for the *Clarion*. I'm here on a story."

He shoved me backward so roughly I stumbled and fell to the ground. "Don't come around here again or I'll have you arrested."

The cop glowered like he was ready to arrest me right now. The coach walked off, as Brandon got in the car and rode away. I stood back up, watching him go, and rubbed my arm where it had been wrenched. *Attacked twice in one afternoon,* I thought.

Somebody tapped me on the shoulder. I whirled, thinking I was about to get grabbed again.

It was the elderly lady. She put a consoling hand on my arm. "Don't worry, honey. Just wear a wig next time and they won't recognize you."

There would be a next time, alright. I'd get hold of Brandon and Danny both.

I'd ask them about Eric's secret—and about the beef between them.

CHAPTER SEVEN

EXHAUSTED, WITH THE sky growing dark, I headed back toward the T station and home. But I hadn't made it a block before my phone pinged. Professor Reynolds had just emailed me back.

I clicked on his email, excited. It took forever to open up. "Come on!" I said out loud.

Finally the email loaded onto my screen. It consisted of one emoji, repeated three times: an upraised middle finger.

Really?

How many people had told me "fuck you" today, in one way or another? I'd lost count. Then the phone buzzed: Mama calling again. I sighed and hit the green button before I realized what a mistake that was. I was in no condition to cheerfully bullshit Mama.

But I would try. *"Zdravo, Mama.* Is everything good?"

"I saw your article, about tempers flaring at City Hall," she answered. "Very nice!"

I heard people talking in the background and pictured Mama stepping away from her dentist's receptionist job for a moment so she could call me. "Thanks, Mama," I said, crossing the street toward the T station.

"How many clicks did you get?"

I had forgotten all about that. But if I said so, she'd realize something was bothering me. "Five thousand."

"O moj Bože, five thousand? Your boss must be very happy!"

My lips tightened. "I gotta go, Mama. Subway's coming. Love you!"

I hung up quickly and headed down the subway steps. I took the Red Line to the Green, and when I finally made it to North Station, three blocks from home, I was so hungry I could hardly stand it.

But now I had to face Jonah and finally come clean.

Walking through the North End past all the newly renovated triple-deckers, I thought, *Is there any way to spin this positively?* After all, I still had a shot at keeping my job.

A *slim* shot. I'd been fired. Again.

Beneath a streetlight, two teenage girls walked past me laughing, arms swinging, carefree. I thought back to my two best friends I grew up with, Alejandra and Sienna. I should have become a nurse or teacher like they did. Why had I imagined I was different, that I was better or smarter somehow than everybody else? It wasn't true.

And what about my college friends—the ones who majored in *anything* besides journalism? They were all working for big tech companies or cool startups. If they didn't pull in six-figure salaries already, they would soon.

I dreaded telling Jonah about my latest shit show even more than telling Mama. Because my relationship with Mama would last forever. But how much more *sturm und drang* could my relationship with Jonah take?

No doubt Jonah would try to be supportive, like every other time I'd lost my job. But sometimes my moods frustrated him. "Dude, shit happens. Lighten up on yourself," he would say. I'd show him newspaper articles explaining how getting fired gives you PTSD just like being in a war, and he'd try to understand. But he couldn't, not really. He was a cutting-edge computer scientist. He would always be in demand.

Our seven months in Boston had been heaven. We lived on the top floor of a newly painted, purple triple-decker in the North End, with bay windows and sunflowers and roses out front. On Saturday nights we'd stroll to Faneuil Hall for ice cream cones, which always reminded us of our very first date ambling down Lamar Boulevard in Oxford. As I thrived at my new job, our relationship thrived too.

Would my getting fired yet again ruin everything? Would Jonah lose faith in me? God knows I was losing faith in me. Jonah might decide he'd never have a simple, easy life with me.

I trudged up the wooden stairs to our third-floor apartment. Jonah must have heard me coming, because before I could even put my key in the lock, he opened the door and stepped out into the hallway. He had a spatula in his hand and a big smile on his face.

"There she is: the incredible Petra Kovach!" He hugged me, holding the spatula away from my clothes.

He smelled like rosemary and lemons mixed with fresh sweat from his bike ride home. I wanted to just grab him and hold him.

But I was feeling too scared. I managed to smile and say, "Hey, babe."

He put on a goofy French accent as he led me into the apartment. "Deenair eez on ze table. Rosemary salmon and pumpkin pesto avec ze red wine."

There were candles too, and flowers. My heart caught in my throat. I hated that I would have to ruin this night Jonah had prepared for us so beautifully.

"Wow, this is amazing," I said. I picked up a glass of wine and had a healthy-sized glug. *I'd rather get hit in the head with a hammer than have this conversation,* I thought. I pictured Jonah's eyes filling with disappointment and even disgust.

He switched out of his French accent. "So I'm dying here. What did Dave say?"

I drank again, through a lump of shame in my throat that almost made me choke. "Well," I began. As I looked at Jonah, desperation welled up inside me. *Maybe I can ease into it.* "He . . . complimented me on the article."

"Yeah, you got so many clicks!"

"And then . . ." I paused.

"Then what?" His face shone with eager anticipation.

Oh God, I have to tell him. I have to—

"I am so proud of you," Jonah said, touching my arm. "I knew you could pull this off—it means so much to both of us. So what happened?"

I can't. Not now. I just can't.

"I pitched him Livvy's story, and he said yes."

I mean, I wasn't exactly *lying.* I just left out some stuff.

He gave me an admiring grin. "Wow, it was that simple?"

I managed a nod. "He wants me to do a podcast."

"Holy crap, Petra!"

"Yeah," I said, grabbing another drink of wine and feeling like shit. I had never lied to Jonah before—even if it was technically an omission, it sure felt like a lie—and certainly never about anything this important. I wanted to take it all back and tell Jonah the whole truth. I opened my mouth, trying to get the words out of my dry throat.

But maybe he'll never have to know. I'll find out Eric's secret and pull this podcast together and everything will work out.

"That's so great!" Jonah said. Then his face wrinkled into a puzzled frown. "Why aren't you more excited?"

"I am, I'm just exhausted. And starved," I added.

"I have just the cure for that. Grab a seat!" As we sat down at the table, he asked, "So did you talk to Olivia's brother today? After you talked to Dave?"

"I'm working a couple different angles now."

He beamed at me. "Major leagues, baby. No more getting laid off, now it's just about … " He raised a suggestive eyebrow. " … Getting laid."

I couldn't help smiling at that. "I should eat."

"Yeah, you'll need *all* your stamina tonight." Then his eyes turned serious. "I just feel like, great city, stable jobs … " He lifted his wineglass. "We can like, start our lives."

I tried to meet his eyes but couldn't. I looked away and started to eat.

The dinner would have been a lot more delicious if I could have tasted it. Jonah chattered away happily and I tried to match him.

After we finished eating, he moved the candles into the living room and turned the lights down low. We set our phones aside on the table and slow danced to gypsy jazz—our favorite foreplay music.

I wished I was one of those people who can use lovemaking to get out of a funk. But I'd learned years ago I needed to be in a good mood already, feeling safe, before I could let myself go. When I was like that, I'd run my hands through Jonah's curly black hair, gaze at his gray eyes that crinkled when he smiled, feel him getting excited, and just melt. Sometimes I would climax the moment he came inside me—a feeling I'd never experienced with anybody else. Just one more way Jonah was the best thing that had ever happened to me.

But tonight the magic wasn't there. Jonah noticed. As we danced, he stepped back from me. "What are you thinking?"

I tried to play it off. "How handsome you are."

"Come on."

"And unbelievably sexy." I reached for his pants and started pulling off his belt. Maybe I could psyche myself into it. He was certainly ready, no question about that—

"Wait." He pulled away from me, but I kept going, unzipping him. "Petra, wait," he repeated.

"That's not what your body's saying."

"There's something I have to ask you."

I blinked. "Okay . . ."

Jonah pulled a small box from his pants pocket. Then he dropped down to one knee and said, "Would you like to engage in an exclusive partnership in perpetuity?"

My mouth fell open.

"I.e.," he said, "will you marry me?"

Oh my God. Tonight of all nights.

But I'd dreamed of this for so long. I'd known almost from the first that he would be the one—

"Yes," I said.

"Whew, thank God," he said. "I was getting nervous there for a minute."

I took his hand. "Jonah . . . *volim te.*" *I love you.*

"I love you more than the moon loves the sky."

We kissed—a long sweet kiss. Then he held out the box to me and I opened it.

The ring was a sparkly diamond set in a circle of sapphires. It wasn't too big but not small either—it was just right.

"Certified non-blood diamond," he said, anxious. "If you don't like it, I can return it."

I put it on my finger. It fit perfectly.

Everything fit perfectly now. All my fears fell away. We were together forever. We would survive my current horror show. "It's beautiful," I said, and kissed him. He kissed me back. Then his lips went lower and he kissed my neck, just the way I liked it—

Buzz.

It was my phone, sitting there on the table. I didn't mean to look. It was just force of habit. But look I did, over Jonah's shoulder, and I saw a message from Dave: HOW'S YOUR BIG LEAD COMING?

My neck tightened instantly, panic jolting through me. I had no lead, big or small. I had nothing. *I'll get fired for real this time. I won't find another journalism job in Boston. Jonah will find out I lied to him. He'll hate me. We'll break up.*

He started unbuttoning my shirt. But there was no way I could get in the mood now. "Wait. Jonah, hold up."

"That's not what your body's saying," he teased, tracing my nipples. They were still hard—but my mind wasn't following my body.

I steeled myself. "I know this is horrible timing, but, I have to go."

He stared at me. "Is something wrong?"

"Olivia's brother just texted me." *God, another lie.* "He's leaving tomorrow for two weeks, and that's my deadline, so I need to talk to him *tonight*—"

"We just got engaged!"

"This is really important—"

"So's this! Are you fucking kidding me?"

I'm such an asshole. "I'm sorry, sweetie. I'll make it up to you when I get home, I promise."

I put on my coat and shoes. If I was really leaving, I needed to do it and get it over with.

Jonah glared at me, pissed off and hurt. But what choice did I have? Engaged or not, if I got fired, our relationship was in big trouble and might not make it. I was trying to save *us*! If only I could explain that to him!

I kissed Jonah, but he didn't kiss me back. "I love you," I said.

He shook his head in disbelief. I wanted to throw my arms around him and never let go.

Instead I hurried out the door. Eric had said he went to the Parting Glass every Thursday night. I needed to get there in time to catch him.

CHAPTER EIGHT

I TOOK A Lyft, figuring it would be faster at night than the T. But the bridge over the Charles was tied up, so I didn't make it to the Parting Glass 'til ten. Praying that Eric would be there tonight instead of at home packing for his trip, I opened the bar's heavy oak door and headed inside.

I sighed with relief when I spotted him sitting at the crowded bar, Guinness in hand, chatting up a young blonde. For a crazy second I thought it was Natalie. Somehow she'd gotten to Eric first and was going to scoop me.

But then I saw the woman was in her early twenties, maybe even still in college. How often did Eric score here on his Thursday nights? It looked like he was getting somewhere tonight: they both looked buzzed and their bodies were close.

Well, I was about to do some serious cock blocking. Wading through a group of guys in Somerville Softball T-shirts, I stepped up to Eric and the young woman. "Hey, Eric," I said.

He instantly glared at me, but I plunged on. "I wanted to give you another chance."

Eric turned to his drinking partner—definitely a college girl, maybe Tufts. "Fucking reporter. This place gets all kinds of riffraff."

Her eyes widened, intrigued. Maybe instead of busting Eric's game, I was helping it. I said, "I'm producing a podcast for the *Clarion* about your sister's murder. The first episode comes out next week."

"Good for you. Now get the hell out of my face."

I narrowed my eyes into slits. My gentle, caring approach at the Red Dolphin had flopped. Tonight I'd try to go tougher, even if it didn't feel natural. "You want me to say you refused to cooperate? It'll look like you're hiding shit about her murder." I'd used a similar line on Eric's stepdad, but now I upped the stakes. Stepping between him and the college girl, I said, "Maybe you *are* hiding something."

The girl backed up. "Whoa, this is heavy."

Eric said, "Bitch, I can get you thrown out of here."

I took out my phone. "That would be awesome for my podcast. Just wait 'til I hit 'record.'"

"Go ahead. You want everyone to know you're a goddamn vulture stalking the victim's family?"

Get-tough isn't working. I put up my hands. "Dude, I'm just trying to find out who killed Livvy. Isn't that what *you* want?"

His lips twisted with sarcasm. "Right, like you'll actually catch the real killer. You're nothing but a lying piece-of-shit hustler."

The real killer. My skin tingled all the way down my spine, just like the night when I first met Eric. "The way you said that, about catching the real killer. You really do think the cops got the wrong guy."

He gave a disbelieving laugh—but his eyes flickered and looked away. That was number one on the "*17 Ways to Tell If He's Lying*" piece I'd written once. "Admit it, I'm right. You used to think Reynolds did it—but you don't anymore."

The college girl watched, enthralled, as Eric said, "What, you're a psychic now? Where's your tarot cards?"

"Tell me what you know. I promise I'll keep you out of it."

"Right—'cause I should trust you."

I looked deep into his eyes. "What would Livvy want you to do right now?"

"Knowing her, she'd want me to pour this Guinness on your head."

The college girl laughed. That seemed to encourage Eric, and he called to the bartender, a beefy guy in his thirties with a cold, flat face. "Hey, Billy, would you get this sleazebag reporter outta here?"

Billy put down the towel he was wiping with and came over. "Eric," I began, about to implore or threaten him, I wasn't sure which.

But Billy cut me off. "Another one, huh?" he said in a thick Eastern European accent. Russian I thought. "Okay, get out of here, lady."

If I left this bar now, I could forget about saving my job—or finding Livvy's killer. Billy stepped around the counter toward me, but I stood my ground. "I'm not going anywhere," I told them. Then, from some place deep inside me that I hadn't even known existed, I said in a low voice, almost growling, "I'm chasing your sister's case like a fucking dog in heat, 'cause that's what you need right now."

Eric looked mesmerized by me. But Billy got in my face, close enough where I could see every black pore on his nose. "You got two seconds before I grab you."

I backed up, bumping into one of the Somerville Softball guys. I was losing again! I'd have to go home and tell Jonah *everything*. Desperation flooded through me as I took one last look back at Eric and the cute blonde college girl. Up close, she didn't look at all like Natalie; she looked more like Livvy.

Like Livvy. That gave me a sudden idea. Without stopping to think if it was a *good* idea, I said, "My sources say you were having an affair with your sister."

Eric's eyes widened with shock. Hell, I was stunned too—I couldn't believe I'd said that. The college girl spilled beer on the table, and Billy stopped in his tracks.

But I was committed now. I continued, "They say that's why you killed her."

"That is total bullshit," Eric said. "You made that up!"

"Maybe, maybe not." I pointed at the girl. "But good luck picking up chicks in bars if they all hear on my podcast how you fucked your little sister and then bashed her head in with a bedside lamp."

I took a business card from my purse and laid it on the bar. "Call me," I said. "And by the way, if you didn't kill Livvy, this piece-of-shit lying hustler is your best chance to find out the truth."

Then I turned and headed past the softball players out the door.

Out on the street again, walking swiftly through the autumn wind to the T station, I still couldn't believe what I'd just done. *Jesus, I am a total bitch. I should go back in there and apologize.*

But what good would that do? Billy would throw me out of the bar before I even got any words out. Eric would just scream at me.

Yes, I had gone over the line in there. I wouldn't do that again. But I was trying to solve a murder. Livvy's murder. If that meant being a little manipulative, hey, cops did it all the time—at least on TV, and I bet in real life too. Same with reporters.

Weariness swept over me. The night was growing colder and I couldn't deal with taking two subway lines. So I decided to take another Lyft, even though God knows I was in no hurry to get home and face Jonah.

I found a dark recessed entryway to a women's clothing store, out of the wind, and called a Lyft. My phone said it would arrive in nine minutes. As I clicked to accept, I heard sudden footsteps—somebody running straight toward me. The thug with the Popeye muscles? I turned quickly.

But not quickly enough. Eric charged into the entryway. His right hand shoved me against the window and his left hand grabbed my throat.

CHAPTER NINE

"Who told you that?" Eric snarled.

"Get off me," I gasped, trying to tear his arms away. But they were steel rods.

"Did somebody really say I was having sex with my sister?"

I wasn't just terrified, I was boiling mad. Why did all these people think they could just manhandle me whenever they felt like it? I'd been a jerk to Eric, but that didn't give him an excuse to physically assault me. I reached into my East LA and jammed my right thumb into his eye.

He screamed and pulled back. I kneed him in the balls, and he groaned and let go of me.

I was debating whether to yell bloody murder or run away, or both, when he said, "Was it my stepfather? He said that?"

What? I moved a few yards away. "Why do you ask?"

He held his groin, evidently still in pain, and glared at me. "Because it's fucking weird," he spat out. I was afraid he'd attack me again, and I got on the balls of my feet, ready to tear off.

Then he shook his head, confused, and turned plaintive. "I don't know what the hell to do. I've never told anybody this."

He went silent. "Told anybody what?" I asked.

He stepped closer and looked hard at my face. Resisting my urge to run, I met his eyes. He said, "Do you swear to keep it confidential where you heard this?"

My pulse roared in my ears. "Of course."

"You have rules about that, right? About protecting your source?"

"Yes." I had an inspiration. "That's why I can't say where I heard that rumor about you. I'm protecting my source."

"That asshole!" Eric slammed his hand against the wall next to the store window. That seemed to focus him, and he looked back at me. "This really might have something to do with what happened to Olivia. It needs to come out. But I can't have anybody knowing it's from me. Especially my stepdad."

What in God's name was going on between Eric and Viktor? "You have my word."

He looked tortured. "You have to understand, he's been good to me. He's the only family I have anymore. Shit is gonna hit the fan, and I can't have this be my fault."

"Eric..." I felt sympathetic, he was in such pain. But I was thrilled by the revelation to come. "What is it you want to tell me?"

He let out a deep breath, leaning against the wall and shutting his eyes. I forced myself to stay patient.

Finally he opened them again. "On Christmas vacation, when Livvy came home from Harvard, she told me she liked to post anonymously on social media. So after she died, I got on Insta and Twitter and everywhere looking for clues. I tried all her nicknames I could think of, but I never found anything."

He wrapped his arms around himself, as if for comfort. "Then a month ago, it was Livvy's birthday. People put up remembrances on her Facebook page. Including some old friends from elementary school. They used her kindergarten nickname, 'Olly Olly Oxen

Free.' You know, the thing you say when you're playing hide-and-seek and it's safe to come out?"

"Sure," I said, though I'd never heard that before. *Olly Olly what?* It must be an East Coast thing, or something rich kids did.

"So I searched social media again, using 'Olly Olly Oxen Free.' And this time I found something. On Reddit."

He stopped. The hair rose on the back of my neck. "What was it?"

"Disturbing shit," Eric said. "Here's what I need you to say: you were reading her Facebook page, and you happened to see her old nickname and tried it on social media. That way you can leave me out of it."

"I'll do that. I promise."

"You better or I'll fucking kill you. Or myself."

Then Eric surprised me by peeling himself off the wall and heading away down the sidewalk. I realized he didn't want to tell me what he'd found on Reddit; he wanted me to read it for myself. Maybe that way he'd feel less responsible somehow.

I still felt bad about coming at him so hard in the bar. I called out, "Eric, I never would've spread those rumors about you. I was just . . ."

He kept walking, not turning around, and my Lyft pulled up just then, so I didn't get to finish my apology. I got in the back seat and greeted the driver, a woman with a determined smile and a silver cross hanging down from her mirror.

I called up Reddit on my phone and searched "Olly Olly Oxen Free."

It was disturbing shit, alright.

Olly Olly Oxen Free's very first post, from seven years ago when Livvy was fourteen, was only one sentence long. It read: *"If you have sex with your stepfather, is it technically incest?"*

CHAPTER TEN

MY HEART STOPPED. *Holy crap, is this real?*

I thought about Viktor staring at my breasts and saying "Nice tits" a minute after he met me. Not proof he was a child molester, of course—but it made me have less trouble believing it. And this would explain why he sent his thug after me—he had something to hide.

As the Lyft rolled past empty storefronts on Mass. Ave., I scrolled down my phone searching for more posts from Olly Olly Oxen Free. For a long time I didn't find any. But there were over a hundred replies to her short post, mostly lewd comments like, *"It's not incest if you're just doing anal."* There were gentler responses too, from women and girls sensing Olly Olly Oxen Free was reaching out for help. One woman, DakotaMary, wrote, *"It sounds like you're dealing with some stuff. Do you want to talk about it?"*

Finally, as the Lyft went over the river, I found a comment from Olly Olly Oxen Free, responding to DakotaMary. *"I know it's supposed to be wrong,"* she wrote, *"but I love my stepdad. And he was having such a hard time after my mom died. He was so lonely. He couldn't sleep so he came into my room, and first we just slept together with our clothes on but then we started doing other stuff. It made us both feel happy again. How can that be wrong?"*

Jesus. No wonder Eric was so stunned when I accused him of having incest with his sister. She was an incest victim, alright—but of somebody else.

I wondered, had Livvy's spirit guided me into asking Eric about incest? Or did I somehow intuit that Livvy had gone through that?

I stared at my screen unable to read it, my eyes cloudy with anger and tears. Livvy was so young then, a ninth grader for God's sake, and dealing with her mom's death. How could Viktor do that to her? So disgusting—and *evil.*

And what else had he done? What if Livvy was murdered by her secret lover, just like everyone suspected—*but the secret lover was her own stepfather!*

What a twist that would be for my podcast!

Because now, for the first time, I believed I could actually pull off a podcast—and save my job. "Fucking incredible!" I said out loud, then realized the Lyft driver with the cross hanging off her mirror was frowning at me. "Sorry."

I felt like a shit, getting excited when I had just learned about this horrible abuse Livvy went through. But really, anything that helped me would also help Livvy get justice at last. They were one and the same thing. I refocused and read on.

Livvy got literally hundreds of replies to her last comment. Besides more internet nastiness—*"What a stupid little girl," "So you're into old farts? Message me privately"*—there was a wide range of opinions and advice. Some people wanted her to go to the police; others suggested a therapist. A number of women described similar experiences. *"It wasn't all bad,"* LadyFly wrote. *"I guess you could say my uncle was taking advantage of me, but it made me feel special. It was way better than some of the first sex experiences my friends had with their same-age boyfriends."*

Olly Olly Oxen Free responded, *"Exactly! I don't see how I'm being hurt, I mean, it's totally consensual. And don't tell me because I'm only fourteen I'm too young. I know what I'm doing. I mean yeah it feels a little weird, but basically it's cool."*

No, it was sick, I thought. *I don't care if you imagined it was consensual, it was rape.* My mind went to all the late-night texts Livvy had sent me for four years. How did I miss it? Did she ever hint her stepfather was sexually abusing her?

No, I was pretty sure she never did, not in any obvious way. She must have felt she couldn't talk to me about it. How lonely, having this terrifying secret you can't share with anyone except your subreddit.

I wondered if her stepfather's abuse partly explained why she turned into an alt-right fire-breather. Maybe her political rants were misplaced rage at Viktor. She couldn't express her anger to him directly, so she found other targets.

As the Lyft stopped at a red light, I got a worrisome thought: *Wait, am I positive Olly Olly Oxen Free is really Livvy? Do I have proof?*

This girl's comments definitely sounded like Livvy. Also, she wrote that she was fourteen, Livvy's age at the time. Then I found a comment where she described her stepfather as "not a troll or anything—he's real handsome with thick wavy hair." That fit too. She said he'd married her mother seven years before—another fit; and he traveled a lot, which was no doubt true of foreign consuls. With all these details piling up, Dave would feel comfortable running with this.

My thoughts got derailed when I found a Reddit comment from March 30, two and a half years ago. Olly Olly Oxen Free had posted a lot when she was fourteen and fifteen, followed by radio silence during her last years of high school. But now, at age eighteen, she wrote, *"Stepfather-incest update: I moved away from home and started college last September. And I have to say my feelings about my stepdad have changed. Yes I still love him. But I'm starting to wonder if our thing was really sick all along. I'm so fucked up about sex. It's messing up my relationship with this guy at school and I keep getting distracted, upset, angry. I tried to break it off with my stepdad over Christmas but he wouldn't let me."*

I stared at these words. He wouldn't *let* me?!

"Or I wouldn't let me I dunno," her comment continued. *"He gets so intense. But now I'm breaking it off for real. Spring break is in three days and I'm ending it before then, I don't care what he says. I can't keep doing this, I just can't."*

Livvy was killed just two nights later. *The night before spring break.* I said out loud, "He killed her. She told Viktor it was over, and he fucking killed her."

The Lyft driver glared at me again. But this time I didn't bother apologizing. "I think I just solved the murder of a girl I loved."

The driver's brow furrowed. "You did what?"

"I can't tell you any more now, but there'll be a podcast in two weeks."

The Lyft arrived at the apartment, so I told the driver, "Have a great night," and jumped out. Her eyes followed me, probably wondering if I was insane.

I bounded up the steps to the third floor. Then I remembered how awful I'd been to Jonah earlier tonight, and slowed down.

But I'd apologize to him. Jonah and I would work it out. Not only had I found a huge piece of evidence, I'd saved my job. By doing that, I might just have saved our relationship.

I unlocked our door and went in. Jonah was on the sofa in a T-shirt and boxers, playing Magic on his laptop. He threw me a pissed-off look. "It's after midnight."

I threw my purse down and sat beside him. Jonah was the one simple, good thing in a life that was way too complicated right now. "I'm sorry I'm so late. I've been thinking about you all night."

"What the hell is the matter with you?" He set his computer aside and stared at me. "Is there some secret you're not telling me?"

"No," I said, looking him in the eye. I still felt bad about lying, but now that I wouldn't get fired after all, he definitely didn't need to know how close I'd come.

"Then how could you walk out on the night we got engaged—"

"I'm just obsessed with solving Livvy's murder. You know how I feel about her." I took his hand and held on, even when he pulled back. "Jonah, please believe me. I love you more than anything in the world. I'm so excited to be getting married to you." I put my other hand on his hip. "Let's start this night over again."

"I really don't see how we can."

"Please, baby. I love you so much." My eyes began to tear up for the second time in the last twenty minutes. My hand slid down his body.

He protested, "Look, you can't just act like—"

"Jonah, you're the handsomest, smartest, kindest, sexiest man I have ever met, and I want to spend my life with you."

His eyes closed, his breath caught, and he got hard faster than I would have thought was physically possible. He gasped a little and said, "I guess you got good news tonight."

"The best. My boyfriend proposed to me."

Then I pulled off my jeans and climbed on top of him.

Fifteen minutes later we spilled off the sofa, spent, and collapsed onto the rug. Jonah ran his hand through my hair. "Damn, what got into you tonight?"

I curled into him. "The world's best cock," I said, grabbing it.

He laughed and cupped my breast in response. "So what did Olivia's brother have to say?"

"Olly Olly Oxen Free."

"What?"

"Long story." Then I sat up on the rug and launched into it. It felt so great being able to share my big success.

He sat beside me and read the Reddit posts. "God, this is *sick*," he said.

"And it's definitely a murder motive for Viktor."

"Yeah."

But there was doubt in his voice and the downward curve of his eyebrows. "Is something wrong?"

He moved away from me on the rug. "It's just, the way you got Eric to talk. Threatening to tell the world he had incest with his sister."

I dropped my eyes. "I felt terrible about it. But it worked. It helped me maybe solve Livvy's murder."

"But it's like extortion."

He was right. Now that he'd put a name to it, a shiver went through me. But I didn't want to go there. "Jonah, don't make me feel any worse." I felt exposed, sitting there naked while he challenged me. I picked up my clothes from the floor and stood up. "I'm a *journalist*. You have to do this kind of stuff if you want to be successful."

He narrowed his eyes, trying to read me. "You're not having problems at work, are you?"

"Of course not. Everything's great."

As I headed for the bathroom, he called, "I'm just worried you'll get in trouble."

"Quit worrying."

I closed the bathroom door and leaned against the wall. Then I brushed my teeth. I began to breathe normally again and calm down.

Today had been an amazing day. My biggest dreams were both coming true: I was investigating Livvy's murder, and Jonah and I got *engaged*. To be *married*. How cool was that? I touched the ring on my finger. I'd been wanting this for two years—and now it had happened!

Everything would be fine. Jonah and I would get over this quarrel by tomorrow.

Tomorrow. I couldn't wait to see Dave first thing in the morning and tell him about my incredible coup.

CHAPTER ELEVEN

SURE ENOUGH, BY the next morning Jonah and I were in sync again. The memory of last night's lovemaking had wiped out any lingering negativity.

And besides—*engaged!*

Even so, I was glad to kiss Jonah goodbye and take off. I didn't need any more ethical debates this morning. Jonah was a computer guy, working in a field where things were binary, black and white. He didn't get the gray.

As soon as I got to the office, I printed out a hard copy of Olly Olly Oxen Free's Reddit posts. I stood over the printer to make sure nobody else came in and read them. Then I knocked on Dave's door, handed him the pages, and waited for his response.

I didn't have to wait long. From the first sentence Dave was hooked. "Evil stepdad has incest with daughter, and son accuses him of murder. This is fantastic stuff. It's fucking Biblical!"

I smiled as only someone who has just saved her job can smile. Dave jumped up and paced the office as he read, jabbing his fist in the air whenever he came to an especially dramatic post. For a chubby guy in his fifties, he moved surprisingly well. I'd never seen him like this. It convinced me I'd guessed right: Dave was petrified of getting laid off himself and hoped my podcast would help save him too. "We'll run the podcast and article simultaneously," he said. "I bet we get more clicks than anything since the Boston Marathon bombing. Terrific work, Petra."

I beamed. "Thank you."

"So what's your next step?"

"I'll get a response from Viktor."

Dave nodded approvingly. "Excellent. And talk to the cops who investigated, see if they ever suspected him."

"Will do. And I'll reach out to Livvy's friends to find out if she ever confided in them."

"Do you have any contacts in the Cambridge police department?"

"Not yet, but I'm sure—"

"Natalie has relationships there. I'll assign her to this story too." He reached for his phone.

Shit! I said quickly, "No, I can handle it." The last thing I needed was to share credit with Natalie. She'd find some way to screw me.

His hand hovered over the phone. "Sure you don't want help? You guys are friends, right?"

I couldn't tell him how little I trusted Natalie, especially since he seemed to think she was the best thing since avocado toast. "I got this," I said in a firm voice. "Just give me Larry to help with recording the podcast, and I'm good."

Larry was a twenty-three-year-old dropout from Reed College in Oregon who did tech stuff for the newspaper. A tall, gangly guy with hair past his shoulders, he wore tie-dye shirts and came in stoned half the time, but he was brilliant. I could never have written my Bitcoin story the previous month without him explaining things to me.

And he was trustworthy. Larry wouldn't steal the story out from under me.

I waited with my heart in my throat while Dave decided what to do. After a few seconds he put his hand on the phone, about to call

Natalie. I jumped in. "We should keep this story under wraps, with as few people involved as possible. We don't want any leaks. That would ruin the impact."

Dave hesitated, tugging at his earlobe. "The thing is, I'm meeting with Abernathy at the end of next week. This podcast needs to come out before then." The earlobe was stretched to the limit. He was probably afraid Abernathy would fire him at that meeting. Then his hand went back on the phone.

I jumped in even faster this time. "I guarantee we'll get this done way before the end of next week. I can write it up this weekend."

Dave looked me in the eye, like he was trying to decide how much he could rely on me. I did my best not to blink or flinch.

Finally he took his hand off the phone. "Okay, we'll see how it goes, but for now we'll keep it on the DL."

I breathed again. Dave tapped his desk. "I can't wait to hear what Abusive Stepdad has to say. I want more than just 'no comment.'"

Given how Viktor had blown me off yesterday, I wasn't sure I could deliver on that. "I'll do my best," I said, and instantly realized I'd screwed up. *Don't show weakness!* In thinking about my past layoffs, I had concluded that if I'd acted more sure of myself at work, I might have been less vulnerable.

Dave frowned, maybe regretting his decision to let me keep the whole story for myself. "We need a statement from him. It's important, Petra."

"I'll get it," I said, deepening my voice.

I left Dave's office and printed out two more copies of the Reddit posts. As I hurried to the T station, heading back to the Swedish consulate, I found myself feeling uneasy, like there was a hollow place in my sternum. My end of the subway car was miraculously empty, and we were aboveground and getting reception, so I took the opportunity to call Mateo. He was alone too, in his office at the law firm.

"Hey, girl, tell me you're not fired yet," he said.

"Far from," I replied. I swore him to secrecy, then read Livvy's Reddit posts out loud.

Mateo was just as enthusiastic as Dave had been. "Damn, way to go, homegirl! I'll be saying I knew you when!"

It was the reaction I'd wanted, but somehow it made me even more nervous. "Mateo, can I tell you a secret?"

"Always."

"I'm scared shitless."

"Why?"

"I don't know. I guess I'm afraid I'll screw this up somehow."

"The old fraud thing," Mateo said.

I frowned. "What old fraud thing?"

"Every time one of the law partners compliments me on my work, I have this quick shot of feeling like a total fake. Like, I'm a poor boy from Oaxaca by way of East LA, what the hell am I doing here in this fancy office with a killer view of all of Boston?"

I nodded vigorously, even though Mateo couldn't see it. "Exactly. Like who am I trying to fool, pretending to be some big shot reporter?"

"Just remember, girl. You're fabulous."

I took a deep breath, feeling better already. "I keep imagining when I go to see Viktor, he'll just make stupid remarks about my breasts again. But he won't. This is a credible allegation made by his own stepdaughter. He'll *have* to respond."

"Petra, you'll destroy that asshole."

"Here's the thing. I really think I might be on the track of Livvy's killer."

"Livvy's up in heaven cheering you on."

The T came to a stop and I got off. "I gotta go. Mateo, you're the best."

"True, but you're a close second."

Three minutes later, I walked up the steps into the consulate. I saw my reflection in the window and felt damn good about how I looked. I'd worn my kick-ass thrift-shop Steve Madden shoes today, and the heels clicked satisfyingly on the concrete.

I walked in and came face-to-face with the receptionist with the ombre hair. She wore a Dries Van Noten dress today, and her professional smile turned instantly frosty. I said, "I'd like to see the consul."

"I'm sure you would," she said. "Shall I have security see you out?"

I looked around the waiting room. Two businessman types in suits sat in one corner and a woman in a tidy black pantsuit sat in another. They were all on their phones. "Could you please tell Mr. Anderson," I said, and then leaned forward and whispered so only the receptionist could hear, "I have information he was having sex with his daughter before she was killed."

The receptionist jumped, startled. The other people all looked up from their phones, sensing something odd was happening. I whispered, "Oh, excuse me, I meant 'stepdaughter.' Would Mr. Anderson care to address the allegations?"

The receptionist found her voice, though she kept it low. "Get out of this office." She pushed a red button on her office phone.

"Also," I whispered, "does Mr. Anderson have an alibi for the night of Olivia's murder?"

She gave an audible gasp, just as the security guard came in from the back room. It was the guy with the Popeye muscles. My neck started to hurt where he had dug into me yesterday, and I took a step back reflexively.

"What's going on?" he asked the receptionist, cutting his eyes at me.

"I was just leaving," I said. "But first I'll give you this." I took a copy of the Reddit posts from my purse and held it out. When the receptionist refused to touch the stapled pages, I placed them on her desk. "My phone number is on there. I look forward to hearing from Mr. Anderson."

Then I turned to the security guard. "And if you touch me again, you ugly cretin, I'm calling the police."

I walked out, head high, with everybody's eyes on me. *God, that felt good.*

But would Viktor take the bait? Or would I come up empty?

On the subway back to the *Clarion* office, I got a text from Dave. HOW'D IT GO WITH MONSTER STEPDAD?

I texted back, STILL WORKING IT.

As soon as I got back to my desk, I scarfed down a raspberry yogurt and looked up contact info for Hope O'Keefe, the detective who had investigated Livvy's murder. Maybe she'd heard rumors about Livvy and Viktor too. I flashed on an image of the two of them in bed together and got thoroughly grossed out.

I picked up my phone and was about to call O'Keefe when it buzzed. I checked the caller ID: *"Viktor Anderson."* Yes!

I hit the green button. "Hello, Mr.—"

But then I heard a noise. I looked up and saw Natalie standing at the opening to my cubicle. Did she have some kind of sixth sense? I was about to say "Anderson," but I couldn't have Natalie hearing the name and somehow guessing what was going on. So I continued with, "Thank you for getting back to me."

Natalie just stood there, listening. What should I do? Even if I got her to leave, she could still eavesdrop from the hallway.

But I wasn't about to ask Viktor if I could call him back. What if right now was the only chance I ever got to talk to him? He might contact a lawyer who told him to keep his mouth shut.

So I jumped up, grabbed my laptop, put my phone to my ear, bumped Natalie out of my damn way, and ran.

CHAPTER TWELVE

As I raced up Cubicle Row and down a flight of stairs, Viktor spoke into my ear. It sounded like he was spitting at me. "I don't know what sewer you got this from, but it's utter nonsense."

I tried to keep from sounding out of breath. "Your daughter put these posts on Reddit. Are you familiar with that website?"

"My daughter did not write these disgusting messages. If you publish this, I will sue."

I opened the door to an old one-stall bathroom that was usually reserved for the two disabled people on staff. "So you deny she had the nickname Olly Olly Oxen Free?"

"That's beside the point—"

I shut the door and sat on the toilet. "How about all the corroborating details: that you moved in when she was seven, that her mom died when she was fourteen, that—"

"For all I know you wrote those posts yesterday."

I balanced my computer on my lap so I could take notes. I wasn't recording our conversation, because it was illegal to do that in Massachusetts without consent. Too bad—a recording of this would be great on the podcast. I considered asking for consent, but what if Viktor hung up on me? I said, "These posts are all right there in the

Reddit archives. I had no reason to write anything bad about you seven years ago."

"Then someone else did it, a political enemy. I loved Olivia like she was my own daughter. I would never have hurt her in the way these posts describe."

"Just from reading them, they sure sound like a young girl wrote them. We'll give everything to our computer forensics people. If these posts came from Olivia's computer, our people will confirm it."

I had no idea if Reed-dropout Larry could really do that. But my threat seemed to give Viktor pause, literally, because he hesitated. I pushed my advantage. "I'm going to record this conversation. That's required at the *Clarion*—"

I didn't get a chance to finish my lie, because Viktor interrupted. "I do not give you permission to record."

Damn. Then he spoke again. I put the phone on speaker and set it on the floor so my hands would be free to type. I transcribed as he said, "Here's what you need to understand: Olivia always loved good stories. She wrote a novel when she was thirteen." That was true; I remembered Livvy telling me about her vampire-zombie epic. "And of course there's her YouTube videos, where she never let the truth stand in her way. Her philosophy was, the more scandalous the better, regardless of what's real. So if Olivia did write these posts—and I'm not saying she did—then they were pure invention, fantasy."

He was speaking so confidently. If he was lying, I needed to trip him up, get him off his game. "So you're saying Olivia . . . fantasized about having sex with you?"

"You know damn well that's not what I said."

"Where were you on the night of her murder?"

"It's outrageous you would even ask this question, but I was home that night. Ms. Kovach, if you publish these unsubstantiated

allegations, that I committed these despicable acts . . . " A plaintive
note entered his voice. "Do you know what that would do to me in
this era? I'd be finished. Cooked. Please, have some compassion."

"Why should I? Your security goon attacked me yesterday."

"I don't know what you're talking about."

"Come on, your guy Popeye with the martial arts skills practically
paralyzed me."

I heard Viktor take a breath. "I asked him to warn you that if you
lied about Olivia, I'd take legal action. I'm sick of you people profit-
ing off her death with slanderous rumors. But I don't know anything
about any physical attacks. I'll talk to him, and if he did what you
said, I'll fire him."

A fuzzy, distorted reflection of my face looked back at me from
the stainless steel wall of the toilet stall. I didn't want to ruin Viktor's life without reason. But I didn't buy his innocence—about
Popeye or Livvy, either. Her posts seemed so heartfelt. "Do you have
any evidence you didn't do what Olivia said?"

"What evidence would work for you? How do I prove a negative?" I didn't have an answer for that. "I'm just not that kind of
man. I was appointed consul in the first place because I have a lifelong reputation for honesty and integrity."

*Right, and all those other creeps had lifelong reputations too—before
they got caught.* My jaw tightened. "Did the police ever ask about
your alibi?"

"I don't recall. They had no reason to."

"Were you alone that night, or was somebody with you?"

"For God's sake." His voice turned hot with fury. "Do you really
plan to destroy my life? Believe me, I will sue you for every penny
you have. And I'll get enough damages from your pathetic excuse
for a newspaper to bankrupt them too. Good luck ever getting another newspaper job again."

I sucked in an involuntary breath, but stayed focused. I typed in Viktor's threat, figuring it would make my podcast even more dramatic. "Since you didn't answer my question, I'm assuming no one can confirm your alibi."

"Go fuck yourself."

Yet another fuck you—but this one I could use to my advantage. "Nice quote. How's this sound: *When asked if anyone could confirm his alibi, the consul said, 'Go fuck yourself.'*"

Viktor hung up. No problem, I'd gotten excellent stuff and Dave would love it.

Now I needed to find some way to confirm the incest—assuming it was true. I opened the bathroom door—

Natalie was stepping toward the door, from the other side. *The bitch.* Had she been eavesdropping?

CHAPTER THIRTEEN

"WERE YOU *SPYING* on me?" I snapped.

"Seriously?" Natalie said in an offended tone. "When you *shoved* me, my arm scraped on something." She held up her right arm, showing a thin cut near the elbow. "I need to clean it up."

I couldn't tell if she was gaslighting me. I didn't think to ask why she hadn't gone to the bathroom on the same floor. Instead I thought, *shit, could I get in trouble for this?* As she swept past me to wash her arm in the sink, I forced my lips into an ingratiating smile. "Sorry about that. It was an important phone call, and I needed somewhere private."

"Yeah, I heard the end of it. Something about an alibi and 'go fuck yourself'?"

This girl never quit. But thank God that was all she heard. "It's a long story. Can I get you a Band-Aid or something?"

"Don't worry about it." Then she reached out and put a hand on my shoulder. "I really wish we could be friends again."

I nodded dumbly. I worried that she was really saying: *Tell me what you're working on, and I won't rat you out for pushing me so hard you injured me.*

"I'm sure we can be," I said, my smile growing even more strained.

"I'd like that." Finally taking her hand off me, she looked at me with big innocent eyes, waiting for me to tell all.

But I said, "Okay, I gotta run." A look of annoyance shot across her face as I turned and headed off.

At the opening to my cubicle, I searched for a rough spot on the wall where Natalie might have scraped her arm. I didn't find anything. I wondered if she had scraped it elsewhere and made up that whole story about me injuring her. Was she that devious?

Screw this, I refused to stress anymore about Natalie. I called the Cambridge Police Department and asked for Detective Hope O'Keefe. They connected me to PR, where I left my name and explained I was doing a story on the Olivia Anderson murder.

The PR woman sounded bored, though, and I figured it would be a long time, if ever, before O'Keefe called me back. I had way too much experience with cops not returning calls. I still remembered Mama waiting for the phone to ring, during the month after Tata was killed.

But little Petra had found a way to fight back against the cops' indifference, and so would I. The internet said Cambridge homicide detectives worked out of police headquarters on Sixth Street. So I took the T to Central Square and walked past pizza joints and Mexican fast-food places. I strode up the worn marble steps into the headquarters, where a giant mural depicted police officers doing a variety of noble tasks, like chasing down criminals and helping an old lady with her groceries. In the far corner of the lobby, three seedy-looking men in worn jeans hung out with a couple of cops. I sensed their eyes on me as I walked up to the cop with big black eyeglasses at the front desk.

The cop was dealing with an irate woman in her sixties complaining about college students in the apartment beneath her smoking pot. "I don't care if it's legal, that smell comes right up through the floor into my kitchen. Last night I got so high, I ate a whole carrot cake!"

I tried to stifle my laugh and got a coughing fit. But the cop managed to keep a straight face. "I can see how that would be upsetting," he said. "We'll send someone out there."

After the woman left, I stepped forward. "Hi, I'm here to see Detective O'Keefe."

"About what?" the cop said.

I decided not to lead with the "I'm-a-reporter" routine. "I have some new information on the Olivia Anderson murder."

He scratched his chin. "What kind of information?"

"I'd rather share it with Detective O'Keefe. It's sensitive."

He looked me over, clearly trying to decide if I was just another nutcase. I was glad I'd worn a conservative outfit today, a high-buttoned navy-blue shirt and gray skirt in addition to my new shoes.

"One minute," the cop said, and got on the phone.

Five minutes later, another cop ushered me upstairs to the homicide squad room. It smelled like burned coffee and was dingier than I'd expected from watching cop shows on TV. I looked around for some kind of big murder board on the walls, but didn't see anything except bulletin boards with messages tacked up like "Cambridge Homicide: Our Day Starts When Your Day Ends" and "I Haven't Had My Coffee Yet, Don't Make Me Kill You."

A civilian receptionist took me through the squad room to Detective O'Keefe's cubicle in the back. O'Keefe rose from her desk to greet me. She was about fifty-five, with thin brown hair and a tired, immobile face. But she had freckles on her nose that made me think about how she must have looked as a kid.

"Hello, Detective," I said.

"Nice to meet you, Ms. . . . "

"Kovach. Petra Kovach."

"Sit down."

As I sat, I saw a close-up photograph of a decapitated man on O'Keefe's desk. I gagged.

"Oh sorry," O'Keefe said, though she didn't look sorry. Her expression didn't change as she put the photo away. "Headless body found in a dump last week. You okay?"

I nodded, hoping I wouldn't throw up.

She laced her fingers together. "What can I do for you?"

Willing my mind away from the decapitated man, I leaned forward. "It's about Olivia Anderson's murder."

"So I heard."

She didn't sound the slightest bit intrigued, so I decided to drop my bomb right away. "Did you ever consider her stepfather as a suspect?"

O'Keefe tapped her desk. "I understand you have information for me?"

"Yes. I believe Olivia's stepfather was sexually abusing her."

I looked for shock on O'Keefe's face but got nothing. Had she heard this rumor before? Except for slightly narrowing her eyes, her expression didn't change. Maybe that was a skill homicide detectives developed.

"On what do you base this belief?" she said.

"On this." I took a hard copy of the Reddit posts from my purse and handed it to her. "'Olly Olly Oxen Free' was Olivia's nickname from kindergarten. Her first post about the abuse is at the top. This document contains all of her posts, covering a three-year period. Toward the end it got extremely stormy."

O'Keefe looked at the top page, and I could tell she was reading the first line: *If you have sex with your stepfather, is it technically incest?*

But her face still betrayed no sign of being disturbed, or surprised, or any other emotion. She looked up. "May I ask how you obtained this information?"

Since I had promised not to reveal Eric's role in this, I answered, "I found her nickname and searched for it on social media."

"You're a reporter, aren't you?"

I gave my best disarming smile. "Sorry, but yeah." I pointed to my phone. "Is it okay if I record this?"

"No."

I tried not to let her blank expression throw me. "That way we both have a record."

O'Keefe leaned back in her chair. "Ms. Kovach, here's the deal. We investigated this homicide two and a half years ago. It was very high profile as you know, so we spared no expense. Everybody here, and at the DA's office, is very comfortable we got it right. The jury got it wrong. So pardon my French, but I'm not gonna spend my time chasing fucking fairy tales." Even when she cussed, her face didn't change. "Now I've got a headless man to deal with. If you have information on *that* murder, I'll be glad to hear it. Anything else?"

Despite my frustration, I found myself fascinated by this woman. Trying to mirror her toughness, I said, "So you won't even look at these Reddit posts? As you'll see, Olivia wanted to break it off with her stepfather. That gave him a powerful motive to murder her."

"Sure, I'll read them, but don't expect anything. You want a quote from me? Fine, here's one: 'no comment.'"

"Actually, I think I'll go with 'I'm not gonna spend my time chasing fucking fairy tales.'" I was pleased with my comeback. Maybe sounding like a steely bitch would make O'Keefe take me more seriously.

Or maybe not. "Suit yourself. Thanks for stopping by," she said, picking up the photo of the decapitated man, ready to go back to work. She tilted the photo so I could see it, probably to get a reaction out of me.

Once again, I fought down my nausea. "Did you ever check Viktor's alibi for that night?"

"Like I said, we already got the dickhead who killed that girl." She eyed me unblinking, waiting for me to leave.

But I gave it another shot. "I'll have to tell the truth on the podcast, that you were unwilling to even consider vital new evidence."

"Podcast," O'Keefe said.

"Yes. We're expecting over five million listeners," I lied.

"So that's why you wanted a recording. Honey, I'll be retired in three months. You think I give a fuck what some reporter peddling bullshit has to say?"

I had taken enough abuse from this woman. She was the bad guy here, not me. "Detective, I knew Livvy in Los Angeles, when she was fourteen. I loved her like a sister. I'm trying to get justice for her."

"You're trying to get clicks. And you'd sell your own grandma for them, just like every other goddamn so-called journalist."

"At least I'm not a goddamn so-called cop." I took my business card from my purse and dropped it on her desk. "If you change your mind and decide to do some actual detective work, let me know."

Then I stood up and walked out. I loved my exit lines, replaying them in my head as I walked to the T.

But later, sitting on the platform waiting for the train to come, I regretted not telling Detective O'Keefe about Tata. Then she would have understood I wasn't just another cynical, uncaring reporter.

All these years later, I still had a recurring nightmare where Tata and I would walk into MacArthur Park and suddenly hear BANG BANG BANG. That black car would charge past us spitting bullets, and Tata would scream. I'd look through the window at the shooter's face, but just as I was about to see it, it would get blurry and I'd wake up.

My conscious mind didn't remember seeing his face, just his arm sticking out the window. But maybe I had repressed the memory, and if I could only get it back, I'd help the police draw a suspect sketch. Maybe I'd even remember a license plate, and they would catch Tata's killer at last. Over the years I had tried everything to shake my memories loose, including three bouts of hypnosis. But nothing worked.

More than anything else, that's what drove me: the desire to make up for that.

And for practically forcing Tata to take me to the park that morning.

I was tempted to go back to the police station and tell O'Keefe all this. But what good would it do? So I got onto the T when it finally came. Thirty minutes later I was just arriving back at my desk when I got a text from Dave, summoning me to his office.

I wasn't worried. Between Viktor Anderson and Detective O'Keefe, I had plenty of great stuff for him.

CHAPTER FOURTEEN

"*I'm not gonna spend my time chasing fucking fairy tales.*"

Sitting in Dave's office, I repeated this line for him along with all the other colorful quotes and dubious denials I'd gotten from both Viktor and O'Keefe. My favorite was Viktor basically claiming that Livvy fantasized about sex with him. Combine this with the Reddit posts and we'd have a great first podcast episode, just as good as all the famous true-crime podcasts I listened to. Not bad for somebody who almost got fired yesterday—God, was it only yesterday?

This episode would hopefully create the public outcry I wanted. Detective O'Keefe would be forced to reopen the murder investigation and take a close look at Viktor.

But as I laid out my quotes, Dave frowned and tugged his earlobe, and I realized my briefing wasn't going over nearly as well as I'd imagined. I found myself talking faster, in a high, nervous voice. Back when I was just starting out, I had been so confident. Honestly, I thought I was hot shit. But getting fired all those times messed with me. *Damn it,* I thought, listening to myself get way too close to squeaking, *if I want to see this podcast through, I need to be fearless.*

Or at least act fearless.

Finally Dave interrupted, running his hand through what was left of his hair. "This is why I wanted to get you some help from Natalie."

Fuck! "It would be a lot better if the cops backed us up. That would give the story more credibility."

"No, this is great for the podcast, that the cops aren't helping," I said, fighting back my panic. "It makes me the courageous lone wolf"—I raised my fist in the air—"going up against a lazy, arrogant cop and a corrupt, unfeeling bureaucracy to get at the truth. That's the story line all these cold-case podcasts use. And then, ultimately, both in real life and the podcast, we'll force O'Keefe and the entire Cambridge Police Department to do some serious investigating."

Dave wrinkled his nose, skeptical. "The whole country saw Detective O'Keefe on our TV screens during the trial. She was a quiet hero. And now you want to turn her into the villain?"

"Exactly! It's a dramatic twist. She'll be a very complex character."

All at once Dave's face cleared, like he was finally getting it. He snapped his fingers. "You're saying we'll be like Netflix, not CBS."

"Exactly!"

He leaned back in his chair and watched me for a moment, then broke into a smile. My nerves unknotted a little. "Cool, I'm with you," he said. "People will say goodbye to the old hero and hello to the new hero: you."

I felt my face reddening. "It's not just about me. If we go up against the powers that be, we'll *all* look like heroes. Including the brave editors like you."

He half-grinned, as if he knew I was kissing his ass but didn't mind. "I like it! Maybe my ex-wife will treat me nicer." Then he turned serious. "You still think you can write up both the newspaper story and the podcast this weekend?"

"Totally."

"Okay, get to it."

I left his office and punched the air, thrilled and relieved. Now I needed to start writing, fast.

I didn't have any worries about the newspaper article; I knew how to write to deadline. But a podcast . . . That was something new. Would I be able, with zero experience, to pull off a show that was dramatic and exciting for a full thirty minutes? I'd be doing the narration myself; that's how true-crime podcasts worked. But I hadn't done any acting or public speaking since high school.

Before I got started, I went downstairs to the basement. Years ago, I'd been told, the basement was full of junior reporters, a hotbed of twenty-something energy. But now that the staff had been reduced, the windowless, beige-walled hallway felt tomblike.

Larry's door was open, so I walked in and found him writing computer code on his laptop, surrounded by posters for Modest Mouse and REM. Larry was dressed up—for him—wearing a bright orange, button-down shirt above his usual faded jeans. Six-four and gangly, Larry seemed all arms and legs, as if he were a high school kid who hadn't grown into his body yet. I got a kick out of him; he was like a little brother. I thought Jonah must have been like Larry when he was twenty-three.

Though without the orange shirts and love of weed. Today, as usual, Larry's pupils looked dilated.

I felt a rush of anxiety. This was the guy I was putting my trust in?

But Larry didn't notice my hesitation. He looked up from his laptop with a welcoming smile. "Hey, California Girl."

"What's up, Mouse?" Whether his nickname was a reference to his favorite band or an ironic comment on his height, I was never quite sure.

He rolled his chair to face me. "So the boss man says you have a top-secret James Bond project for me, and if I tell anybody what it's about he'll cut my nuts off."

"At the very least," I said, then proceeded to lay out the whole story for him. It was good practice for writing up the podcast, and

narrating it too. Maybe I wasn't a born actor, but I felt like I was doing a great job of storytelling, getting all the pauses and emphases in
just the right places. Larry looked rapt from beginning to end.

When I was done, he slapped his hand on the desk. "Man, this'll
be lit, doing another podcast."

"Another?"

"Yeah, I did one my freshman year at Reed."

I couldn't believe my luck. "That's awesome! I need some hard-
core technical help."

He took out his phone. "I'll play you an episode. The podcast was
called *Magic Doors.*"

"What's it about?"

"Mushrooms unlocking the universe. A little esoteric but we were
popular on small liberal arts campuses in the Northwest."

Not exactly the kind of vibe I was looking for. But when I listened, I had to admit *Magic Doors* sounded pretty professional, even
if the sound effects were on the trippy side. And Larry was into murder mysteries; he told me he'd read the complete works of Sherlock
Holmes in fourth grade.

"I'm glad you're so enthused," I said. "The one thing you should
know is, we have a serious deadline."

He grinned. "Cut back on the weed? Got it."

With my new ally squared away, I went back upstairs freshly confident. First I sat at my desk, put my earbuds in, and re-listened to
the pilot episodes of my three favorite cold-case podcasts: *Serial,
Convicted,* and *In the Dark.* I felt like I totally got the formula: earnest, idealistic young woman fights to right the world's wrongs.

That's me, I thought.

At four o'clock, just before the weekend began, I was ready. I took
out my earbuds, set a handful of Hershey kisses on my desk, and
started writing.

CHAPTER FIFTEEN

THAT WHOLE FRIDAY afternoon, the words flowed. I wrote the first draft of most of the article and began on the podcast script. It was after seven o'clock before I even checked the time again.

The one bad part was, it squashed my hopes for a quiet weekend with Jonah. I came home late, then woke up early and wrote all day. We had to postpone our Saturday night date at Soave Faire, our favorite romantic restaurant.

So much for celebrating our engagement.

Jonah was understanding; he'd pulled a couple of all-nighters himself lately, getting a machine learning model ready to demonstrate to investors. He was dying to tell his parents we were engaged—"They'll be so thrilled!"—but he agreed we wouldn't tell anyone just yet. I couldn't handle all the phone calls and congratulations now, not with this deadline.

"We'll tell everybody next weekend," I said, as we lay intertwined on Saturday night after I finally got home from the office. "My mind will be clearer then." I stroked Jonah's cheek, with its three-day stubble. Jonah wasn't perfect; his ears stuck out and he didn't like chocolate. But the sound of his voice could still make me melt. And he had been so loyal through all my ups and downs.

We made love and I went to sleep spooning him, and on Sunday morning, when we both called our parents, we stayed mum. I did tell Mama about the podcast, though. It took her a while to understand what a podcast was, but she sure understood the words "millions of listeners."

"*O moj*, Bože! And you're in charge of this?"

"That's right, Mama."

I heard a small sound on the other end of the line and realized she was crying. "I'm so proud of you, *mišić*. Things are finally working out for you."

I teared up myself. I was so glad I wouldn't have to put Mama through any more pain.

Assuming everything went well.

As I'd expected, the podcast script was a bear. I read it out loud to myself on Sunday afternoon and hated it. So I rewrote the whole thing, said it out loud again—and still hated it. I did another rewrite, and finally hated it a little less.

That night, Jonah sat at the kitchen table listening to me read it and said he liked it. But he was a tech guy, what did he know? Besides, he was my boyfriend—fiancé. "You'd say it was good no matter what," I said, as I made notes on the paragraphs I wanted to change.

"True, but trust me, your script is killer."

I still didn't know if I believed him. I wanted to run the script by Mateo, but he and his boyfriend were in Vermont for the weekend, leaf peeping.

On Monday morning I got to the office at seven and was amazed to find Larry there already. He usually didn't put in an appearance 'til ten at the earliest. Not only that, his pupils looked normal. He bounded upstairs to my cubicle and greeted me with a boisterous, "Good news!"

"Keep it down." The office was almost empty this early, but still, we needed to guard against any leaks until the podcast aired.

"Got it." He said quietly, "I found us a free recording studio."

I was expecting to record in a walk-in closet, like I'd told Dave. "Are you serious?"

"Yeah, this harpist I know has a soundproof room in her basement. I helped her record some songs, so she said we can use the place whenever we want."

"Oh my God. Thank you, Mouse."

He beamed. "So how's the writing going?"

"Almost done," I said. Rereading my script on the T this morning, I had found six or seven rough spots. As soon as Larry left, I got to work fixing them. I'd promised Dave to have the script finished by Monday morning, and I wanted to hand it to him right when he walked in, so I'd look on top of things.

I was making good progress, getting to the point where I was just checking punctuation. But then, without warning, my brain froze up. Every dash and semicolon looked wrong to me. I spent three minutes taking out a comma and another three putting it back in. My rational mind told me these changes I was making now didn't matter. But my irrational mind was firmly in control.

I took one last look at the opening paragraph. Suddenly I decided it was crap, nowhere near punchy enough to hook listeners—

"How's it going?" Dave asked, startling me. He entered my cubicle with a Starbucks latte in his hand. His hair looked messy and there were bags under his eyes, like he'd had a rough weekend.

"Great!" I said without thinking.

"You all set?"

"Yup," I answered, and immediately wanted to take that back and tell him I needed another five minutes.

But it was too late. He said, "Good, send it over. I'll read it right away."

He walked out and headed for his office. I figured I had one or two minutes before he opened his email, so I took a quick pass at the offending opening paragraph. I made three small changes, then emailed him the script.

As soon as I pressed SEND, I immediately became convinced that by making those three changes, I had destroyed the whole script and now Dave would hate it. *Jeez, quit being so fucking neurotic,* I told myself, but I didn't listen.

As the seconds crawled by slower than dead bugs, I waited at my desk, playing online Boggle to try and kill the time. Five minutes. Seven. Ten. Twelve. Thirteen. *What's taking him so long? Why the hell did I change the lead? And I should've sharpened the ending!*

At last my phone pinged. COME ON BACK, the text from Dave read.

I headed down Cubicle Row to Dave's office, my legs heavy, swallowing down all the saliva and fear that had collected in my throat, and knocked on his door.

"Entrez vous," he said.

Speaking French—was that a good sign? It was when Jonah did it. I went in, hoping I wasn't marching to my doom.

Dave was holding his latte to his lips, which meant I couldn't see his whole face well enough to read it. Two documents sat in front of him: the hard copies of my newspaper story and my podcast script.

Don't squeak. "Hey, boss."

He put down the coffee. "It's good, Petra. Both the article and the script."

Oh God thank God. I could have burst into song. I sat down and said, "Thanks, I'm glad you're happy with it."

"But I do have one question."

The skin on my neck prickled. His eyes looked hooded somehow. "Okay."

Dave stood up and put a foot on his chair, then looked straight into my eyes for the first time. "In both the newspaper story and the podcast, you left out a key fact: that Eric suspects his own stepfather committed sexual abuse and murder."

"Right. Like I told you, I promised him I'd keep that out of the story."

"I get that. The thing is, it gives our story credibility, that the son himself believes it."

I blinked. "Are you saying I should burn my source?"

"I just wish there were some way around this. Can you go back to him and ask for permission?"

"I'm pretty sure he'll say no."

"Tell him we can't put this story out there unless we can say he suspects his father."

My jaw dropped. Would Dave really kill this story? Or was he just threatening Eric—and me—so we'd do what he wanted? "I don't think Eric will change his mind. He was very clear about staying out of it."

Dave shook his head and sighed. I read disappointment on his face, or disgust. Like I was another in a long line of obstinate reporters he'd been forced to deal with over the years, who had turned his hair gray. My throat went dry. My moment of triumph with the boss was going downhill fast. He held up my newspaper story, like he had once held up the manila folder when he was intent on firing me. "Petra, we could publish this, but people would say exactly what Viktor said: 'This is all BS. Livvy didn't really write these posts, or she made it all up. Face it, the Killer Professor is guilty.'"

I managed to get some words out. "But you said yourself, Livvy's posts are—"

"They're great—but only if we give the context. We need to be able to say, 'Livvy's brother doesn't think the professor killed her after all. He thinks his own father did it.' That's what will make people believe this story. That gives it pop. Without that . . . " He tossed my story down on the desk. "It's not page one material. Or a podcast."

My heart flipped and plunged. "I really think—"

"I've had two other podcasts bomb on me already. I can't have another dud right now, not with—" He stopped himself, but I assumed he meant, not with his meeting with the publisher coming up. "Look, I'm just very concerned about it."

Sweat broke out on my forehead. "If I burn my source, that would make the newspaper look bad."

"I'm trying to make sure this paper even *survives*."

"But it's such a cardinal rule of journalism, to protect your sources and honor their anonymity—"

"Who knows what the rules are anymore? They're changing so fast I can't keep track."

"I can't go back on my word," I said, trying to sound firm and unbending. "I promised Eric."

Dave nodded. "I respect that. But let me ask you a question: What would Olivia want you to do?" The same question I had asked Eric at the bar. Dave stood up and paced behind his desk. "The more listeners our podcast gets, the more pressure we can put on the cops. And we increase the chances that some student or security guard hears the podcast and it gets them to remember a key detail. That they saw Viktor outside Olivia's dorm on the night of the murder. Or an old high school friend of Olivia's will finally come forward and say, 'Yeah, Viktor abused her for years.' Petra, you're right that you have a responsibility to your source. But we also have a responsibility to tell this story and tell it well." He tapped my podcast script. "Think about what we owe the public and Olivia herself."

My mind churned, taking it all in. I had never heard Dave give such a long speech. It seemed heartfelt—but also desperate. I thought he believed everything he said, but now I was positive: he was facing the job guillotine too.

But setting that aside, he had a point. Really, it was close to the same point I'd been thinking all along: If my story got a lot of attention, it would get the police off their asses, just like my Letter to the Editor had done twenty years ago. They'd investigate the man I strongly suspected of the murder.

I heard myself say, "I'll ask Eric again. Maybe I can turn him around."

Dave nodded approvingly and sat down. "Tell him if he wants to solve his sister's murder, this is the way to go."

"Will do," I said.

I walked back to my cubicle, gulping down my fear and anxiety. How would I get Eric to say yes? I sat down at my desk and decided to jump right into it without thinking too much. I found the phone number he had given me at the Red Dolphin and texted, HI ERIC, I HOPE YOU'RE ENJOYING CALIFORNIA. WE NEED TO TALK ABOUT THIS STORY BEFORE IT GOES OUT.

It was early in the morning in California, but Eric must still be on East Coast time, because a minute later, I saw the text bubbles on my screen. Then his text came in: I'VE ALREADY TALKED TOO MUCH.

I responded, SOMETHING CAME UP THAT WE REALLY NEED TO DISCUSS. PLEASE CALL ASAP.

I waited. For ten minutes. Finally, I called him. A robotic voice said I could leave a message here for Eric, so I did. "Eric, please call me. It's important."

I waited twenty minutes this time. Then I went downstairs and outside to the sidewalk so no one would overhear me and called Eric again. This time when the robot voice told me to leave a message, I laid it all on the line.

"Eric," I said. "We're about to put out the story and here's the deal. My editor wants to include the fact you told me about Livvy's Reddit posts. And I think he's right. If we want to solve your sister's murder, we need to light a fire under the cops and get new witnesses coming out of the woodwork. That means we need a lot of listeners, hopefully millions, and the best way to get that is for you to be okay with me telling the whole truth. So please think about that and call me back this morning. Because we need to start recording this podcast."

I went back into my cubicle and waited.

And waited some more.

I got onto Twitter to DM Eric. But he had disabled his DM feature.

I went out and took a walk. I left him three more phone and text messages. Hours passed. Clearly he was putting his head in the sand about all this. I wondered if he had blocked me on his phone. I had no other way to reach him in California.

At two thirty, in my office again, my phone buzzed. I jumped to answer it, but it was Mateo. I hit "accept" and said, "Hang on a second," then raced back downstairs to the sidewalk.

"Mateo, are you still there?" I said breathlessly.

"Still here, sweetie, and bored stiff by this brief I'm writing, so entertain me. How's my favorite soon-to-be podcast star?"

"Confused," I said, and proceeded to tell him why. I stepped into an alley to escape the street noise.

"Your problems are way more interesting than Medwick Jones Limited versus Draper Sterns Limited," Mateo said when I finished.

There was a garbage can near me that smelled like rotting vegetables, so I moved farther into the alley. "But what should I do? I feel like I'm so obsessed with saving my career, I can't tell what's right anymore. What's more important, being loyal to a source or possibly solving a murder?"

"Okay, so: abstract code of journalistic ethics, versus nailing a guy who sexually abused and very likely murdered his young stepdaughter? For me it's not a tough call."

"Would it even be legal to break my promise to Eric?"

"That was not a binding contract. And certainly not enforceable. Anybody who speaks to a reporter, even confidentially, is fully aware their secret might be revealed one day."

That makes sense, I thought.

"What's your gut telling you?" Mateo asked.

"I wish I knew."

"Then think about this: If your podcast helps get justice for Livvy at last, how will Eric feel?"

As soon as Mateo said that, I felt a lightness flow through my shoulders and chest and spread over my whole body. "He'll be grateful," I said. "When this is all over, he'll be thrilled I did it."

"Exactly."

The rotten vegetable smell wasn't bothering me anymore. "If someone ever caught Tata's killer, I wouldn't give a fuck how they did it or what rules they broke."

"So maybe you should break your promise to Eric for *his* sake."

"And Livvy's too."

I got off the phone feeling a lot better. But as I went back upstairs and headed down the hallway toward my cubicle, my chest grew heavy again. I found myself staring at the loose strands on the gray acrylic rug. What I was thinking of doing . . . Even if it was the right thing in a way, it felt sleazy. I knew my motives weren't completely pure. Yes, I wanted to get justice. But also, I wanted a hit podcast.

That made me smile a little. So I wanted to do good in the world and also be famous. Sounded an awful lot like Livvy at fourteen!

And it was pretty freaking normal. It didn't make me some kind of terrible person.

As I sat down at my desk, I picked up a small wind-up dragon that Jonah had given me for my birthday a month after we met. This dragon had been with me in Oxford, Bozeman, Seattle, and now here. It had seen all my heartaches and pain and my moments of victory, as well. I wound up the dragon, then set it down and watched its tiny metal legs churning as it made its way across the desk. I picked it up before it fell to the floor and wound it up again, staring into the dragon's fiery red eyes. Did I really believe I'd be able to solve a murder? That seemed crazy. Arrogant.

But why *shouldn't* I be able to? I had been on the case less than a week and already I'd discovered an important clue that the police missed. I reminded myself of successes I'd had: exposing a college admissions scandal when I was in high school. Uncovering a housing scam targeting scholarship students when I was at UCLA. Here in Boston, I discovered the butterfly smuggling—even if Natalie got the credit.

I can do this. I can help Eric get closure.

Eric had had all day to call me back. He clearly wasn't going to. I had tried my best. And I needed to get this podcast out fast, before Dave's big meeting on Friday.

I woke up my laptop. My fingers poised over the keys for a long time. Then I typed, *"Eric Anderson has a terrible feeling deep in his bones. He thinks something truly awful happened between his beloved sister, Olivia, and his stepfather, Viktor.*

"*Eric believes Viktor sexually abused Olivia for years, starting when she was fourteen. Less than a week before she died, she tried to finally put an end to it. That may be what led to her murder.*

"*And here's the thing: Eric can back it up with hard evidence. Today on this podcast we will share this shocking new material, which has never been revealed in public before. You can decide for yourselves if there's a new suspect in town.*

"*A suspect with a horrible but convincing motive.*"

PART TWO
"MURDER OF THE CENTURY,"
THE PODCAST

CHAPTER SIXTEEN

THE NEXT SIXTY hours were insane.

I dropped my rewrite on Dave's desk at seven p.m. I was sure he'd like it, and I was right. He had only minor notes, and he accepted that I had given Eric every opportunity to say no to my naming him as the source.

Now it was time to record the thing. So Larry and I headed over to the basement studio of his friend Erinne in Southie. Erinne was a six-foot-tall jazz harpist and scat singer who wore electric blue bell-bottoms. Everything about her was big, from her teeth to her breasts to her music when she played a couple songs for me. "Bop poppa chop deedladee dop!" her voice boomed over the Bose speakers. The studio was full of cool instruments she'd collected on her international tours: a Thai mandolin with a peacock for a head, a mahogany board from France studded with different size wineglasses . . . I was a little intimidated by Erinne, but inspired too.

I sat down in front of the microphone on a faded Hindu throne from Sri Lanka that was a little uncomfortable but forced me to sit up straight. Larry did a sound test while Erinne brought me ginger turmeric tea. Then I pulled out my script and got to work.

Since I hadn't recorded any interviews, most of the podcast would basically be me doing a monologue. Talk about daunting. "I'm a reporter, not an actor!" I complained to Larry around midnight, after he made me repeat the sentence "Viktor Anderson has no alibi for the night of the murder" five times in a row. He said I kept going up at the end, turning it into a question instead of an emphatic statement. I started to hate my voice. I sounded so young.

"Hey, you're doing amazing. You're very rootable," Erinne assured me, smiling with those broad teeth. Despite her large personality, she was down to earth and encouraging. She was invaluable in other ways too. She played the part of Olivia, reading her Reddit posts aloud for the podcast. Also, by swirling her fingers on the wineglass rims, she created eerie, disturbing sound effects for when the podcast got heavily into murder and incest.

Between all the retakes and adding in sound, we didn't finish until Wednesday afternoon. I emailed Dave the audio. Half an hour later he called me into his office, and once again I was scared shitless.

But when I walked in, he was beaming. "Nice work, Petra. You have a good voice for this."

I sat down and beamed back at him. But I couldn't help asking, "You don't think it's too high?"

"Not at all. And I like it that you stumble over your words sometimes. It makes you sound more natural. Like a regular person who just feels passionate about justice."

"I hope our listeners agree." I wished it was easier for me to accept compliments.

"Have you thought of a name for the podcast?"

"How about we keep it simple, like: *Murder of the Century*."

He slapped the desk. "Excellent!"

Dave played the podcast for the head of the advertising department, an ultra-competent woman in her fifties who sold an ad for the podcast on her very first try, to a company that sold women's bras online. They insisted I read the ad myself. *I guess I'm not so bad at this podcast thing after all!*

Larry and I went back to Erinne's studio to record the ad. I felt weird reading the script: "You know, I've been wearing Comfy Bras for two months now, and I gotta say, they live up to their name. Not only super comfortable, but you'll feel good about how you look." I had never heard of Comfy Bra before, let alone worn one of their products. But Larry and Erinne both complimented me on how sincere I sounded.

That made me laugh. *"Sincere?"* I held up a bra the company had sent over. It had two more straps than I was used to. "I'd never wear one of these."

But the Comfy Bra people listened to my testimonial that night and signed off on it, and that was all that mattered. They were paying forty dollars for every thousand people who listened to the podcast, which was on the high side. It felt like all the stars were aligned for *Murder of the Century.*

The only person who said anything critical was Jonah. I proudly played him the episode when I got home late Wednesday night. When we came to the part where I revealed Eric was my source for the incest allegation, he paused the episode and narrowed his eyes at me.

"I thought you promised to keep Eric out of the podcast."

I'd been afraid Jonah would react like this; that's why I hadn't told him before. "I left multiple messages for Eric, but he never called back." As Jonah frowned, I continued, "Dave thought we should do it this way, and I agree. We'll get a lot more people listening to the podcast, which increases the momentum for solving the case."

"But isn't protecting your sources like, the number one ethical thing for you guys?"

I gave an aggressive shrug. "I'm not saying I feel great about it, but there's gray areas. I'm trying to make sure the cops do their fucking jobs."

Jonah's brow furrowed. "You're destroying Eric's relationship with his stepfather."

I didn't try to hide my irritation. "Who cares? Viktor is a freaking murderer!"

"Come on, you don't know that."

"He's definitely a child abuser."

"You don't know that either."

"Sure I do, we have the Reddit posts." I was so exhausted after my long nights of working, I was ready to kill him. "This is the biggest story of my life. I may have discovered Livvy's killer! Don't get all negative on me!"

Jonah hesitated, and I wasn't sure which way he'd go, but finally he said, "Okay. Sorry, I didn't mean to rain on your parade."

I put my hand on his arm. "I didn't mean to yell at you, Jonah," I apologized, and we made nice to each other. But I still slept restlessly, and at five a.m. I woke with a start.

Today was the day. My newspaper story, "Startling New Revelations in the Olivia Anderson Murder Case," would come online in exactly two hours. My podcast would drop then too.

I slipped out of the apartment, then stopped at Starbucks for fresh coffee and a chocolate croissant. I made it to the office at six thirty and sat alone in my cubicle, waiting for the numbers to come in. I hoped we'd get a hundred thousand readers and ten thousand podcast downloads the first day. That would be amazing.

Seven o'clock finally came. My story popped up on the *Clarion's* home page with a link to the podcast.

I gripped the edge of my desk and waited.

CHAPTER SEVENTEEN

I GOT A hundred readers in the first two minutes, a thousand in the first ten, and *twenty thousand* in the first hour.

And the podcast downloads were already over the three thousand mark. *"Oh my God,"* I said out loud to myself. *"Holy crap."*

Maybe one of these people would know a key piece of evidence about Livvy's murder, that they hadn't realized until now was key.

Dave came into my cubicle at eight a.m.—the first time he'd ever hung out with me there. Together we watched the numbers explode. By nine a.m., we'd hit ninety thousand readers and ten thousand downloads.

"Boy, am I glad you talked me out of firing you," he said.

We both laughed like it was the funniest thing either of us had ever heard.

After Dave left, Mama called. She had just listened to the podcast. "Petra!" she exclaimed. "You sound just like a real reporter!"

I rolled my eyes. "Mama, I *am* a real reporter."

"I know, but you sound like Jane Simpson!" This was absolutely the highest praise Mama could bestow. Jane Simpson was the Channel 2 anchorwoman who had been Mama's favorite newscaster since forever.

I sat at my desk refreshing the page, overwhelmed but ecstatic as the numbers rose faster than the likes on a Katy Perry tweet. At nine fifteen I received a four-word text from Eric: YOU'RE A FUCKING SCUMBAG. I texted back, I TRIED TO CALL YOU ABOUT THIS, but he didn't respond.

I tightened my jaw and told myself that Eric would realize one day I had done the right thing. I called up a photo of Livvy on my phone, from the summer I met her. I had organized a beach outing for the campers, and she was wading out into the ocean with a huge smile on her face. "This is for you, Livvy," I whispered.

As the *Clarion* staff came into work, they learned about my big triumph. Soon everybody in the whole newsroom, from department heads to assistants, was making a pilgrimage to my cubicle to congratulate me. I got a warm glow inside me that I hadn't felt since . . . well, since I co-edited the *Daily Bruin*.

At nine thirty, Natalie came to my cubicle and said, "Nice work! How's it feel to be the star of the day?" There was a big smile on her face, but it wasn't hard to see she was burning up with jealousy inside.

Eat your heart out, Natalie, I thought, but I smiled back and said, "Pretty good. I'm sure you know the feeling."

Doug, a movie critic and arts reporter with a sloping forehead and New York accent, stood next to Natalie. "Petra, fabulous podcast! So what do you think: did Olivia's stepdad really kill her?"

"Stay tuned for the next episode," I said coyly.

"Do you have your next one figured out?" Natalie asked with innocent, wide-open eyes.

"Of course." *Don't show weakness!*

Giles, an assistant editor in a wheelchair, had rolled up just in time to hear Natalie's question. He asked, "So what else do you have up your sleeve?"

Soon everybody was asking me different versions of this same question. I kept repeating my mantra, "Stay tuned for the next episode." But by the seventh or eighth time, it began to sound like hollow bravado to my ears.

Because the truth was, I didn't have a clue what my next episode would be.

Dave had made it clear he wanted at least six episodes. He expected me to follow up with number two next week to keep the momentum going. But what if I couldn't come up with any more good episodes? Yes, I'd gotten lucky with Eric—but now what? What if the trail leading to Viktor ran dry?

I tried to shut off my self-doubt. This was the biggest success of my life! *Bask!*

But my feelings of glorious victory began to ebb. I needed to find more great stuff on Livvy's murder, fast. Not only for her sake and Eric's, but mine. With the incest angle out in the open now, other reporters with more experience and connections on the crime beat could seize my story and run with it. I wanted my warm glow to last. I was starting to realize that I wanted Livvy to get justice—but I wanted to get it for her myself.

So when Mama called to congratulate me again and hear the latest click and download stats, I got off the phone as quickly as I could and packed up to leave my cubicle. I would hit the street right away and get to work. I'd outwork everyone else, just like I did at UCLA. This was my big shot and I wasn't about to blow it.

I needed proof that Viktor sexually abused Livvy and she was planning to break it off. That would nail down his murder motive, and be the ideal escalation of the story for Episode 2.

But where would I find proof? I couldn't go back to Eric for help.

Maybe I could get Livvy's boyfriend, Brandon, to talk. In her final Reddit post, she wrote that the incest was *"messing up my relationship with this guy at school.*" Did she ever tell Brandon about the incest? Now that it was publicly exposed, maybe he would open up about it.

I walked across the newsroom, accepting congratulations along the way, and found Chuck Kling, the old sports reporter, sitting in his cubicle immersed in a football video game. "Hey, Chuck," I said.

He paused the game. "Hey, it's the woman of the hour. Incest is best."

I hated hearing Livvy joked about in that disgusting way, but I forced myself to ignore it because I needed his help. "So listen, what's the best way to get hold of Brandon Allen?"

Chuck laughed. "If you figure that out, let me know. I've been trying to hook him for three years."

I frowned. "What kind of person is he?"

"A very quiet person."

Gee thanks. I turned to go—and practically ran into Dave, coming up the hallway behind me with a spring in his step. "Did you see the latest?" he said. "Twelve thousand livestreams and thirty-six thousand downloads."

I reminded myself everything was going great so far. "Freaking awesome!"

"I bet we hit a million by the weekend, which means forty thousand quick bucks from Comfy Bra."

"Nice!" I held up my fist and we knocked knuckles.

"And Jennifer"—the head of advertising—"says we can double our rates for the next episode and put in two or three ad breaks instead of one. Plus who knows what this'll do for our subscriptions. When I have lunch with Abernathy tomorrow, I'm telling him if we go ten episodes, it'll bring in a million bucks easy."

Wait—*ten?* Just trying to come up with the second one was hard enough! But I covered my anxiety, saying, "Damn, I guess I'll ask you for a raise after all."

Dave laughed. "So how's Episode 2 coming?"

"Lookin' good. Following a lead right now, I gotta run."

He put a hand on my shoulder. "Go get 'em, tiger. Report back this afternoon."

"You got it."

He took off, and two women from advertising headed my way. I tried to remember their names. The older one, with big red-rimmed glasses, said, "Hey, that was terrific, Petra. When's Episode 2 coming out? We should tell the advertisers."

"I'll let you know. Gotta run," I said, and made it into the stairwell.

I left the building through a side exit and walked five blocks to a Peet's. This should be far enough away that I wouldn't see anyone else from the *Clarion* here. I'd grab some coffee and quiet time and decide my next move.

But after I got my drink and sat down, my mind was still too scattered to think clearly. Maybe I should take a few minutes to just celebrate. Jonah had left me a congratulatory phone message and texts, and I'd texted him back. Now I called him.

I felt some trepidation, because of our argument last night. But Jonah had let go of his moral qualms, at least for now. "I always knew you'd be a star one day," he said. "From the very first night I saw you at that coffee shop in Oxford, and you were so focused on your writing you didn't look up for like, thirty minutes."

"Good thing I did. Otherwise I wouldn't have seen the world's sexiest guy."

After we said goodbye I called Mateo, who couldn't get over the fact I had just launched a potentially million-dollar enterprise. "Damn, *chica,* that's more money than I'll make for my law firm in three years!"

Then I googled "Olivia Anderson" to see how my story was playing in the media. I discovered that *every single* major news site, from the *Wall Street Journal* to *E Online,* was covering it. Most of the stories mentioned my name: *"investigative reporter Petra Kovach."* *TMZ* featured a photo of Viktor, captioned, *"Shocking New Podcast Reveals: Scumbag Stepdad!"* The *Washington Post* declared my podcast "a blockbuster."

A blockbuster!

My nerves relaxed. I got on Twitter and discovered #Olivia-Anderson was trending. There were hundreds of tweets from people either intrigued about the new suspect or furious that I was pretending the Killer Professor was innocent. On a whim I tried #PetraKovach, and it turned out that was a thing too. They had the same kinds of tweets, plus a few about how sexy my voice was. I checked my emails and found congratulatory messages from old friends around the country: former colleagues, UCLA classmates, and even friends from elementary school. My old second-grade teacher wrote me, *"You go, girl!"* and attached a picture of a female bear with a bow in her hair riding a motorcycle.

I saw an email from a name I didn't recognize—"renatacoon"—and wondered what old friend this person might be. I clicked on it and read: *"Everybody knows that shithead professor killed Olive Oil. Where do you get off saying he didn't? Are you a TYPICAL LIBERAL BITCH protecting a FELLOW LIBTARD?"*

Okay, so not an old friend. But I read on. *"The jury said innocent because they loved that he murdered a TRUE AMERICAN HERO who was NOT A FEMINIST and TOLD THE TRUTH. Somebody should've smoked that fuckhead piece of HARVARD SHIT two years ago, and you too, you CUNT. Bye-bye for now, Not A Coon."*

My chest grew tight. I scanned my inbox and found more emails from addresses I didn't know. I hoped some of these emails would provide tips about Viktor or the murder, but none of them did—and the majority were hate mail. I'd received messages like these on occasion before, but never a hundred at once. The most vicious were from QAnon followers accusing me of being part of a Harvard sex trafficking ring that had killed Livvy.

As I gulped down some coffee, I got three new emails from unknown addresses. How many more would I—

Wait, I knew the address on that third email. It was Professor Reynolds!

I opened it quickly and read, *"Hi Petra, So I guess you're legit. Sorry about that middle-finger salute the other day, I get a lot of emails from crackpots. Anyway, I've got information you should probably have. You want to meet?"*

I couldn't believe my luck. I wasted no time emailing back, *"Sure, when?"*

Thirty seconds later I got a reply: *"How about now? Where are you?"*

So he still lived in Boston? *"At the Peet's on Clarendon."*

"Be there in twenty."

My heart pounded. *An interview with Professor Reynolds?* He had never spoken to the press, ever.

I'll actually have a second episode!

CHAPTER EIGHTEEN

I DOWNED MY coffee and crumpled and uncrumpled my napkin as I looked through the front window of Peet's, waiting for Reynolds to appear. After twenty-five minutes I was positive he had changed his mind, and I was about to email him again when a man with a thick beard and glasses, who must have come in through the side door, walked up and said, "Hi." I jumped, startled. It took me a few moments to register the guy's high forehead and realize this was Reynolds.

"You've changed your look," I managed to say.

"Yeah, there's a lot of folks who are kinda pissed off at me." He had a pleasant nasal twang, Minnesota maybe. "Looks like you got coffee already. I'll get myself some. You want anything else?"

I jumped up. "I'm the reporter. This'll be my treat."

He thought about it, then sat down. "I won't say no. Money's tight."

"You want a latte?"

"Regular's fine, thanks."

As I went to the counter and ordered his coffee and a refill for me, I took another look back at him. Behind those glasses, I could see his dark, serious eyes. His posture was good but not *too* good—he had an ease about him. I could imagine a freshman girl getting a crush on him.

But why was he so taken with Livvy? Sure, she was young and pretty, and I'd been taken with her too. But he took a big risk going out with a student, even one who wasn't in his class. Was he a born risk taker?

Was he the kind of impulsive guy who would grab a bedside lamp in a fit of fury and bash somebody over the head with it?

I hoped none of these thoughts showed on my face. I needed Reynolds to feel good about talking to me. So I wore a warm smile as I came back to him with the coffees and asked, "Would you like cream or sugar—"

Suddenly, the front door of the coffee shop burst open. A tall, burly man in his early thirties, with wide, flaring nostrils and a black T-shirt that said "America Forever" in white letters, stormed up to us. He held his phone to his eye like he was shooting video with it. "I know you," he declared triumphantly. "You're William fucking Reynolds."

Reynolds turned to me, frowning. "You were followed."

The man glared at me. "So you're conspiring with the killer, just like we thought." He stepped closer, looming over me. "A beautiful girl like Olive Oil gets killed, but you get to live?"

Was he threatening me? My heart raced. The other customers backed away from us. But the manager, a woman with long black dreadlocks, walked up. "Excuse me—"

From two feet away, the man trained his phone camera on me. "Don't you care this guy brutally murdered an innocent young woman?"

Reynolds said, "Let's get out of here."

"Yeah, run, you fucking pussy."

I tried to push my chair back and stand up, but the man was blocking me. I looked up at his pointy teeth and smelled beer on his breath. "Answer me," he snarled. "What's the matter with you? You don't care this guy killed Olivia?!"

I grabbed my cup of hot coffee and threw it in America Forever's face. He howled and jumped back, the dark liquid spilling down his chin and onto his shirt. I jumped up and ran out of the coffee shop, throwing the front door open as I went. Reynolds came right behind me.

America Forever barreled out the door after us, phone held high, shouting, "You bitch, I got your picture!"

"Nice move with the coffee," Reynolds said as we broke into a full-on run.

"Thanks," I said, breathless.

America Forever chased us, yelling, "Enemy of the people!" But he was built for intimidation, not speed, and we started pulling away from him. He kept shouting, but I couldn't hear all the words. After four or five blocks, we turned around and he was gone. We were both huffing and puffing. "I think we're okay now," Reynolds said.

A shiver went down my spine as I wondered if America Forever was one of the creeps who had sent me hate mail. Something about the phrase "America Forever" scratched at my mind, but I couldn't place it. I turned to Reynolds. "I'm sorry I didn't notice someone was following me. It didn't even occur to me." I hoped Reynolds wouldn't be too mad at me for putting him in danger. There was another coffee shop right across the street. "Shall we go in there?"

Reynolds didn't answer; he was still checking behind us. I said, "I feel bad he was videotaping. I guess now the crazies will know what you look like, with the beard."

Reynolds was clearly upset, his eyes pulled downward. Then he gave a shrug. "Hey, it was bound to happen sooner or later." He tugged at the hair on his cheek. "This thing was getting scratchy anyway. Maybe I'll shave it off and leave the 'stache."

I smiled at him, grateful he still seemed to want to do the interview, and we headed across the street. *This guy doesn't act like a murderer,* I thought, but I knew that wasn't very scientific. He held the door open for me, and we walked into the coffee shop. As I ordered for both of us, I asked, "Does this kind of thing happen to you a lot?"

"Used to be at least two or three times a day. Then I grew this beard and went underground, and it got better."

"What do you do for a living now?"

"Anything I can do online. Adjunct teaching, freelance articles under a pen name, even beta testing. I'm hoping one day my life gets back to normal, don't ask me how."

Even more clearly now, I saw how this man could have appealed to Livvy. You could tell he was super smart, but he also seemed vulnerable and approachable. We got our coffees and sat down close to the side door, in case America Forever showed up and we had to take off again. Nobody was sitting near us. I asked as casually as I could, knowing the answer would be no but having to ask anyway, "Is it okay if I record this?"

"Be my guest," Reynolds said—as if he hadn't refused this exact same request for two years, ever since his trial.

I tried not to act shocked, for fear he would change his mind. But inside me, my heart turned cartwheels. *An on-the-record interview, with audio, of William Reynolds!* And he was doing it for free. He could probably get six figures for this interview. Why was he *giving* it to *me?*

Hell, don't look a gift horse in the mouth. If this went well, Episode 2 would be an even bigger blockbuster than Episode 1. I turned on the recording app.

Reynolds said, "So let's get the first thing out of the way."

"What's that?"

"Everybody I meet, whether they say it or not, wants to look in my eyes while I maintain my innocence. So they can see if they believe me." He held up his hands. "Go for it. Look in my eyes."

I laughed nervously. "Okay . . ."

I looked in his eyes. He gazed back at me. "I didn't kill Olivia."

For a few moments neither of us spoke. Then he asked, "You believe me?"

"Yes," I said. And I meant it.

Mostly.

He nodded thoughtfully and rubbed his chin. "I think you maybe sixty percent believe me."

I had no idea how to act. *What if this man did kill Livvy?* But I ignored my doubts and raised an eyebrow, flirting a little. "Direct, aren't you?"

"Hey, I'm just grateful you're up at sixty. There's a lot of evidence against me."

"Now there's evidence against Olivia's stepfather too."

"Just her Reddit posts."

"And the fact he doesn't have an alibi." I set down my coffee. "You said you had something to tell me. Do you have more evidence against him?"

Reynolds put his coffee down too. "It's hell being falsely accused."

"I can imagine."

"My own mother only ninety-five percent believes I'm innocent. So I'm really glad you're taking a fresh look at the case. That's why

I'm talking to you. I could tell from your podcast you have an open mind. Maybe you can get the cops to reopen their investigation." He ran his hand through his hair, suddenly hesitant. "But here's the thing. I hate to tell you this, but the lead you have now is bogus."

I blinked. "What do you mean?"

"Viktor Anderson did not sexually abuse his stepdaughter."

CHAPTER NINETEEN

My jaw dropped. This was the last thing I expected—or wanted—to hear. "What makes you so sure?"

Reynolds shifted in his chair. "Look, I'd love to sit here and tell you, 'Yeah, Viktor had sex with Olivia and he might've killed her, and I've got evidence to back that up.' Obviously that would take the heat off me. But as much as I've been hurt by false accusations, I can't just sit by and do nothing while somebody else gets his life ruined the same way. And I don't want you going down some rabbit hole when you could be chasing the real killer. So I gotta tell you the truth."

He took a deep breath. "Let me tell you how Olivia and I met. It was at Tatte in Harvard Square, on a Saturday morning in October. I was sitting there reading the paper and this very attractive young woman walks up. She says, 'Professor Reynolds. I recognize you from the picture on your first book. I loved that book. May I sit down?' I said sure. I didn't even know she was a student at Harvard, didn't find that out 'til later. 'Til we'd already kissed."

Reynolds' lips turned downward and he rubbed his eyes. Then he went on. "As you may know, my books are about how we use social media to invent new identities and try out new personalities. Olivia was all about that. She said she had invented a persona on Reddit as an abused girl, and she showed me her posts. She wrote them just to see what reactions she'd get. She wanted to shock people, like she shocked them later with her YouTube videos." Reynolds paused and shook his head. "But her persona on Reddit wasn't real. None of it. Her stepfather never abused her. She told me that."

I couldn't breathe. *I am so fucked.* If Reynolds was right, then my big breakthrough on Livvy's murder had just turned to ash. Episode 2 would be about how utterly wrong I'd been in Episode 1. People might tune in to hear this idiot girl apologize for getting fooled, but after that, who would trust me anymore?

And it wasn't like I had any leads for an Episode 3. My podcast would be dead. Not only that, I had flat-out committed libel. Would Viktor sue both me and the newspaper, like he'd threatened? And would Dave decide he had to fire me—for real this time?

My dream of getting justice for Livvy would never be fulfilled. Instead, the dream would be a lead weight sinking me and my career.

Reynolds seemed to have some sense of what I was feeling. "Sorry about this."

My instincts for self-preservation kicked in, just like when Dave tried to fire me last week. I thrust my chin forward. "What makes you so sure Olivia was telling you the truth about not being abused? Maybe that was a pickup line. She knew you wrote books about creating fake identities, so she pretended to have a fake identity herself so she'd have something to talk to you about."

Reynolds shook his head. "That's pushing it. She recognized me from my book, and the only reason she read it in the first place was because she'd already created a fake identity, so she was interested in the subject."

"But maybe she was in denial about the abuse."

He gave me a pitying look. We both knew I was grasping at straws. "Are you saying she *thought* she was creating a fake identity as an abuse victim, but she really *was* an abuse victim? I don't buy it for a second."

I couldn't think of a comeback. I changed the subject, desperate to salvage *something* out of this meeting. "Then who do *you* think killed Olivia?"

Reynolds looked down at his coffee, then out the window at the cloudy sky. "Obviously I've spent a lot of time thinking about this." He turned back to me. "I loved Olivia. I loved her passion about politics, even though we disagreed on just about everything. But she did get a lot of people riled up. I think somebody got pissed off at her videos and killed her."

"But if that was true, wouldn't they have come prepared? With a gun?"

"Maybe they just meant to confront her and got carried away."

"Was there anybody who was especially angry at her?"

"Sure, every feminist on campus. People were outraged when she publicly named Sarah Fain, the freshman who accused a guy of rape. I thought that was over the line myself. I gave Olivia grief about it."

I rubbed my head, trying to think of my next question. Again, Reynolds seemed to sense the stress I was under. "I wish I could give you a specific name to investigate, believe me. I'm dying for you or somebody to solve this thing."

I thought back to the Reddit posts. "Even if Olivia was creating a persona, there must be some truth in what she wrote. Like when she wrote, '*I feel like I'm fucked up about sex. It's messing up my relationship with this guy at school.*' Do you know what that was about?"

"Honestly, our sex was pretty good. I mean . . ." He lifted his shoulders, either embarrassed or humblebragging. "Really good. That post about a messed-up relationship could've been just another part of her false persona."

"Oh come on." I was surprised by how sharp my voice sounded, but I didn't back off. "She was screwing you on the side. Clearly her relationship had issues."

He gave me a sheepish look. "Okay, you have a point there."

"Did she ever talk about Brandon?"

"He wasn't exactly our number one topic of conversation." Reynolds leaned back in his seat, and his feet met mine under the table. I quickly pulled my legs back. "But there was one thing I always found kind of odd."

"What was it?"

"Olivia tended to come by my apartment late on a Friday night, like, for a booty call. Lots of times it would be right after a date with Brandon."

I got an image of this bearded guy in his thirties in bed with the fourteen-year-old Livvy I used to know, and I winced. I forced myself to remember she was eighteen when she met this guy. And he was younger then. "So she'd have sex with Brandon and then you?" *Ick.*

Reynolds looked away, uncomfortable. "I asked her about that, but she would, you know, deflect. I kinda blew it off, because I didn't want to stress about it. But she never smelled like sex, or like she'd taken a shower. So I figured Brandon must have some weird training rule about no sex before a big game. Or maybe they had a tempestuous relationship and sometimes their night ended badly. But like I say, the whole see-Brandon-then-have-a-booty-call thing was very weird."

I stared at him, my mind racing. I had just gotten an idea that might salvage my investigation after all. I said, "Maybe Brandon was gay."

Reynolds stared back at me. I said defensively, "Hey, I'm sure there's lots of gay football players."

He shook his head. "It's not that. It's just, Olivia was such a sexual person, I can't imagine her with a gay guy." He hesitated. "But . . . "

"What?"

"The last time I saw her . . . alive, I mean . . . she told me she was gonna do a video about gay men trying to act straight. And how terrible that is for the women they're with."

I sat bolt upright. "Maybe that's what she meant about her last video being 'super personal.' She was planning to reveal she'd been fooled by her gay boyfriend."

We both sat there thinking. Reynolds spoke first. "It's the kind of thing Olivia would do. That video would've gotten a shitload of clicks."

"What would it have done to Brandon's football career?"

Reynolds' eyes were bright, intrigued. "There's only one player in the NFL who ever came out. And he waited 'til he was twenty-eight and had already signed a twenty-five-million-dollar contract. For a college player to come out . . . Well, there was a famous prospect who got outed a few years ago, and it kept him out of the NFL."

"So you're saying if Livvy outed Brandon, that could've cost him millions of dollars!"

"No question. Instead of getting picked in the first round, he might not even get drafted at all."

I gave a slow smile. "Now that's what I call a murder motive."

Reynolds bit his lips, looking suddenly pained. "You gotta be careful with this. If you out Brandon on your podcast—well, there's no going back."

I said, "Brandon may be the guy who bashed Livvy's head in with a fucking lamp and killed her."

"It's possible." Reynolds reached out and put his hand on top of mine. I was too surprised by his gesture to move my hand away. "But promise me you won't ruin his life 'til you're sure. Too many people have already been falsely accused of killing Olivia."

I nodded, then withdrew my hand and had a sip of coffee. I could picture it: *Livvy discovers the truth about Brandon. She's furious at him for lying to her and making an idiot out of her. She decides to drop a YouTube video to get back at him—and because it would go super viral. He goes to her dorm room late at night to talk her out of it. She refuses. He's desperate. They fight . . .*

Holy crap, had I just solved Livvy's murder?

I thought to myself, *sorry, Professor Reynolds, it's not like I want to out Brandon, but there may be no way to get justice for Livvy without doing that.*

And then I thought: *Episode 2 will be killer.*

CHAPTER TWENTY

"WILLIAM REYNOLDS?" DAVE said, his eyes bright with excitement. We were sitting in his office with the door closed. "You got an interview with the Killer Professor?!"

"Yup," I said, trying not to grin from ear to ear, because that wouldn't be cool.

"Incredible. Did you get anything?"

"I sure did," I said, and played him the interview. I started at the halfway point, when Reynolds and I began talking about Brandon Allen.

Dave loved it, like I knew he would. "Holy mother of God, Boyfriend Number Two says Boyfriend Number One wasn't having sex with her? That's money!" He held up his hands like he was laying out a newspaper headline. "*Did Gay Football Star Kill Olive Oil?*"

I'd been worried he would consider my evidence of Brandon's sexuality too thin to go with, but all he said was, "Keep working it. I'm sure you'll come up with corroborating evidence."

"Will do," I said, thrilled that my boss trusted me so much. But I still felt shaky about one thing. "I need to play you the first half of the interview too," I told him, and clicked on it.

On the recording, Reynolds began explaining that the incest never happened. My hands turned clammy with sweat, and I looked away from Dave's eyes. How upset would he get when he learned that my other big lead, my entire pilot episode, was utter bullshit?

But Dave surprised me. "So what if Reynolds thinks the incest didn't happen? There's no need to make a big deal of that in your next podcast. He could be wrong."

I blinked. "He was pretty convincing."

Dave gave a puzzled lift of his eyebrows. "Not to me. He doesn't have any evidence."

"But Olivia told him there was no incest—and she would know."

"Maybe she lied to him about it because she was ashamed. I'm sure a lot of girls feel that way."

"Then why bring it up to him in the first place?"

Dave shrugged. "A cry for help? I don't know. The point is, don't you think it would be irresponsible to let Viktor off the hook unless we're sure he's innocent?"

My head swam. It wasn't like I *wanted* to let Viktor off the hook, since that would mean debunking Episode 1. Dave's next words echoed my thoughts. "And it won't be good for the podcast if we lose our prime suspect—the suspect everybody in the country is talking about."

"But now we have a whole new prime suspect—"

"Good. Two is better than one."

It threw me that my editor wasn't more focused on getting The Truth. I had done some questionable things in the past few days, but this was a step too far: letting a guy twist in the wind for having sex with his fourteen-year-old stepdaughter when my gut told me he probably didn't do it. "Dave, I'm not saying I'm a big Viktor fan, but don't we owe it to him to tell the other side of the story?"

"The other side is from Reynolds, who's still a suspect himself and not exactly reliable." Dave leaned back in his chair and regarded me. "I'll leave it to you. Your podcast. My suggestion is, sure, say

Reynolds has doubts the incest really happened. But maybe down-play it a little. Don't make him sound positive. Say we're not positive either." Dave slapped the desk. "That might work out perfectly. If we get a controversy going about whether the Swedish consul general was sleeping with his beautiful blonde stepdaughter . . ." His face broke into a smile. ". . . And meanwhile, we start a whole new fire about the boyfriend. I bet we break three million!"

I rubbed my neck, trying to think. Dave was right about how to get the most clicks. He was also right that we didn't know the truth about Viktor for sure. I didn't have proof there was no incest.

Though as Viktor had said, how do you prove a negative?

I let out a breath. I needed to quit arguing with myself and keep it simple. *Do what's best for the podcast. Because that's what's best for the investigation. And for Livvy. Who knows, maybe next week some-body will provide further evidence the incest was real.*

"What do you say?" Dave said.

But still, to leave Viktor hanging like this . . .

I looked up at Dave. "I'll think about it. But unless we get more evidence against Viktor, then pretty soon, Episode 3 or 4 at the lat-est, we should give the full quote from Reynolds about how he's certain Viktor is innocent."

Dave nodded. "Works for me. Now go see what's up with this boyfriend."

CHAPTER TWENTY-ONE

LEAVING DAVE'S OFFICE, my legs felt as unsteady as my mind. I headed to the break room for some chocolate. When I went in, ten or twelve people were gathered around the TV monitor on the far wall. I stood in the back and watched.

On CNN, Viktor Anderson was walking down the front steps of the consulate toward a crowd of reporters waiting in ambush. His silver hair was uncharacteristically ruffled and his sport jacket hung askew. But he stood firm, eyes direct and voice ringing, as he declared, "There is no truth to these outrageous allegations. They dishonor the memory of my beloved stepdaughter."

A male reporter in a blue suit thrust a microphone at him. "Your stepson believes these allegations."

Viktor's chin quivered slightly. "Nonsense. Now if you'll excuse me, I'm late for a meeting." He walked toward a waiting car as the reporters chased him, shouting questions. One voice rose above the din: "Have you talked to Eric since these allegations came out?"

On the TV screen, Viktor escaped into his car. Watching him, I wished I could have kept my promise to Eric. Then Viktor wouldn't know his own stepson had turned on him. He had been a single parent to Eric and Livvy all these years, never remarrying. Then he lost

Livvy; and now he must feel like he had lost Eric. How could their relationship ever recover from this?

But there's no way I can solve Livvy's murder without opening up some old wounds, I told myself. *I can't help that, even if it means a couple innocent people get hurt.* And this was assuming Viktor was innocent. Maybe he wasn't.

CNN cut to the anchor desk, where their star anchorman, Joel Caldwell, addressed the camera. Caldwell hosted my favorite true-crime show: *Dead to Rights*, a daily hour-long show devoted to sensational crimes and court cases. He had a strong chin, a British accent, and a touch of street toughness, and I had a bit of a crush on him. Right now he was saying, "In this stunning new development, reported by Petra Kovach of the *Boston Clarion* . . ."

I could hardly believe Joel Caldwell had just said my name on national television. It was like when I first saw my name in the *LA Times*. I strained to hear the rest of his sentence, but my colleagues had noticed me behind them. Eddie Lopez, who wrote a twice-weekly column with local feel-good stories, called out, "There she is! The marvelous Ms. Kovach!"

"You just made CNN, girl!" said Louise from circulation.

My body grew warm with pride. *Joel Caldwell!*

When CNN went to commercial, I headed back to my cubicle so I could get to work on Brandon Allen. My excitement about Joel Caldwell began to ebb as I thought, *time to wreck Brandon's life too.* I wound up my dragon and watched him crawl across my desk.

I wondered how Mateo would feel if I outed Brandon. In college, I had watched Mateo struggle for two years while he built up the courage to come out to his conservative religious family. I strongly believed people should be free to make their own choices about coming out.

But Brandon was a legit murder suspect. It had been drummed into me over and over again at UCLA: Your job as a journalist is to get the truth and let the chips fall where they may. I needed to find out who killed Livvy. End of story. *The truth shall set you free.*

The reading I'd done indicated that Brandon didn't have a good alibi for the night of the murder. If it turned out he did have one, then I wouldn't need to out him, but otherwise . . . I'd have a tough decision to make.

My immediate task was to corroborate that Brandon was gay and Livvy was about to tell the world. Ideally, I would go straight to the source: Brandon himself. But as I'd learned, that would be supremely difficult.

"Hey, Petra, guess what?" It was Larry, ambling into my cubicle wearing a leather peace-symbol necklace over a yellow tie-dyed shirt. "We just hit a hundred thousand downloads!"

I pushed a metal folding chair toward him. "Sit down, we've got work to do." Then I thought about how little privacy we'd have. I stood up. "Better yet, let's get out of here. Bring your computer."

After my experience with the guy in the America Forever T-shirt, I didn't want to leave the building through the front door and risk somebody tracking me. We walked out through the loading dock instead. Keeping an eye out for America Forever or any other sketchy types, we headed left, then took a right on a one-way street going the wrong way. That should get rid of anybody following us by car.

We ended up at Pope's Pizza. My weight had gone up three pounds since the morning Dave almost fired me. But I figured as much stress as I was under, I deserved a couple slices.

We got on our laptops, searching for any tidbits that might reveal Brandon's leanings. First we simply googled *"Is Brandon Allen gay?"*

We were intrigued to get twenty-two hits. But they were all silly, and when we googled the same question for other college football stars, we got about the same number.

We found tons of photos of Brandon with his high school and college friends and teammates, but nothing compromising. His Facebook, Insta, and Snapchat accounts were private. He had a Twitter handle—"BACrimson"—but he'd never tweeted. We didn't find any mentions of girlfriends for Brandon post-Olivia, but maybe that was just part of his desire for privacy.

I DM'ed him on all four platforms, but I wasn't optimistic he'd hit me back—especially if he had something big to hide. Then we searched his friends' and teammates' social media. But we didn't find any hints that somebody in Brandon's circle harbored a deep secret or a special love of gay culture.

"I feel like a fucking homophobe, looking for mentions of *Pose* or Judy Garland," I said.

"Me too," Larry said. "You want to just forget it?"

I sighed. "We're trying to establish a murder motive here. Let's keep going."

We spent another half hour checking sports sites and fansites. "It says here Brandon's favorite TV show is *Breaking Bad* and favorite movie is *Caddyshack,*" I said.

"Not very gay," Larry said.

"Don't be stereotypical."

The counter guy came out and bussed our table, a pointed hint we'd been here too long and it was time to go. I stood up, discouraged we hadn't made any progress, while Larry checked for messages. "We just got a text from Dave," he said.

As we headed for the door, I groaned. "What's he want?"

"He wants you to write tweets for the newspaper feed, teasing the next episode."

I nodded wearily, then all at once stopped short. Larry bumped into me from behind and dropped his phone on the floor. "Oh shit," he said, picking it up and checking to make sure it wasn't cracked.

But I barely heard him. I had just gotten a brilliant idea.

I knew exactly how to pressure Brandon Allen into talking to me.

CHAPTER TWENTY-TWO

In general, when you're a reporter doing a story, people want to talk to you. They're hoping for their three sentences of fame.

But not when you're doing investigative journalism. The people you most want to talk to stay as far away from you as they can. Your biggest challenge isn't intellectually piecing the truth together, or writing perfect sentences, it's getting these people to surrender their darkest secrets.

Sometimes that means manipulating people, and it can get a little ugly, but when it's the only way to get to the truth, and you're working on something really important, you justify it to yourself. Brandon was so protected as Harvard's biggest football star, I couldn't think of any other way to get through to him. So when I got back to the office, I tweeted out from the *Clarion's* account, "Big revelations in next podcast! Olivia's romantic life was NOT what it seemed!"

Then I tweeted, "Brandon Allen, where are you? We've been reaching out. Please talk to us! We're trying to solve Olivia's murder and we need your help!"

The danger was that these tweets would set other reporters on Brandon's trail. But they were probably after him already, because he was such an obvious potential source. I had to hope that since I was ahead of them with the gay-Brandon lead, I'd be able to beat them. Also, since I was the one calling Brandon out, maybe he'd come to me first.

Hopefully these tweets would smoke Brandon out of hiding. The "romantic life was NOT what it seemed" tweet would make him scared I was about to reveal his sexuality, and he'd want to be on top of that. Calling him out publicly in my second tweet would push him even harder to contact me, because if he didn't, people might think he didn't care about solving his old girlfriend's murder.

They might think he killed her.

But I didn't hear anything from Brandon. An hour later I tried again: *"Brandon Allen, let's do this together! Your assistance is needed!"*

In the next hour my tweets went viral. Famous athletes, politicians, and other celebrities retweeted me. ESPN.com, SI.com, and all the other sports sites, along with a lot of mainstream news sites, speculated about why Brandon hadn't responded to me yet. Some pundits declared he should be allowed to leave that painful part of his life behind; but others intimated he must have something to hide. All in all, most people felt he should call me already. How could it hurt?

Brandon stayed silent, though, and shortly after three p.m., the press office of the Harvard Athletic Department put out a statement. *"As a condition of their scholarships,"* it read, *"we require that our student athletes not speak directly with the media. Therefore, Brandon Allen will not be available for interviews. We in the Harvard community believe that the tragic murder of Olivia Anderson was already solved by the Cambridge Police Department two years ago. Olivia's death was traumatic for Brandon, and he should not be forced to relive it for the sake of some sensationalist podcast."*

Some sensationalist podcast?

Public opinion, based on comments, internet stories, and #Petra-Kovach, which I checked obsessively, began swinging back in the direction of Brandon being allowed his privacy. The poor young man had been through so much, people like me should leave him alone!

Damn, I thought. I passed Dave in the hall on my way to the bathroom and impulsively asked, "Dave, am I looking like the bad guy in this?"

He stopped. "How so?"

"People will think I'm pushing Brandon too hard."

"Quit being a girl," he said.

I couldn't believe Dave would make such a sexist remark. "Say what?"

"Don't worry if people like you. You're being an aggressive reporter and there's nothing wrong with that."

He was right. And I should know better than to let myself be vulnerable in front of my boss.

Back at my desk, I decided to go through Livvy's tweets and social media posts from the month before she was killed. I'd done that before, but now, armed with the new information Reynolds had given me, I went through them again.

I struck gold. Two weeks before Livvy died, she tweeted, "Gay guys get so much sympathy and love when they come out. Okay. But what about their wives and girlfriends? They deserve even more after all the shit they went through."

Then, a week later, Livvy quote-tweeted a post that read: "Gay men who deceive their wives deserve to be outed." Livvy's own added message was, "Fucking right!"

It wasn't proof, but it was pretty good corroborating evidence. Buoyed by these discoveries, I set to work contacting Livvy's friends from freshman year. I had phone numbers, email addresses, or social media info for five girls, including two who had lived down the hall from her. Maybe she'd confided in one of them about Brandon.

I was in the middle of messaging them when Dave texted me to come to his office. Now what? I still felt a little uncomfortable after our last conversation. I walked in and asked, "What's up?"

Dave said, "Sherry from PR will email you, but I wanted to give you the heads-up myself. She set up interviews for you on three local newscasts."

I just stared at him. *Interviews? Me?* I should've expected this, but—

Dave smiled at my inability to speak. "Pretty cool, huh?"

I smiled back, picturing myself on TV. "Yeah, it's freaking awesome."

"So be ready in fifteen. We'll have a driver take you around."

I gave him a thumbs-up. "Nice!" Then I looked down at my orange and white striped shirt and thought: *I'm not dressed for this. Aren't you supposed to wear blue on TV?*

Dave eyed me for a long moment, like he was sizing me up. "Now when you're on the set talking to these people, you gotta project confidence. Leave all your doubts behind." *Quit being a girl.* "You'll nail this Brandon Allen story, no worries. And if you get stuck, we have people who can help you."

No thanks. "I already have a good lead on Brandon," I lied. "An old friend of Olivia's."

Dave nodded approvingly. "Excellent. Now go ahead and have fun."

"Will do."

Leaving his office, I resisted an urge to burst out laughing. Just last week I'd wondered if my journalism career was dead. Now I was wondering what to wear for my three TV interviews.

At my desk, I took out my compact and started putting on lipstick. Wait—should I go for something brighter? The Panama Red? What kind of lipstick looked best on TV? As I sat there indecisively, Natalie walked up.

"Hey, I heard about your interviews. Congratulations," she said.

"Thanks."

Then she looked at my blouse. "Wait—you're not wearing that on TV, are you?"

I wanted to rip that concerned look off her face. "It's all I've got." Actually, I had another shirt in my drawer, but it would look even worse.

"I wish I had something to lend you. Those stripes will look a little garish on TV." She gave a chagrined look. "Sorry, didn't mean to bum you out. You want to borrow some makeup? Your face is gonna look all washed out."

Suddenly I realized Natalie was trolling me and I was panicking for no reason. The networks would have makeup artists. Hell, they probably had racks full of clothes, to make their interviewees look great. "I'm fine, Natalie. Do you mind? I'd like some quiet time."

"Oh sure." Natalie looked abashed, and maybe she even was, a little bit. "Good luck."

Twenty minutes later, my driver showed up. *I have my own driver!* He was a slender Chinese guy in his thirties named Christopher with a big Adam's apple, and he was excited to be driving the famous reporter investigating Olivia Anderson's murder. "Not that I had any love for Olive Oil," he said. "No offense, but to me she was no good. I'm an immigrant myself."

"I get it," I said. Again I thought about Livvy's bizarre lurch toward the alt-right. Nothing I'd learned about her could explain how that happened. I wondered if it would help me solve her murder if I understood that.

The first TV station was located in an industrial park just off the river. Almost as soon as I gave my name to the receptionist, I was swept up by a young, perky makeup artist. Everything I had imagined came true—and more. She touched up my makeup, blew my hair out, and found a pale blue shirt that complemented my dark brown hair. Eyeing myself in the mirror, I was amazed at how fabulous I looked. I looked like ... well, like somebody you'd see on TV.

Then I was brought onto the set. The TV lights were so bright it was daunting. This interview wouldn't be like the podcast, where if I screwed up I got another take. It would be broadcast live on the local news at six thirty.

At least my chair was soft and comfortable. As soon as I sat down, my interviewer, Chip Martin, spent the whole three-minute commercial break putting me at ease. I recognized his blandly handsome middle-aged anchorman's face from billboards all over the city. He treated me with practiced warmth, clearly used to working with nervous first-time interviewees. "Where are you from, Petra?" he asked.

"Los Angeles."

"No kidding! What do you think of In-N-Out Burgers?"

"Best hamburgers in the world."

He flashed me a grin. "Absolutely!" We shared our other burger preferences, and then, when the recording light came on, he introduced me to the TV audience.

"This is Petra Kovach, the *Boston Clarion* reporter and podcaster everybody's talking about." I shifted in my seat, proud but nervous. "Petra has reopened the Olivia Anderson murder investigation and captured the attention of the entire world with some very startling allegations. Welcome to Channel 4 News."

I gave a smile that I hoped didn't look stilted. "Thank you."

Chip started me out with a softball question. At least, to him it was probably a softball. To me it was a radioactive bomb. "So you believe Olivia's stepfather was sexually abusing her?"

Oh God, I don't believe that. I mean I'm not sure but I think probably not. But I can't admit it.

Confidence. Project confidence.

CHAPTER TWENTY-THREE

I GAVE CHIP a confident nod. "Olivia's Reddit posts certainly indicate an incestuous relationship. We expect to have a follow-up on this very soon."

Chip raised his eyebrows. "So you have additional evidence of the incest?"

Did I say that? I didn't mean to! "I can't comment on that at this time. Stay tuned for our next podcast," I said coyly. Afraid that might sound frivolous, I added, "Obviously sexual abuse is a serious issue. We want to get to the bottom of this."

"Yes indeed," Chip agreed solemnly. "Let me ask you the question everyone's asking today. Until now, pretty much the entire country believed the jury got it wrong and Professor Reynolds was the killer. But you think he didn't do it?"

"I think it's very possible Professor Reynolds is not guilty."

"And the culprit was Viktor Anderson?"

I think he's innocent! Of everything!

Get hold of yourself. He could be guilty as sin.

"It's one possibility we're investigating."

Chip nodded. "I know you're trying to reach Olivia's boyfriend, Brandon Allen. Do you believe he has knowledge of the incest?"

"We believe he has information relevant to this investigation." *I sound like a lawyer*. But that was probably good. It was safe.

"Earlier today, you tweeted that . . . let's put it up on the screen here." An excerpt of my first tweet appeared on a monitor in front of us. Chip read out loud: *"Olivia's romantic life was NOT what it seemed!'* Tantalizing. Can you tell us more about that?"

"Not at this moment." But then I realized this interview was a golden opportunity to put even more heat on Brandon. "I will say, though, that if Brandon cooperates, it may be an important step in solving Olivia's murder." I turned to the camera. "Brandon, if you're watching this, please call me. We need your help."

Perfect—if anything could smoke him out, this would.

"I certainly hope he does cooperate," Chip said, "because you've got me on the edge of my seat! Do you think you can actually solve this murder once and for all?"

Confidence. "Yes, I believe we will."

The interview kept going for another few minutes. I was getting way too hot under all that makeup. Sweat rolled down my armpits and I was positive the TV audience would see it.

Finally, the interview was over. As a commercial came on, Chip shook my hand. "Well done. You come across as very earnest and caring." I looked into his eyes, trying to figure out if he meant it. Then three producer types congratulated me, followed by the makeup artist, the receptionist, and Christopher the driver when I got back in the car with him.

"Was I really okay?" I asked.

"Yeah. Must-See TV."

"I sounded sincere?"

Christopher looked puzzled at the question. "Sincere? Of course," he answered, as we started off to the next TV station.

Before we even got there, I received congratulatory texts from Mama (DRAGA, I AM SO PROUD OF YOU), Jonah (DAMN, YOU LOOK HOT ON TV. CAN'T WAIT TO FOOL AROUND WITH A TV STAR!), and Mateo (CHIQUITA, DON'T FORGET THE LITTLE PEOPLE). Nobody mentioned my armpit sweat.

So I was feeling good when I sat down for my next two interviews. They were being taped for the late-night news, which felt less pressured than going live. Also, my interviewers, both of them women in their forties with blunt haircuts, asked me pretty much the same questions Chip did. So I was prepared. I started to feel less guilty about shining suspicion on Viktor. After all, as I kept reminding myself, he was still a suspect.

After the third interview, Christopher drove me back toward the *Clarion* office. I finally watched my first interview with Chip on my phone and thought, *I do look sincere. And yeah, pretty hot.*

Before I finished watching, Dave texted me. I was expecting congratulations, but instead he asked: ANY PROGRESS ON BRANDON? JUST TALKED TO ABERNATHY AND HE AGREES WE NEED MORE BEFORE WE GO WITH IT.

Great, now I was dealing with the publisher too. I came down from my high and texted back: YUP, LOOKING GOOD.

The sooner I found more evidence Brandon was gay, the better. It was still only nine thirty, so I decided to try once again to get through to Livvy's old friends and dormmates. First I checked Insta and Facebook. Plenty of people had contacted me, but none of Livvy's friends. Half the messages were hate mail. I didn't linger on them.

As Christopher drove through downtown, I got on Twitter. #PetraKovach was booming. I really was getting famous. Most people seemed to love me, except for the right-wing nutjobs tweeting things like: *"Petra Kovach is a tool of the Harvard elites, conducting a fake* '*investigation*' *to pursue their Defund the Police agenda.*" Then I checked my DMs. They were a mix of fan mail and hate mail, with a couple death threats mixed in. I scrolled down the screen, finding nothing useful—

Until I came to a DM from BACrimson: CALL ME. PLEASE KEEP CONFIDENTIAL. Then there was a phone number.

BA Crimson—that's Brandon!

I called him right away.

CHAPTER TWENTY-FOUR

AFTER THREE RINGS, a man—Brandon!—picked up. "Just a second while I get somewhere private," he said.

"Okay." I realized I shouldn't have Christopher listening in, so I asked him to pull over. I jumped out of the car and waited on the sidewalk in front of a Chipotle, my heart racing.

After half a minute or so I worried that Brandon had hung up, but finally he said, "Hi, you're Petra Kovach?"

"Yes, I am. Thank you for reaching out."

"Please don't tell anyone I did."

I hesitated, then went with honesty. "Well, I *am* a reporter. It's my job to tell people stuff."

"I realize that. But I can't have anyone from Harvard finding out about this. Can you keep it confidential, at least for now?"

"I can do that," I said, thinking I'd made a similar promise to Eric and broken it. I hoped I wouldn't have to do that to Brandon.

"Can we meet in person somewhere?"

Hell yes! "Wherever's good for you."

"I'm in a tutoring session until ten. Let's meet at ten thirty at one of the benches by the Charles River. Say, the first bench in from DeWolfe Street on the western side."

"Wait a second."

"What?"

A homeless man stumbled past me, muttering to himself. "Let's be up front here. You're a murder suspect. I'm not meeting you in a dark, secluded location. I've seen that movie."

"I don't want anyone to know we're meeting. I'm not gonna hurt you."

"That's what they all say. How about we meet at a coffee shop in Harvard Square?"

"You don't get it. Everyone will recognize me. Look, I'm taking a big risk here. You want to meet me? Take it or leave it."

No way I was going to leave it. "Fine, but first I'm informing three people about this. I promise they won't tell anyone. But if something happens to me, they'll know it was you and they'll all call the cops."

There was a silence, which I had to restrain myself from filling. At last he said, "See you then," and my line went dead.

I was so thrilled I wanted to shout. I satisfied myself with a loud "Yes!" as I threw my fists in the air, Rocky style.

"Is everything okay?" Christopher asked as I got in the car.

I was confident Brandon wouldn't do anything to me, not after I'd warned him that I was alerting three people. So I just told Christopher it was a confidential source. I didn't call Jonah or Mateo; I didn't want to worry them. Instead I texted Jonah that I'd be home late again, inserting frowny faces. Then I asked Christopher to drive me to Cambridge.

We got to DeWolfe Street a half hour ahead of time. There was a sports bar on the corner, and to the left was the riverside park where I'd be meeting Brandon. "You can take off. I'll get a Lyft home," I told Christopher.

"No, I can wait here."

But I didn't want him to scare Brandon away. Also, Christopher had been chauffeuring me for hours and I felt weird about it. The

East LA girl inside me wasn't used to this kind of treatment. "I'll be fine," I said. "My interview might not be over 'til eleven thirty."

Christopher argued a little while longer, then drove off. The night was cold, so I went in the bar and ordered onion rings and a Coke. At ten twenty-five, I left and headed for the park. The first bench was about forty yards in from the street, and I sat down on top of some faded gang graffiti, warming my hands in my jacket pockets. The ground underneath me was covered with fallen autumn leaves. In the distance, the dark river flowed west. There weren't many people in the park this late, just a couple of drunken partiers way down on the riverbank.

I scanned the night for Brandon, checking the bridge and then looking back toward DeWolfe. Ten yards in from the street I saw a man step out from behind a tree in the darkness. He was built like Brandon, tall and broad, so I raised my hand to wave.

Then the man brought up his right hand. It looked like there was something in it.

A gun?!

I dove off the bench just as the man fired.

CHAPTER TWENTY-FIVE

I HEARD A loud blast, then another one, and felt a sharp pain in my right shoulder. I'd been hit!

I was on the ground with the leaves and branches, rolling away from the bench, trying to stay low and get away from where I'd been when the guy fired.

But what if he could see me rolling around? Would I be safer lying still?

Then I heard him racing through the leaves toward me. I got up and ran, clutching my shoulder. It didn't hurt so much anymore. Must be the adrenaline—

"Hey!" he shouted.

I ran faster than I'd ever run before, toward the nearest street-light. But he was fast too. There was a hedge of bushes in my way and I had to veer to the right. I heard his footsteps racing closer. I screamed.

"Petra!" the man said, and he grabbed my left arm. I screamed again and tried to wrench free. But his grip was too strong.

I turned and saw who it was: Brandon Allen. "Let go of me!" I yelled.

"All right!" He let go. "But just so you know, I didn't fire those shots."

I stared at him, my heart pounding. His face seemed concerned. Then I looked down at my right shoulder. The light was dim, but I didn't spot any blood and my jacket wasn't shredded. I felt my shoulder and it didn't seem damaged.

Maybe I hadn't been shot after all! I thought back to what had happened. Maybe when I was rolling on the ground I went over a sharp stick.

"Are you okay?" Brandon asked. "I was coming toward you and I heard those shots. Then the guy ran away toward DeWolfe."

Brandon's distressed face said he was telling the truth: he wasn't the shooter. My throat was still tight with fear, but I said, "I'm okay. Thanks for coming after me."

"No problem." He looked around the park. "Let's get onto a main street where it's safer."

We walked quickly toward the closest street, thirty yards or so away, with bright streetlights. Checking behind us, I asked, "Did you get a good look at the guy?"

"He was running too fast."

For a moment I wondered if the guy was an accomplice of Brandon in some way. But that didn't make sense. Brandon wouldn't want to draw attention to this meeting. The shooter must have followed me from my last TV interview.

We reached the street and I breathed more freely. Across the way was a 7-Eleven. Brandon said, "Do you want to go in there and call an Uber?"

I blinked at the store windows, reorienting myself. I so wanted to go inside that safe, shiny store. Instead I turned back to Brandon. "We still have to do our interview."

"We should get out of here. What if he comes back?"

"You said he ran away. And he won't try to hurt me with you around."

"Look, we can do this another time."

Residues of terror were still ricocheting through my body, but I wasn't about to let Brandon Allen get away from me. I stepped off the sidewalk into the park a few feet. "That guy's long gone. We can talk right here."

Brandon hesitated, scanning the area. "I guess that's okay, but keep your eyes open."

"Thank you for agreeing to meet with me," I said, trying to get him focused.

Finally, he looked back at me. "I want to help you find Olivia's killer, if I can."

I felt guilty for what I was about to ask Brandon. He had been kind of a hero, running toward me in the dark with a shooter on the loose to make sure I was okay.

But he was still a murder suspect. "Brandon, I have a lead I need to talk to you about."

"That's why I'm here. What is it?"

I thought I detected a slight tremor in his voice, and his shadowed eyes might be showing fear, but I wasn't sure.

"I'm sorry to ask you this, but are you gay?"

His face, even in this light, registered dismay but not surprise. I felt sure he'd known all along this was the reason I wanted to see him.

"No," he said emphatically. "That's ridiculous."

My chest grew tight, full of uncomfortable feelings. I plowed on. "I'm following a lead that Olivia found out you're gay, and she was about to out you on YouTube when she was killed."

He shook his head back and forth. "That is wrong in so many ways. Who told you that?"

"I can't say."

"You're not planning to put a stupid, unfounded rumor like that in your podcast, are you?"

"I'm considering it," I said. "That's why I wanted to talk to you first."

Anger, pure and visceral, flashed in Brandon's eyes. His hands turned into fists and I remembered he might be someone who had killed on impulse. I looked back toward the 7-Eleven, gauging my escape route.

"Do you know how much that rumor could hurt me?" he said.

"I understand that—"

"Olivia's murder put a stain on me. I've had to play at an all-American level for three years to get past it. Now if you add in some gay thing, and make me out to be a killer—"

I gathered my courage. "It's true, isn't it?"

He didn't respond for a moment, just eyed me with fear and fury mixed, and I knew I was right.

"It's *not* true," he snapped, "and I'll tell you what's *especially* not true. Olivia wasn't going to out me. She wasn't planning anything like that."

"Did she suspect you might be gay?"

"No!" He took a breath, and when he spoke again he was quieter. "Look, if I give you another lead—a real one—would you use that and forget this bullshit lie? Do you really want to destroy my life over this?" His voice turned plaintive. "I've dreamed of playing in the NFL ever since third grade."

My throat caught. I was in third grade when I got my own impossible dream of becoming a reporter. "If your lead is good enough, I'll do what I can," I said, though I wasn't sure how I'd convince Dave to keep the gay-football-star-boyfriend angle out of the podcast. "It would help if you had an alibi for the night of the murder."

Brandon looked down and shook his head. "I don't. I was in my dorm room packing for spring break, then I went to bed early."

"Why don't you tell me your lead, and I'll do my best."

"You promise me that?"

"Yes." *I'm telling the truth,* I thought. *If Brandon has something really big, maybe the podcast can go right there and skip the gay-boyfriend angle.*

Brandon eyed me for a few moments. I met his gaze, trying to look trustworthy. Then he said, "What I'm about to tell you, it's a serious fucking lead. But don't tell anyone you got it from me. My coach will suspend me for talking to the press, and besides, I can't keep getting involved in Olivia's murder. I'm trying to put it behind me."

"What's the lead?" I asked.

He took another deep breath. "You're right that she was about to out somebody. But it wasn't me, and it wasn't for being gay."

"Who was it?"

Suddenly a police siren wailed. It sounded like it was coming toward us. "I gotta get outta here," he said. He touched my shoulder, and the closeness made me squirm inside. "Please don't tell the cops or anyone else I was here when you got shot at. The internet will twist it into some crazy shit."

"Just tell me who Olivia was outing."

The siren came closer. He said quickly, "Sarah Fain, the girl who accused Danny. Olivia found more dirt on Sarah, and she was gonna drop another video. Sarah got furious and threatened her. I told the detectives, but they were so sure Reynolds was the killer, they never followed up."

"What was the dirt?"

The siren stopped close by and a car door slammed. Brandon said, even more rapidly, "Sarah was a serial accuser. She claimed another guy sexually assaulted her in high school. It's how she got attention."

Over by DeWolfe, two men in police uniforms entered the park.

Brandon touched my shoulder again. "Don't tell them. Please. It'll ruin my life."

He ran off, just as the two cops came racing toward us. "Hey!" one of them yelled. "Halt! Police!"

I was afraid they'd start shooting. I called out, "It's okay, Officers, I'm alright!"

Brandon was out of sight down the street by the time the cops got to me. The cop who had shouted was a light-skinned Black guy with a short Afro; the other one was a White guy with a mustache who was breathing hard and seemed out of shape.

"What happened?" the Black cop said sharply. "There were reports of shots fired."

"Yeah, somebody shot at me. But I'm okay. He ran away."

The White cop asked, "Who was the guy that took off just now?"

Should I honor Brandon's wishes and not reveal who he was? With no time to think, I came out with, "Just a passerby who heard me scream." Instantly I felt good about protecting Brandon, as much as I could.

"Why'd he run away from us?"

"I guess he's scared of cops for some reason."

"Do you know who shot at you?" asked the Black cop.

"No." I pointed toward DeWolfe. "He was by that big tree. He shot twice and then ran."

The White cop eyed me. "You look familiar."

I started to say I didn't think we'd met, then realized he had probably seen me on TV tonight. Despite everything else that was going on, I smiled inwardly: *I'm a celebrity now.* "I'm Petra Kovach, the reporter who's investigating Olivia Anderson's murder."

"Oh yeah," the Black cop said. "You're the one who claims the guy who did it didn't do it."

I blinked in confusion at his slightly convoluted comment, then got angry. "Somebody just shot at me, and you're giving me a hard time?"

The White cop held up his palms in a gesture of peace. "So what do you think happened tonight?"

"Somebody may have followed me from WBZ. You should check the security video from their parking lot."

"We'll do that," the Black cop said. "Are you having any boyfriend problems, anything like that?"

"No. But I've been getting a lot of hate mail about my podcast."

"Any death threats?"

Cold though I was, I felt sweat break out on my forehead. "A couple of the emails came close."

The cops asked me to forward them the worst hate mail. Then they escorted me into the 7-Eleven and headed back to DeWolfe to look for video from nearby stores. Maybe they'd get footage of the shooter running away. Hopefully they wouldn't also get footage of Brandon.

Meanwhile, two more sirens blared and other cops arrived, along with TV reporters, a *Globe* reporter, and some freelancers who must have been listening to police radio. I belatedly realized I was in the middle of an *"active shooter situation." Whoa, talk about lucky!* This would be great for the podcast. And the new Sarah Fain lead was intriguing. My investigation was doing exactly what I'd wanted: stirring things up so we'd get closer to catching Livvy's killer. Standing outside the 7-Eleven, I was about to text Dave when he called me.

"Petra, I heard you got shot at. Are you okay?" he asked.

My name must have been on the police radio, another side effect of being a little famous. "Better than okay. I'm coming into the office right now," I said. "I've got one hell of a story."

CHAPTER TWENTY-SIX

IN THE LYFT back to the office, I forwarded hate mail to the cops. Then I called Jonah.

"How's my famous fiancée?" he said. His voice sounded sleepy; he was probably reading in bed.

"Well, I'm fine, and that's actually why I'm calling. To let you know I'm fine."

"Cool, I'm fine too. What's up?"

"I was doing an interview and somebody shot at me. But they missed," I added quickly, "and the cops came. So everything's good."

I heard a sound like he'd dropped something, and imagined him sitting up in bed, his Kindle tumbling to the floor. "Oh my God, where are you?"

"I'm safe. I'm in a Lyft headed for the office."

"Who was it? Who shot at you?"

"I guess somebody who doesn't like my podcast."

"You must be freaking out!"

I hadn't felt like I was freaking out. But now I heard the fear in Jonah's voice and some spigot opened up inside me. "I guess I kind of am," I said haltingly, tears forming in my eyes.

"You need to come home."

"I can't. I need to write this up tonight."

Jonah's voice rose. "What did the cops say? Next time they might not miss!"

I shivered. "I'll be safe at the *Clarion*."

"Look, write the story from home."

"I told Dave I was coming in. I'm almost there anyway."

I heard Jonah give a frustrated sigh. "Fine. I'll come to the office right now and make sure you're okay."

Such a sweetheart. "I promise, I'm really not that stressed. You can make me a cup of chamomile tea when I get home."

"I'll bring it to you."

"Honey, I want Dave to look at me like I'm tough, like I can handle anything on my own."

Jonah hesitated. "You're insane. Text me the second you get there."

"I will. I love you, peach blossom."

"I love you too, sprite. Promise me you'll be careful."

"I promise."

After I got off the phone, I realized Mama might find out from TV or the internet that I'd been shot at. So I called and left a message I was alright.

From the front seat, the Lyft driver, a bubbly, aspiring-actor type named Lianne, said, "Excuse me, did I hear you say you were *shot at* tonight?"

"Yup."

"Wow. How can you be so calm?"

I practically burst into tears just now, and this girl thinks I'm calm? Am I that good at faking it? "Hey, it's all in a day's work," I drawled, feeling like the coolest girl imaginable. My body grew lighter. This story would be hella fun to write—a big step up from reporting on the Zoning Board in West Newton!

I still wasn't sure how to deal with the Brandon issue, though. Was there some way to avoid revealing that he was gay? Maybe I could hold off on that for now and focus the podcast on Sarah Fain instead. Although throwing suspicion on a possible rape victim wasn't exactly appealing either.

"Look at it this way," Dave said thirty minutes later, as I sat in his office and told him the story. He'd come in at midnight expressly to meet with me. "In your heart of hearts, who is the most likely killer?"

The answer came to me right away. Sure, Sarah was possible, but this kind of violent, brutal murder didn't seem like something a woman would do. Also . . . *it's always the boyfriend.* "I think Brandon's more likely."

"Then that's who we need to focus on, right? No matter how much we hate outing him."

"I just wish there was some way to tell his story without that."

"If you can think of one, let me know."

I ran my hands through my hair. "I'll hide the fact he was there tonight, meeting me in secret. I can at least give him that."

Dave frowned. "Okay, but the thing is, the secret rendezvous gives your story a spy-intrigue flavor. Also, the way he came to your rescue makes him look like a hero, which is actually good for him."

Dave was right about that. And I'd never promised Brandon to keep his presence a secret. "How do we deal with the fact I lied to the police? I told them Brandon was just a random passerby."

Dave beamed at me. "Brilliant!" I instantly felt great, though I didn't get what was so brilliant until he explained. "Now we don't have to worry about some cop leaking to the *Globe* that Brandon was there. We'll have an exclusive."

"Yeah, that's what I was thinking," I lied.

Dave nodded. "So we'll need you to put out a written piece right away and the next podcast episode by nine a.m."

Nine a.m.?

"I know that's a fast turnaround but this is a breaking story and we gotta jump on it. You think you can handle it, or do you want help?"

Help—aka Natalie. "No, I got it."

This late at night, the newsroom was quiet. I grabbed coffee and headed back to my cubicle, where I called Jonah and told him I might not make it home tonight for chamomile tea after all. Mama had left me a message, but I didn't have time for another phone call. So I texted her that everything was really, truly okay and I was working late with a super-tight deadline.

Then I got down to it. *"This is an emergency podcast,"* I wrote. *"A lot has happened in the last two days. We have a new suspect."*

Actually Brandon was an old suspect with a new motive, but no need to overcomplicate things.

"And on top of that . . . I got shot at.

"But before I tell you about all that," I wrote, thinking, *yeah, make 'em wait for it—"we have yet another surprise development. After over two years of avoiding the media, Professor William Reynolds, the man who was tried for killing Olivia Anderson, consented to an interview with this reporter. We met at a coffee shop in Boston, where Reynolds still lives."*

Earlier tonight, while I was doing interviews, America Forever had posted anonymously his video footage from Peet's. The footage included close-ups of Reynolds in his new beard that quickly crossed over into the mainstream media. So I felt okay disclosing he still lived in Boston and describing his looks. *"His thick brown beard would make a lumberjack proud,"* I wrote.

But now came the delicate part. I couldn't reveal that Reynolds told me emphatically the incest never happened. So I wrote, *"Professor Reynolds isn't sure if Olivia really was a victim of incest. He says that sometimes Olivia, like other young men and women, would post outrageous things on social media just to get a reaction. She may even have done that on Reddit."*

Perfect, I thought.

"So we still don't know for sure what happened between Viktor and Olivia. But incest wasn't the only thing Professor Reynolds and I discussed." My fingers hovered above the keys, then I typed, *"This will come as a shock to a lot of people, but there is a very real possibility that Brandon Allen, the star Harvard football player and Olivia's boyfriend at the time of her murder, is not who he seems to be."*

My eyebrows furrowed. In all the excitement of the live shooting incident, Dave and I had forgotten about getting further corroborating evidence of Brandon's sexuality, beyond those two tweets Livvy had sent out.

But if Dave wasn't going to bring that up, then neither would I. From the way Brandon reacted to my questions in the park, I was convinced I was getting this right.

My fingers paused again. With what I typed next, I might be about to wreck a man's life.

I pictured Brandon's sensitive eyes. He seemed like a nice guy. I had instinctively liked him.

But he might have taken Livvy's life. I owed it to her to go through with this.

I typed, *"I have reason to believe Brandon is gay."*

Now that I'd taken the plunge, I took a deep breath and kept going. *"Not only that, but according to Reynolds, Olivia was about to drop a YouTube video on gay men hiding their sexuality from their wives and girlfriends. Her video would likely have exposed her relationship with Brandon.*

"But Olivia was killed before she got a chance to record this video."

Reading what I'd written, I thought: *It's true. It's all true.* I pictured Brandon's big hands swinging that heavy lamp at Livvy's head. *Forget your feelings about this guy.* I got on a roll, writing without stopping about how Livvy's video could have cost Brandon *"tens of millions of dollars. That must have been infuriating. Maybe infuriating enough to kill over."*

I suddenly remembered I'd never gotten the chance to ask Brandon about his beef with his old friend and teammate Danny Madsen. Too bad; I was pretty sure Brandon would never agree to talk to me again.

Now came the action-adventure portion of the podcast. I wrote about how Brandon and I were planning to meet in secret, and I got shot at. *"From the shadow of the tree, the man stared straight at me. Then he raised his arm, aimed his gun at me, and fired. I dove for the ground, rolling away as fast as I could, then jumped up and ran."*

I described how Brandon raced up to me—*"heroically, I must say, with no regard for his own safety."* After all the damaging things I'd written about Brandon, it made me feel a little better to be putting in something nice about him.

I had a drink of coffee. Then I began writing about Brandon's new allegation: that Livvy was about to drop a video exposing Sarah Fain as a "serial accuser" who did it for attention—

Wait. I stood up from my desk. Maybe I shouldn't even mention Sarah Fain in the podcast for now. Episode 2 should be about: *Hey, Viktor may be innocent, hard to tell, but check this out. We have a fresh, even more exciting suspect for you: the gay football star.* Throwing yet a third suspect into this episode would complicate it too much, making listeners' heads spin. Sarah Fain belonged in Episode 3.

She could definitely carry a whole episode by herself. I had looked her up. Not only did Sarah have lustrous pale skin and striking red hair, she was on the crew team. It was still hard for me to imagine a girl committing this murder. But Sarah was six feet tall with big biceps, plenty strong enough to bash somebody with that lamp. Her height and strength worked against her when she made her rape accusation; the public had trouble taking in the fact this big girl might have been thoroughly drugged at the time. But as a murder suspect, her looks made her ideal casting. And girl-on-girl violence was always a winner. Come to think of it, maybe *Murder of the Century* would get optioned for TV. Wouldn't that be amazing! Who would play me? How about Anya Taylor-Joy, I thought with a laugh—

Then I stopped. What was happening to me? *Fuck the fame and career shit. This is about justice for Livvy.*

It's about the justice my Tata never got.

I sat back down and thought things through again. What should I put in this podcast?

I went back to my touchstone: whatever attracted the most listeners would also be best for pressuring the cops and solving Livvy's murder. So I cut the Sarah Fain bit. Then I composed the rest of the piece.

As I wrote the episode's final sentence about *"the savage murder of Olivia Anderson,"* I closed my eyes. My mind saw the crime scene photo I had first seen on *TMZ* several days after the murder: Livvy lying dead on her bed, legs splayed, blood oozing from the fracture on the side of her head.

I remembered a detail from this photo that had always stuck with me. Across the room from Livvy's body, by the door, was a pair of red running shoes with black laces. The shoes sat on top of a shoebox looking brand new, like Livvy had just bought them and was still debating whether to keep them.

But she never got a chance to make that decision.

I closed my eyes and thought, *Livvy, I will find out who did this to you.*

At one-thirty a.m., I finished my script and read it over. Even though it was a first draft it was tight, I thought. And I'd written it in less than two hours. I was getting the hang of this podcast business!

I had one more thing to do before taking the script in to Dave. I texted Larry and asked him to look into the identity of America Forever when he came in this morning. Maybe Larry could work his magic and figure it out from America Forever's anonymous video posts. Unmasking the man who had attacked Professor Reynolds and me would make for a nice sidebar in the newspaper. I'd work it into the podcast as well.

Then I printed out my script, checked again for typos, and brought it to Dave's office. I knocked on his door.

"Join the party!" he called out.

Join the party? I opened the door and started inside.

Then I stopped.

Natalie was in Dave's office. She sat in the chair where I always sat. And she had a big smile on her face.

What the hell is Natalie doing here, in my chair?

CHAPTER TWENTY-SEVEN

"Hey, Petra, grab a seat," Dave said. He was sitting behind his desk with a smile even broader than Natalie's.

"O-kaay," I said dubiously, because there was only one other chair in the room and it was off to the side, an old, pockmarked, wooden folding chair that looked like it came from a yard sale. It made a screeching sound when I sat down and felt unstable, like I was about to fall off. Dave and Natalie were perched in their padded seats across from each other at the desk. I wondered if Dave noticed how uncomfortable I was.

"Hi, Petch," Natalie said cheerfully.

I nodded tightly to her, then put the hard copy of my podcast script on Dave's desk. "I just finished the script. I think you'll love it."

But he left it sitting there. "We'll need to make some changes to it."

We? A ribbon of fear squirmed in my chest. "What's going on?"

Dave said, "Why don't you tell her, Natalie?"

"Sure," she said, her perfect white teeth glistening and showing every dollar of the orthodontia she'd had growing up. "So I decided it wouldn't hurt to follow up on your story a little."

I didn't ask for your help! a voice inside me screamed. But I tried to calm my racing pulse. Maybe Natalie had found something that would help my investigation. There was nothing wrong with a fellow reporter chipping in a little, if they got a lead.

Natalie continued, "I got on Eric Anderson's Twitter feed and saw he goes to a bar called the Parting Glass every Thursday night." She said in an aside to Dave, "I've found the first place to go in any crime investigation is Twitter."

Dave nodded his approval, like Natalie had just said something incredibly wise. *What's so brilliant about getting on Twitter? That's exactly what I did.*

"So tonight after work I went to the bar. Eric was by himself, drinking Guinness and shots and looking wasted. I sat near him, and we start talking. He's in a crappy mood, asking if I'm a reporter and telling me women are lying bitches and you can't trust 'em." She looked at me. "I guess that was you he was talking about."

I nodded, impatient for her to get to the point. She continued, "So Eric is drinking and ranting, and then the front door opens . . ." She stood up like she was giving a performance and paused for dramatic effect. "And in comes Viktor. He walks up to Eric and he's shitfaced too. I could smell the wine on him from where I was."

Dave clapped his hands. "Love that detail about the smell. Put it in the podcast."

"You got it, boss," Natalie said.

I thought, *Natalie is on my podcast now?!*

Her voice went deeper, as she acted out the part of Viktor. "So Viktor says to Eric, 'You ungrateful piece of shit, did you really tell that reporter I was having sex with Olivia?'

"Eric yells back, 'It's true, isn't it? You were fucking her!'

"Viktor switches to another language, Swedish I'm guessing, and yells back at Eric. So Eric says in English, 'Why'd you kill her, Viktor? She had enough of you?'

"Now everybody in the bar is watching. They scream at each other in Swedish, and Viktor shoves Eric off the seat." Natalie pushed an imaginary Eric off the chair where she'd been sitting. "He hits the floor and Viktor starts beating the crap out of him. The bartender tries to stop him but Viktor punches him, and the cops come and before you know it . . ." Natalie put up her wrists like they'd been handcuffed. "Viktor is under arrest for assault. He's in the Cambridge city jail right now."

What? "Doesn't he have diplomatic immunity?"

"Apparently, diplomatic immunity doesn't extend to having a drunken brawl with your stepson in a local dive bar."

Dave laughed. "Fabulous! Say it just like that in the podcast."

"You got it," Natalie said, sitting back down.

I was too stunned to speak. My actions had set this brawl into motion.

Dave turned to me. "So here's the plan. We'll lead off the podcast with Natalie telling her story: how our number one murder suspect totally lost his shit, exposing what a violent, dangerous guy he is. Capable of murder."

I had to admit, Natalie had lucked into a great story. I told myself to quit being jealous: Maybe Viktor really was the killer, and Natalie's scoop would be another step toward proving it.

Dave said to her, "I can't believe you got an eyewitness account. You have what we used to call 'a nose for news.' That's something you gotta be born with."

As Natalie beamed and I gritted my teeth, Dave turned to me. "After Natalie builds up Viktor as a suspect, you come in and knock that down a little—just a tad—with what Reynolds said about maybe no incest. Then you go: 'Surprise, listening audience! Boyfriend Brandon—gay—millions of dollars—holy crap, did *he* do it?' Big cliffhanger, and we're out. Nice, huh? Like the kids say, this episode will be fire."

Dave was outdoing himself tonight. Natalie rewarded him, laughing like he'd said something hilarious.

I tried to stifle the anger uncoiling inside me. "This is all great stuff, but we should start the podcast with how somebody shot at me. That's still the most dramatic part of our story: a first-person account of me almost getting killed."

Dave said, "Petra, it turns out there's a little problem with your story."

I stared at him. "What do you mean?"

"We got new information about your incident. As you know, Nat"—*Nat?*—"has police sources. So she made some calls." He turned to Natalie. "You want to fill her in on what you found out?"

"Sure," Natalie said. "According to my sources, an eyewitness walking down DeWolfe Street saw the shooter in the act of shooting. This was a nurse getting off her shift at Mt. Auburn Hospital, so she's reliable. And she's positive this guy wasn't actually shooting at you. He was aiming up at the sky."

My jaw dropped open. "I don't care if she's a nurse, she's mistaken. He was aiming at me. I saw the barrel of his gun!"

Natalie's voice turned condescending. "Petch, the thing is, the cops have other evidence too. There's a tree branch right above where the shooter was standing, and it has what looks like an entry wound and an exit wound. They're still running the forensics, but my guy is sure it'll turn out to be a gunshot through-and-through."

I was about to protest. But then I saw the scene again in my mind's eye, when the guy lifted his gun. I assumed he was aiming at me. But now that I thought about it, maybe he was lifting it higher—

"This is good news, Petra," Dave said. "He wasn't trying to kill you, just scare you."

Yeah, great—except it made my story a lot less exciting. I felt a flush creep across my cheeks. I'd been so emphatic the guy shot at me. Now I didn't feel I could back down. "I'm positive about this. I know what I saw!"

Dave eyed me a little pityingly.

"Maybe he fired one shot at me and one in the air," I said, realizing immediately how lame it sounded.

Dave said, "Petch"—oh God, he'd picked that up from Natalie— "don't stress about this. I'm sure when someone's aiming a gun right near you, it's easy to get things wrong. And of course we'll use this story, I just don't want to lead with it. We can't say he shot at you and then have the cops knock that down the next day."

Natalie rubbed her chin thoughtfully. "How about this: we'll say the guy pointed his gun at Petch to scare her, then lifted his gun and shot in the air."

Dave aimed an imaginary gun at Natalie. "Excellent idea, Nat. There's no way anyone can disprove that." He looked at me. "Maybe it's even true."

All I could manage was, "Yeah."

He tapped his desk and stood up, signaling an end to the meeting. "So why don't you two hash this out and come up with a script and send it to me. I'm going home, but I'll make some espresso and stay awake 'til you guys have it done."

Natalie stood too. "Cool," she said, then turned to me. "It'll be fun to collaborate on this."

Now this bitch was winning points for being a team player? Through my clenched jaw, I said, "Yeah, it'll be great."

"Terrific," Dave said, holding the door open for us.

As I took my script off the desk, Natalie said, "How about giving me your piece after you rewrite it and I'll look it over?"

"Awesome idea," Dave said.

I'll have to answer to Natalie?! Trying not to explode, I said pleasantly, "Sure. And I'll be happy to look over what you write."

"Thanks, Petch."

As the three of us left Dave's office, he said, "Okay, I'll leave you guys to it. Look forward to reading what you come up with."

"Thanks, Dave," Natalie said, as he took off for the parking garage.

Not to be outdone, I called loudly, "Yeah, thanks, Dave!"

Now that he was out of earshot and the newsroom was empty, I let go. I snarled at Natalie, "My name is Petra. You know I fucking hate 'Petch.'"

But my timing was terrible. A frizzy-haired assistant editor named Isabel, the only editor here this time of night besides Dave, came around the corner just at that exact moment. She must have heard me, because she threw me a startled look. I froze. Oh hell, would she mention this encounter to Dave? Natalie shrugged as if to say, *Yeah, Petra's being kind of a jerk.*

After Isabel disappeared down the hall, Natalie turned to me. Her eyes looked earnest, even a little hurt. "If it weren't for me, you would've done a podcast about how you got shot at, and you would've ended up with egg on your face. I did you a favor."

I didn't buy her act. "Right, because you're such a good friend."

"Petra, I know we've had some issues in the past—"

"Like you stealing my story, which you're trying to do again."

"I didn't steal your story. You're just sensitive because you got laid off so many times. It's understandable. I'd feel the same way."

If there were a Pulitzer for gaslighting, this woman would win it hands down. Or was it possible she was telling the truth?

No. "Spare me the sympathy," I said.

Natalie rolled her eyes impatiently. "I'm just trying to be a good reporter for the newspaper we both work for. Look, we're gonna be working together—"

"—for *one* episode—"

"—so we might as well get along. That'll be best for both of us," she said, throwing me a meaningful look.

Was that a threat? That if I didn't make nice, she'd tell Dave? I seethed in silence as we walked down the hallway toward our respective cubicles. "I'll let you know when I'm done writing," Natalie said. "Then we can read each other's halves."

Halves? No, no way you're stealing a full half of my podcast.

I did a quick rewrite on my pages, changing them to reflect the new story that the shooter aimed at me and then shot in the air. I had no idea if that was what really happened, and I wondered how my old journalism profs would have felt about my looseness with the truth. Actually, I already knew.

While I waited for Natalie to finish writing her section, I went to the downstairs bathroom for privacy and called Jonah, even though it was two a.m. His alarmed voice answered after one ring. "What's wrong? Are you okay?"

"I'm sorry to wake you up, honey. I'm just so upset."

I could hear him taking a sip of water from the glass he kept by his side of the bed. "Why, what's going on? Do they know who shot at you?"

"That's not what I'm worried about right now." Pacing back and forth in front of the sink, I told him about Natalie's power moves. "This is my podcast! And now this conniving slimebucket is trying to make it hers!"

"I think you're overreacting."

My voice rose an octave. "Overreacting?!"

"I'm just saying it'll be okay. Everybody knows *Murder of the Century* is your baby. You've been on TV three times."

I rubbed my head. Jonah was right. And so was Natalie. My PTSD from all my career traumas was making me hypersensitive. I needed to chill.

"It's gonna work out," Jonah said. "Hang in there. You're the best."

"No, you're the best. You win the good person prize by like, three hundred percent."

I went back to my desk feeling calmer. But then Natalie appeared at the opening to my cubicle. She held out a few double-spaced pages and said, "Here's my half."

Half. Did she somehow intuitively know how much that word pissed me off?

We split up and began reviewing each other's pages. I grabbed a pen from my drawer, eager to shit all over Natalie's script. She'd written it quickly, so it would probably be garbage.

I switched to a thick, red, felt-tip marker, figuring that would make my negative comments look even scarier, and got to work.

CHAPTER TWENTY-EIGHT

FIFTEEN MINUTES LATER, I still hadn't done a lot of ripping.

I hated to admit it, but Natalie's script, which I estimated would run about nine minutes, almost as long as mine, was tight. She wrote great descriptions of the Parting Glass—"working-class urban with a touch of college girl"—and Eric's state of mind—"semi-homicidal brooding." Viktor was "the Swedish diplomat, reeking of expensive red wine." The fight scene was gripping, and she managed to insert herself into it. She claimed she tried to get between Eric and Viktor, but Viktor shoved her, knocking her down. I doubted it was true, but it was effective. And the actual scene at the bar was probably so chaotic, none of the people there would be able to say for sure that she was lying.

In the end, my efforts to trash Natalie's script were limited to suggesting a few picayune word changes, like "dubious" instead of "doubtful." It was exasperating.

When I finished my edit I went to her cubicle, where she was listening to Beyoncé. She had put on fresh lipstick, and I felt shabby next to her. I gave back her pages and said grudgingly, "Good work."

She gave me a smile I couldn't decipher, then handed my own pages back to me. "You too. I had a couple suggestions."

A couple? Red ink *covered* the first two pages. Natalie had had no problem at all finding things to rip.

I went back to my desk to look at her comments. No doubt they were all stupid and I could ignore them. My script was solid.

But when I read Natalie's changes, I got where she was coming from. Mainly what she'd done was make cuts in my account of what happened at the park. Now that the incident was no longer a murder attempt, but somebody firing in the air, my section felt overwritten. Natalie's cuts right-sized it.

What killed me was, with these cuts my half would actually be shorter than hers.

The other thing Natalie pointed out was that I could have done a better job describing how terrified Brandon was when I confronted him about being gay. *"You can punch up the drama of this scene,"* Natalie had written in the margin, *"which is Brandon realizing you have him by the balls and his secret is about to explode."*

I realized I had downplayed this aspect because I still felt uncomfortable about outing him. I needed to be more cold-blooded.

Like Natalie. Much as I was skeptical of her, I had to admit her remorselessness had virtues when it came to being a good journalist.

I took my laptop and went back to Natalie's cubicle, where I immediately thought: *why did I come to her instead of the other way around? It gives her the power!* She greeted me with a bright smile and said, "Shall we dive in?"

"Sure." As we went through my script, I tried to act cool about it, accepting almost all of her suggestions. We finally finished and combined our two documents into one—which Natalie proceeded to send to Dave herself, without asking me first. I felt sure it was another way for her to assert dominance.

Dave called us—on Natalie's cell—and gave us the thumbs-up, praising her section effusively. Then he asked us to record the episode right away, because Viktor's arrest would be all over the news in the morning. So we took a Lyft to the recording studio and met Larry there. It was two thirty a.m. and I was exhausted. I'd been up since five in the morning, riding a roller coaster of fame and fear. Now I had to sound fresh for this podcast.

Larry's friend Erinne the harpist was on a concert tour down South, so it was just Larry, Natalie, and me. He turned on the mic and soundboard and asked, "Who wants to go first?"

"I will," Natalie said with a flip of her blonde hair, at the same time I said, "I can go."

Larry said, "Why don't we start with Natalie, because she goes first in the podcast."

I didn't have a logical comeback to that. But I wondered, *does Larry have a crush on Natalie?* It did seem like his eyes were lingering on her luscious, lying lips. She sat down on the Hindu throne in front of the mic and exclaimed, "This throne is perfect!"

I tried to sleep while she recorded her piece. But I couldn't doze off while hearing my rival's voice, especially with no comfortable beds or sofas around. She sounded so damn polished, lowering her pitch and coming off as authoritative without losing the drama. Larry fawned all over her.

Finally, an hour and a half later, it was my turn. After listening to Natalie, my own voice sounded incredibly young. I tried to deepen it like she had, but Larry stopped me. "What are you doing with your voice? You sound kind of uptight."

So I went back to my regular voice, or tried to. Larry said, "Now you sound flighty."

Aargh!

The throne was killing my back. When I said out loud, *"I have reason to believe Brandon is gay,"* my throat constricted and I had trouble getting the words out, as I confronted the fact that I was changing Brandon's life forever, without his permission, and likely for the worse. *It's for Livvy,* I told myself, several times.

I finally finished at six o'clock. I was too burned out to know if I sounded any good. Larry sent the audio to Dave, and we waited to see if he'd want us to record anything over again. I lay down on the floor and finally nodded off.

An hour later I was shocked awake by a dream. Little fourteen-year-old Livvy had blood on her head and she was floating in the air, waving to me like she was trying to get my attention. "I'm over here," she called out. "Over here!"

My heart was racing and I half expected to see Livvy still hovering above me. But before I could think about what my dream meant, I was distracted by Larry and Natalie talking quietly to each other. They were setting up to do more recording. "What's happening?" I asked.

"Good news. Dave was cool with the podcast," Natalie said.

"Excellent. So what are you guys doing? Did he want you to re-record something?" I was hoping Dave hadn't liked part of Natalie's segment and was making her do it over again.

"No, I'm recording the ads."

I jumped up. "I should do that. It's my podcast."

The words were out before I thought about them. But it was true—I *should* be the one doing the ads.

Larry said carefully, "I think the sponsors will be okay with Natalie. It's what Dave wanted."

Natalie said, "Dave thought you sounded tired."

Larry said, "It's true, you kind of did."

It took every ounce of self-control to keep from screaming.

CHAPTER TWENTY-NINE

THE PODCAST WOULD drop at eleven, so I decided to take a Lyft home to snatch a couple hours of sleep first. I passed out in the car and barely made it up the stairs. I threw my purse on the kitchen table, set my alarm for ten fifteen, and fell into the bed next to sweet-smelling Jonah.

The next thing I knew, Jonah was gone and my alarm was chiming. I shut it off, then stumbled into the kitchen foggy-headed for a glass of water.

Jonah was there. He was at the table reading the stapled pages of my podcast script. It's not like it was secret or anything, but still, I was taken aback to see him reading my stuff without asking me first.

"What are you doing?" I said.

He looked up at me. His eyes looked flat. "Your script was on the table." I realized what had happened: it must have fallen out of my purse. "I couldn't stop reading."

Something was off. Even in my bleary state, I was pretty sure I knew what it was. I got a glass from the cabinet and filled it. "Did you like it?"

He held up my script. "Did you get his permission?" When I looked away without answering, he asked, "You're outing this guy in today's podcast?"

I'd never seen Jonah like this, squinting at me with disbelief, or horror. "He may have killed Livvy," I said.

"Do you even know for sure that he's gay?"

"Yes!" I said, walking over to him. I did feel sure.

He tossed the script onto the table. "How? You don't give a lot of evidence."

"Look, I didn't love doing this either, but it's the best way to get information. You put out what you've got and hope it stirs the pot."

"Why not investigate for a couple weeks first? You could've found out he was innocent. Then you wouldn't have to out him."

"I didn't have a couple weeks."

"Why not?"

I slammed my glass down and water sloshed out onto the script. "Do I tell you how to do your job?"

I knew that was childish, and he called me on it. "I don't destroy people's privacy on my job. You're fucking with this guy's life."

"I'm a journalist trying to solve Livvy's murder. People are gonna get hurt, that's just a fact."

"That's your excuse every time you do something questionable."

"I had a podcast to get out this morning. You have no idea the shit I've been going through!"

"So that's why you're outing this guy. Because it's good for your podcast!"

His eyes were so hard, I wanted to cry. But I was burning up inside. "What do you know? You grew up in the fucking suburbs! You've never had a career problem in your life! I was fired four times!"

"Get over that already. That was over a year ago—"

"I was fired last week!"

It came out just like that. I didn't think about it. I was still standing. He looked up at me from the table. "What are you talking about?"

"I was fired, okay? This whole podcast, it's how I got Dave to let me keep my job."

"When was this, the day you pitched? The day we got engaged?"

"Yes."

I was hoping he'd have sympathy for me. Instead he said, "And you didn't tell me?" He stood up so fast his chair fell over. It clattered on the tile floor. "The day we got engaged, you lied to me? A huge fucking lie?"

I tried to find the words. "I was ashamed. And I thought you'd hate me if I got fired again. I wanted to fix everything so I'd never have to tell you."

"What about outing Brandon? You lied to me about that too—"

"No I didn't—"

"You never even *mentioned* it. What kind of relationship is that, where you won't talk to me about anything that's really important?"

"I didn't want to upset you."

"You don't want to upset me, but it's perfectly okay to destroy Brandon's career?"

"He's the most likely suspect!" I couldn't take Jonah's anger anymore. "I have to get dressed and go to work. My podcast drops in thirty minutes."

He shook his head, disgusted. "Fine. Knock yourself out."

He grabbed his backpack and started toward the door. Then he looked back at me. "I don't know who you are anymore. You're not the idealistic young woman I met in Oxford."

"Of course I am," I said. "I'm trying to get justice for Livvy."

"No, you're trying to get justice for your Tata, and that's never gonna happen. The only question is how many people you drag down with you."

We stood there eyeing each other like boxers after a fight. Did he include himself as one of the people I was dragging down? I felt

I had more to say, but I wasn't sure what. Jonah looked like he felt the same.

Then he walked out.

*   *   *

I listened to the episode in the Lyft on the way to work. It was true, I did sound tired. Especially compared to Natalie's resonant voice.

Or maybe it wasn't tiredness I heard, it was stress, about Brandon.

Regardless, Episode 2 jumped out of the gate with forty thousand listens and a hundred thousand downloads in the first hour. When I made it into the office, a parade of *Clarion* staffers came to my cubicle to congratulate me. Larry and I gave each other a big hug.

But I'm sure I didn't give off the best vibes, because I was replaying that scene with Jonah in my mind. I'd been a jerk. But why couldn't he try to understand what I was going through?

And what did my dream about Livvy mean? Waving her hands and calling out, "I'm over here." Over where?

I wanted to text Jonah, but I still didn't know what to say, and he didn't text me. I tried to forget about him, for now. It felt like we'd just had a huge, destructive, relationship-changing argument, but maybe I was tired and overreacting, and we'd work things out tonight.

I heard loud laughter down the hall—people congratulating Natalie. I could tell she had more well-wishers than I did, either because her half of the podcast was better or because people could tell I was in a weird mood.

I tried not to be petty. The most important thing—the only truly important thing—was that this episode might get us closer to the truth about Livvy's murder.

And it was still my podcast, even if it was a little bit Natalie's too now. I had every reason to expect it would bring me some job security in this insane business. These podcast episodes and newspaper articles would be the killer clips I'd needed, giving me an open sesame to my next job.

But I couldn't relax.

Partly it was about Jonah. But also, I didn't know how to relax. I'd been scrambling to get ahead ever since I was a high school kid trying to get a scholarship to UCLA. Long before I got fired all those times. Now I couldn't shut my motor off. I wasn't programmed to accept compliments. Maybe it was the fraud thing kicking my ass, especially after another night with almost no sleep.

And maybe I was more upset about Brandon than I knew. I kept telling myself what I did was justified, but then I would feel Brandon's touch on my shoulder in the park, as he said, "Don't tell them. Please. It'll ruin my life."

Shortly before noon, when my office had emptied out and Natalie's office was still full of laughter, my phone buzzed. I hoped it would be Jonah, but it was Mateo. I took a deep breath and decided to get it over with. He used to be a journalist too. Maybe he'd understand that I had to out Brandon. I had no choice.

"Hi, Mateo," I said hopefully.

"What the fuck," he said. "What the fuck, Petra."

Our conversation went downhill from there, and I got off the phone feeling less certain than ever that I had done the right thing. I wished I had made a close woman friend in Boston, someone I could rely on at a time like this to give me some perspective and get me out of my head. But my job was so demanding, I hadn't had time to socialize—

Chuck Kling, the sports reporter, poked his head into my cubicle. "Hey, Petch," he said. Great, would the entire newsroom call me that now? "Everybody's celebrating in the break room. There's donuts."

I wanted to be there so it wasn't just Natalie accepting congratulations. But just then my phone buzzed: Mama. "I'll be right in," I said, as I clicked ACCEPT. "Hi Mama."

"*Draga,* are they giving you a bodyguard?"

Dave had offered me one, but I'd decided the shooter was just some nut trying to scare me. I thought I'd get extra points for acting tough—*don't be a girl.* So I told Dave no.

But Mama would be upset if she knew that. "Mama, I'm sure there's nothing to worry about, but yes, I got a bodyguard. He's six foot three with lots of muscles, so I'm good."

"*Vrlo dobro,* but don't go in any dark places at night, stay on the main street."

"Will do, Mama. Did you listen to the podcast yet?"

Her voice turned lighter instantly. "Yes, I'm so proud of you. You sounded great! A little tired, but not too much."

Gee thanks, Mama.

"And that other girl on the podcast, is she a friend of yours? She was terrific!"

I swallowed the anger that rose up inside me. I tried never to tell Mama about problems at work. So I told her I needed to get off the phone, and I had just clicked off when Dave walked into my cubicle—followed by Detective Hope O'Keefe.

What the hell? O'Keefe's face was expressionless as usual. But Dave was in a great mood. "Petch, you have a visitor," he said.

I stuck out my hand. "Hello, Detective."

O'Keefe gave my hand a perfunctory shake.

"Detective O'Keefe has some questions for you about Olivia's murder," Dave said. "You guys can have the conference room."

I gave O'Keefe a broad smile. "Sure. Sounds good."

No, it sounded *fantastic*. O'Keefe might be acting cold, but the fact she was here meant she now took my investigation seriously. I had accomplished my goal of getting the police to reopen their investigation of Livvy's murder.

Now I felt vindicated about all the decisions I'd made. For the first time today I felt optimistic again. Dave escorted us into the conference room, then lingered with me at the doorway and whispered, "Make sure you get some good stuff out of her."

"Will do," I whispered back.

CHAPTER THIRTY

O'KEEFE STOOD BY the table observing me silently as I walked into the conference room. "Would you like some coffee?" I asked.

"No thanks."

I looked at her stolid, unlined face and wondered if she might be using Botox. No, of course not—she didn't give a damn how she looked. I would enjoy describing her on the podcast, right down to her smattering of childlike freckles that looked so incongruous.

I said, "Won't you sit down?"

"No thank you."

Okay, whatever. I stayed standing too. "So what did you think of our new podcast episode?"

"Haven't listened to it."

I blinked. "Yeah, it just came out this morning. What did you think of the first one?"

"Didn't listen to that either. Why should I, since we already know who the killer is?"

My heart sank. I put my hands on my hips. "Why are you here?"

"My captain ordered me to interview you. So give me your pitch, then I'll go back to the station and report you had nothing useful to tell me."

I glared at her. "That is outrageous. I've already discovered two pieces of key evidence that you missed in your rush to judgment. I found the Reddit posts, and I found out Livvy was going to out Brandon—"

"Why should I believe anything you say?" O'Keefe pointed a thick finger at my chest. "You lied to the police last night. In the middle of an active shooter incident."

"I did not." *Sure, I said he was aiming at me, not the sky. But that was a "fog of battle" thing—*

"You told the officers on the scene you were talking to a random passerby. But really it was Brandon Allen, wasn't it?"

Oh right, *that* lie. "He asked me not to say it was him."

"But you ratted him out this morning in your podcast, I'm told."

"I changed my mind."

"Let me repeat: *active shooter incident.* If the police had known Allen was there, they could've interviewed him. Maybe he had vital information about what direction the shooter was going, or what he was wearing."

She was right. I hadn't thought of that. "Well, you could ask him now."

"It would've been better to ask when his memory was fresh and the shooter was close by. For all I know, you staged this event for publicity. I wouldn't put it past you."

Enough apologizing. "Why are you so closed-minded you won't even consider the possibility somebody besides Reynolds committed this murder?"

O'Keefe held up her fingers one by one, ticking off evidence. "His prints on the murder weapon. The victim's blood on his jacket. Obvious motive. No alibi. If it's the truth you're after, then do a podcast about the jury letting an obviously guilty man go free because they didn't like his victim. But since you don't give a fuck about the truth, go ahead, get your little clicks, knock yourself out."

Now was my chance to tell this woman what I should have told her last time. "My father was shot to death when I was eight. The police were dickheads, just like you. You think all I want is clicks? I want you cops to do your freaking jobs. I want you to finally find Livvy's killer."

It was a damn good shot, but O'Keefe didn't blink. "Sure, tell yourself that. You're a princess in shining armor." She checked the time on her phone. "Okay, I've been gone from the station for an hour. Long enough to convince the captain I interviewed you. Have a nice day."

She headed out the door. I didn't want to let this meeting end without getting at least something. I called, "Wait!"

She half-turned, barely looking at me. I asked, "Did anyone ever tell you that when Olivia died, she was about to drop another video attacking Sarah Fain, the girl who was the subject of 'Who Raped Who'?"

"You wanna turn her into a suspect too? Spare me."

"Hey, she was plenty strong enough to—"

But O'Keefe was already out the door and gone.

Great, now what?

Well, if the police weren't trying to solve this crime, then I damn well better do it myself. My adrenaline was still firing and I paced, trying to figure out my next investigative move. I should focus on the best suspect, which I still thought was Brandon, not Sarah—

My phone pinged with a text from Dave: LET'S MEET IN MY OF-FICE IN FIVE AND TALK STRATEGY. He had copied Natalie. Obviously she was now part of the podcast going forward. I clenched my fists. I was still reeling from everything else, and now I'd have to deal with this. It would be the contraband butterfly story all over again, with Natalie trying to steal the best leads and all the kudos. Between that and having to confess to Dave that O'Keefe had stonewalled me, this would not be a fun meeting.

But then it hit me: there was a way I could screw over Natalie and at the same time keep Dave from getting on my case about O'Keefe.

I headed for Dave's office to do battle. Investigating Livvy's murder was my mission. If anyone was going to find out what happened to her, I wanted it to be me.

CHAPTER THIRTY-ONE

I DECIDED TO hit Dave's office in three minutes, not five, so I'd get the good chair and not be stuck off to the side. But as I walked toward his door, I saw Natalie coming up the hall from the other direction. Obviously she'd had the same idea.

We were both the same distance from Dave's door. I quickened my step, trying to be cool about it and not run, but Natalie quickened her step just as fast.

Fuck it, I thought, and broke into a full-on sprint. She was taken by surprise, and it took her a couple seconds before she started running too.

Those short seconds made all the difference. I got there first, knocking on Dave's door just as Natalie came up.

"Come in," Dave said.

Then Natalie elbowed me in the ribs, throwing me to the side, and started through the door ahead of me.

I grabbed the belt at the back of her dress and pulled. As she stumbled backwards for a step, I moved ahead of her and walked through the door.

"Hey, Dave," I said, and sat in the prized chair across from him.

His eyes were on his computer, probably checking the latest click stats from the podcast, and he didn't seem to have noticed anything untoward. Natalie entered and cast me a venomous look, then headed for the folding chair.

"Hi, boss," she said, her composure back in place. "I hear we just hit a hundred fifty thousand."

"You guys killed," Dave said, looking up from the computer so he could beam at Natalie. "I talked to Abernathy. He couldn't be happier."

"That's great," Natalie said enthusiastically.

"Freaking fabulous!" I said, trying to outdo her and sound even more gung ho. I clapped my hands together.

"And you guys are both majorly trending on Twitter. Natalie, you're number three, and Petra, you're number eight."

Just what I needed to hear. "Terrific," I said.

Dave nodded. "So what did you get out of O'Keefe?"

I sat up straight in the chair and made my play. "Juicy stuff about Sarah Fain."

"Really."

"Detective O'Keefe confirmed that Olivia's last video was going to be about Sarah." I leaned forward. "And not only that: just before Olivia was killed, Sarah apparently threatened her."

Making direct eye contact with both Dave and Natalie so I'd look trustworthy, I said, "Besides Professor Reynolds, Sarah was the cops' most promising suspect. But when they arrested him, they dropped everybody else. So all this evidence against Sarah is low-hanging fruit for us."

"I like it. Definitely worth pursuing," Dave said.

"Totally," said Natalie.

I nodded vigorously.

"So which of you guys would like to tackle it?" Dave asked.

I didn't speak, desperately willing Natalie to take the bait and say she'd jump on the Sarah Fain angle right away. But she just sat there looking at me. We locked eyes for a moment.

I turned to Dave. "Much as I'd like to do it, I should probably stick with Brandon and see that through."

Natalie held up her hand. "Petra sounds so passionate about this angle, I'd hate to take it from her." She turned to me. "Why don't you go with Sarah, and I'll take Brandon and Viktor."

Fuck! "I don't want to be greedy," I said. "I'll be happy with Brandon and Viktor, since I've already been working them, and let Natalie have Sarah."

Natalie threw me a fake smile. "No, that's okay, really. You can do Sarah."

"It's nice you ladies work so well together," Dave said, rubbing his hands. "So it's all settled. Petch, you got the girl."

Trying to salvage at least a small victory, I said, "I should help on Brandon too. I'm identified with that story line after today's podcast."

Dave said, "I don't think that's a problem. Our listeners can make the adjustment to a different reporter telling that story." He tapped his desk. "Okay, anything else you need from me? We're counting on you guys."

"We won't let you down," Natalie said.

"That's right," I said, trying to hide my panic. I had nothing on Sarah Fain except for what Brandon said—and he could have been lying to protect his ass.

As Natalie and I walked out of Dave's office, she whispered, "You were trying to sucker me into taking Sarah, weren't you?"

I acted offended. "Of course not. I'm thrilled to have that story."

"You shouldn't have been so greedy. You could've had Viktor or Brandon. Now I've got both."

* * *

A few minutes later, after checking my phone—still no messages from Jonah—I headed outside. It was just after noon and the temperature was up in the sixties: an ideal late September day. I needed to take a walk and clear my mind, and hopefully figure out a way to tackle the Sarah Fain story. Maybe I could put that to bed quickly and get back to investigating more fruitful avenues.

But I was so lost in my own head, I forgot to check my surroundings when I left the building. I hadn't gone ten steps before a familiar figure stepped in front of me on the sidewalk, blocking my way. It was the big, burly guy from Peet's, wearing the same black America Forever T-shirt. Or a duplicate, since the white logo didn't have any stains where I threw coffee at him. Larry had told me this morning that he was trying to track down America Forever's identity, as I'd asked him to, but he hadn't succeeded yet. I edged backward, ready to run.

"So you're still at it," he snarled, eyes red and feverish like he hadn't slept much last night either. "Conspiring to cover up the murder of a great American heroine."

I stared at his hefty frame. There was something about it I couldn't quite put my finger on. Then it hit me. "Oh my God."

He kept talking, spittle flying, oblivious to the revelation I'd just had. "Acting like you're God's gift to Olivia. Well, I knew her for two years, and—"

"It was you, wasn't it?"

He looked confused. "What's eating you, bitch?"

I looked around to make sure I was safe. The sidewalk was full of people heading to lunch.

I turned back to America Forever. "That was you last night. You shot at me!"

CHAPTER THIRTY-TWO

AMERICA FOREVER'S LEFT eye twitched. "What are you talking about?" He took a step back and his right arm flew upward, so suddenly it banged into a No Parking sign. "Fuck!" he said, bringing his arm up and checking it. The sign must have had a sharp edge, because he was bleeding from a cut on his wrist.

His backward retreat, combined with the nervous twitch and how upset he was about a minor cut, emboldened me. *This guy's a bully and a clown, but not someone to actually be afraid of.* I said, "You're a fucking nut, aren't you?"

Sweat broke out on his wide, large-pored face. "Nobody shot at you. I read in the *Clarion*. They shot in the air."

"Admit it. You're the shooter!"

He bent his knees and put his weight on one foot, getting set to run away. If he did, then how would I identify him to the cops? I quickly said, "I took your picture."

His mouth opened, bewildered. "When you were chasing us from Peet's. I turned around and got a full-on picture of your face." That was bullshit, but he didn't know it. His eyes widened. "I can show it to the cops. They'll arrest you. They'll find more evidence and throw you in prison."

He gulped and said urgently, "Whoever did that last night, they weren't gonna hurt you. They just wanted you to stop this fake investigation. If you really care about Olivia, Reynolds was her killer!"

I said, "How do I know you won't aim at me next time instead of the sky?"

"I won't!"

I smiled grimly, as we both realized he'd just admitted it was him.

"Show me your ID," I said.

"No fucking way!"

He turned, once again ready to run. I grabbed him by the arm—shit, his blood was getting on my shirt—and said, as sympathetically as I could, "I get that you care about Livvy just like I do, and that's why you did it. I don't want to call the cops on you. Show me your ID and I won't have to."

He frowned. "What do you mean?"

"I'll have protection. I'll write down your name and the fact it was you last night and put it in my desk, and if I ever get shot for real, the cops will know it was you."

He narrowed his eyes at me. "Why should I trust you?"

"'Cause if you don't, I show them that picture."

We stared each other down for a long moment, and I thought he would run after all. I'd have to chase him screaming and hope somebody called the cops.

Finally, shaking his head like he wasn't sure he was doing the right thing, he reached into his pocket for his wallet. He fumbled for his driver's license and handed it to me.

Robert Heath, I read. *1437 Holmes Avenue #206, Revere, Massachusetts.*

Got him!

I handed the license back. "Okay, Mr. Heath. Stay away from me or I call the cops immediately."

"I was just shooting in the fucking air," he growled petulantly.

"Starting right now. Go."

"Fine, I'm sick of your face too."

America Forever—Robert Heath—took off down the street. I smiled, satisfied—

Wait a minute. "Come back here!" I yelled, running after him.

He turned. "What do you want?"

"You said you knew her for two years. From where?"

"I don't have to tell you."

"You do if you don't want to go to prison."

He shook his head, frustrated. "Fine. Different patriotic websites."

I translated "patriotic" to mean "right-wing extremist." "Which ones?"

"I don't remember. All of 'em."

I pointed at his T-shirt. "I'm guessing one of them is called America Forever." I had just remembered that "America forever" was part of a phrase Livvy had used in her first YouTube video: "protect America forever."

Heath glowered at me and said, "Yeah, so fucking what?" Then he walked away.

I'd check the America Forever website as soon as I got a chance. Maybe it would give me new insight into Livvy and the question that still dogged me: how sweet Livvy turned so extreme.

Right now, I needed to call the cops. That had been my plan all along: get as much information from America Forever as possible, then call Detective O'Keefe on him.

I dialed O'Keefe's number and waited for her to pick up. But as the phone rang, I started to wonder if I was doing the right thing.

Robert Heath had known Livvy for two years, at least online. She might have shared things with him that she didn't share with IRL friends like me. Not only that, what if none of my main suspects was the killer, and her online life held the key to the crime? Livvy's two big mysteries, her murder and her extremism, might be somehow connected.

It all added up to: I should let Heath stay free so I could use him as a confidential source. If he refused to talk to me, I'd turn him in to the cops then.

Over the phone, I heard O'Keefe say, "Yeah, what?"

I clicked off without answering.

CHAPTER THIRTY-THREE

I WALKED A block and stepped into a Trader Joe's, where I bought sugar snap peas and apples. Those are my favorite foods when I'm trying to fight off chocolate cravings. I still hadn't heard from Jonah. He was the one who had walked out of our argument. Didn't that mean he should text first, not me?

On the other hand, I was pretty sure I'd been the one who was most in the wrong. Once again I felt my lack of sleep. I decided I'd apologize later, when I hopefully felt less stressed. I didn't trust myself to say the right things now.

As I bit into a tart McIntosh apple, I headed toward the same Peet's where I'd been yesterday morning. I decided I should leave Heath and America Forever aside for now and get back to my current assignment: Sarah Fain. I gathered up my courage and called Professor Reynolds from the Peet's parking lot.

Reynolds answered on the first ring. "Yeah," he snapped.

I ignored his apparent anger. "Hi, this is Petra. How are you doing?"

"You misquoted me in your podcast."

"I did? How?" I asked, as innocently as I could.

"I told you, Olivia stated clearly that Viktor never abused her. You left that out. It's kind of key."

"I said in the podcast that you *believed* Viktor didn't do it. Everything else is just hearsay—you saying what you remember her saying."

"This is bullshit."

"Look, I'll get more specific about your comments in a future episode. I have a boss to deal with. He edited me."

"So it's not your fault. Poor little you."

"Do you have any idea, the risks I'm taking with this story? I got shot at yesterday."

"Why are you calling me?"

Reynolds' voice was still rough, but I sensed him softening a little. "What do you know about Sarah Fain?"

He hesitated. "What do you mean?"

"I've been told that Sarah threatened Livvy, shortly before the murder. Did she ever say anything to you about that?"

"No. Where did you hear this?"

"Detective O'Keefe." Really the answer was Brandon, but I thought Reynolds would be more impressed this way. And I was afraid that now might be my only shot to get him talking.

A derisive snort came over the phone. "So that's bullshit for sure. Detective O'Keefe never tells anyone anything."

Busted. "Look, I can't reveal my actual sources."

"Right, 'cause you're so ethical all of a sudden."

I didn't have a good comeback for that, so I moved on. "Did Livvy tell you she was dropping another video about Sarah?"

"Can I ask you something?"

"Sure."

"Why did you get into journalism?"

"That's kind of a big question."

"No, it's simple. Did you become a reporter because you like finding out the truth about things?"

I decided to try flattering him. "That's a very good way of putting it."

"Then what the hell happened to you?"

I shook my head, frustrated, though of course he couldn't see that over the phone. "William, I'm aware I've been pushing the boundaries in this investigation. But I'm trying to prove you're innocent. And catch the person who killed a girl you loved. I loved her too. Not a day has gone by for two and a half years when I haven't thought about her."

Reynolds was silent for a moment.

"So what can you tell me about Sarah?" I continued.

He still didn't answer. "Hello? William?"

Shit, he hung up.

Now what? Brandon and Eric would hang up on me too. Jeez, I had to quit burning through all my sources.

I considered going into Peet's, but decided to keep walking until I came up with a plan. I'd read somewhere once that ninety percent of people's good ideas come when they're walking, and that was definitely true of me. As I headed down the sidewalk, I glanced down at the spot of blood from Heath on my sleeve. It wasn't too bad; I'd deal with it when I got home.

Seeing the blood made me think about the blood in the crime scene photo. If Sarah killed Livvy, it went like this: In January, Livvy named and slut-shamed Sarah, telling the world about her drug history and the *"Fuck 'em"* and *"Fuck me"* tattoos on her butt. In April, according to Brandon, Livvy was planning to depict Sarah as an attention-seeking wacko who got off on accusing guys and had been doing it since high school. Sarah found out and stormed into Livvy's room late at night, just when she was recording that video. Sarah yelled at Livvy for ruining her life all over again, but Livvy refused to back down. Sarah lost her shit, grabbed the nearest weapon . . .

Maybe it wasn't so unrealistic after all. I should get hold of the other rowers on Sarah's crew team and ask if she acted erratic sometimes, or was obsessed with Livvy. Maybe one of them would know the same dirt about Sarah's past that Livvy knew—

A car horn screamed at me. I was so preoccupied, I had walked right into the middle of the street. As I backpedaled to the sidewalk, the car drove past me. It had a red bumper sticker supporting the Harvard football team, *"Go Crimson."*

Suddenly it hit me: What about Danny Madsen, the Harvard football player Sarah accused of rape? He must know all kinds of good dirt about her. After almost three years of legal battles, no doubt he hated Sarah. He'd be happy to dish on her.

While I was at it, I could question Danny about himself. After all, he'd been my favorite suspect at first, two and a half years ago when the murder occurred.

But how would I get hold of Danny? Harvard had that ironclad rule against their athletes talking to the media.

I checked the Crimson fansites on my phone and discovered there was another practice this afternoon at three. So I hurried to the T and made it to the Harvard athletic complex forty minutes ahead of time. Hopefully I'd catch Danny on his way to the locker room. Campus security might be on the lookout for me, so I got an old baseball cap out of my purse, where I kept it in case of rain. It was a crusty old Bozeman Bucks cap with a purple deer on the front. I pulled it down low on my forehead.

Fifteen or twenty people were already outside the gym, waiting for the players to arrive. But these weren't teenage groupies, they were reporters and cameramen. I realized they were all here because of my story outing Brandon. It was what I had wanted, to rev up the investigation, but now it was also making me feel guilty as hell. It was so unfair, so retro, that NFL teams might not draft Brandon, at least in the early rounds, just because he was gay. I hoped they would, and it would turn out that my outing him hadn't wrecked his career after all.

Assuming he was innocent, of course.

I recognized three or four reporters from TV. Then I saw Chip Martin, the blandly handsome anchorman who had interviewed me last night—*God, was it just last night?* Chip saw me too and immediately walked up, signaling his cameraman to come along. "Hey, Petra," he said pleasantly. "Fancy seeing you here. Nice hat."

"Thanks for the segment last night. I thought it came off great."

He nodded. "So what are you up to? Waiting for Brandon, like us?"

"Yup." I wasn't about to reveal my real reason for being here. No need to get rival reporters racing down the same trail I was on.

"I imagine Brandon's not too happy with you, is he?"

"I can't really speak for him," I told Chip through tightened lips. More reporters were coming our way: the TV guys I recognized and other, scruffier people who I tagged as print and online journalists. They must have recognized me.

"How did you feel about outing him?" Chip asked.

That's when I saw his cameraman was shooting me. I probably looked horrible, after barely sleeping for two nights. To say nothing of my Bozeman Bucks cap and the spot of blood on my sleeve.

"This isn't about me feeling whatever," I said. "It's about discovering the truth at last on Olivia Anderson's murder, and bringing closure to her family."

Two other TV cameras were on me now, and no doubt several phone cameras as well. The reporters kept moving closer, like zombies from *The Walking Dead*. A young woman with short blue hair and tattoos of blue birds on her arms asked me, "Are you concerned that by outing Brandon Allen, you may have damaged his standing in the upcoming draft?"

I reminded myself to square my shoulders and stand tall. "Again, this is about Olivia. I'll follow the evidence wherever it leads."

"So you believe Brandon may have committed murder," Chip said.

"Yes. I also believe Viktor Anderson may have done it. And there are other suspects as well."

"You mean William Reynolds?"

"Stay tuned for our next podcast," I said.

A reporter in a faded denim jacket, with a wispy beard and hawk-like nose—probably a website reporter, based on the jacket and beard—said, "What are you gonna ask Brandon about? I can't imagine he'd ever talk to you again."

"We'll see," I said tightly.

The reporter came closer, breathing in my face, his coal black eyes boring into mine. "You wrecked this kid's life to make your podcast more exciting."

The hairs on the back of my neck rose. All of these cameras were shooting me. I was being attacked in front of the whole world. But what had any of these sanctimonious reporters ever done to find out what really happened to Livvy? *Nothing.*

I said, "All I care about is solving this horrific murder. I'm sorry if it's hard for Brandon, but hey, it's the twenty-first century. Nobody can keep secrets anymore, especially if you're a celebrity."

As soon as I said it, I knew I probably sounded insensitive. *I should've kept my mouth shut.* The young woman with the bird tattoos frowned at me. So did Chip, usually so amiable and nonjudgmental.

I needed to get out of here before I said anything else stupid. "If you'll excuse me, I have to make a phone call."

As I walked away, the bird-tattoo woman followed me. "Your stories seem a little thinly sourced. Would you agree?"

"I can't reveal all my sources," I said, realizing this would be a useful phrase in the coming days, and also realizing I sounded like Natalie.

"Is that because you don't have any? Look, I get it. I'm trying to make it in this business too."

Which means you'd jump at the chance to write an exposé of me.

"Sorry, I need to make my call." I dialed numbers at random as I headed down the sidewalk. The reporter finally gave up, and as I turned the corner I was finally alone.

Walking past coffee shops and pizzerias full of Harvard students, it hit me that being semi-famous had drawbacks. My every move from now on would be publicly dissected.

As I approached yet another student pizza joint, I thought how frustrating it was that Danny Madsen must be so close to here, on his way to practice or maybe finishing lunch, but I had no way of connecting with him.

I looked through the window of the pizza joint and did a double-take. A shiver ran down my spine. Maybe Livvy's spirit had guided me here. Or else, to quote one of Tata's favorite sayings: *"It's better to be lucky than smart."* Because that big guy with big ears and wide-set eyes, sitting by the window with two other guys who also looked like football players . . . *That's Danny Madsen!*

I took a deep breath and smoothed my hair, then headed inside.

CHAPTER THIRTY-FOUR

As I walked up to Danny's table, he was laughing at a joke from one of his two buddies. I said, "You're Danny Madsen, aren't you?"

His eyes darkened and he put down his pizza slice. No doubt he got accosted all the time—sometimes by people who just wanted his autograph or to talk football, but other times by people yelling at him about his alleged rape.

"I'm Petra Kovach. From the *Boston Clarion*."

Danny broke into a welcoming smile. It put a big dimple in his chin. "Good to meet you," he said. "Olivia basically saved my life. I'm so glad you're reopening her case."

So he's not pissed off at me for outing his teammate. Interesting. "Thank you," I said. "Do you have a minute?"

He looked regretful, pinching his lips together. "Coach Jackson doesn't allow us to talk to the media."

"We can speak off the record," I said, telling myself that this time I would actually keep my promise. "I have a new lead on Olivia's murder and I think you might be able to help me."

Danny hesitated. "I wish I could, but Coach is hard-core. I'd get an automatic suspension." He stood up and said to his buddies, "Let's get to practice."

I was not about to let Danny get away. "Olivia had your back. Now you need to have *her* back. Help me find out who killed her."

"I'm sorry, Ms. Kovach." He started for the door with his friends. I followed after him. "I think she was killed because of you."

He turned and stared. "What is that supposed to mean?"

I stepped closer and whispered, quietly enough so no one else could hear, "I think Sarah Fain may have killed her."

Danny blinked, startled. I sensed the wheels in his brain spinning. Finally he turned to his friends. "Why don't you guys go on without me?"

"You sure?" said one of them, a heavy offensive-lineman type with a squashed nose that must have been broken at least once. "If Coach finds out—"

"Yeah, so don't tell him, okay?" Danny turned to me. "And let's go someplace private. There's a hallway downstairs, just past the restrooms."

"You got it," I said, acting calm even though my every nerve cell was firing with excitement. And fear—if he was a rapist and possibly a murderer, following him into a private downstairs hallway wasn't the smartest move.

But I went. Danny led me to the back of the pizzeria, where we descended some steps to the basement, then walked down a long cement hallway past the restrooms. We turned left into another hallway with a utility room and janitor's closet coming off it.

It was quiet down here and the walls were damp. The basement smelled of bleach and something else, some combination of urine and mold. I watched Danny's broad back as he walked in front of me and wondered if he did rape Sarah Fain.

The story Sarah had told about that night was a modern-day classic. She went to a frat party that attracted male athletes and freshman and sophomore girls, including several of her crew team-mates. She and her friends got split up. She wasn't drinking alcohol anymore, so she stuck to ginger ale. But she woke up the next morning in an upstairs bedroom that smelled like dirty socks, next to Danny Madsen. She had no idea how she got there. Her head was fuzzy like maybe she'd been drugged and her private parts were raw and aching. Danny woke up at the same time she did. He leered at her and said, "Wanna go for round three?"

She bolted out of there and spent two months tormented by anger and shame, not wanting to make a thing out of this. She called Danny to ask what happened that night, but he wouldn't give her a straight answer. She went to see a therapist, then a rape counselor. Finally she went to the campus police and filed a complaint.

Danny's story was very different. He said he passed out in the bedroom, alone, and when he woke up the next morning Sarah was all over him, fondling him. Hungover and confused, he sat up and pushed her away. She said, "You still too drunk to get it up, or are you just a fag?" Appalled, he staggered out to the bathroom, then left the frat.

For the next two months Sarah called him and stalked him, still wanting to go out. Finally, he yelled at her and threatened to call the cops. She retaliated by going to the cops herself and making wild accusations.

So whose story was the truth? It hit me that if this guy was a rapist, he could attack me right now in this moldy basement and nobody would hear it.

We had reached the end of the hall. He turned around, and I involuntarily stepped back. Luckily he didn't seem to notice. "Okay, we should be safe here," he said. "So why do you think it was Sarah? I gotta tell you, I always thought it could be. But I never told the cops, 'cause who would believe me? Everybody would've said I was just trying to get back at her."

"What made you suspect her?"

"'Cause she's freaking insane! Look what she did to me, lying like that. I'm not sure if she even knows she's lying. Maybe she's a sociopath. Or maybe she was high that night and dreamed all that shit up. She says she's been clean and sober since high school, but I don't buy it for a second."

"Did she ever physically attack you?"

"You mean, besides grabbing my dick?"

"Besides that."

"No, but I wouldn't put it past her. And you know, she threatened Olivia."

So Danny was confirming this part of Brandon's story! "Threatened her how?"

"After 'Who Raped Who?' dropped, Sarah went to Olivia's room one night and said all kinds of disgusting stuff, like, 'You woman-hating bitch, maybe I should drug you and rape you and see how *you* like it.'"

Holy crap, maybe Sarah did kill her! Ignoring the slimy-looking bug crawling up the wall behind Danny's head, I asked, "How do you know about this?"

"Olivia told me." He shifted his weight to the other foot. "See, after Sarah made that accusation against me, Olivia thought I wasn't getting a fair shake. She wanted to hear my side. She was Brandon's girlfriend, so I said, 'Okay, I'll talk to you.' After the video came out, I thanked her, and she told me about the threats. Then the week before she died, she said she was doing a new video about Sarah." *So Brandon was right about this too.* "She was gonna call it, 'The Fuck 'Em, Fuck Me Girl.'"

"What was Olivia planning to say?"

"She was gonna talk about Sarah's threats, and also she'd found out some new really bad stuff about Sarah. She wouldn't tell me what it was, but she said I would love it."

Yet another match with Brandon's story. "Did Olivia tell anyone else about this bad stuff?"

"She told Sarah, three days before she was killed. She wanted to let Sarah respond to the accusations."

"How did Sarah react?"

"Same kind of threats as before, except worse."

How could Detective O'Keefe not have investigated this?

"Ms. Kovach—"

"Call me Petra."

Danny's face was open and earnest. "If you knew Olivia, you wouldn't be surprised she called Sarah for her side of the story. Everybody thinks of Olivia like this hard-ass, take-no-prisoners kind of person. But the thing is, she did a lot of research and thought hard about stuff. Even though she was conservative, she wasn't against the Me Too movement. She just didn't want to see innocent people get hurt. In your podcast, I wish you could say what a kind person she was. She *listened* to me, at a time nobody else did, except my family and closest friends." Tears glistened at the edges of his eyes. "I'm really glad you're taking this on. I never believed William Reynolds killed her. He just seemed like a typical professor, not some crazy guy who would lose his shit like that. That's more Sarah's style." He wiped away his tears. "I hope to hell you can finally find out the truth."

Then he gave me a hug. I froze, a residual of wondering if this guy was a rapist, or maybe I was trying to keep a reportorial distance. But then I hugged him back.

He was right about Livvy. The girl I'd known was a kind, warm person who cared about journalism and wanted to do it right. It was good to hear that some of her idealism survived even after she became a radical alt-righter.

I would approach my podcast just like Livvy approached her final story.

"I should go to practice," Danny said.

Even though my mind was still buzzing with suspicion of Sarah, I remembered the other question I'd come here with. "By the way," I said, "are you and Brandon friends these days?"

Danny looked puzzled. "Me and Brandon? Yeah, we're tight. Why?"

"'Cause when I saw you guys at practice the other day, it seemed like there was some kind of tension between you."

"Not that I know of."

I wondered why he was lying.

*   *   *

Danny didn't want to risk any coaches seeing us together, so he left the pizzeria first. A minute later I left too, striding down the sidewalk with a spring in my step. Wouldn't it be hilarious if, after trying so hard not to get stuck with investigating Sarah Fain, it turned out she was the killer? I pictured myself actually succeeding in my mission: solving the crime, bringing justice to Livvy's family—

Suddenly my phone buzzed and pinged frantically with recent texts and messages. It must not have been working down in the basement. My first thought was relief that Jonah had tried to reach me. I grabbed my phone out of my purse. But all the texts and messages were from Dave. CALL IMMEDIATELY, one text read. Another said simply, ASAP!!

I called and he picked up right away. "Petch, we needed a quote from you, and you weren't around, so we came up with one we figured you'd be cool with. We were in a hurry."

"Why, what's going on?"

"I gotta run, Abernathy's calling. Check the website and you'll see."

I jumped onto the *Clarion's* website and found a huge headline: "*Reporter for* Clarion *Leads Police to Shooter.*" The byline belonged to Natalie Blair.

Before I even read the story, I felt sick.

"*The Cambridge Police Department today arrested a suspect in last night's shooting incident near the Charles River that briefly terrorized the city. Robert Heath of Revere was put into custody and charged with the crime.*

"*In an unusual series of events, this reporter led the police to the shooter.*"

This reporter—that meant Natalie. How the hell had she caught Robert Heath?

My fist tightened so hard around my phone it's a wonder it didn't break. *I'm such an idiot. Why didn't I tell the cops myself about Heath, right away? What the fuck was I thinking?*

I had let Natalie beat me again.

CHAPTER THIRTY-FIVE

STANDING ON THE sidewalk outside the pizza joint, I made myself read on. *"Yesterday evening, as part of our podcast on Olivia Anderson's murder, I asked our investigative staff—"*

Investigative staff? Was Larry working for her now?

"—to identify the unknown man who harassed our reporter Petra Kovach at a Boston coffee shop, while she was interviewing a murder suspect. This man anonymously downloaded a video of his harassment. We were able to determine that the video came from the YouTube account of Robert Heath, a thirty-eight-year-old man from Revere."

This is bullshit, I thought. *I'm the one who asked Larry to identify America Forever.* I must have looked furious, because a couple of teenage boys coming out of the pizza joint circled widely around me to avoid me.

But then I realized what must have happened. I hadn't texted Larry 'til I was done with my interviews. In the meantime, Natalie must have texted him. She beat me by maybe thirty minutes.

Today, while I was busy chasing down Danny, Larry must have passed the information along to Natalie. Maybe he was too much of a stoner to get the office politics of this. And now the bitch was taking all the credit.

"Mr. Heath's YouTube account featured several videos of himself with firearms, including one of him shooting into the air. When this reporter noted that, along with the fact he matched the physical description of last night's shooter, I brought this information to the attention of the police. They went to see Robert Heath at his residence, and he immediately confessed.

"When informed of the arrest, Kovach said, 'I'm grateful this dangerous man was taken off the streets thanks to the quick action of my colleagues here at the newspaper, as well as the Cambridge Police Department.'"

I couldn't stand it. Now I was quoted as *thanking* Natalie for protecting my life?

Though I had to admit, thinking about it, she probably hadn't done anything I wouldn't have.

Heading down the street, a wave of exhaustion swept over me. I'd been going nonstop ever since last week. No wonder my judgment wasn't perfect now. I wished I could call Jonah and pour my heart out to him. He'd know just what to say.

I hit the T station and headed back to the newspaper. As I held onto a pole in the crowded train car, Mama called. She had just read online about Heath getting arrested. "Thank God your friend Natalie caught that man!" Mama said. "You should buy her some flowers."

I bit my lip. "Good idea, Mama. I'll do that."

Then Jonah texted, GLAD THEY CAUGHT THE GUY. A little cold, I thought, but at least we were communicating again.

I debated how to respond, and finally texted, THANKS! SEE YOU TONIGHT!

He texted back, YUP.

Not much of a text.

The T ground to a halt and a man said over the loudspeaker, "There will be a short delay due to track maintenance." The "short delay" turned out to be thirty minutes, which I spent checking the internet. Viktor Anderson had been released from the jail he was taken to after brawling with Eric. But he wasn't going back to his job, because the Swedish government had relieved him of his duties. Detective O'Keefe was quoted as saying that given the seriousness of the assault charges, and the new developments in the murder case, she had requested that he not leave the jurisdiction and that the Swedish government not allow him to return to their country.

Does O'Keefe really suspect Viktor of the murder now? No, she was probably just paying lip service to reopening the case. But regardless, Sweden acceded to her request. Viktor would remain here for the foreseeable future, facing criminal charges.

Meanwhile, social media crackled with discussions of whether Brandon Allen was gay, along with discussions about whether they should even be discussing it. The sports pundits debated how low Brandon would fall in the coming draft, and would he even get picked at all? Two guys came out of the woodwork claiming they'd had Grindr dates with Brandon. They didn't seem to have any proof, except one of them claimed to know a distinguishing characteristic on Brandon's penis. It always amazed me, how often people in these types of situations talked about the "distinguishing characteristics" on some guy's penis. In my limited experience, most penises were pretty much the same, except for size, of course.

I thought about the three men whose lives I'd forever altered this week: Brandon, Viktor, and Eric. I wondered, did Natalie ever have qualms about ruining the lives of people who turned out to be innocent?

Probably not. I might be a better reporter if I got less emotional about this stuff. I told myself that all I'd done was speak the truth. And where I hadn't given the full, complete truth, I would rectify that in the next episodes.

I gave my head a shake. I needed to center myself.

Or maybe forget myself. On my phone, I called up my photo of Livvy at fourteen, wading out into the ocean. *So young.* I would do everything I could to find her killer. That would make it all worthwhile. I wouldn't let anything get in the way of that.

I finally made it back to the *Clarion* at five fifteen. I tossed my blood-spotted shirt in my bottom desk drawer; luckily I had a clean shirt stashed there. Then I headed straight for Dave's office. Natalie was already there—of course—in the good chair—of course.

"Hey, Petch," Dave said. "You feeling good we caught the shooter?"

"Sure am," I said with a fake smile.

"That was a nifty piece of reporting by Natalie here."

"Thank you," Natalie said.

I felt compelled to say, "Yeah, I texted Larry too last night. Asking him to do that research."

"Well, good job," Dave said. Then he tapped the desk. "So I was just about to tell Nat: we've got three more TV interviews tonight."

"Sweet!" Natalie said.

"That's awesome!" I said, and I knew it was, even though what I really wanted to do tonight was pursue my Sarah Fain lead. I needed to keep my focus on investigating, not the star-making machinery of it all.

Dave studied me. "Now, if you want," he said, "since you did the last round of interviews and you must be exhausted from how hard you've been working, we can have Natalie handle this round. That's actually how I booked them."

I sat bolt upright in the wooden folding chair, alarmed. The chair groaned and squealed like it was about to break into pieces and dump me on the floor. "No, I can do the interviews." When Dave looked skeptical and pursed his lips like he was about to say no, I forced myself to add, "We'll do them together. It'll be fun."

"Whatever you guys want is good with me," Natalie said, the perfect politician.

Dave eyed me. "You sure you're up for it?" I tried to answer, but he kept going. "You were a little low-energy in the podcast last night, and I saw your interview outside the gym today, when they asked you about Brandon. You sounded . . . well, honestly, you seemed a little off, like you were dismissing his pain. It wasn't a good look. They're killing us on Twitter."

I reddened. "Lesson learned. They caught me by surprise, but now I'm good. Another espresso and I'm ready to roll," I added, and instantly regretted it. I sounded frivolous.

Dave folded his arms. "We can't afford to screw up the PR on this—"

"I understand—"

"Abernathy is concerned that we don't come across as homophobic with Brandon. He's a star, and a lot of people feel bad for him. After all, his girlfriend was killed."

"I get it. I'll make sure we treat him with respect."

At last Dave nodded his acceptance, and that's how I ended up spending the next several hours in way-too-close quarters with Natalie. The company car was once again driven by Christopher, who rapidly developed a crush on her, of course. We went to the three TV stations where we had interviews, and I watched with envy as Natalie took to TV like a copperhead snake takes to water. The makeup artists all fawned over her flawless skin and thick blonde hair.

I felt like I did a good job. No gaffes. Whenever an anchorperson asked me anything remotely controversial, I stuck to my "We're searching for the truth" and "We want to get justice for the victim and closure for the family" mantras.

But maybe I was too uptight. As the interviews proceeded, all three interviewers gravitated toward Natalie, directing most of their questions her way. She seemed so comfortable in her skin, like she'd been born into this job. Which was true. Her father, as editor-in-chief at *Travel + Leisure*, must have given her all kinds of help over the years. No wonder she understood this game so instinctively.

If only my Tata were still alive to guide me.

The last interview was the biggest: a CNN remote interview, not with Joel Caldwell but another anchorman who was just as famous. My first national TV appearance! My mind flashed to fourteen-year-old Livvy saying to me, "I can totally see you on CNN!"

But as I sat on the couch next to Natalie, listening to her sound incredibly smart and charming, I felt like I was shrinking into myself. I had done so much better in yesterday's interviews.

I tried to be less hard on myself. Here I was on freaking CNN, being watched by millions, when only last week I'd come this close to getting tossed in the dumpster.

When we got back to the *Clarion* a little after nine and headed to the break room for coffee, Dave was there grabbing a stale donut. Waving it at us, he said, "I just watched the clips. You guys were great!"

Not really, I thought, but I said, "Thanks, Dave," at the same time Natalie did.

"What's your plan for the next couple days?" he asked Natalie.

"I should be able to get more evidence against both Brandon and Viktor."

"Nice," Dave said.

I cut in. "With Viktor, we need to tell the whole story about what Reynolds said. How he's positive Viktor didn't sexually abuse Livvy."

Dave gave me a frown.

"We said we'd do that in the next episode," I continued stubbornly.

"I don't recall that." He rubbed his chin thoughtfully, and I sensed he was telling the truth. Maybe he had willed himself to forget our agreement.

"It wouldn't be fair to Viktor to keep withholding the other side of the story," I said.

"Well, we'll think about it," Dave said. "So how's it going with Sarah Fain?"

I decided there was no point in pushing the Viktor issue right now. I wanted something cool to talk to Dave about. So I stood up straighter and dropped my bomb. "I've got excellent news."

Dave's eyebrows went up. "Really."

"I located a second witness who completely confirms Brandon's story. Sarah Fain found out Olivia was putting out another video trashing her. So she confronted Olivia and said, 'You woman-hating bitch, maybe I should drug you and rape you and see how you like it.'"

Dave whistled. "I love it. Who's your witness?"

"Danny Madsen," I said proudly. "He's not supposed to talk to the media, but I got him."

Dave frowned and pulled at his earlobe. Out of the corner of my eye I saw Natalie smirking. Instantly I went on alert.

"The thing is," Dave said, "of course Danny's gonna trash Sarah Fain—she accused him of rape. He's not exactly a reliable witness—"

"I know that," I interrupted. "I'm getting backup witnesses."

"If we put Danny on the podcast attacking Sarah, nobody would take his opinion seriously. A lot of people would be offended we were giving a platform to an accused rapist."

"I wasn't gonna put him on the podcast. The interview was off the record."

Dave's frown deepened. "So it's an interview with a heavily biased party that's not even on the record?"

My face grew warm. I sensed Natalie to my left swelling up with enjoyment. Even though it was over a week since Dave fired me, it was still nerve-wracking being around him. "Like I said, I'm getting another witness."

"Who?"

"At least one of Olivia's freshman friends," I said. "Maybe more."

"I'm just concerned about spending too much time on a dead end. I mean, I hope I'm not being sexist here, but it seems highly unlikely a young woman would commit this kind of crime."

If Dave had a beef with Sarah as a suspect, why hadn't he said so in the first place? "I think Sarah's a very viable suspect," I protested. "She's highly unstable with a history of drug abuse, and she's got shoulder muscles bigger than yours." *Oh shit, did that sound like I was insulting Dave?*

He sighed. "All right, give it a day or so and see what you get. If you come up dry, maybe help Natalie with her stuff."

I nodded, too outraged to speak.

He rubbed his hands together. "Okay, ladies. Go out there and make another killer episode!"

"You got it, boss," Natalie said, standing up.

"We're on it," I said.

I went back to my office, where I unwrapped a Kit Kat I'd stashed away and wondered, *why does Natalie get my goat so much?* There was nothing so unusual about reporters helping each other on their stories.

I didn't see myself as a jealous person. It wasn't like I had a sibling who got all of our parents' love and made me prone to envy for the rest of my life. But somehow, all of my fears and self-doubt about my troubled career, all my anxiety that I should have picked something *siguran* like being a teacher, had boiled down to: *I gotta beat Natalie, and make Dave love me so much he'll never let me go.*

I wondered, *is that it?* My Tata died and abandoned me, and now I was afraid Dave would abandon me too?

I finished my Kit Kat. *Screw the psychodrama,* I thought. *Just do a great job on this podcast. Find out the truth about Livvy's murder and you'll be such a star, you'll never get fired again.*

Livvy, if she can see me now, would get a huge kick out of that.

CHAPTER THIRTY-SIX

But before I did anything else, I needed to gather my courage and reach out to Jonah already. Sitting at my desk, I texted, When are you getting home? Dinner together?

He texted back, Working late on the model.

That would be the machine-learning model he and his colleagues were working on. They were supposed to unveil it to a major potential investor this weekend. So it made sense that Jonah needed to work late.

Or maybe he just needed a little time away from me.

I texted, I'm sorry if I was a jerk this morning. I couldn't remember anymore who had been worse, him or me. But I had definitely been a jerk in the days leading up to this morning, keeping secrets. Also, I suspected the real reason I'd gotten so pissed at Jonah was because he voiced the same doubts about outing Brandon that I was feeling.

Jonah texted back, Hope you're having a good day.

Well, at least it was friendly. I typed, You too, and then impulsively added, Love you! I hit send.

Then I waited. My pulse pounded in my throat. Maybe I shouldn't have said *Love you!* It was too soon. But finally his text came back: Love you too.

That made me feel better . . . though it had taken way too long for that text to arrive. I couldn't do anything more to fix me and Jonah for now, so I threw myself into my work. I started searching for contact info for Sarah's crew teammates and ex-teammates.

But then I stopped. With everything else that was going on, I hadn't had time yet to check out the America Forever website. I should do it now. If Livvy's posts there were half as intriguing as her Reddit posts, I'd have something big. So far as I knew, nobody else had ever uncovered Livvy's connection to that corner of the internet.

AmericaForever.com and AmericaForever.net didn't exist; their home pages had domain messages from Go Daddy. But when I tried America-Forever.com, I hit pay dirt. The site featured a huge American flag with the words, "Patriots unite to keep our country free forever!" Underneath it were articles about supporting the "Greco-Roman tradition," defunding public universities, and stopping "trans Nazis." To the left was a menu where I clicked on *"Groups"* and found all kinds of subgroups devoted to everything from smoked meats to Bitcoin to politics.

I clicked on the biggest politics subgroup, *"Live Free,"* which claimed to have eighty thousand members. They had an active discussion board with over a hundred messages per day. I searched for posts from *"Olly Olly Oxen Free"* but found nothing. Then I tried *"Olive Oil," "Olivia," "OliviaA," "Livvy," "OAnderson . . ."* Still nothing.

Heath had claimed he knew Livvy for two years before she died. So I went back and read posts from that time period, searching for ones that sounded like her. This was my first time ever on a website like this, but I wasn't too overwhelmed by the hatred I found. During the past week I'd read hundreds of anti-woman, anti-immigrant, just plain anti-human messages in my email and social media. That

somewhat prepared me for the message board's poorly drawn car-
toons of brown-skinned immigrants getting shot and dumped in
ditches.

What did surprise me was the amount of serious-sounding discussion I found: people posting about *"ethnostates"* and *"civic na-
tionalism"* in ways that made it clear they thought deeply about
these subjects, even if they were deeply deluded.

I also found a lot of just plain friendly chatting: people sharing
their feelings about the world, and how stressful it could be when
families and friends violently disagreed with them. For instance, one
kid who called herself *"Orphan Girl"* posted how nervous she was
about going to college next year. Everyone was so liberal at college,
and how would she ever fit in? The other chatters were encouraging,
telling her to just be herself and things would work out. She wrote
back, *"Thank you so much for your kind words! Basically I want to do
good in the world, and also be famous—"*

Wait—Livvy had said these exact same words at boot camp!
This was her!

I typed in *"Orphan Girl"* and began reading her posts. I wondered
if they were another attempt by Livvy to create a false identity.

"This is my first post on this website," Orphan Girl wrote, *"but I've
been reading it for a month now. My mom was killed in a hit-and-run.
The police never found the guy, but a witness who was right there said
he looked Mexican."* Had Livvy ever told me that? If so, I'd forgotten;
maybe I thought "looking Mexican" wasn't much of a lead. *"Now
I'm reading on here about all these illegals who are really bad drivers
and don't have licenses, and they run away if there's an accident. And
they do all kinds of other terrible things too."* I remembered Livvy talking on her videos about immigrants "committing thousands of unsolved crimes," but I hadn't known she suspected her own mom was
killed by an immigrant. *"My stepdad says I shouldn't blame all*

immigrants just because of this one thing that happened. But if that piece of shit had stayed in Mexico, like he was fucking supposed to, my mom would still be alive."

This post brought two hundred thirty-four responses. One came from *"Rheath"*—Robert Heath, no doubt. He wrote about how immigrants made America "dirty." A lot of the other posters told Orphan Girl not to be ashamed of her feelings, no matter what liberals like her stepdad said. Some of them shared bad experiences they'd had, or claimed to have had, with "illegals."

The comments Livvy got were supportive—but they were also sick. I looked up from my laptop and thought: *This would explain it. The mystery of how Livvy got radicalized. This is the key I've been searching for!*

I played it through: Livvy blames her mom's death on an undocumented immigrant. Then she finds this website and reads all the anti-immigrant rants. She's full of pent-up rage at her mom's killer that she can't fully express to her stepfather, or me. She's afraid I'll get mad if she speaks honestly about her anti-immigrant feelings. So she ends up getting emotional support from these screwed-up, racist people.

I read more of Livvy's posts and became convinced this was her speaking her truth, not creating some other identity like she did on Reddit. I sensed her growing confidence in her budding alt-right beliefs, as they were validated by her new online community. Somebody posted BS statistics about immigrants and crime, and she responded, *"Yes! See, this is the kind of real talk you never find on LSM!"* That was the abbreviation they all used for "lamestream media."

How could somebody as smart as Livvy get fooled by this crap?

But she was in pain. Her birth father had walked out when she was three, and her mom died when she was fourteen. She loved her big brother, but he was off at Boston University, living his life. She was alone in the house with her stepfather, and who knows what that relationship was really like, and if he sexually abused her, but I was pretty sure he worked all the time and traveled a lot.

So she was lonely and vulnerable—a ripe target for recruitment. *Poor Livvy.* I felt terrible she'd landed on this site full of twisted minds. Most of the people who wrote back to her were men: *"Darth Hayek," "felix fuckburger," "Providence . . ."*

Actually, Providence was by far the most frequent responder to Orphan Girl. Often he replied right after Rheath. He used a lot of Heath's favorite phrases, like *"kick their fucking asses," "immies"* instead of *"immigrants,"* and *"p4k libs,"* whatever that meant. But unlike Heath, he sprinkled his comments liberally with encouraging words for Livvy. *"You'll love college! Best years of your life!"* he promised in one comment. And: *"That college you're going to won't know what hit it!"*

I read Providence's comments in chronological order and found they got more and more personal. He asked, *"What college are you going to? (You don't have to say* ☻ *),"* and Livvy responded, *"Well, I feel funny saying this, but Harvard."*

This brought on a cascade of congratulations but also people warning her how hard life would be for a conservative at Harvard, surrounded by "snowflakes." Providence was undaunted, though. He posted, *"Hey I live in Boston! There's lots of people like us here, you just have to find them. If you want some support we can get together IRL. You can DM me."*

Livvy posted back, *"Will do* ☻ *. Actually coming to Harvard next week for pre-orientation."*

Huh. So did Livvy ever meet up with Providence? I read her subsequent posts, which continued all the way up until her death. Most of them were about the liberal "hypocrites" she was meeting in college, who "care more about immies than average white Americans who love this country and have lived here all their lives." Considering how much Livvy loved publicity, it was interesting she never revealed her YouTubing on this site. Maybe she wanted to participate freely on a white nationalist board and say whatever she felt like without worrying about her image.

From Livvy's posts and Providence's responses, I got a growing sense they did meet up—and more than once. It was never explicitly stated; maybe she didn't want other guys thinking she'd hang out with them too. But Providence posted little inside jokes and dancing Pepe the Frog emojis, and she responded in kind.

Was Livvy juggling yet another secret life? Maybe even a third lover?

Then I read a comment from Providence dated a month before the murder. There was a chat thread about Antifa attacking alt-righters, and Providence wrote: *"That's why revolutionaries hate living on the first floor. Too easy for the bad guys to get at you, right OG?"* OG was his nickname for Livvy, short for Orphan Girl. She responded, *"You said it P!"*

How did Providence know she lived on the first floor? He must have gone to see her.

Who was Providence in real life? I googled "Providence alt right," then searched "Providence" on Reddit and Twitter, but came up empty.

I needed to find this guy. At the very least, he could help me understand how a smart, personable teenage girl with so much going for her got sucked into this alt-right pigsty.

And at the very most . . .

This asshole might have killed Livvy.

CHAPTER THIRTY-SEVEN

I GRABBED MY laptop and headed downstairs to see Larry. He was hunched over his own laptop. "Hey, Mouse," I said.

Larry jumped, startled. "Oh, hi." He lowered the lid on his computer. "You surprised me."

"What are you workin' on?"

"Just some stuff." He looked away guiltily. *Porn?* "What's up?"

"I think Olivia was seeing a guy she met on a white nationalist website."

His eyes returned to me, widening. "You're shitting me. Possible suspect?"

"I'm hoping. So I'd like you to work your magic and locate him for me."

"Sure. Send me the link and I'll get to it as soon as I can."

"It's really important. Could you do it now?" I held up my hand. "Oh, and don't tell Natalie. Let's just keep it between us."

"Funny you should say that."

"Why?"

"'Cause I'm in the middle of doing something for Natalie that *she* wanted done right now. And she asked me to keep it between me and her."

I stood there with my mouth open.

"Sorry," Larry said.

I tightened my lips. "No problem. Just get my thing done as fast as possible."

Then I walked out before I said anything I'd regret. Stepping into the stairwell, I slammed the door open so hard it dented the wall.

Stalking back to my desk, I noticed Natalie's cubicle was empty. It was ten o'clock. Had she gone home to bed, or was she out following some incredible lead?

I hoped not—which felt weird. Worse than that, it felt wrong. If I truly cared about Livvy, I should be rooting for Natalie's success. But I wasn't.

Well, but we all have bad thoughts. That's just being human. As long as I didn't do anything to impede Natalie's investigation, then my emotional blip wasn't hurting Livvy in any way.

Several cubicles away from mine, a new part-time intern named Rose sat at her laptop. Rose was a sophomore at Northeastern who came in three nights a week to help with the Calendar section. She had a weak chin but a shy, winning smile, which she shone on me now.

"Hi, how's it going?" she asked.

I wanted to confide in this girl. In *someone.* "What a day," I began. But then it hit me: *what if she turns around and tells Natalie everything I say? If I were trying to break into this business, I'd probably ally myself with Natalie.* So all I said was, "But it'll be over soon, thank God."

"It's so great what you're doing with this podcast," Rose said.

"Thanks." I sat down at my desk and sent the America-Forever link to Larry, along with a request that he ID Providence. As soon as I hit SEND, I feared he might betray me with Natalie too, telling her everything. It felt like he'd already gone over to her side. He had a crush on her, after all, or he'd been blown away by her reporting and narrating style, or both. I reminded myself there were no sides, we were all working toward justice for Livvy. But even so, I quickly hit UNSEND on the email to Larry. I would figure out some way to ID Providence myself.

On my laptop, I searched "Providence p4k libs," "Providence immies," and other combinations. I felt there was something about his posts I was missing. Some detail itching at my subconscious that might help me identify him. But I didn't come up with anything.

I checked the time: 10:10 already. How had that happened? I should try calling Livvy's old friends and dormmates, before it got too late. Then I'd get back to work on Providence—

My phone buzzed: Jonah. An electric jolt went from the phone right down my spine. I picked up. "Hey, babe."

"Hi, Petra," he said in a voice that seemed somewhere between neutral and friendly. In the background, people were shouting. "Let me get somewhere quieter."

"Where are you?"

"Still at work. Jesse and Wang Lei are playing Nerf basketball and trash talking."

"Who's winning?" I asked.

Jonah laughed. Hearing it made my heart ten pounds lighter. "The basketball or the trash talking?"

"Both."

"Too early to tell." There was a pause, then: "Listen, I think I'm gonna stay here and pull an all-nighter. Wang Lei found a couple bugs in the model, which we need to get fixed before end of day tomorrow."

Like before, it sounded like he was telling the truth. Their meeting with the potential investor was a big deal. But . . .

"Are you still mad at me?" I asked.

I couldn't hear shouting in the background anymore. Jonah said, "More than anything, I'm confused. Have you ever lied to me before? I mean, about anything big?"

My throat caught. Had I? Well, early in our relationship I'd gone to a party with another guy and hadn't told Jonah—but that was before we'd said we were exclusive, and anyway, I went home alone. "No. Never. I'm really sorry."

"And then this afternoon I saw that clip of you outside football practice. Where you acted like outing somebody was no big deal."

"I didn't mean it that way, Jonah. You know me."

"I still have trouble with you outing him in the first place. Would it have been so terrible to spend another few weeks or whatever to see if you could get at the truth without doing that?"

I took a deep breath, fighting back equally powerful urges to yell and cry. "Jonah, it's late and I'm tired, and I don't want to say something stupid I'd regret. Can we both just go home? I want to go to bed with you. We don't even have to talk."

Jonah didn't answer right away. I was pretty sure he'd say yes.

"I really need to work tonight," he said. "Let's talk tomorrow."

My heart froze. My mouth opened but no words came out. Finally I said, "Okay. Bye, peach blossom."

"Bye, sprite."

Well, at least I got a sprite out of him.

I heard Rose coughing in her cubicle, and felt funny that she might have heard my call with Jonah. If I really wanted my calls to Livvy's friends to be private, I should go outside. So I grabbed a few sugar snap peas and headed up Cubicle Row.

But as I walked past Rose, I noticed she was wiping her eyes. "Are you okay?" I asked.

She looked up, and her eyes were red. "I'm sorry," she said. "I'm fine."

"You sure?"

She hesitated. "I know you're super busy . . ."

"No, that's okay. What's wrong?"

She gulped, and then everything came out in a rush. "We're getting all these angry comments from people. I got the date on a concert wrong. I said it was tonight but it was really last night. So all these people are there now and they're super pissed off. The editors are gonna come in tomorrow and find out I fucked—I mean, screwed up. And this is only my second week on the job and what if . . . what if . . ."

I knew exactly what she was worried about. "Honey, nobody's gonna fire you."

She burst into tears. "Really?"

I came into her cubicle and leaned against the desk. "My first job in journalism, at the *Los Angeles Register*? I did the Calendar section too, and oh my God, I made so many mistakes. One time somebody sent in a listing for a tiddlywinks tournament, and I didn't realize it was a joke, so I put it in. My editors laughed so hard at me."

I laughed, and Rose managed to laugh too.

"Another time I wrote that Christian Bale was doing a book signing, and two hundred people showed up, but it was really Christian Dale, some Australian playwright nobody ever heard of."

Now Rose's tears were gone. "Are you serious?"

"Unfortunately." We both laughed again.

She looked up at me gratefully. "Thank you, Petra."

"No problem. I'll see you later."

I headed outside, feeling better now. Damn it, Jonah and I would work out. This time I remembered to check around me for crazies as I left the building. To be even safer, I stood right outside the front door where the security guard in the lobby could see me through the glass window.

Then I got to work, calling and texting. None of Livvy's old cohort had responded when I contacted them last night. But maybe tonight I'd have better luck. It was late, but hopefully not too late for college students.

On my second call I reached the current president of the Harvard Young Republicans, who had been described in several newspaper articles as one of Livvy's closest friends. But she refused to talk to me. "William Reynolds killed Olivia. Get over it," she said, and hung up.

What if Reynolds really is the killer after all? Wouldn't that be the shit.

Then I tried Livvy's old hallmate Alexis Campbell. From what I had gleaned on social media, Alexis was an anthropology major from New Zealand who, like Reynolds, disagreed with Livvy on all matters political but felt close to her personally.

Alexis answered on the second ring. I could hear a jazz vocalist singing in the background. Billie Holiday, somebody like that.

"Hi, this is Petra Kovach from the *Boston Clarion.* If you have a couple minutes, I'd love to talk with you about Olivia Anderson."

There was a pause on the other end, as Billie Holiday ended abruptly. "You're the one who started that podcast," Alexis said.

"Yes, that's me." Hopefully, this girl approved of the podcast. "We're trying to find out the truth about what happened to your friend."

"Her stepfather was really molesting her? I knew she had problems with him, but I never would've guessed anything like that."

"Her Reddit posts are pretty convincing."

"I just wonder if she made it up, for shock value. I loved Olivia, but she did like to screw with people."

The wind was blowing, and I turned to keep it at my back. "I'd like to talk with you about something else related to Olivia's murder."

"I'm kinda sick of this. I still think Professor Reynolds killed her, and your podcast is bringing up a lot of bad memories."

"Alexis, I'm sure it's difficult, but—"

Her voice turned petulant. "Also, I have a paper due tomorrow, and I just talked to the other woman from the *Clarion* for half an hour."

The other woman? Fucking Natalie. "I'll be quick, I promise—"

"Maybe call me tomorrow—"

"Did Olivia tell you she planned to drop another video exposing Sarah Fain?"

"That other woman already asked me that."

Natalie asked about Sarah? She's working both Brandon and Viktor, and now she's trying to steal Sarah away from me too?

Alexis was saying, "I'm sorry, I really have to go—"

"Just real quick, what did you tell Natalie? She's out of the office now so I can't ask her."

I heard Alexis sigh. "I don't know what Olivia was working on. She was private about that stuff. She liked to spring her videos on the unsuspecting world."

"Is there anyone else she might've confided in?"

"Not that I know of. Like I told the other reporter, maybe Olivia wrote something down in her computer."

Of course!

But where would her computer be?

"Okay, goodbye," Alexis said, and clicked off.

I stood on the sidewalk thinking. No doubt Natalie was chasing down Livvy's computer, if it still existed. Somehow I had to beat her to it.

CHAPTER THIRTY-EIGHT

A DRUNK GUY staggered toward me on the sidewalk. I waited for him to pass by, checking through the window to make sure the security guard was still at the front desk. Then I took out my phone and called Detective O'Keefe.

If I was lucky, she'd be working late tonight. Since Livvy's murder case was never officially closed, the police must still have all the evidence locked away in storage. That's where Livvy's computer would be. Maybe O'Keefe had even copied Livvy's files and would email me the ones about Sarah Fain—if I played this right.

O'Keefe answered on the first ring. "Yeah, what?"

At least there was no bullshit with this woman. All of her negative vibes were right up front. "Do you still have Olivia's computer?"

"No."

Damn. "Where is it?"

"With the brother. He reclaimed her stuff after the case was over. It *is* over, by the way."

I had zero desire to go see Eric again. "Did you make copies of Olivia's files?"

"Yes."

Thank God. "Could you send them to me?"

"I'm busy. Got some nostril hairs that need trimming."

I had known she would say no, so now I played my hole card. "Your captain ordered you to interview me. He would want you to cooperate."

"Not anymore. He ordered me *not* to cooperate."

"You're full of crap."

"Bad enough you lied about a witness to an active shooter incident. But today when we arrested Robert Heath, he said he had already confessed to you. You withheld that from the police. Talk about obstructing an investigation."

While I tried to think of a comeback, the phone connection ended. O'Keefe had hung up.

I stood there staring at the phone. I wanted to call Mateo. He always made me feel better. But our last conversation, about outing Brandon, had ended so badly.

I heard a woman laughing and looked up. Two women about my age walked past me on the sidewalk, hand in hand. The one on the left, with a red paisley top, was carrying two paperback books, and I wondered if they might be teachers. Were these women happy and free of care?

Well, screw it. My job might be a pain in the ass, but I was willing to bet it was a lot more exciting. Neither of them was chasing down a murderer tonight. I slapped the wall of the building and said out loud, "Get your shit together." I knew what I had to do, like it or not.

I would go back to Eric.

It was the obvious move. Maybe he had saved his sister's computer. That was the kind of thing a cynical but sentimental guy like Eric would do. If I convinced him the solution to Livvy's murder might lie inside her laptop, maybe he'd get over his anger at me and let me see her files.

I went back inside the building determined to locate Eric myself, without Larry's help. Waslking past Natalie's cubicle, I saw she was still gone—but she had left her laptop behind. I was tempted to sneak a peek at it, but I was afraid she might have installed some sort of software that would catch me.

Back at my desk, I got onto Twitter and searched for clues about where Eric lived. His feed had been silent lately, except for one photo of him with a Guinness in each hand, eyes at half mast, looking completely sloshed. Going further back, I found all the same tweets I'd seen last week, about his favorite bars and restaurants.

But now I googled those bars and restaurants and discovered an interesting fact: most of them were in the Porter Square area, where Cambridge and Somerville met. Maybe Eric lived near there.

From previous searches I knew his other social media all had tight privacy settings, so I decided to google images of Eric. I found several photos of him during Reynolds' trial and a gif of him standing next to Viktor and shouting that Reynolds was guilty.

There were also two photos of him and Livvy together. One showed him graduating from high school and the other showed her graduating. In both pictures they had their arms around each other, smiling broadly. It reminded me that getting closure for the family wasn't just a cliché, it was deeply real. God knows I still longed for it, with Tata—

Wait. I stopped at a third photo. Eric and Livvy were sitting on the front porch of a gray two-story house, on the corner of a tree-lined street. With their feet up on the railing, they hoisted bottles of beer. They looked at home, like one of them might live here. Livvy looked older, like she was already in college. In the upper right corner of the photo was a street sign. I enlarged it and read *"Mackenzie Street."*

I knew there was a Mackenzie Street near Porter Square. This house could be Eric's!

I found Mackenzie on Google Earth and started checking street corners. The fourth one I tried—Mackenzie and Beekman—had a gray two-story house that looked exactly the same. I grabbed my jacket and practically ran out of my cubicle.

I called a Lyft to drive me there. The whole ride, I strategized about what I'd say to him. I decided to simply tell him the truth: whatever he thought of me, I was the one who had reopened his sister's case. I was on his side.

Finally, we turned onto Mackenzie and headed for Beekman. I saw red lights flashing up ahead. What was that about?

It was a police car, parked on the corner. Next to it was an ambulance.

Two EMT's were carrying a gurney out the front door of the gray house.

My heart stopped. Lying on the gurney, not moving, was Eric. One of the EMT's was putting an oxygen mask on his face.

Coming right behind them, wearing a dark jacket and carrying a big red purse, was Natalie.

I jumped out of the Lyft and ran up to her, as the EMT's lifted Eric into the back of the ambulance. "What happened?" I asked, breathless.

Natalie turned toward me, eyes shining with horror and excitement. "Eric tried to kill himself."

CHAPTER THIRTY-NINE

"*This is Natalie Blair of the Boston Clarion, with another special emergency podcast,*" Episode 3 began.

It was eleven o'clock the next morning. I sat at my desk alone, listening to the episode with my head in my hands. It was a Saturday, so there weren't as many people dropping by my cubicle today, which suited me. I was miserable.

Once again it made sense that Natalie should lead off the episode. She had found Eric and saved his life. I should be grateful. I *was* grateful. But . . .

"*Last night I was on my way to see Eric Anderson,*" she continued. "*I had questions about his sister's murder. When I got there, the front window was open and I smelled—well, to be blunt, I smelled human excrement. I got a really bad feeling, it's—it's hard to describe. So I tried the door. It was unlocked, so I went inside.*"

She sounded so sincere, but I didn't buy it. She was on the front porch and smelled shit all the way from the bedroom? No way. Probably she found the door unlocked and decided to go in and do some snooping. She figured Eric was out of the house, but if he came home and caught her, she'd charm her way out of it.

That's what I would have done.

"I followed the smell to Eric's bedroom. And I found him . . ."
Her voice caught, filled with emotion. I had seen Natalie practice this voice-catching thing again and again at the recording
studio.

*"I found him hanging from a ceiling beam. With an extension cord
tied around his neck. His legs were stretching, trying to reach the floor,
and his hands grabbed the cable trying to untie it, but he couldn't. His
mouth was making this horrible sound, like . . ."* Here Natalie gave a
gasping kind of groan. She and Larry had worked hard on that
groan, deepening it and making it longer so it would be effective in
the podcast.

*"So I grabbed a chair and put it under his legs. Finally he was able
to stand again, and he quit making that awful noise. Then I stood on
another chair and somehow we got the extension cord loose and took
his head out. He fell to the floor and passed out, unconscious. I gave
him CPR and tried to slap him awake, but he wouldn't move. He was
just . . ."*

Natalie stopped, overcome by emotion, and if I hadn't seen her do
ten takes of this in the studio, I would have gotten emotional too. I
guessed that was how the millions of people listening to this podcast
would react. *Natalie, a goddamn hero.*

*"So I called 911 and the ambulance came, and thank God he sur-
vived. Before they came, I found a piece of paper on the bed. It was
Eric's suicide note. I don't feel right interfering with his privacy and
telling you the exact words."* Actually, she was dying to say the exact
words. She had taken a picture of the note before the ambulance
got there, and she thought reading it verbatim would be the high-
light of the podcast. If I'd been in her shoes, I would have wanted
the same thing. But Dave was afraid people would find it in bad
taste. *"I can tell you, though, the note expressed deep sadness about
his sister's death, and his stepfather's . . . situation."*

The note's exact words were: *"My sister's dead and my stepdad's in the shit. Life is so fucked up, but fuck it, I don't give a shit. Sorry, everybody. Goodbye."*

For the hundredth time since last night, I thought: *if Natalie had showed up at the house just two minutes later—or one minute—Eric would be dead right now.*

I gripped the edge of my desk and closed my eyes. I never should have revealed publicly that Eric was my source for the incest story. And when I found out Viktor probably didn't do it after all, I should have called Eric right away. Maybe then he wouldn't have felt so overwhelmed that he tried to kill himself.

It's my fault.

"Eric is now recovering at Mass General, and I'm happy to say the doctors anticipate a full recovery. But please keep him in your prayers. Also, before I continue with this podcast, I want to say on behalf of all of us here at the Clarion: If there's anyone out there who's thinking of hurting themselves, don't do it. Get help. Call the National Suicide Prevention Lifeline at 1-800-273-8255. There's hope. There's a lot of love out there, for you."

"Oh screw you," I said out loud. But as Natalie repeated the hotline number, I forced myself to take a breath. *Don't be a jealous bitch. Just be glad she showed up in time.*

Come to think of it, how did she know where Eric lived? Larry must have found out. That's why he couldn't help me last night—he was tracking down Eric for Natalie.

She had been hunting for Livvy's computer too. It was still out there somewhere—

"Now the question that always gets asked at a time like this is: why? Why did Eric try to do this to himself? For possible answers, let's bring in Petra Kovach, the reporter for this newspaper who interviewed Eric last week. Hello, Petra. Welcome to the podcast."

I cringed, listening. I hated *"Welcome to the podcast."* That made it sound like I was a guest on Natalie's show.

"Hello, Natalie." That had been scripted as *"Thank you, Natalie,"* but I couldn't bring myself to do it that way.

She said, *"Did Eric seem in any way suicidal when you spoke with him?"*

"Not at all," my voice responded. *"He was eager to find out once and for all what really happened to his sister."*

"So why do you think he took this terrible step?"

"I think Eric came to believe that his stepdad, who he loved deeply, sexually abused Olivia and might have killed her. Eric was tortured by that possibility."

At this point in the podcast, I made a statement that Natalie and Dave had both protested against. But for once I was so adamant that they gave in.

"I would like to say," I declared, *"that I now believe Viktor Anderson was innocent. There was no incest. According to Professor Reynolds, who has no reason to lie about this, Olivia explained to him that her Reddit posts about the incest were fictional. She was creating an alternate identity for herself on social media, pretending to be a sexually abused teenager as an experiment to see what kind of reaction she'd get. She was curious, doing it for kicks. That's why she was attracted to Professor Reynolds in the first place: she was intrigued by his research on alternate internet identities."*

Natalie hadn't asked any follow-up questions. Instead she went for the jugular. *"Petra, do you feel guilty that Eric attempted suicide? That maybe you caused his despair?"*

I said, *"All I've done since I started this investigation is search for the truth. I'm devastated that Eric made this terrible decision to take his life, and I'm grateful he's alive and recovering."*

I clicked the pause button and pushed my chair away from my desk. I couldn't take listening any longer.

I knew this episode would kill. Episode 2 had gotten over two million livestreams and downloads already, and I was positive this one would hit at least five million. The ad money was pouring in; we had a second sponsor now, a new movie called *Warriors of Ganymede,* paying top dollar. No doubt subscriptions to the *Clarion* would take a jump. Dave was happy. Abernathy would be happy.

But I had left such a path of destruction behind me.

And after all this, were we really any closer to knowing who killed Livvy?

I was scared people would find out about some of the questionable things I had done. Eric might reveal how I'd bullied and lied to him, which played a part in his suicide attempt. Reynolds might accuse me of lying too. And what if there was a backlash against me for outing Brandon?

If all that happens, or even some of it, will I get canceled?

I clicked on Twitter, then closed the tab before reading the latest on #PetraKovach. I was too afraid of what I might find. I had thought creating this blockbuster podcast would solidify me at the *Clarion* and make me highly marketable for my next job. But I might be a lot less marketable than I'd imagined.

It didn't help that I'd been awake most of the night again, recording this episode. I shook my head vigorously. *Quit beating yourself up. This is just your PTSD from getting fired all those times. You found the clues that broke open this whole investigation!*

I drank some coffee and thought about Jonah. Earlier this morning, he had called me from his office. I'd been afraid he would blame me for Eric's suicide attempt. But instead he'd said, "Look, I haven't agreed with all your choices, but don't get too down on yourself.

You didn't tie that extension cord. Eric did it himself. And he's alive. It'll be okay."

That had made me feel better about our relationship, for the first time since our fight. So now I decided to give Jonah a call. When he picked up, I said, "Seeing as we both worked most of the night, do you want to go home and grab some Zs?"

"Funny you should ask. I was just thinking I needed a break from this freaking model."

Thirty minutes later, his bicycle and my Lyft arrived at our apartment simultaneously. We embraced on the front porch for a long time, without speaking.

Then I pulled back and looked into his eyes. "So you don't hate me?"

Jonah took my hand. "Of course not. But I'm concerned. I always thought we shared the same values."

"We do, Jonah. If it makes you feel any better, I'm not so sure I like all my choices either. Especially how I've treated you lately."

Jonah gazed at me a moment longer, then kissed my forehead. "Let's go upstairs."

The last thing he said to me, before we fell asleep in each other's arms, was, "But one thing. If we're gonna be married, don't lie to me again."

"I won't," I said. "I promise."

*　*　*

I woke up from a dream I couldn't quite remember, but it included walking on a sandy beach with Tata, and then him disappearing. I looked over to Jonah's side of the bed and realized he had disappeared too. I rubbed my eyes, disoriented, and checked my phone—7:30. I had wasted the whole day, not doing any work at all since this morning. I went to the bathroom and saw a note from Jonah taped to the mirror: *"P, I'm back at work with Jesse and Wang Lei, will be home as soon as our model obeys orders! L, J."*

L, J. He had decided to forgive me, for now, though I knew we weren't back on solid ground yet. I was still fuzzy-headed but there was no way I could go back to sleep. What should I do?

The answer hit me so hard it was like somebody slapped me in the face: *solve Livvy's murder.* I needed to quit worrying about everything else and focus on the mission I'd had ever since childhood.

I threw on jeans, T-shirt, socks, and shoes. Then I searched the closet for my darkest sweater or jacket and found an old black hoodie of Jonah's. *Perfect.* I put it on.

I left a message on the refrigerator for Jonah that I was headed out to do some work and I'd text him. Then I took off out the door.

CHAPTER FORTY

I TOOK A Lyft to Somerville, several blocks from the corner of Mackenzie and Beekman, and walked the rest of the way. There were no police cars or ambulances outside the gray house tonight, and no Eric either; he had been transferred to a psych facility for three days of evaluation.

But even though tonight was dark and quiet, I had to be careful. On the night after police cars and an ambulance had shown up, Eric's neighbors were likely to be hyper-aware of their surroundings. I stepped softly onto Eric's porch and saw two mailboxes, for "Anderson, Apt. 1," and "Hamada, Apt. 2." That probably meant Eric lived on the main floor and Hamada, whoever they were, had the upstairs. All the lights were off; they must be out of the house, enjoying the Saturday night.

I reached for the doorknob and turned. It was locked.

My breath turned shallow. Until now, so far as I knew, I hadn't broken any laws in this investigation. I'd never broken any significant laws in my life. This would be crossing a line.

For good reason, I told myself. If Eric hadn't gotten rid of Livvy's laptop, he probably kept it somewhere in this apartment. He was already living here when the cops gave him Livvy's stuff back.

I stepped over to a window and the floorboards creaked. I hoped they weren't really as loud as they sounded to me. I put my hands on the window and pushed upward, with all my strength.

It didn't budge. I tried a second window. Still no go.

I walked around to the narrow side yard. The neighbors' house was only a few feet and one thin hedge away, and their lights were on. I peeked through their window and didn't see anyone. So I tried to force one of Eric's two side windows open. *Don't let some stupid locked windows stop you.* But they held tight.

I went to Eric's small, treeless, rear yard. The three-story house in back was way too close for comfort. Their lights were on too, with laughter spilling out from inside. I slipped through the shadows to the back steps. Then the toes of my right foot banged into something, and I strangled a sharp cry. It was a cinderblock lying randomly next to the steps.

Suddenly a dog barked next door, an angry, full-throated growl. I got on the balls of my feet, ready to run. But someone said, "Quiet, Francie! Shush!" At last the dog grudgingly stopped barking.

I didn't move for a full minute, then stepped onto the back stairs. Still no barking. I walked past a potted plant, a ficus it looked like, and tried the back door. Locked. So was the back window, and the two windows on the other side of the house. I could only think of one plan that might work: break a window and pray the neighbors didn't hear.

I peered down at the ground, searching for something to smash a window with. That cinderblock was probably *too* heavy. What about the ficus pot? I lifted it up, wondering if I had the guts, or desperation, to do this.

But then I saw, underneath the pot, a shiny object.

A key.

I picked it up and turned it in the lock. The door opened and I went in.

I had crossed that line and I wasn't going back.

I was in the rear hallway. I didn't see a burglar alarm. It was even darker inside the house, but I kept my phone flashlight off to keep any neighbors from seeing it. I edged my way forward, and as my eyes began to adjust, I saw a living room in front of me, complete with sofa, TV, and chairs.

I didn't think Livvy's computer would be out in the open; Eric would keep it someplace more private. I opened a closed door and found myself in his bedroom.

My gaze rose involuntarily to the big wooden beam near his double bed. I pictured Eric with his sandy hair and wounded eyes, hanging there moments from dying. I imagined those eyes watching me now.

I tightened my jaw. *Enough.* I shut the door behind me and checked the windows. The shades were down, unlike the rest of the apartment. Maybe Eric drew them closed before he hung himself, so nobody would see him and try to stop him.

With the shades down, I felt a little safer turning on my phone flashlight. Keeping it pointed away from the window, I opened all four drawers of Eric's desk. Mainly they just contained office supplies and old files. In the bottom right drawer, I found a thick Alcoholics Anonymous book and a printed list of AA meetings in Cambridge; apparently Eric had decided he might have a drinking problem. *You think?*

I went over to the small closet and opened the door. It was full of khaki pants and oxford shirts that Eric no doubt wore to work. Then I looked up at the top shelf.

There was a big cardboard box.

My heart jumped. Somehow I knew.

Getting on tiptoes, I reached up and grabbed the box. It was heavy enough I had to be careful not to drop it. I set it on the bed and shone my light on the cardboard lid. An official sticker from the Cambridge Police Department read: *"Docket # A40738, People v. William Reynolds, State Exhibits H1 – H19."*

Inside this box I would find the prosecution's trial exhibits, which would include Livvy's personal effects—like her computer.

The packing tape had already been broken open, so the lid came right off. I shined my light inside.

Lying on top were the gray sweatpants and purple "I Don't Give a Fuck" T-shirt Livvy wore the night she was killed. I felt shivery, seeing them. The sweatpants and shirt both had big pieces cut out. There were sheets, a blanket, and a pillowcase, also with missing pieces. I assumed they were stained with blood and got sent in for DNA testing. The cops had been banking on the nail file theory: that Livvy stabbed the killer with her now-missing file, and his blood dripped onto her clothes and bedding. But the blood they tested all turned out to be Livvy's.

Underneath the sheets and blanket were Livvy's socks, underwear, and red running shoes, with no pieces cut out. Evidently, the police hadn't found any bloodstains on these items. I picked up the shoes and recalled from the crime scene photos that they were sitting on top of a shoebox by the door, a few feet from Livvy's body. They looked brand new, like she'd only worn them once or twice at most.

Next to the shoes I found the jewelry Livvy wore that night: earrings and a thin silver necklace. I also found some keys that must have been in her pants pocket.

But there was no computer.

Why not? Where the hell had it gone? Since several of Livvy's emails were introduced at trial, her computer would have been included in the exhibits and made available to the defense lawyer and jury to examine. I was pretty sure that was how trials worked.

So what did Eric do with Livvy's computer? I wondered, if I had a sister who was murdered, what would I do with her laptop? Would I use it myself, or would that feel ghoulish? Would I sell it? Hold onto it as a keepsake?

I wasn't sure. All I knew was the laptop wasn't here, and it seemed like my mission had been a failure.

I slipped out the back door and placed the key back under the ficus pot. Just then my phone pinged. I hurried away from Eric's apartment and read the text: I JUST GOT HOME. WHAT'S YOUR ETA?

If I went home now I'd have to tell Jonah about breaking and entering, since not telling him would feel like a lie, and I'd made that promise to him. And to myself. But I couldn't bear getting into a big discussion with him right now, not after all the turmoil we'd been through.

Also, I wanted to do some work and salvage something from this wasted day. So I texted Jonah that I was still working and I missed him, and then I walked a couple more blocks and called a Lyft to take me to the *Clarion*. When I got there it was after ten and totally dead except for Chuck Kling typing away in his cubicle. He was writing up a puff piece on Boston College's new freshman running back. "How's it coming?" I asked.

Chuck laughed. "Are you kiddin'? I could write these things in my sleep. 'Joe Shmo grew up poor with gangs all around, but thanks to his mama's love here he is today, blah blah blah, etcetera.'"

God, if only I could be half that comfortable in my work. A third.

Back at my desk, I shifted gears and began searching for Providence. He was a viable murder suspect, but I'd been so busy with everything else that I still hadn't found Providence's real name.

I googled for an hour but didn't get any closer to finding it. I wanted to throw my computer at the wall. Maybe I should ask Larry for help after all. I'd feel him out, see if I felt like I could trust him. Like a true programming nerd, Larry kept idiosyncratic hours, so maybe he was still here. I headed downstairs.

He wasn't in his cubicle. But a laptop with a pink case and a Taylor Swift sticker sat open on his desk.

Pink? Taylor Swift? Larry didn't strike me as a pink Taylor Swift kind of guy. He must be borrowing some woman's—

Wait. *When Livvy was fourteen, her computer had Taylor Swift stickers.*

Could this be . . .

Oh my God.

My pulse quickened as I thought back to last night: Natalie coming out of Eric's apartment carrying her big red purse. Maybe Livvy's laptop was inside that purse!

After Natalie saved Eric, but before the EMTs got there, she had the presence of mind to photograph his suicide note. Maybe she was also ballsy enough to do a quick sweep of the bedroom—and find the box with the computer in it.

Where was Larry now? I called and reached him on the second ring. People were talking in the background. "Hi, where are you?" I asked. "I need your help on something."

"I'm having pizza with Natalie. We'll be back in half an hour."

"You know what? No rush. Take your time. I'll ask you in the morning."

I grabbed the laptop and took it upstairs to my desk. Since I only had half an hour, I set my phone timer for twenty-five minutes. I opened the laptop and saw it was already on. But the screen said, *"Log in. Password required."*

I understood right away what had happened. Natalie couldn't get into Livvy's files, so she asked Larry for help. He hadn't found the password yet, but he would give it another shot when he came back from pizza.

So what might the password be? I quickly tried the obvious ones, that Natalie and Larry had probably tried already. Then I got an inspiration. I typed in "OrphanGirl."

I was in.

I shouted "Yes!" Then I looked around, afraid somebody would come by. I didn't want anyone seeing me with this stolen laptop, even if it wasn't me who stole it, it was Natalie.

Well no, actually I stole it too. From Natalie and Larry.

I turned back to the screen. Livvy's screensaver was a mountain range, in Sweden maybe. The desktop had folders with names like *Econ Paper*, *Soc Notes*, and *Anthro*. I skipped those and went straight to a folder labeled *YouTube*. But it just contained files about marketing, with titles like *"Maximizing Clickability."*

Only nineteen minutes left. I clicked on the *Microsoft Word* icon at the bottom of the screen, then hit *File* and *Open Recent*. The most recent files had been opened two and a half years ago in May, the month after Livvy's murder. The police must have gotten into this computer too, somehow, and read these files.

I found documents titled *Identity Politics Identify Nothing* and *Pseudo-Microaggression*. Then I came to a document called *The Fuck 'Em Fuck Me Girl*. My hand raced to click on it.

The second I began reading, I realized this was solid gold.

Brandon had said Sarah Fain was a serial accuser, who accused one of her fellow high school students of assault. But he got that wrong.

In reality, Sarah had done something *way* more disturbing.

CHAPTER FORTY-ONE

As most of you guys know, Livvy wrote in her *Fuck 'Em Fuck Me Girl* document, *back in December, Harvard freshman Sarah Fain accused Danny Madsen, a football player and fellow student, of raping her at a frat party. She told a horrifying story of sex, drugs, and violence. Another heartbreaking example of rape culture running rampant on college campuses.*

I checked when Livvy wrote this: March 27, six days before she was murdered. This must be the video script she was planning to record.

Only one problem with this tragic tale: I'm pretty sure it's total bullshit, like everything else these left-wing nutjobs say about college campuses. As we described in our video "Who Raped Who," Sarah Fain has a pretty fucked-up backstory. She developed a heroin addiction in ninth grade. The tattoos on her ass, "Fuck 'em" and "Fuck me," that's who she is. So who do you trust: this screwed-up drug addict or Danny, who's never been in trouble in his life, an Eagle Scout for God's sake, he was a Big Brother to a foster kid in high school. I mean, take the red pill, right? But guess what? The "fuck 'em, fuck me" girl gets a free pass from the college administration and the media—well done, feminazis—while the All-American Eagle Scout almost gets thrown out of Harvard.

Thanks to my video, and all the pressure from you guys, Danny wasn't expelled and he's doing great. Except he still has to deal with the stigma. And that's why I'm dropping this new video today. Once you hear it, you'll know for sure this outrageous accusation against him is just another bunch of victim-culture crap. 'Cause let me tell you, Sarah Fain is even sicker than I thought.

Two weeks ago, a document came into my possession from an anonymous source. This document purported to be an arrest record from the St. Louis Police Department three years ago, when they busted a fifteen-year-old girl named, you guessed it, Sarah Fain. I contacted the Sex Crimes Unit and spoke to the captain and one of the detectives. Both men would neither confirm nor deny; that was their legal obligation. But I came away from these conversations with no doubt this doc was legit.

Now ordinarily I'd say hey, she was a minor, give the girl a break. But Sarah Fain is trying to destroy a friend of mine's life. So fuck that. I'm gonna read you the summary portion of this record, written by the arresting officer. You ready?

"Complainant, Juvenile M, stated that he was attending a party in the basement of a friend's home and drank both bourbon and beer, whereupon he passed out. He stated that he awoke the following morning with his penis attached to his testicles with Superglue. He experienced severe pain when he tried to urinate. He claimed to have no idea how the Superglue got there. He was able, however, to give the names of the other party attendees.

"This officer questioned all the attendees accompanied by their parents and, when requested, a lawyer. Three witnesses confirmed that Juvenile M's penis had been Superglued when he awoke. Two of these witnesses stated that Juvenile M had a verbal altercation the night before with a fifteen-year-old girl named Sarah Fain, henceforth referred to in this document as Juvenile S. This officer questioned Juvenile

S further and she confessed, stating that she was angry at Juvenile M for 'trying to stick his dick down my throat.' After he fell asleep, she decided to 'teach that dickhead a lesson.'

"Juvenile S has been arrested for sexual assault and committed to the Elm Street Juvenile Facility awaiting disposition."

Now this arrest record goes on for twenty pages and I'll post it on oliviaanderson.com, but you get the idea. Maybe Juvenile M was an asshole, but this crazy bitch Superglued the guy's dick to his balls. She's fucking insane. And we're gonna let Superglue Girl fuck up Eagle Scout's life? Sarah Fain is the one who should be thrown out of Harvard for sexual assault, which is what Danny accused her of. And if her radical feminist pals don't like it, they can leave too.

So that's today's red pill, guys. Speaking out on behalf of freedom and justice in this crazy world of ours, this is Olivia Anderson. Fight on, friends!

As I came to the end, my heart pounded. Not only did this video script explain why Sarah was furious at Livvy during that final week; it also proved she had the temperament to commit a violent, vengeful act.

Sarah Fain had just jumped to the top of my suspect list.

I checked the time. It had only been twenty-two minutes, so I was still okay if I hurried. I didn't want to email the script to myself and leave an electronic trail, so I printed it out. I checked Livvy's other files and found a PDF titled "Juvenile Case #2483." I opened it, saw it was the arrest record she had quoted, and printed that out too. I headed down the hall to the copy room to get the pages—

But then I heard Natalie's voice, followed by Larry's. They were walking up the hallway that intersected with this one. *Shit, I bet they're heading downstairs to Larry's office. They'll see Livvy's laptop is missing and realize I stole it!*

"There must be some way to get in without the password," Natalie was saying. They were coming closer. No way I could run back into my cubicle fast enough to avoid them. I heard Larry say, "I got a couple hacker friends. I'll ask them for help—"

Then they appeared around the corner, slowing when they saw me. Larry looked away, no doubt feeling guilty about switching his allegiance to Natalie. But she had no shame, smiling brightly and asking, "How's it going, Petch? Working late?"

I did a quick calculation. If they found out I stole that laptop from them, Livvy's video script wouldn't be my discovery anymore, it would be Natalie's. She'd get all the credit. I'd be the jerk who tried to steal Natalie's scoop. Dave would be outraged at me. Not only was Natalie his pet, but he'd think I was the opposite of a team player.

Natalie and Larry were already walking past me on their way downstairs. I said, "They got some yummy pastries from Madeline's in the break room. Chocolate éclairs," I added, going straight for Natalie's weak spot.

"Ooh, let's do it," Natalie said to Larry. Then her forehead knitted in surprise that I was doing her this good turn. "Thanks, Petra."

I nodded, noting that for once she was using my full name. Then, as they headed toward the break room and out of sight, I ran as quietly as I could on the thin carpet back to my desk. I grabbed Livvy's laptop, raced downstairs, and placed it back on Larry's desk the way I'd found it, or as close as I could remember.

I ran back upstairs, where I once again encountered Natalie and Larry. Natalie eyed me suspiciously. "There weren't any chocolate éclairs."

I gave her a sympathetic look. "Oh shoot. Chuck must've eaten the last one. Sorry!"

Then I walked past them to the print room. I swept the pages out of the printer and headed back to my cubicle, holding them close.

These pages were my treasure. No one would take them away from me.

CHAPTER FORTY-TWO

I KNEW I better show my pages to Dave, fast. As soon as Larry hacked into the laptop, Natalie would find the same docs I'd found and claim them for herself.

It was too late at night to call Dave. So I sent him a text: GOT OUR NEXT PODCAST ALL SET—SECRET DOCS—BLOCKBUSTER!!!

Then I got to work searching for Sarah Fain's contact info, so I could get her response. But her info was locked down, just like Reynolds' info had been.

So I searched for Sarah's crewmates. Through People Finder, I found a phone number for a senior named Rachel Reiser. She answered on the first ring.

"Who is this?" her irritated voice said.

"Hi, sorry to call so late. My name's Petra Kovach. I'm a reporter for the *Boston Clarion,* and I need to get in touch with Sarah Fain."

There was a pause, then Rachel said, less grouchy, "Yeah, I listened to your podcast. What do you want from Sarah?"

"I'm working on a story and I'd like her input. It's urgent."

"She doesn't talk to reporters."

"Rachel, the thing is, I was given some information about Sarah's past that could be, well . . . damaging. So I want to get her side before I put it out there. If you could give her my number and ask her to call me, I think she'd appreciate it."

Rachel hesitated. "I guess I can do that."

"And please, I know it's late but, if you can try to reach her now. My boss is pushing me to put out this podcast first thing tomorrow."

"She's right down the hall. I'll see if she's up."

"Thanks."

I clicked off and had some coffee as I waited. Fifteen minutes later my phone buzzed with a call from an unknown number. I picked up. "Hello, this is Petra Kovach."

"What the hell is this?" a young woman's voice said. "Are you threatening me?"

This had to be Sarah. "I just want your side of the story," I said, trying to sound calm and matter-of-fact.

"What story? It's the middle of the night!"

"The story of your arrest in St. Louis for sexual assault."

I could feel Sarah's panic in the pause before she spoke. "How did you get hold of that? It's supposed to be sealed."

Nice—she had just confirmed the arrest record was real. "We should talk about it. We're putting it out in a podcast tomorrow morning."

"You have no right to do this. Juvenile records are supposed to be sealed," she repeated. "I'll sue you."

I hesitated. No question, I had opened up another moral can of worms. But I felt, as I had before, that solving Livvy's murder trumped everything. I said, "We've already vetted this with the newspaper's lawyers. I think it would be helpful to you if we discuss this. You can put what happened into context."

"Fuck you, you people ruined my life. If I could do it over again, I would've kept my mouth shut and let Danny walk around campus gloating that he got away with raping me. That's what happened anyway."

"You knew Olivia was about to drop a video revealing this story, didn't you?"

There was another pause before Sarah replied, "What are you saying? What's your point?"

"You must've been pretty pissed off at her."

"Oh my God, are you trying to say *I* killed her?"

"You have to admit you had motive. That's why we need to talk."

"Unbelievable. You bitch."

"Look—"

"Fine, let's talk. In person. If you're gonna fuck me, look me straight in the eye and tell me you're gonna fuck me."

An in-person interview? *Hell yes!* "Where do you want to meet?"

"Cambridge Common, by the playground."

I was about to say yes when I realized I'd already been shot at once during a late-night outdoor meeting in Cambridge. Sarah seemed volatile enough to make it twice. "No. How about that all-night diner on Mass. Ave.? El Greco."

"Fine. See you in thirty."

Thirty minutes was pushing it, but my Lyft got there in thirty-two. Sarah Fain was already inside, sitting in a corner booth.

CHAPTER FORTY-THREE

EVEN IF SARAH'S eyes hadn't been aiming angry blue venom at me, I would have recognized her instantly from her photos online. She was striking. Though she was sitting down she *looked* tall, with her thick biceps and forearms and strong forehead and chin. Her skin was pale and her hair was flame red, with corkscrew curls cut close to her head. She'd taken off her denim jacket and wore a black tank top with a colorful dragon's tail tattoo climbing up her chest.

I walked up to her. "Thanks for agreeing to see me."

Up close I saw redness in her eyes, like she'd been crying. But her words were as belligerent as they had been over the phone. "Where'd you get my juvenile record?"

A middle-aged waitress in a blue uniform who looked like she'd been working in this diner for thirty years came up and asked, "Coffee?"

"Sure," I answered, and Sarah nodded. As the waitress stepped away, I said, "I got your record from the same place Olivia got it."

Sarah curled her fist around a napkin. "The cops swore up and down it was confidential."

"So what's the deal with that? Supergluing a guy's dick to his balls—that's hard-core."

Then I realized the waitress was standing next to us again with the coffee-pot. She looked stunned by that last remark.

"Sorry," I said.

"Superglue, huh?" the waitress said as she poured. "Might try that myself. You guys ready to order?"

"Give us a minute."

"No problem."

As the waitress left, Sarah said, "That asshole had it coming. The whole night he kept trying to stick his dick in my mouth, even after I told him I'd bite it off. Then he was bothering this other girl that came to the party—an eighth grader. So when he passed out, I decided to teach him a lesson about keeping his dick in his pants."

"One hell of a lesson."

"Yeah, I overdid it. Best thing that ever happened to me."

"How so?"

Sarah rubbed her cheek. "I got busted and forced into rehab. Most people just do their time and get high again as soon as they get out. But for me, it took. I stayed clean, joined the crew team, and got addicted to rowing like I used to be addicted to heroin and cranberry vodka." She looked up at the waitress, who was back at our table. "You know, just coffee'll be fine. I'm in training."

"Same here," I said. "Well, I'm not in training, but just coffee."

The waitress said, "No worries," and after she left, Sarah continued her story. "So freshman year I'm on crew, no partying, but the other girls convince me to go to this frat one night. Okay, I'll go for an hour, drink my ginger ale, and go home. Except I never leave. I wake up in the morning next to this fucking creep with vomit breath, and I'm sore in places I shouldn't be. I know right away what happened. No other explanation." She shifted in her chair. "Now of course I remember how I Superglued this other guy's dick and that didn't turn out well. So this time I figure I'll just leave and forget the whole thing, stay out of trouble. Only it doesn't work. Nightmares and depression. So two months later, I call the cops. And you know the rest of it. Olivia Anderson goes on a crusade to destroy me. The whole country starts talking about what a mentally deranged slut I am."

She sounded utterly believable.

But then again, I had believed Danny Madsen too.

"In the past two years," Sarah continued, "things have gotten back to normal a little bit. But if you put out my juvenile arrest record— which it's illegal for you to have, and I'm sure you did plenty of stupid shit when you were a teenager—if you put my juvie record in your podcast, you might get more clicks. Congratulations. But you'll make me look like even more of a wacko. It'll be impossible for me to ever get a job coaching crew, which is what I want to do with my life. Help other young women find a purpose."

She was finished now. She sipped her coffee and looked at me over the rim of her cup.

I wasn't sure what to say. I sipped my coffee too. Then I asked, "So Olivia told you she had this crime report?"

"I'm not answering that."

"Why not?"

"If I say no you won't believe me, and if I say yes you'll put it in your podcast and twist it in some sick way." She put down her cup. "I haven't done anything wrong. Not since I got sober anyway, nothing serious. I'm living an honorable life."

I put my hands on the table and leaned forward. "Sarah, I'm not out to hurt you. All I want is the truth."

She gave a sharp laugh. "Yeah, right."

I tried a new tack. "Where were you the night she was killed?"

"Give me a break."

"If you don't give an alibi, it'll make you look guilty."

"Do you seriously think I would ever kill somebody? Hit a girl's head so hard I bashed her skull in?"

"I don't know. That's what I'm trying to find out."

Sarah eyed me closely. "Give me one good reason to trust you."

I opened my mouth, but was embarrassed to see I was stumped.

"That's what I thought," Sarah said. She stood up. "Well, now you've seen me. If you want to fuck up my life for no good reason except to advance your own career, then I'll sue you for invasion of privacy, and I'll hope you rot in hell."

I found my footing again. "Look, I was Livvy's camp counselor when she was fourteen. She was like a little sister to me. I'm trying to find her killer. That's all I'm after here."

"Sure, tell yourself that." She took out her wallet.

I said quickly, "No, I'll pay."

But she put three dollar bills on the table. "Don't do me any favors. Just treat me the way I deserve."

Then Sarah headed out of the diner. I was left behind with nothing but a half-full cup of coffee and a headache seeping into my skull.

As I raised the coffee cup to my lips, I looked out the window and watched Sarah walk through the parking lot. She was looking down, preoccupied, so she didn't see a white minivan coming straight at her. My heart stopped. Three feet away from her, the minivan screeched to a halt.

Sarah jumped back. Then she bounded forward and slammed the front of the minivan with her hand. She screamed at the driver and banged the windshield so hard I was sure it would break. I couldn't hear her words, but her face twisted with fury. The driver, a young woman, looked petrified.

Then Sarah stormed off, still screaming.

CHAPTER FORTY-FOUR

As I LEFT the diner and headed for home, I thought about Sarah.

I was guessing she truly had turned her life around after being a serious drug addict. Several of my old classmates from East LA hadn't been so lucky.

But that didn't mean she wasn't the killer. She had obvious anger management issues, and she'd been beyond furious at Livvy. Even if she was clean and sober, I could easily imagine this six-foot athlete impulsively smashing Livvy on the head.

So even though it felt sleazy using someone's sealed record from when she was only fifteen, I knew what I had to do, as a journalist: tell the truth and whatever happens, happens. *The truth shall set you free.*

When I finally got home, Jonah was already in bed asleep. I brushed my teeth, took a shower, and left my clothes off as I curled around him. It felt so good to feel his body again. So simple and sweet. Hopefully we wouldn't get into a discussion about Sarah Fain tonight. I tried to be as quiet as possible so I wouldn't wake him.

But he shifted his body backward, pushing up even closer against me, and said, "Hey, babe."

Well, since he was awake anyway . . . "Hi, gorgeous," I said, and reached for him.

"Mmm," he said. "Where have you been?"

"Talking to a source."

"After midnight. Must have been an exciting source."

"Not as exciting as you."

"So who was it?"

I ran my hand down his chest. "Do you really want to hear it now?"

He turned to face me. "Yeah, now I definitely do."

Well, so much for uncomplicated sex tonight. "I should probably start at the beginning," I said. "I was at Eric's apartment."

"Eric's? What were you doing there?"

"Well, I promised to tell you the truth. I kind of did some breaking and entering."

"Some *what?*" He raised himself up on his elbow.

I proceeded to tell him my adventures at Eric's house, getting through it as quickly as I could and hoping he wouldn't get too riled up. I could see the outlines of Jonah's face in the light that crept in through our curtains, but I couldn't catch his expression.

When he finally spoke, there was shock in his voice. "I can't believe you did that. That really was breaking and entering. A felony for sure."

"I know it was dangerous, but I couldn't think of any other way to get Livvy's laptop."

"Are all journalists this insane?"

"Just the good ones. The only reason the laptop wasn't there was because Natalie already stole it herself."

Jonah got out of bed and looked down at me. "Next time you do something that might land you in prison, how about you talk to me first?"

Was this what it would be like, being married? I'd have to clear things with him first? But I could see how he felt. "You have a point."

He shook his head. "What about this source you talked to. Who was that?"

"That's another long story. Can you sit down?"

He sat back on the bed. "Go ahead."

I sat up too so he wouldn't be above me and told him how I got hold of Livvy's laptop and found Sarah's juvenile record. I sensed Jonah's body tensing, and he interrupted.

"So you're using her record from when she was a minor?" he said.

"This is information that needs to come out. Legally speaking, it shows a pattern of prior bad acts."

"She was fifteen."

"Which was only three years before the murder. You should've seen her tonight. She has a hair trigger temper." I told Jonah how Sarah blew up at me.

Jonah said, "If she was innocent, no wonder she blew up."

"Then she went totally berserk in the parking lot. I thought she'd kill this woman who was driving." I told that story too.

Jonah said, "Well, she was upset. I don't blame her."

I'd had enough. Now it was my turn to stand up and look down at him. "Great, I'm glad you don't blame her. But she's still a murder suspect. That's what I'm gonna say in my podcast. I promised I won't lie to you again. But I can't promise you'll agree with everything I do."

"First you out a guy, and then you use a juvie record that some cop probably stole in the first place—"

"When you come up with a better way to find Livvy's killer, I'm all ears."

We argued for a while longer, then I went to the kitchen for some milk and never came back to the bedroom. He never came out of there. I fell asleep on the living room sofa.

*   *   *

My alarm woke me at seven thirty. I shut it off before it woke Jonah. I wanted to beat Dave to the office so I could talk to him as soon as he got in.

My back muscles twinged from sleeping on the sofa, but a shower fixed that, and after I got dressed and put on makeup I felt like myself again. I went into the bedroom and looked down at Jonah. He was sleeping, his long, lean body stretching all the way to the foot of the bed.

A river of warmth flowed through me. He was the love of my life and we would get back on track. Once I caught Livvy's killer, Jonah would see that I had to do everything I'd done. I kissed him lightly on his curly hair and took off.

I ordered a cappuccino to-go at an indie coffee shop and still made it to the *Clarion* before the others. But as I sat in my cubicle, I worried that Larry might have accessed Livvy's laptop last night. What if Natalie had already texted Dave about Livvy's files?

So I sent him another text: DAVE! KILLER STUFF RE SARAH! IN OFFICE WRITING IT UP! 😊 😊 😊 !

As soon as I sent the text, I felt stupid for having included all those smiley faces. On the other hand, maybe he'd appreciate my youthful enthusiasm. I turned on my laptop and got down to work.

Ever since Olivia Anderson was brutally murdered, I wrote, *her fans*—I deleted that and typed *the world—has wondered what her final YouTube video, that she never got a chance to record, was supposed to be about.*

Well, wonder no more. We—here I stopped for a few moments, then decided to be ballsy and change "We" to "I"—*I have the answer.*

I wanted to skip lightly over the question of how I attained Livvy's documents. So I temporarily switched from the *"I"* to something more general—*This podcast has obtained a copy of the video script Olivia wrote the week she died. Was somebody desperate to suppress this video? Is that why they murdered her?*

I'll let you be the judge. Actor and musician—what was the name of Larry's harpist friend? Oh yeah—*Erinne Dobson will now read*

Olivia's video script for you, from start to finish. We should warn you there will be profanity and a description of coarse sexual behavior.

I took my hard copy of Livvy's script from my purse and transcribed it. Then I wrote, *I met with Sarah Fain last night. She refused to say whether she knew about Olivia's upcoming video. She also could not provide an alibi for her whereabouts on the night of the murder.*

I went on to describe how furious Sarah had been at Livvy. *So the question,* I wrote, *is: Was Sarah angry enough on that fateful night to kill Olivia in the heat of the moment? Was she still the same impulsive, hot-tempered girl who criminally assaulted a boy when she was fifteen?*

I reread my piece and decided it was damn good. As I made a couple of small changes, my skin tingled like I was being touched by a soft breeze. I had the strongest feeling Livvy was hovering right there in the room with me, guiding my fingers to the right laptop keys. Like I was about to solve her murder, and she was helping.

I looked up toward the ceiling as if I might actually see her. I whispered, "If you're here, I love you—"

"You're here early," I heard Natalie say.

She was standing in the opening to my cubicle. I quickly shut my laptop so she couldn't read anything. But she reached out and grabbed the hard copy of Livvy's script sitting on my desk. She brought it up to her face to read it.

Lightning fast, I snatched it out of her hands and held it below the desk so she couldn't grab it again. "This is private."

She rolled her eyes. "Well, excuse me. I thought we were working together."

"Oh, so you tell me everything you're doing? No secrets?"

She threw me a snarky smile. "Good point. Speaking of which, I gotta run. I have a lot of juicy stuff to write up."

As she headed off, I thought, *What kind of juicy stuff? Did she somehow beat me again?*

I stressed for the next half hour until Dave finally texted us to come back to his office. I'd kept my ears open for his arrival, but he had made it in without my noticing. No doubt Natalie would already be in the power chair when I got there.

Walking into Dave's office, I discovered I was right about that. But his office had a new addition: a third good chair. It was off to the side, so not great strategically; but still, it was an equalizer. Maybe Dave wasn't as oblivious to my feelings as I'd thought, and he'd noticed my frustration about getting stuck in the crappy chair.

Thinking about Dave being sensitive reminded me how much he cared about his staff getting along. I should be careful to pretend to like Natalie.

"So what do you guys have?" he asked, taking the lid off the Starbucks latte that he armed himself with every morning. "I got a pretty excited text from Petra a little while ago."

I said, "I'll be happy to start." Glancing at Natalie's pursed lips, I realized I had nothing to worry about: she didn't have me beat this time. I sighed with relief inwardly and said politely, "Unless you'd like to go first."

"Go for it," she said genially. "I'm eager to hear what you've got."

"I got it late last night or I would've texted you." I turned back to Dave. "Shall I read you guys what I wrote up?"

He grinned, in a good mood this morning, probably due to the podcast's success. "Story time, I love it. Lay it on us."

I did. I read my entire piece. For once I didn't worry about not being perfect, because Dave kept interrupting with exclamations like "Holy shit! Superglue?" and "Fucking fabulous!"

Natalie tried to act excited too, but I knew her envy was burning her up inside. It put the cherry on the whole experience.

When I finished, Dave literally slapped his knee. I'd never seen anyone actually do that before. "Man, we'll hit *ten* million on this! How'd you get this stuff anyway?"

My throat tightened. This was the one part I was nervous about. Out of the corner of my left eye I saw Natalie watching me. "I'd rather not say."

Dave frowned. "Why not?"

Because I basically stole it from Natalie. "I think it's better I not say anything."

He gave a nervous laugh. "How many laws did you break?"

"Not that many." I leaned forward earnestly. "I want to give you deniability. If the police ask you how we obtained these documents, you can say you don't know."

Dave tugged at his earlobe, uncertain. Natalie stepped in and asked, "Are you positive they're legit?"

She was obviously hoping to trip me up. But I had my response ready. "Detective O'Keefe can confirm they're authentic."

Dave smiled like he'd just figured it out. "So O'Keefe is your source?"

"I'd rather not say."

"Playing it close, huh?" But then his face darkened and he looked me hard in the eyes. "If you're wrong about this, you're walking us straight into a legal firestorm."

I looked right back at him. "These documents are the real deal. Ask O'Keefe."

Dave eyed me for a few endless moments, then finally tapped his desk and stood up. "Good, let's do this."

Yes!

He paced behind the desk. "Now ordinarily I'd say, let's build up the suspense and put this out next week. But who knows when the

Globe will find the same stuff you did. And CNN, all those guys. Joel Caldwell is in town sniffing around. So let's get right back to the studio." He stopped. "Wait a second. Natalie, what do you have for us?"

I watched her shift in her seat and knew right away the answer was: nothing one-tenth as good as what I had. She put the best face on it she could. "I'm getting great dirt on both Brandon and Viktor that'll make for an episode all on its own. But for Episode 4, I think we should focus on Sarah Fain."

Dave nodded, then turned back to me. "Okay, Petra, I'll edit your piece real quick, just diddlyshit stuff. Then hit the studio." He eyed Natalie, seeming to realize he hadn't given her anything to do. "You keep working Brandon and Viktor."

"Got it," she said cheerfully.

Dave held out his knuckles to me. "Really kick-ass job."

I knocked them. "Thanks, Dave."

As we left his office and walked back to our cubicles, Natalie asked quietly, "How *did* you get that stuff?"

"Hard work."

She threw me a more malignant glare than I had ever received in my life. "I'll find out."

"Good luck." I strode to my desk, leaving her behind.

Natalie didn't even come to the studio that morning; there was no need for her. It felt like old times, just me, Larry, and Erinne, who had gotten back from her concert tour and was in bell-bottoms again, orange and black this time.

"Thank you for helping out with this," I told her.

"Are you kidding? Thank *you.*" She reached out one of her long arms and touched my shoulder. "I mean, performing the very last thing Olivia wrote before she died—that's powerful juju."

With her and Larry supporting me, I felt at ease when I sat down to the mic. I did a lot of it in just one or two takes. Larry's eyes held renewed respect.

We were done so fast, Dave decided to drop the episode that very afternoon. This way people could listen to it during their Sunday evenings. By eight o'clock, when I made it home, we already had over a million livestreams and two million downloads—to say nothing of the millions of clicks on the newspaper article. I worked out on the calculator how much money that would make the *Clarion*. Comfort Bra was paying sixty-five thousand dollars per million listens now, and *Warriors of Ganymede* was paying eighty. Multiply that times three, and the podcast had just made the newspaper *four hundred thirty-five thousand dollars*.

Holy tomato juice.

As I walked up the steps to our apartment, I worried what Jonah's reaction to all this would be. In my heart I felt I had done a good thing. If Sarah was the killer, today's podcast was a good way to stir up evidence against her. In my opinion, the best way. Tonight I'd check my phone for messages or emails from people who had information about Sarah they hadn't shared with the police, or that the police had ignored.

When I opened the door, Jonah was in the living room watching TV on the big flat-screen he'd bought last month. At the time the purchase surprised me, since we didn't watch TV much. But now I thought that subconsciously, he'd been getting ready for married life.

"Hi, Jonah," I called out. As I kicked off my shoes, I fantasized about what we'd do when this whole podcast craziness was over. Maybe we'd spend a long weekend together on Cape Cod, just the two of us. I'd heard that Provincetown was so romantic after all the summer tourists had gone. We'd skip rocks on the ocean at sunset.

Then, as we rode home from the Cape, we could call our parents from the car and tell them about our engagement—

Jonah looked up, expressionless. "Joel Caldwell's doing a special show tonight. About your case."

"Wow," I said. I got onto the sofa beside him and kissed him. He kissed me back, a little.

"You're still mad at me," I said.

"I heard your podcast. I feel very mixed."

I would have to accept that for now. The pre-show commercials ended and Joel Caldwell came on-screen, hosting his true-crime show. "Welcome to this special edition of *Dead To Rights*," he said. "Great show tonight. We'll be talking about the Olivia Anderson murder. And we have a very special guest: a young woman who's all over the news today. Ladies and gentlemen, please join me in welcoming: Sarah Fain."

I sat up straight on the sofa. Why had Sarah agreed to appear on CNN?

She walked onto the set. She looked amazing—of course she did, with the TV makeup artists softening her red hair and brightening her blue eyes.

The studio audience applauded, hesitantly. No doubt many of them had once rooted for her in her public battle against Danny Madsen. But now they had learned about the whole Superglue thing. On top of that, she was a murder suspect.

But Sarah's tall-girl gawkiness made her sympathetic. She gave the audience a vulnerable smile, and the applause grew stronger as she sat down.

Then Sarah began to speak.

CHAPTER FORTY-FIVE

JONAH AND I watched as Sarah said "Hi" to the studio audience with an awkward wave.

"Welcome to the show, Sarah," said Caldwell.

"Thank you."

"Thank you so much. I understand this is your first appearance ever on television, even though you've gotten a lot of requests. I know we've asked you at least twice."

"Five times, actually," said Sarah, and the audience laughed, warming up to her.

I frowned. I wasn't sure how I felt about the audience liking Sarah, since I had just accused her in my podcast of maybe being a murderer. In truth, I liked her too, despite my suspicions.

Next to me on the sofa, I felt Jonah stiffen. I didn't look at him.

"So why did you agree to this interview now?" Caldwell asked.

"I just decided enough's enough. First I get raped. Then the media attacks me for reporting the guy who raped me. They tell the whole world about my substance abuse. My love life. Even my tattoos. Then they get hold of my sealed juvenile record, which is, excuse me, sealed. And now, I get accused—I mean, really?—they accuse me of murder! And all because I got raped and stood up for myself!"

She stopped, breathing hard, nostrils flaring. She looked impassioned. But not wild-eyed crazy, or like it was fake outrage.

Caldwell gave a solemn nod—not seeming to agree or disagree, just being there with her. The camera swept over the audience. They all looked rapt.

"Let's start with the murder," Caldwell said. "Sarah, did you kill Olivia Anderson?"

She gave an abrupt laugh. "No, I did not kill Olivia."

"Do you have proof of that?"

"Yes, I do," Sarah said.

I sucked in a sharp breath. She's lying. If she had an alibi, she would've told me!

"What is your proof?"

"It's right here." She held up a piece of paper, typed partly in boldface, that looked like an official document. "This is my record of admittance to the Harvard Medical Hospital Mental Health Unit on the afternoon of April 2. I was an in-patient, in their lockdown unit, until April 5. As you know, Olivia was killed on the night of April 2. So it would have been impossible for me to kill her."

I stared at the screen and thought, *are you serious?*

Caldwell asked, "Why haven't you told anyone before?"

"I did. I told the police at the time. They had the decency to keep this information private."

"What about Petra Kovach, from the *Clarion?* Why didn't you tell her?"

Exactly! If you had told me your alibi, and it checked out, I never would have put out that podcast!

"I didn't trust her. She's a reporter." Sarah looked at Caldwell and added, "No offense."

The audience laughed, releasing tension. "None taken," Caldwell said.

"I was hoping Petra would show a little common decency and not run with this story. It was based on my juvenile record. That's bull-crap, to use that against someone. It's not right." She looked at the camera, and I felt like she was looking right at me. "And what if I did tell Petra my alibi? How do I know she wouldn't twist it in some crazy way?"

I wouldn't have twisted your story. I'm not some monster!
Am I?

"That's what reporters do," Sarah said. "I mean, she already stole my juvie record somehow."

I looked to Jonah for support, but he just sat there watching the TV intently.

Caldwell gave Sarah a sympathetic nod, and she continued. "I'm gonna tell you why I admitted myself to the hospital, because now I'm sure it'll come out anyway. I was suicidal. I don't like to admit that. It's embarrassing. There's a stigma. I'd rather the world didn't know about it. But I guess I have no choice now. So the bad news is: yes, I was suicidal. The good news is: I'm not a murderer."

Sarah smiled in a way that lightened that up, and Caldwell smiled with her. Watching them, I felt crushed. I had revealed this poor girl's juvenile record and accused her of murder for no reason.

Caldwell said, "If I may ask, why were you feeling suicidal?"

"Before I answer that, there's one thing I'd like to say to Olivia's brother, Eric." She looked straight at the camera again. "Eric, I've never met you, but I'm guessing you may be watching right now. I know you tried to take your life a couple days ago, and I just want to let you know, my heart is with you. It'll get better, I promise. Don't give up, please."

Somebody clapped, and then the entire audience applauded. Oh God, she was coming across like Mother Teresa. Everybody would hate me. I kind of hated me.

Then she continued, "The reason I felt suicidal was because, yes, I did know that Olivia was planning to drop another video about me. She called me up on that Tuesday and asked if there was anything I wanted to say. I told her I felt like she was raping me all over again. She started giving me the same old stuff: 'Why didn't you report it right away? Why wait two months?' So I told her to go screw herself."

At least I'd gotten that part of the story right.

"I hung up on her. But then I started shaking. I couldn't stop. I kept thinking about all the goddamn crap I'd have to deal with all over again after this new video dropped. I couldn't sleep for three nights, and finally I signed myself in to the hospital."

"That sounds like a very wise decision." Caldwell addressed the camera. "At the end of this segment we'll give help numbers and websites for anyone who might be having these kinds of dark thoughts and feelings." He turned back to Sarah. "So I take it that was your last contact with Olivia."

"Actually, no."

Caldwell raised his eyebrows in surprise. But I suspected they had rehearsed this whole surprise earlier. "Really. When was your last contact?"

"At the hospital, before the nurses took my phone away, Olivia DM'ed me on Snapchat. This was two or three hours before she was killed. Her message said, 'I just tried to break up with a guy and he threatened to kill me.' Then she sent another message: 'I just realized he's been abusing me for a lot longer than two months, and I never reported it either.' Then came a third message that just said, 'I'm sorry.'"

My mouth fell open. *I just realized he's been abusing me for a lot longer than two months.* That had to be Viktor!

Wait, it could be Brandon, or Professor Reynolds . . .

"Wow," Caldwell said. "Do you have proof of these messages?"

"No. It's Snapchat."

"Right. So did you message her back?"

Sarah shook her head. "It was too much. I couldn't deal with it right then. But that night, after they gave me some sedatives and I was half-asleep, I got another Snapchat message. I was just starting to read it when the nurse came in and took my phone."

"Do you remember what it said?"

"I think so, but I'm not positive. I was heavily medicated by then and the nurse distracted me. I told the detectives what I remember but it didn't make any sense to them or me. They decided not to use my testimony because it was, you know, unreliable."

"So what do you remember?"

"Two words. The first one was the F word, and the second one was 'Providence.'"

I was so stunned, my throat closed up and I started coughing.

Caldwell said, "'F Providence.'"

"Right."

"Did she mean Providence like the city? Or as a synonym for God?"

"I don't know."

They kept talking, then stopped for a commercial break. I was still in shock. *Fuck Providence.*

No one else knew what that meant, but I did. Livvy was talking about the guy she'd met on America Forever.

Beside me on the sofa, Jonah said, "So what do you think?"

My mind was racing. *Livvy said somebody abused her and threatened to kill her. Then she said, "Fuck Providence." Put that together and it's obvious: The abuser who threatened her wasn't Viktor or Brandon or Reynolds. It was Providence.*

But who's Providence? What's his real name—

"That was some pretty heavy stuff," Jonah said.

I nodded. I felt numb, barely registering the expression on his face. "I know who killed her," I said quietly. "I mean, I know his internet handle."

Jonah stared. "Are you shitting me?"

"I just need to find out his real identity—"

"Did you hear what Sarah just said?" He jumped up from the sofa and glared down at me. "You stole her juvie record and told the whole world, but she's obviously innocent!"

"She should've told me about the hospital. Then I wouldn't have done that!" I couldn't deal with this right now—or with Jonah's disapproval. "Did you hear *me?*" I grabbed his arm. "I finally know who killed Livvy!"

Jonah pulled back from me and laughed, a sharp bark. "Do you know how many times you've said that in the past week?"

"But this time I'm right!"

"You're destroying lives just because you get a bug up your ass!"

I wanted to scream. "You try solving a murder without hurting anybody's feelings!"

"You have the self-awareness of a fucking flea."

"I don't need this right now."

"Neither do I." He grabbed his jacket off a wall hook and yanked open the door.

"Jonah." He turned. "I really have solved Livvy's murder. It's an internet friend of hers named Providence. I just need to get proof."

"Knock yourself out," Jonah said. Then he walked out. The door slammed shut behind him.

I sat there frozen. I felt my breath go in and out, way too stunned to cry.

My phone buzzed. It was Dave. I picked it up, like an automaton. "Hi, Dave."

"Are you watching what I'm watching?"

"Yeah."

"Come to the office. Now. We need to talk."

Then Dave hung up.

CHAPTER FORTY-SIX

HAD JONAH JUST broken up with me? I didn't know. But I had to set it aside. I couldn't have my personal and professional lives both fall apart at once. I'd never survive that. I went downstairs and ordered a Lyft to the office.

I knew Sarah's interview had made me look terrible. Jonah's reaction told me that. But I didn't get how truly awful things would be until a little while later, in the Lyft. I was watching a clip of the last few minutes of Sarah's TV interview. The driver, a thirty-something woman named Ellie with a Jamaican accent, said, "That woman is some piece of work, huh?"

I looked up from my phone, interested in the POV of an average person. "You think Sarah Fain is lying?"

"Nah, I'm talking the other woman, what's her name, Petra?"

I sank lower in my seat, hoping Ellie wouldn't recognize me.

"Lord, stay away from that one. She'd eat you alive and feed your bones to the dogs," Ellie said.

I was relieved when my phone buzzed, so I could escape this conversation. "Hi, Mama."

"Petra! Are you okay?!"

Oh no. I willed myself to ignore the panic in Mama's voice. "Yeah, I'm good. How are you?"

"They're saying such horrible things about you on TV. And the internet too!"

"Don't worry, Mama, it'll be fine."

"Is it true? Was that girl in a mental hospital?"

I was pretty sure she was, but I said, "We'll check that out."

"Why didn't you check it before you did the podcast?"

Now Mama was a critic too? "I tried to. I met with her, but she didn't tell me."

"Why not?"

I gritted my teeth. "I don't know, Mama, people are weird. Listen, I gotta run. My boss is calling," I lied.

"I hope he's not mad at you."

"Thanks, Mama. Love you."

After I clicked off, Ellie eyed me in the mirror. "Do I know you from somewhere? You seem familiar."

Why did I ever want to be famous? "A lot of people say that."

I looked down at my phone to hide my face from Ellie. Without any conscious decision by me, my fingers clicked on Twitter. #SarahFain was trending topic number one, and #PetraKovach was number two. I found some tweets heralding me as a no-bullshit reporter who did whatever was needed to uncover the truth. But they were in the distinct minority. According to most people, I was either a homophobe and I'd attacked an innocent rape victim, or I was a libtard. Apparently, the one thing Americans of all political stripes could agree on was: the hell with Petra Kovach.

We pulled up to the *Clarion* and I got out, with Ellie still frowning, trying to figure out who I was. I went up to Dave's office. Natalie was already there—in the better positioned seat, of course.

I pasted on a smile. "Hi, Dave. Hey, Natalie."

Dave tapped the desk like he was calling the meeting to order and got right into it. "We are so screwed right now. I can't believe we didn't know about the hospital. Why didn't O'Keefe tell you?"

I didn't have an answer for that. Dave shook his head. "If we'd known, we could have avoided this whole fuckup."

From the corner of my eye, I saw Natalie subtly smiling, loving my humiliation. But I had a card to play. "Dave, I feel bad we put Sarah through this, but I don't see how it's such a big fuckup. We made over four hundred thousand dollars in one afternoon—"

"Except we look like jerks. Some people still actually care about journalistic ethics—"

"I didn't do anything unethical." *At least, nothing you know about.* "And whatever pushed the boundaries, we agreed on together."

Dave waved that away. "Here's the problem. People care about the *appearance* of journalistic ethics."

"We can put out a retraction on Sarah—"

"I understand this isn't totally fair, but right now you're seen as the woman who outed a guy, caused a suicide attempt, and falsely accused a college girl of murder without checking your facts."

Natalie smirked. I wanted to punch Dave in his sanctimonious face for refusing to acknowledge his role in outing Brandon and betraying Eric.

I wanted to curl into a little ball.

No, what I really wanted to do was tell Dave I had a new murder suspect, and this time I was positive I was right. But he wouldn't listen to me. He'd react the same way Jonah did, by laughing in my face.

So I said, "I think you're overstating. People understand you can't make an omelet without breaking some eggs." *Oh God, what a pathetic metaphor.*

Dave said, "Let me state the issue clearly. Our sponsors don't want to be associated with a product that seems sleazy. Comfy Bra and *Warriors of Ganymede* both called us in the last half hour. They threatened to withdraw their ads from the next podcast."

"Oh fuck."

"I convinced them to stay"—I exhaled with relief—"but they made me promise something." He looked away from me, pained, like he didn't want to say more. Natalie pursed her lips in a sad way, but her eyes told me she was gloating. *About what? What's going on here?*

Dave continued, "They feel that you're associated with the ethical excesses of the podcast. They're scared off by all the crap on Twitter. So they don't want you narrating anymore."

My heart stopped. I could barely register his words. "You'll still be listed as a producer, but Natalie will be the face—and voice—of the podcast."

I'm getting kicked off my own show?!

And then what? Would I be such a PR problem that Dave would feel obligated to fire me?

After all this, I'd be right back where I started.

Except worse. Because even though I'd created a hit podcast, I was in danger of being canceled. How would I ever get a newspaper job after this?

Dave was waiting for my response. I felt like a little kid in the principal's office. All I could think of to say was, "Okay."

He softened. "You can still work on the show, of course. Do research, work behind the scenes."

I nodded, crushed.

But then something hardened inside me. I thought: *I'll show these fuckers.*

I'll prove Providence was the killer.

CHAPTER FORTY-SEVEN

DAVE LET OUT a loud breath, clearly relieved to get that part of the meeting over with, without me getting screaming mad or bursting into tears. He folded his hands on the desk. "Okay. So what's our next podcast about?"

I kept my mouth shut. Providence would stay my secret for now.

Natalie said, "I'll start out by apologizing for the Sarah story. Then I'll segue real quick into the next suspect. And that suspect is . . ." She leaned in toward Dave. *"Danny Madsen."*

"Danny Madsen?!" I hadn't meant to call out my incredulity so loud. I was in no position to sow discord in Dave's presence. "Why would *he* be a suspect?"

Natalie answered triumphantly, "I discovered the real truth about Olivia's final video. It's not what we thought. Olivia was planning to reveal she'd changed her mind about Danny. She now thought he was a rapist after all."

I stared at Natalie. So did Dave. If she was right about this, it was our biggest blockbuster yet.

"What if Danny found out?" Natalie said. "He comes to Olivia's dorm room, heated argument . . ." She slammed a fist on the desk. "He kills her. A little extreme, but he's a rapist, he's an extreme guy."

Dave asked the question I would have asked if I'd felt comfortable enough. "Do you have any evidence for this?"

"Yes I do—as of one hour ago. Larry and I found something Olivia wrote the day she died. It's basically an outline for her final video. Very short, just three lines." She reached into a manila folder and took out a piece of paper that was blank except for the very top. "I printed it out. I'll read it to you."

I waited, my heart sinking. Natalie must have found something on Livvy's laptop that I didn't, because I ran out of time. She cleared her throat and read: *"TONIGHT'S VIDEO: 1) I feel weird, but this is gonna be super fucking personal."*

Natalie looked up at Dave. "Those are the exact words Olivia said in her final video."

Then she resumed reading. *"2) I think I was wrong about Sarah Fain. And the rape. 3) My own personal shit."* Natalie looked up again. "That's all Olivia wrote. But clearly she was planning to say some things Danny would have found extremely upsetting."

Awfully thin as a murder motive, I thought, but maybe I just felt that way because I was so sure Providence was the killer. I hoped Dave would agree with me and take Natalie down a notch. Instead he asked, "Where did you get hold of that?"

"From Olivia's computer."

I blinked, astonished. Would Natalie admit she stole the computer from Eric's apartment? Dave would be furious. That was going *too* far. Sure, I had tried to steal it from Eric's apartment myself—but I would never have admitted it.

"How did you get hold of her computer?" Dave asked.

Natalie said, "That night when I went to Eric's place? Before I went in, I checked his garbage cans. I always do that. It's totally legal. And it turned out that, for some reason, Eric threw out Olivia's computer that night."

Bullshit! I wanted to scream. *You snatched it from the box in Eric's closet!* But if I said that, I'd be revealing I broke into his apartment.

Dave laughed. "That's brilliant, checking the garbage can. Nice work, Nat."

Ever the team player, she responded, "Larry did great work too. He spent twenty-four hours hacking that computer and finally got in."

I knew I was supposed to compliment Natalie too, but I couldn't bring myself to do it. Meanwhile Dave's face clouded over and he tugged on his earlobe. One day that thing would fall off. He said, "I like it. But I'd hate to accuse a new suspect and have that blow up in our faces too. We just went through that."

Natalie leaned back confidently in her chair. "This is the best way to clean up our PR damage. People will say hey, these guys were rough on Sarah, but now they're hitting Danny too. They're being fair, going after both sides, just trying to get the truth."

Dave broke into a broad smile. "You're right. Our sponsors will love it."

This podcast had become a cesspool of bullshit. Why had it taken me so long to realize this? Why did I have to fall into the muck first and lose everything I loved?

I needed to haul myself out. I was desperate to get back to my cubicle and start the *real* work. Nailing Providence for murder.

At last Dave dismissed us from his office. As we headed out, Natalie turned to me. "Sorry about all this. Tough break, Petch."

In case Dave could still hear, I said, "Thanks." Then I fast-walked down the hall, leaving her behind. I went past my cubicle, because on second thought, I didn't think I could work here tonight. The office felt too poisonous right now. I wasn't sure I could handle working at home either, with Jonah's things all around me. I went to a Starbucks that was open 'til midnight.

I sat down in the almost-empty coffee shop with my double espresso and thought: *how do I find Providence?*

CHAPTER FORTY-EIGHT

I WAS TEMPTED to call Mateo for advice, but we still hadn't spoken since our big argument, and it would take more groveling than I had time for. So I took out a pen and wrote down everything I knew about Providence on my napkin.

"*Alt-right asshole*," I began. "*On America-Forever.com. Met w/ Livvy in Boston (how often?). Knew she lived on first floor (was in her room?). Abused her for 'a lot longer than two months' and 'threatened to kill me.*'"

It was nowhere near enough to ID him. The best plan would be to track down his ISP. That's what a super-tech-savvy person would do. But I didn't want to ask Larry for help, and certainly not Jonah. My stomach flipped when I thought about him. I decided to take another, deeper look at Providence's posts on America-Forever, searching for clues to who he was.

A lot of his posts were in response to Orphan Girl. Once again, I was struck by how kind and sympathetic he sounded.

But reading his posts now, I saw he often gave them a twist at the end to pull Orphan Girl in closer. A typical post was: "*I feel so bad for what happened to your mom, getting killed by an illegal immie like that. I've found the best solution to private pain is community action. We need to stand up to the p4k libs! I can help you with ways to do that.*"

I wondered if it was Providence who encouraged Livvy to start her YouTube career, as a way to deal with her "private pain." Of course, she wouldn't have needed much encouragement; she had always dreamed of being famous.

I noticed again that Providence and Robert Heath used a lot of the same language, including rare words like "immies" and "p4k," which I learned meant "pitchfork," though why liberals would be associated with pitchforks I didn't get. Why did Providence and Heath's vocabulary overlap like that? Maybe they hung out together—

Wait a minute. The thing that had itched at my subconscious when I first looked at America Forever finally came to the surface. *How did Heath even know that Livvy was on this site?* She wasn't Livvy here, she was Orphan Girl. As far as I could tell, the only person on this site who ever met her in real life was Providence.

Maybe Providence and Heath knew each other—and Providence told Heath about Orphan Girl's real identity.

Which meant Heath would be able to tell me who Providence was!

But first I'd need to get Heath to talk somehow. He must be out on bail by now. Unfortunately, he hated me.

I checked the time: 11:15 p.m., giving me another forty minutes at Starbucks before they closed. What approach should I use on Heath?

I didn't know much about him, except he was a jerk who liked guns and lived in Revere, a mostly white, working-class section of Boston. I looked him up on Facebook, but his settings were private. He didn't have an Insta account or Twitter feed that I could find.

Then I googled "Robert Heath Revere" and found a blog: *America Arising.* That sure sounded like him. I clicked on the home page and saw it was devoted to the same alt-right stuff I'd been reading way too much of lately: "protecting Western civilization," "they will not replace us," etcetera.

I went to his bio page and read: *"My name is Robert Heath and I'm just a working-class kid from Providence. In the military that was my nickname, Providence—"*

My jaw fell open.

Providence and Robert Heath are the same person? How does that make sense?!

But the tingle in my spine told me I was right. This would explain why Providence always seemed to post a reply to Livvy right after Heath did. They were the same guy!

Maybe by having "Providence" and "RHeath" echo each other's thoughts, saying pretty much the same thing to Livvy twice, it made what they said sound more powerful and believable. Like a miniature groundswell. Maybe he even had other personas responding to Orphan Girl too. He targeted her because she sounded vulnerable—and because she was a teenage girl.

He seduced her into getting together in person, pursuing his plan of being the one guy in liberal Boston that she trusted. They became lovers—except to Livvy it ended up feeling more like abuse.

Then Livvy started going out with Brandon. That must have been hard enough for Heath, but then she did something even worse: she hooked up with a fucking "p4K lib" Harvard professor. Heath must have been furious.

Maybe furious enough to kill her in a moment of passion.

I had judged Heath as a scary but ultimately harmless nut. But really he was the alt-right version of an ISIS recruiter.

My adrenalin roared. Right now might be the perfect time to talk to him. He had probably watched Sarah's interview and freaked out at the "Fuck Providence" revelation. Maybe he was sitting alone in his apartment tonight, scared that cops or reporters would figure out who "Providence" was and come knocking on his door. Speaking of vulnerable, he could be at his weakest point now. Ready to open up.

But I wasn't about to go to his home this late at night, considering he'd already shot at me, or above me, and might very well be a murderer. I tried People Finder and found his phone number. I decided I would record our call. Sure, it was illegal, but I'd sort that out later. This was too important.

It was still a quarter to midnight; I had fifteen more minutes at Starbucks. Ignoring the barista with two nose rings who was cleaning tabletops all around me, I turned on the recording app and dialed Heath's number.

His phone rang once, twice, a third time, and then he picked up.

CHAPTER FORTY-NINE

"Petchura Kovass," Heath said, either slurring his words or mispronouncing my name. "What the hell do you wannnt?"

Slurring, I decided. Drunk. *Good.* My pulse raced. I would be direct and try to cut straight through his defenses. "I know who you are. You're Providence."

He gave an odd laugh, a loud "Huh-huh-huh." It confirmed my opinion he was wasted. "Well, aren't you clever. So fucking what?"

He just admitted he's Providence! I kept pushing. "Speaking of the F word, what did Olivia mean by 'Fuck Providence'?"

He snorted. "How the fuck should I know?"

"Because you talked to her that day, and she told you it was over."

"What was over?"

"Your affair."

"You dumb bitch. I never had an affair with Olivia."

"Sure you did. That's what she meant, when she said someone was abusing her. You started having sex with her when she was still underage."

He said angrily, "It was Reynolds she had the affair with. I only had sex with her once."

Yes! Even if he was drunk, I couldn't believe I was getting him to talk so easily. "Then why did Livvy tell Sarah, 'Fuck Providence'?"

"'Cause I'm the one who convinced her to do the 'Who Raped Who?' video. I said it would get three million clicks. And it did!" There was triumph in his voice, but now it turned to outrage. "But then Olivia decided she was wrong and that girl really did get raped. She was gonna apologize in her next video. Of all the stupid ideas."

"You were against it?"

"Hell yeah, I said don't be an idiot. First rule of political warfare: Never apologize. Always attack."

I was the last customer at Starbucks, and the nose-ringed barista came closer with her cleaning rag. I turned away. "Did you always tell Olivia what to put in her videos?"

"I was her advisor. We DM'ed each other twenty times a day. And we'd meet in person every weekend. I saw her potential. I made her. She woulda been bigger than Ann Coulter, Kayleigh McEnany, any of them. She coulda been president one day."

"So when she decided to go against your advice, that must've really upset you."

"That dickwad professor got in her head."

"You felt she should only listen to you."

There was a pause, accompanied by a gulping sound. He was drinking something. "I loved her, you know. Just 'cause we only did it that once . . . She was the most beautiful person I ever met." I heard the drinking again. "Now she's dead, and everybody'll know about us. I'll have to talk about how much I loved her to bitches like you and the fucking cops. You'll all make it sound like we had some kind of sick relationship."

"Robert . . ." Despite the pain in his voice, I was excited. I felt so close to getting a confession. I tried to make my voice gentle. "I know you loved her. You didn't mean to hurt her. But you did, didn't you?"

Heath laughed. "Huh-huh-huh." A chill raced down my back. "Are you asking if I killed her?"

"I know you did. You were already pissed off she was dating Brandon Allen. Then you found out about the liberal professor."

"That fucking guy. It's his fault she's dead. I saw a message on her phone about how she liked sucking his cock."

Whoa. "I can see where that would be too much for you."

"I always thought one day she'd split up with Brandon, and then we'd get together for real. But when I saw that message, I knew it would never happen. It was all bullshit. All of it. Just bullshit. She was leaving me behind." I heard him drink and wondered if it was beer or something stronger. Then he answered that question for me. "You know, I'm sitting here in my bedroom drinking Jack Daniels and thinking. All these people that were part of this thing almost committed suicide. First Sarah ... Then Eric ... You think anybody will actually do it?"

The hairs rose on the back of my neck. Was he talking about himself? "Listen, Robert, you must be under a lot of pressure."

"Pressure's my middle name, bitch."

"Can I make a suggestion? Why don't you turn yourself in?"

He gave a short bitter laugh, but I kept going. "Olivia deserves that. You made a mistake in the heat of passion. People will understand. I think it'll help you turn your life around if you get honest."

"I'll tell you something funny. The cops took my Glock 17 after they caught me for that little shooting incident the other night. But they didn't touch my Glock 9."

As I thought about how to respond, the barista said, "Excuse me, ma'am, you'll have to leave."

"Wait just a minute," I told the barista.

Heath seemed to believe I had directed that to him. "No, I don't think I can wait," he said. "Fact is, I shoulda offed myself as soon as it happened. I can still see her body lying there on the floor."

"Robert, hold on—"

I thought I heard a sob. "It's never gonna end, you know. The pain will just get worse. You and your fucking podcast are bringing it all back."

"Please, don't do anything stupid—"

I heard a noise that sounded like he was gagging.

"Robert?" I said. He didn't answer. "What's wrong? What are you doing?"

Then I heard a gunshot come over the phone.

"Robert?!"

There was no reply.

PART THREE
THE GUILTY PARTY

CHAPTER FIFTY

I SAT THERE in Starbucks shaking. The barista had heard the gunshot too. She stood there, rag in hand, staring down at me in horror.

"What was that sound?" she asked.

"I have to go." My legs were wobbly, but I managed to make it out of the Starbucks, feeling the barista's eyes on me the whole way.

People were spilling out of the bar next door, laughing and drinking in the warm, Indian-summer night. It was Sunday, but they were stretching out the weekend as far as it would go. Two young women in short skirts sang a K-pop tune about falling in love with the man on the moon.

Walking past them, I tried to get my brain working again. I knew I should call 911. It was conceivable Heath was still alive. Based on that gagging sound, I thought he had put the gun in his mouth; but even so, some people must survive that. I dialed the three digits and was about to hit the green button.

But I couldn't bring myself to do it. My phone call with Heath would become public knowledge. I'd have yet another black mark against me, even worse than all the others: I got on the phone with a man and drove him to suicide. He was a murderer, but still, how would people view it?

I felt like a shit, but I couldn't take that chance, not now, not when my career and my life were so precarious. Besides, I knew from Robert Heath's driver's license that he lived in an apartment. No doubt the other people in the building, awakened from sleep by a midnight gunshot, would call 911 themselves.

In the end, I didn't call. Another choice I would have to live with.

I took a Lyft home and walked up the stairs. Jonah was still gone, as I'd feared but expected. He was probably sleeping at his office. I poured myself a glass of wine and sat down on the living room sofa. I didn't want to call Jonah for advice, so I bit the bullet and tried Mateo.

Since it was so late, I didn't expect him to answer, but I got lucky. He picked up on the second ring. "Petra, I've been following you on the news. You seem busy." He didn't sound particularly warm, but at least he sounded wide awake.

I gripped the armrest of the sofa. "Mateo, I know you're still mad at me for outing Brandon, and I really do apologize about that. I fucked up, especially because now I know he's innocent. But I need help, Mateo."

"What's wrong, besides what I've been reading about?"

I started to sob.

Finally his voice softened. *"Chica,* what is it?"

I got control of myself and told him everything. I played my recording of that final phone call.

"Holy shit," Mateo said after the gunshot.

"I know."

"Honey, you did everything you could to stop him. It's not your fault."

The tears began falling again.

Mateo said, "It sounded to me like when you called, he already had a gun in one hand and Jack Daniels in the other, getting ready to pull the trigger."

I nodded and sniffed, my nose all stuffed up from crying. Then we checked the internet. I was hoping that somehow the whole thing might turn out to be a hoax Heath had played on me. But we found reports of a shooting in Revere. A suspected suicide. Details to follow.

I hugged my knees. "Am I the world's worst person?"

"No. Do I think you've been overaggressive in your reporting? Especially with Brandon? Yeah. But you're far from a bad person."

"I'm afraid I'll get canceled and never get another job."

"Look at the bright side."

I laughed despite myself. "There's a bright side?"

"You solved Olivia's murder. I know this sounds harsh, but that guy dying is no great loss. He's a murderer."

"He is, isn't he? I mean, he basically confessed, right?"

"Yes, he did. You wanna play it again?"

"Yeah, but let's stop it before the gunshot." I hit the button on my app and we listened all the way up to when Heath said, *"Fact is, I shoulda offed myself as soon as it happened. I can still see her body lying there on the floor."* Then I hit STOP.

Mateo said, "Sure sounds like a confession to me."

I took a big sip of wine. "I wish I had something more airtight. People will say maybe he was talking about seeing her body on the internet the next day."

"That's really reaching, *chica.*"

"But people do that. I don't want Dave or Natalie or Detective O'Keefe challenging me. If I go public with this and the whole world starts debating whether I drove an innocent man to suicide, I'll never live that down. *Never.*"

Mateo's soothing voice came over the phone. "Petra, I know you've been through a lot lately. But I think you're better off just being straightforward. Play the recording for Dave and the cops, and whatever happens, happens. You haven't done anything wrong. It'll work out."

I wanted to believe him. But Mateo's only reporting experience had been in college and one brief year afterward. He didn't get journalism in the real world, where careers flourished and foundered on unquantifiable winds of human emotion, and if you made one false move you were dead.

"I'll sleep on it," I said.

But when I went to bed that night, sleep didn't come. I wanted to feel great about catching Livvy's killer at last. But that gunshot kept ringing in my ears. Along with Heath's more-or-less confession.

I felt sure my instincts were right: Heath's words on that phone call wouldn't be enough to end this. Half of the country would think it was fake news. They'd still believe that Professor Reynolds killed Livvy and I was some kind of Typhoid Mary who caused people to attempt suicide—and in Heath's case, succeed. There would be no closure for Livvy's family. And I would be canceled, and unemployable—maybe forever.

I got up and ate a bowl of cereal, drank more wine, paced the living room, lay on the sofa, got up again, and lay back down on the rug. I felt more hopeless as the endless night wore on. Finally, I closed my eyes.

But then they sprang open again. I had an idea.

I'll frame the guilty man!

Then I thought: *I've had so many brilliant ideas in the past two weeks that backfired. Don't get sucked in again.*

But I couldn't stop thinking about my plan. The more I considered it, the more I liked it. It was risky—*but really not that risky,* I told myself. *And it should work.*

Mainly, I was beyond desperate. It was the only way I could find to get uncanceled and save my career. At the same time, I'd be getting closure for Eric and Viktor, who I'd hurt so badly. All the people who had been falsely accused of killing Livvy, largely because of my own actions, would no longer have to live under a cloud.

Livvy could finally rest in peace.

It's perfect, I thought. *But will I really go through with it?*

I jumped off the rug. *Hell yes. And I better start right now while it's still dark.*

It was three-thirty a.m. I grabbed Jonah's black hoodie from the closet and called a Lyft, giving an address three blocks from Eric's house. I walked the rest of the way. Eric was still an in-patient, so his apartment should be empty. It certainly looked that way. I hit the back porch—and the dog next door began barking.

I froze. But the barking died down. I reached under the ficus pot, grabbed the key, and let myself inside.

I hadn't felt so focused since—since when? Since I was a kid, writing that Letter to the Editor. I knew exactly where to go. I opened Eric's bedroom closet and pulled down the big box of Livvy's belongings. I took out the red running shoes with black laces that had been on top of the shoebox by the door, the night Livvy was killed.

I put the shoes in a plastic bag I'd brought with me, and stuffed the bag in my purse. Then I left the house.

It wasn't yet dawn. I walked a few blocks away and called a Lyft to the *Clarion*. When I got there, the building was mostly empty.

I went up to my cubicle and opened my bottom desk drawer. My shirt was still there, with the spot of Robert Heath's blood on it. I felt a wave of terror but forced it down. I put the shirt inside my purse next to the shoes and headed for the old restroom downstairs, the one with just one stall. I wouldn't have to worry as much about the night janitor barging in on me.

I knew I was committing felonies—tampering with evidence and obstructing justice. But I didn't think I would get caught. And what choice did I have, for me and for everybody else?

I took out Livvy's right shoe and put it next to the sink. It still looked brand new, spotless except for maybe one tiny speck of dirt on the black shoelace. I examined the insole of Livvy's shoe. It was the same shade of wine red as the outsides of her shoes.

Then I took out my shirt, found the spot of Heath's blood, and began rubbing it hard against the insole of Livvy's shoe, at the heel.

Heath's blood was long dry, and I worried none of it would transfer. So I turned on the sink and wet down the blood a little, then rubbed it even harder on the heel of the insole. That area was a slightly darker shade of red now; I hoped it was partly from blood and not just from being damp. After two minutes of rubbing, the spot of blood on my shirt was much lighter; presumably some of the blood had transferred to the insole.

Satisfied I'd done what I needed to do, and it was the only thing I *could* do, I put everything back in my purse and returned to my cubicle. I stuffed my shirt back in the bottom drawer, then set Livvy's right shoe on the floor underneath the desk where nobody would see it if they came in. I sat and waited for the shoe to dry.

A shiver went through me, as I thought about what I was doing. But I told myself, *this wrong thing I'm doing will correct all the other wrong things I've done.*

An hour later, the insole was dry—and still discolored, very slightly. *That* has *to be blood.*

Now I just needed to convince Jonah to help me.

I hated to get him involved. But as far as I could see, there was no alternative. Also, I was confident that if I did get in trouble with the police—which wouldn't happen—none of the blame would land on him.

My heart, I thought, was in the right place.

CHAPTER FIFTY-ONE

THE SUN ROSE as I walked the mile and a half to the WeWork office on Charles Street. I was shivering from the autumn cold, but the glowing pink in the sky made it worth it. When I got to WeWork, I texted Jonah, HI, ARE YOU AT THE OFFICE?

He didn't respond. But a young woman wearing a tie-dyed shirt and sandals came along and opened the front door with her key card. She didn't object when I walked in behind her.

I went up to the fourth floor and entered the common room. As I'd hoped, Jonah was sprawled out on the sofa asleep. I went over to the espresso machine and brewed a cup.

The noise woke him up. He blinked a couple times, looking confused, like he couldn't remember where he was. Then he saw me. His lips parted with puzzlement, then pursed into a tight, foreboding line.

But I thought maybe I detected a bit of longing in the way his eyes watched me. "I made you coffee," I said. I brought it over and held out the cup.

He sat up. "Am I supposed to thank you?"

"No. Just listen, that's all."

Finally he took the cup from me. I started in. "You know how the police always thought Livvy must have stabbed the killer with her nail file? And he took the nail file with him because his blood was on it?"

Jonah lifted his eyebrows, suspicious. "What's the punch line?"

"The police tested the blood on Livvy's clothes, looking for the killer's DNA. Unfortunately, they only found Livvy's DNA. But here's the thing." I brought Livvy's shoes out of the plastic bag in my purse. *"They never tested her shoes.* Probably because they were all the way across the room, and the cops took a look and didn't see anything. But I got a chance to look at them myself—and check this out." I held out the insole of the right shoe. "Doesn't this look like it could be blood? On the heel?"

"What are you up to now, Petra?"

"Just look. Please."

Jonah reached for the shoe, but I moved it away. "Don't touch it. It's bad enough my DNA is on it."

Jonah leaned forward and eyed the insole. "I guess that could be blood maybe." His eyebrows narrowed. "It's a big long shot though, that he would bleed a couple drops right into the shoe."

I knew what I was saying was shaky, but it had to be just barely logical enough. "It was a new shoe and it's totally clean except for this one discoloration. And it was right by the door. I'm thinking when Livvy stabbed the killer, he didn't start bleeding that much right away. Or he kept his cut covered, wherever it was, on his arm, say, so it wouldn't bleed. But then when he had to open the door, his arm got jostled, and a little blood dropped into the shoe."

Actually, when I say it out loud, that kind of makes sense.

Jonah said, "I mean sure, it's possible—"

That was the only opening I needed. "Could you test it for me?

His eyes widened. "Me?"

"Your company. Isn't that something you guys can do?"

He shook his head. "God, you're relentless."

I sat beside him on the sofa. "Look, I know I've been a shit to you." My eyes got wet, and I swear I wasn't trying to manipulate him, they were honest tears. "I don't know if you're ever gonna forgive me. But I need this. I can't tell you how much. This is my one chance to really, truly, no-bullshit, catch Livvy's killer. Yeah, it's a long shot. But what if we get lucky? I've messed up so many times on this. Maybe I can finally make it right."

He looked away from me. "We do genetics for drug companies. We've never done any work like this."

"But you could, right?" I put my hand on his arm. "Please, Jonah. I don't know who else to turn to."

"Why not just go to the cops?"

"O'Keefe won't listen to me."

"Why not ask Dave?"

"He wouldn't have any idea who to contact. And I don't want him and Natalie to know about this, not until it actually works out."

"Is this even legal, what you're asking me to do? Where did you get those shoes anyway?"

I didn't answer directly. "They were in an evidence box from the trial. The police aren't even interested in them anymore. Nobody is—except me. And I hope you."

Jonah put his cup down on the floor. "Pretty ballsy, coming here and asking me for a favor."

"I know."

"How do I know you're not lying to me again?"

Oh God. I *was* lying to him yet again.

I told myself he'd never know. No one would. And no one would be hurt. People would only be helped. Their names scrolled by in my mind: Eric. Viktor. Brandon. Sarah. William Reynolds.

And yeah, me. I'm not denying that.

I said, "I understand your not trusting me. But if this test succeeds, think how much it would mean for everyone involved. And there's one more thing you should know. Robert Heath, the man who shot at me, committed suicide tonight. But before he did, he confessed to killing Livvy."

Jonah's jaw dropped open, then he frowned. "If he confessed, then why do you need his DNA?"

"Because it's not a full-on confession. I'll play you the tape."

I clicked PLAY and walked over to the other side of the room so I wouldn't have to hear it again. When the gunshot blasted out from the phone, I came back to Jonah. He was still on the sofa, looking up at me in shock. I waited.

"Oh my God, Petra. That's horrible. Are you okay?"

"Trying to be. But that's why I need to do this. I need to know."

Jonah gazed at me. Finally he said, "Okay."

I wanted to throw my arms around him and thank him. But another part of me wanted to spill everything and quit deceiving him and tell him I was so sorry. Instead I just said, "Thank you."

Maybe he wanted to put his arms around me too, or maybe he was mad at himself for giving in, but he looked away, uncomfortable. "No problem. I'll ask Jesse and Wang Lei to help."

"That sounds great."

His eyes darkened for a moment. No doubt he was thinking how pissed off he still was at me. Then he gave his head a little shake, as if sloughing that off so he could get down to business. "Like you said, there might be DNA from you and Olivia on the shoe. We'll need DNA samples from both of you, so we know what to exclude."

"I already thought of that. Livvy's DNA profile was in one of the prosecution's trial exhibits, when they were proving it was her blood on Reynolds' jacket. I'll get that from the courthouse. And, of course, for my DNA, I can just spit in a cup."

Jonah nodded. "Now if we do find DNA from a third person, we'll need the police to get us Robert Heath's DNA so we'll know if it's a match."

"I'll work on that," I said.

CHAPTER FIFTY-TWO

JONAH'S COLLEAGUES PROMISED to do a rush job and extract the DNA from the insole in twenty-four hours. So I went to the Massachusetts State Court on Suffolk Street as soon as it opened. After filling out endless forms in three different offices—the court reporter, the chief clerk, and the court secretary—I finally got my hands on the trial exhibit with Livvy's DNA profile. I emailed Jonah a copy.

Now I had to pray that Jesse and Wang Lei really could recover Heath's DNA from that insole. I worried that all the rubbing I'd done, or something else I hadn't thought of, might have degraded the DNA in some way. Meanwhile, I was supposed to meet with Dave and Natalie at eleven. But I spent too long at the courthouse, so I ran into Dave's office breathless, twenty minutes late. I had prepared an excuse, but he didn't seem to even notice my lateness. He was too engrossed in what Natalie was saying.

Sitting in the chair off to the side, I felt like a hostage, forced to listen to Natalie hold forth about her amazing successes. Last night she had finally gotten one of Livvy's old dormmates, a comp sci major named Karina, to open up. What Karina said had further implicated Danny Madsen in the murder.

I shifted uneasily while Natalie pulled out her phone and played a recording of the interview. *"A couple nights before Olivia was killed,"* Karina said, *"we were hanging out in the hall, and she told me Danny was a creep and maybe he did rape that girl. It wouldn't surprise me one bit if she was planning to trash him in her next video."*

"I like it," Dave said. "But we need more evidence than that—"

"I got more," Natalie said confidently. I groaned without thinking, so loud I was afraid they'd hear it. The more "evidence" Natalie got, the harder it would be for me to convince people that Robert Heath killed Livvy. Without the DNA, it would be impossible.

"Lay it on me," said Dave.

"I got hold of a third-string Harvard linebacker named Elvin Johnson. He says that the week Olivia died, Danny told some guys in the locker room she was a, quote, 'two-faced bitch.' That's why he and Brandon quit getting along, 'cause Brandon heard about it."

Dave nodded. "Nice—"

"And I'm saving the best for last," Natalie said. "I got through to Eric."

My head snapped back. "I thought Eric was still in the psych ward."

Natalie smiled. "Yeah, but I got him anyway. He comes out tomorrow, and he promised me an interview."

Dave shook his head admiringly. "Nat, you're unstoppable."

She gave a modest shrug. "Well, he does owe me something. After all, I saved his life."

I pictured ramming Natalie's blonde head into Dave's desk.

All in all, it looked like Episode 5 would be another hit—and I would have almost nothing to do with it. When I passed Dave in the hall later that afternoon and said hi, he didn't meet my eyes. He said "hi," while looking at the wall. I felt like I was already being canceled, right there in the office.

I still couldn't believe I was in this situation, after I'd earned the newspaper so much money. A lot of TV news shows and newspapers asked to do interviews with me, but Dave said no to them all. "I'm sure they just want to ask you about screwing up the Sarah Fain story. And they'll probably give you a hard time about the other stuff too, if you don't mind me being blunt."

"No problem," I said, as I died inside. In less than a week my reputation had exploded into the stratosphere and then plummeted into the mud. I only had one hope of surviving. I spent the afternoon eating chocolate and pacing, unable to concentrate. Finally, at seven o'clock, while I sat at my desk biting my thumbnail down to the nub, my phone buzzed. It was Jonah. "Please, God," I whispered to myself. I could barely breathe as I clicked the green button. "Hi, what's up?"

"Guess what!" Jonah said, and I knew right away my prayers had been answered. My breath came out in a rush as he continued, "We found your DNA, Olivia's DNA—and also a *third* DNA profile in the insole of the right shoe! And it's not from sweat or hair—it's from straight-up blood."

"Oh my God." I wanted to cry. "My God."

"So you need to get Robert Heath's DNA profile right away."

"I'm on it. Send me the lab report."

I got off the phone and immediately called Detective O'Keefe. I was hoping she'd take my call simply to gloat at how bad I looked on the whole Sarah Fain thing.

I was right. She picked up on the first ring. "It's my favorite reporter," she said. "What's your latest ridiculous theory?"

"My latest theory is you fucked up. You never checked Olivia's shoes for DNA."

There was a brief pause, then O'Keefe said dismissively, "Her shoes were on the other side of the room."

"By the door. And a drop of the murderer's blood fell into the right shoe."

"Oh really. And you know this how?"

"Because the highly regarded DNA lab Authentic Genes tested Olivia's shoe at my request. You guys missed it, but the dark red insole was very slightly discolored with dried blood. The lab found DNA from Olivia, me—and a third party. With the third party, it was blood."

"Kovach, what game are you playing?"

"I'm emailing you the lab report as we speak. You'll see this is no game. And now I have something else to tell you. You know Olivia's final Snapchat message to Sarah Fain? 'Fuck Providence'?"

"You got a crazy theory on that too?"

"Check the chat board for America-Forever.com. Olivia's handle was Orphan Girl. Robert Heath had two handles: RHeath and Providence. He got to know Olivia intimately through that chat board. I have reason to believe he's the man who killed her."

"Oh, for Christ's sake."

"You know what, O'Keefe?" I stood up in my cubicle. "I'm sick of your shit. Yeah, sometimes I've been right on this case and sometimes I've been wrong, but I have always been motivated by finding out the truth. I was right that Olivia posted on social media about incest. I'm pretty sure I was right that her boyfriend was gay. I was right she was gonna talk about Sarah Fain in her last video. Now I have evidence against Robert Heath, and I'm right about that too. It's evidence I won't tell you about just yet, but you better believe it's powerful as fuck. So I need you to go to the morgue and get Robert Heath's blood and do a DNA profile, and compare it to the profile I'm emailing you. I need you to do it now. Because tomorrow night I'm doing a podcast, and you better be on board with solving this murder, because if not, I will unleash a fiery shitstorm on your lazy

ass and I know you only have a few months 'til retirement but I will
make sure those few months are hell."

I stopped, breathing heavily with anger. I had just raised my voice
way more than I should have, but luckily no one was in the hallway
now. I stood there and waited for O'Keefe to respond. If she said no,
I had no idea what I'd do.

Finally she spoke up. "Tell you what, Kovach. Like you say,
Heath's body is in the morgue. Soon as we get off the phone, I'll take
his blood up to the lab myself and get them working on the profile
right now. And you know why I'm doing that?"

"Because deep down you want to be a good person and do the
right thing?"

"No."

"Because you're scared I really will make your life hell?"

"No. Because I'll enjoy throwing it in your face when you're
wrong once again."

O'Keefe hung up, leaving me to stare at my dead phone. I could
hardly believe I'd gotten her to do what I wanted. I pounded the
desk with my fist and did a little whirling dance in my cubicle.

How long would it take the police lab to get Heath's profile and
compare it to the one I'd sent them? Jonah said that theoretically
you could do it in as little as eight hours. Tired though I was, I had
trouble sleeping that night. It didn't help that I was alone, because
Jonah was staying at Jesse's place. I wondered, if my DNA ploy succeeded, would Jonah ever come to forgive and trust me again?

The next morning at the office, I couldn't sit still. I wound up my
toy dragon over and over, creating an obstacle course on my desk
that he would have to crawl through. Then, at eleven thirty, when I
was in the break room brewing yet another cup of coffee, my phone
buzzed. It was O'Keefe. The coffee pot fell from my fingers.

"We got the results back," she said.

I couldn't tell anything from her voice. Had I screwed up somehow? "And?"

"You really got that DNA from the insole of Olivia's shoe? And you can prove it?"

"Yes, of course. Authentic Genes took a video of their whole extraction process. What did you find?"

"You sure you didn't plant the blood on that insole?"

My heart missed a beat. "Detective," I said, trying to sound offended, "do you really think I'm that fucking sleazy? And besides, how would I get Robert Heath's blood?"

Over the phone, I heard O'Keefe sigh. It was the first sign of any kind of weakness I had ever heard from her. Finally she said, "Yeah, well listen, Kovach. You got a match. I have to admit, I think you may have just caught Olivia Anderson's killer."

My throat caught. *I convinced O'Keefe!*

My plan had worked!

"You still there?" said O'Keefe. "I said it looks like you might be right."

"Thank you, Detective. I appreciate that."

"Let's not pop the champagne just yet. You said you had more evidence this asshole's guilty. What is it?"

I knew I couldn't put it off any longer. "I'm gonna play a recording for you. It's a phone conversation I had with Robert Heath two nights ago."

"A recording. Did you have permission?"

"Don't ask," I said, and proceeded to play O'Keefe the recording. It was still painful to hear, especially the gunshot. But the confession was sweet. *"I shoulda offed myself as soon as it happened. I can still see her body lying there on the floor."*

After the recording was over, O'Keefe said, "Talk about ending with a bang. I'll need a copy of that."

"You got it. Could I ask you for a favor? Would you mind not going public with this until I put out my next podcast, which I promise will be very soon?"

"You and your clicks," O'Keefe said. "Yeah, whatever, we'll work something out."

CHAPTER FIFTY-THREE

As soon as I got off the phone, I headed for Dave's office and knocked on the door.

"Come in," he said.

I did, and found Natalie there, settled into the chair across from him. I assumed they were plotting out the next episode and hadn't bothered to include me. I decided not to sit down. I would stand tall. "Hi guys," I said brightly. "I have interesting news."

Dave raised a dubious eyebrow. "Yeah, what's that?"

"I just found out who killed Olivia."

Natalie laughed out loud. "I'm sorry, but what is this, the fourth time you've caught the killer?"

"I have DNA evidence. Blood from the killer inside Olivia's shoe."

They both eyed me with disbelief. I continued, "And guess what? Detective O'Keefe agrees with me."

Dave frowned, like it was dawning on him this just might be something he needed to take seriously. But he kept his tone light. "So who's the killer now?"

"Here's a recording from two nights ago. A phone call between me and him."

I hit the button and played it for them. They listened in growing amazement, then cringed at the gunshot. I did too, inwardly, but kept my cool. I folded my arms and said, "So what do you guys think?"

Dave hesitated, then drawled, "Natalie, we might need to rethink that next episode." He turned to me. "Sit down, Petra. Tell me the whole story. From the beginning."

So I did. For once I didn't mind sitting off to the side, because I would have had Dave's full attention no matter where I was. I told him everything—leaving out the part about planting the blood, of course. By the time I finished, he was up on his feet bouncing around the office. "Holy crap, we are actually solving the murder! No podcast *ever* does that. We'll be the biggest podcast in history!" He beamed at me. "Petra, I underestimated you. You are one ballbusting hound dog of a reporter!"

I beamed back at him.

Natalie stepped in, trying to poke holes in my story. "But it doesn't make sense. If Heath was the killer, why would he make that video at Peet's? Why fire shots above your head? Wouldn't he want to lay low and stay out of trouble, instead of calling attention to himself?"

Luckily I'd been thinking about this, so I had my answer ready. "Partly, he wanted to scare me into not investigating any more. But mainly I think he felt guilty for killing Olivia. So in his mind, he twisted it so the murder was all Reynolds' fault. Like the whole reason he and Olivia got in that big fight and she ended up dead was because she was going out with Reynolds. So he wanted to punish Reynolds."

Natalie frowned. "That sounds kind of—"

"If it works for O'Keefe, it works for me," Dave interrupted. "Between the DNA and the confession, we've got plenty of evidence."

Natalie gave a little smile and nodded. But I knew she was bursting into flames inside.

Writing the podcast, and recording it that night, went like a dream. Especially because I got to work without Natalie again and bask in Larry's and Erinne's admiration.

I sat on the Hindu throne and read aloud into the mic, *"Yesterday morning, at eleven thirty, Detective O'Keefe called me. We had a match, with a certainty of over ninety-nine point nine nine nine nine percent. The man who killed Olivia Anderson, beyond a doubt . . ."* Dramatic pause. *"Was Robert Heath."*

Larry and Erinne both started clapping, and when we were done we all drank champagne.

When I got home that night, a little tipsy, I walked up the stairs to my apartment and saw light coming from underneath the door. My heart sped up. I opened the door and, sure enough, Jonah was there. He sat on the living room sofa, drinking wine. There was a bottle and a second glass on the table in front of him. He looked up as I sat down on the sofa beside him, but not too close. I didn't want to presume. From the way his legs spread out loosely, I got the feeling he was already a little drunk. But his eyes studied me.

He said, "I truly don't get you."

I poured some wine. "I'm easy," I said. "I'm just a girl from East LA who wants to do good in the world and also . . . " I was about to say "be famous" but then I thought it didn't feel totally accurate. ". . . do my job without worrying about getting fucking fired all the time."

Jonah said, "Sometimes you hurt people."

I swallowed. "That part I hate."

Jonah nodded. Then he leaned over and kissed me. I threw my arms around him like I'd been wanting to since forever. His kiss tasted like wine. His body felt so solid, so strong, as I held him and melted into him.

But then he pulled away. His lips were parted with what I was sure was desire, but his eyes looked a little haunted. "I think I should still sleep on the sofa tonight."

"Okay," I said. I didn't want to seem too needy, so I stood up. "If you change your mind . . ."

He nodded and I went into the bedroom. He didn't change his mind, but when I woke up, he was in the kitchen making us bacon and eggs.

"You want orange juice?" he asked when I came in, still wearing the T-shirt I'd slept in.

"Thanks," I replied, hugging him from behind as he stood at the stove. *We're weathering this storm.*

I went to the office and did a few touch-ups on my newspaper story. Then, at four p.m., the *Clarion* published the story and dropped my podcast. At the same time, Detective O'Keefe gave a press conference at Cambridge Police Headquarters announcing that the police had a new suspect, "thanks to the work of *Boston Clarion* reporter Petra Kovach."

Dave came to my desk and asked, "You wanna come by my office and enjoy the chaos that's about to break out? I bet we get fifty calls in the first half hour from news outlets wanting to interview you."

I was about to say yes, reflexively. *Never say no to the boss!* But then I changed my mind. Maybe it was bad office politics, but what the hell. "I'll come by in a few minutes, Dave. Right now I want to just sit here and soak it in all by myself."

Dave was surprised but not annoyed. If anything, I thought he looked at me with new respect. "No worries. Come by whenever you want."

Sitting in my cubicle, I listened to the podcast. My voice was so loud and strong today. *"I will never forget,"* I heard myself say, *"the sound of that gunshot when Robert Heath killed himself. I will always regret that I could not save him.*

"But I will never regret finding justice at last for Olivia Anderson, and closure for her family: her beloved brother, Eric, and father, Viktor. Most of the world knows Olivia as an angry young woman who threw hand grenades and created controversy. But I knew her as a sweet girl who was a lot like me. She wanted to do good in the world. I loved Livvy, and not a day goes by that I don't miss her and think about the woman she might have become."

I listened to myself crying, in the podcast. I hadn't had to practice those tears. I wasn't proud of everything I'd done these past two weeks. But now that I had climbed out of the cesspool, I'd returned to what journalism really was, at its warm, beating heart: telling the stories of people you cared about, who for whatever reason couldn't tell their own stories.

People like Livvy, and like my Tata.

CHAPTER FIFTY-FOUR

EPISODE 5 WAS—TO no one's surprise—even more successful than our previous episodes. In one day we hit seven million listeners. Dave was so cheerful he looked twenty years younger. The publisher Colin Abernathy, on his way back to Scotland, even put in an appearance at the office so he could shake my hand. With his white hair and twinkling smile, he looked like a fun uncle—not the ruthless, cost-cutting mogul who had almost been responsible for me getting fired.

Dave was right about the media crush. It seemed like every news outlet in the world was desperate to interview me. This time Dave said yes, and I did five TV interviews that first night and five more the next day. I felt like I was shining on-screen. I'd finally gotten the hang of it.

On Twitter, the negative sentiment against me reversed itself. Canceled no more. Some guy tweeted "PETRA WILL KETCH YA!" and got ten thousand likes and counting. A woman tweeted a photoshopped gif of me dancing through flames, captioned, "THERE'S A METHOD TO HER MADNESS!" That got twenty thousand likes.

Even sweeter was when Mama called. "*Moj mišić,*" she sniffed. "To have such success and happiness. I just wish your Tata was still alive." Then she broke down.

I broke down too. "I love you, Mama."

It was just as affecting, in a different way, when I got to see Professor Reynolds again. Chip Martin from Channel 4 set up an interview with both of us together. This was Reynolds' first TV appearance since Livvy's murder, and he was clearly overjoyed to be out of hiding at last.

"People may not like me," he told Chip on-air, "and I get that. I fell in love with an eighteen-year-old college freshman when I was thirty, and that bothers a lot of people. But at least they don't want to kill me anymore." He turned to me. "Petra, you gave me back my life. I can never thank you enough."

I put my hand on his arm. "You just did," I replied.

I never got to see Brandon again, but I saw his famous press conference at the fifty-yard line of the practice field, attended by over a hundred reporters. The Harvard Athletic Department had finally agreed to let him speak publicly. His first two sentences were replayed on TVs, phones, and laptops all across the country. "Okay, guys," he said, "so let me just get this out of the way. Yeah, I'm gay."

He didn't look happy about having to say it, but he didn't seem distraught either. "It's not anybody's business really, and I don't think Petra was right to out me. But I am glad that now we know who killed Olivia. I won't lie in bed wondering about it, like I've done every night for two years."

That very weekend, Brandon played the best game of his life, getting two interceptions and forcing a fumble. Maybe he played more freely, since he was released from the lies and uncertainties that must have caused him so much stress. Or maybe he was extra aggressive because he was so pissed off about getting outed. In any case, the experts now predicted that despite his revelation, he would still get drafted by the third round. The fourth at the very latest. Brandon wouldn't go broke anytime soon.

And then there was the guy I felt most guilty about.

Three days after Episode 5 dropped, I was invited to appear on *Dead to Rights,* Joel Caldwell's CNN show. I was thrilled. I had no idea there would be a surprise guest: Eric.

Coming onto the stage, he looked better than I'd ever seen him, in jacket and tie, smiling, apparently sober. I reached out nervously to shake his hand.

But instead of shaking, he pulled me in for a long hug. I felt my chest fill up inside. After we sat down, Caldwell asked, "So, Eric, what was that hug about?"

Eric looked in my eyes. "When Petra came and started poking around, I'll admit I wasn't sure about her. Then when she told all my family's secrets, I was, you know, devastated." After this obvious reference to his suicide attempt, he went silent for a moment. "But now I realize, she was just doing what she had to, to get the truth. She can't be stressing about people's feelings all the time. She's gotta be like a heavyweight boxer knocking down lies. That's what makes Petra so great. And it all worked out."

Caldwell said, "Yes, it did. I know I speak for everyone all over this land when I say: we're so glad you survived."

"Amen," I said.

The audience applauded solemnly, and Eric nodded to acknowledge them. "Thank you, I'm glad too."

"May I ask how things are going now between you and your father? I mean, you accused him of some pretty terrible stuff."

"All of which I was wrong about. As you can imagine, we have things to work through. But the main thing is, we finally know who killed my sister. And the son of a bitch who did it is dead. Olivia can rest in peace at last. And it's all because of this young woman here," he said, pointing to me.

The audience applauded again, and Caldwell joined them. He said, "It's true. Petra is quite an impressive young journalist. What I love most about Petra is her heart. She's tough and relentless, but it's because she cares so deeply."

I blushed. I thought Caldwell was piling on the compliments just for dramatic effect, but then he invited me to stick around after we finished taping the show. I met with him in the production office, along with the show's two executive producers, a good-looking woman in her fifties with red hair, a short dress, and a rough smoker's voice, and a man in his thirties who wasn't very personable and seemed like a numbers guy.

Caldwell opened the conversation. "Petra, seeing you in person confirms what I thought. You have great presence. You radiate earnestness and compassion. People love you."

In my TV interviews, I'd been training myself to accept compliments graciously without putting myself down. So I just said, "Thank you."

"Now you're probably wondering what this meeting is about . . ." I was. "Well, Sandra here"—he gestured toward the woman producer—"has been after me for the past year to hire some female talent."

Oh my God. I started to get the drift of this conversation. My pulse beat so hard, I could feel it in my ears.

Sandra said, "People are tired of looking at Joel's face all the time. Dashing and debonair though he may be."

"And our demographic is skewing a little old these days."

"Median age fifty-three," said the male producer.

"So what we're wondering is, how would you feel about being co-anchor?"

I was too stunned to speak.

The woman said, "We'd like to try you out. We'll give you a three-month contract."

Caldwell said, "But I'm sure you'll be great at it, and we'll want to hire you permanently. So what do you say?"

I said, "Yes."

* * *

The next night, Jonah and I went to Faneuil Hall for ice cream. As we sat on a bench licking our cones and listening to a street performer play classical guitar, Jonah said, "Two hundred thousand bucks for three months. Not bad."

That was the number the producers and I had agreed on, along with an option for eight hundred thousand a year. I'd gotten advice from both Jonah and Mateo during the negotiations, and I felt like I'd gotten a reasonable deal. I would have taken the job for a lot less.

I said to Jonah, for maybe the tenth time, "I feel bad that I'll be away from you in New York for five days a week."

"I'll be happy to work from there sometimes. Really." He kissed me, and we laughed about the ice cream on our lips. We had made love the night before for the first time since our big fight, or fights. We hadn't talked anymore about getting married, and telling our parents we were engaged, but things were definitely heading in that direction.

Dead to Rights wanted me to start work the following week, while I was still the most famous journalist in America. So the next morning I went into Dave's office at the *Clarion* and gave notice. He tried to get me to stay, talking about matching my salary offer. But when he heard how much money *Dead to Rights* was paying me, he gave up.

"Well, so it goes," he said, his eyes cast down. "I guess we'll stick with Natalie."

My jealousy of Natalie had left me now that my career had taken such an awesome turn. Both of us were just trying to do our jobs in a very stressful business, and she had been trying to catch Livvy's killer too. "She'll do great. The paper will make another million dollars before this is through."

Dave looked up at me and smiled. "You saved my job, you know."
I smiled back. "Yeah, I had that feeling."

"Funny, considering how I tried to fire you."

"*Sort of* funny," I said with a grin, and we shook hands.

Natalie wasn't at the office, so I just wrote her a goodbye email, wishing her well. I was glad neither of us would have to run into each other in the halls anymore.

I did run into Rose the intern, though. I invited her to come down to New York to watch a taping. She said she was interested in working in TV news one day, so I thought that might help her.

My life had become a dream. Five days later I was sitting in the makeup room at the studio on Broadway where *Dead to Rights* was taped, getting ready for my first-ever appearance as co-anchor.

As Elaine, the middle-aged makeup artist, touched up my cheekbones, I gazed up at the TV monitor on the wall. It showed the studio audience, with my mama in the center of the sixth row. With all that money about to come pouring in, I had broken out the credit card and paid for her to fly in from Los Angeles. We were staying in the same Manhattan hotel together, and I'd bought Mama a brand-new dress and treated her to a fancy New York haircut.

Sitting in the audience, beaming, Mama looked so happy. Next to her was Rose. On her other side was Detective O'Keefe, wearing an actual skirt. She had agreed to come here and be interviewed on the show, pushed into it by her captain, who wanted the Cambridge police to get some of the credit for solving the murder. Tonight's show was a live, prime-time special that would run an extra hour and recap the entire murder investigation from start to finish. The show would include new evidence that had surfaced during the past five days against Robert Heath, like the fact he and Livvy shared a hotel room in downtown Boston one night. Also, credit card records put them together two nights before the murder, at a

restaurant in Cambridgeport. The waitress remembered them
shouting at each other. It was further evidence, not that I needed
any, that I had "framed" the right guy.

The five rows in front of Mama and O'Keefe were a big sea of
purple with islands of Livvy. At least that's how it looked to me on
the TV monitor. These rows were occupied by girls and young
women wearing identical purple T-shirts with a photo of fourteen-
year-old Livvy on the front. That was Joel Caldwell's idea. The photo
reminded me of the eager, fresh-faced kid I first met, who was writing an article on how to take care of wounded birds.

Jonah's voice interrupted my musing. He'd come to New York,
too, to be here for my first show. Now he was hanging out with me
in the makeup room. "Wow, will you have to spend this long putting
on makeup for every show?" he asked.

I gestured toward my makeup artist. "Elaine says it gets quicker."

"That's right, honey," Elaine said.

Jonah's phone buzzed. He looked at the display and said, "This is
my office. I gotta take it."

"No worries," I said.

He clicked the phone on. "Hey, what's up?" Moments later he
said, "Why, what's wrong?" Then he said, "Hang on a second."

He turned to me. There was a strange look in his eyes, like he
didn't quite recognize me. "I'm gonna take this in the hall."

I frowned. "Is everything okay?"

Jonah hesitated. "I'll be right back." Then he walked out with his
phone.

I figured there must be some kind of problem at his job.

I was right about that. I just had no idea how bad the problem
would be.

CHAPTER FIFTY-FIVE

Fifteen minutes later, Jonah was still gone. Elaine had just about finished making me TV-beautiful. It was almost time for me to go onstage.

"Oh God," I said.

Elaine gave me a knowing smile. "Nervous?"

"Petrified."

She laughed. "You'll do great."

"You promise?"

"Honey, I've seen your interviews. You're a natural. And you're talking about something you're an expert on."

"You're right, damn it," I said. "Thanks, Elaine."

Just then the door opened and Jonah walked in. Elaine's arm blocked me so I couldn't see his face right away. "Hey, babe, what's up?" I asked.

He stepped toward me. His lips were set in a grim line. "We need to talk."

I frowned, worried. "Sure, go ahead."

He said, "Elaine, do you mind stepping out for a minute?"

"I just need to finish this here," Elaine said, pointing at my left eye.

"Just for a minute," Jonah said.

She looked back and forth between us. "Whatever you say."

As soon as Elaine walked out and closed the door behind her, I glared at Jonah. "What the hell—it's my first day of work!"

"Jesse called."

"I'm supposed to go on in five minutes—"

"You know how there were three DNA profiles on that shoe: you, Olivia, and Robert Heath?"

What the hell is this about? "Yeah."

"Well, Olivia's DNA profile was always a little hinky, Jesse said. Not the technical term, but close enough. Her genetic markers on one part of the black shoelace weren't quite right. So today at the lab he was thinking about it, and he took another look at the report."

I still had no idea where this was going. "Okay, so?"

"So that DNA profile of Olivia was contaminated with *another* profile. And this other profile . . . belonged to a male sibling of hers."

"What? You mean Eric?" That made no sense.

"He's her only sibling, right?"

"How could Jesse possibly know—"

"Same way you know anything with DNA. The patterns of the genetic markers. The degree of sharing."

"But Eric was nowhere near Livvy's dorm room that week. Look, you said the sample was contaminated. Things must've gotten screwed up a little."

"Jesse was certain. He sent me the data and I'm certain too. The profile says that DNA had to belong to a male sibling, not a parent or child or cousin. The sibling spilled a tiny drop of blood on that shoelace."

My heart stopped. *Eric's blood? On Livvy's shoe?*

Jonah said, "Those shoes were brand new, right? We think she never even wore them outside."

I managed to get out, "But Eric wasn't there that night. He was at BU, at business school."

"It's Eric's DNA," Jonah repeated. "From his blood."

I started to protest. Then I shut up. My head was spinning. *That bit of dirt I saw on the shoelace—it was really Eric's blood?*

Jonah said, "So what I'm asking you is, how did Eric's blood *and* Robert Heath's blood both end up on that shoe?"

I knew full well how Heath's blood wound up there. But Eric's— *Oh fuck, is that possible?!*

Elaine poked her head in. "Honey, you're on in three minutes—"

"Okay, thanks," I said robotically.

"I need to finish up—"

"Not now!" I yelled.

Elaine finally shrugged and left a second time.

Could Eric have bled onto Livvy's shoe after he brought it home? When it was inside the cardboard evidence box?

That seemed so unlikely. The shoe was at the very bottom, underneath a lot of clothing and other stuff. Eric would have had to lift up everything else, not bleed on anything, and then bleed from some sort of cut right onto the shoe.

But if that wasn't what happened . . .

My mind raced. I bit my fingernails and went through it all again. From the very first time I met Eric, at the Parting Glass.

Eric, drunk, tells me he knows a secret about the murder. Some "serious mind-blowing shit."

A week later at the Parting Glass, I tell Eric there's a rumor he had incest with his sister. He absolutely freaks out. What if I accidentally got that right? That sixth sense I always felt I had about people— what if it was working overtime that night? Maybe when Eric said he and Livvy used to get drunk together, and then I saw him with that blonde girl who reminded me of Livvy, that got my subconscious mind going.

Jonah said, "Petra—"

"Quiet." I looked away from him and pulled at my lips as I thought.

Eric thinks his stepfather must know about the incest and must have told me. That would explain why I'd said what I said. So Eric fights back. He pretends Livvy was having incest with his stepfather. The Reddit posts back him up.

But Livvy was being cagey with those posts. She wrote them as if they were about a stepfather, when really they were about her brother. Maybe the truth was too uncomfortable to put in writing directly. When their mom died, Livvy needed comfort. And Eric gave it to her, in a very sick way. Maybe at some point the stepfather began to suspect. Maybe later on he even suspected Eric of the murder—but didn't want to tell anyone.

The incest left Livvy feeling dazed and powerless, and alone. She didn't feel she could tell anyone about it, even me. She couldn't release her anger at Eric—she sort of loved him. But her agitation left her vulnerable to the seductiveness of the America Forever community and Robert Heath. She vented her fury at unseen forces, like illegal immigrants.

Well, not totally unseen. She believed one of them had killed her mother.

Then she went to college. She dated other men, including a gay man who didn't place sexual demands on her. That must have been a relief in a way, but also confusing. She started a relationship with Professor Reynolds—another older man, like her brother.

She was finally ready to end things with Eric. She tried to do it over Christmas. But as she said in her barely fictionalized Reddit post, he refused to let her go. So she called him right before spring break. She told him that this time she was finished with him for real.

Something happened during that conversation. Maybe he yelled at her. Made threats. Used violent language. And for the first time, Livvy realized how truly sick their relationship had been. Hell, Eric started having sex with her when she was fourteen and suffering from trauma.

Now she understood that she'd been sexually abused for years and never told anyone. This opened the door to her identifying with Sarah Fain, who also took a long time before speaking up. Livvy realized at last that Sarah was probably telling the truth. She DM'ed Sarah on Snapchat and apologized.

Livvy got ready to do her video. It would be about Sarah—and also about herself. This was the "super fucking personal" stuff she planned to reveal: that she had been abused.

Eric showed up, knocking on her door, still furious at her for threatening to break it off. Probably drunk. She opened her window shade because when he was drinking, he scared her. They got in a fight. She exploded, years of rage bursting out. She told him he was an abuser, a statutory rapist, and she would say so in her video. And then . . .

Then Eric hit her, she stabbed him with the nail file, and he killed her.

He sobered up fast. He got the hell out of there before the blood started leaking out of his shirt or pants, or wherever she stabbed him. Except one drop spilled out when he reached to open the door, and it landed on Livvy's black shoelace.

Ever since then, he'd been drinking. Pretending to be furious at Professor Reynolds to cover up his own crimes. And because it made him kind of forget that he was the killer himself.

But part of him wanted to be punished for what he'd done. His guilt leaked out in strange ways. In his hints to me that there might be more to the murder than the world knew. In his silent admission that he didn't totally believe Reynolds was the killer. In his suicide attempt.

Above all, in his suicide attempt—

"Petra?" Jonah asked. "What are you thinking?"

I opened my eyes. "I think Eric did it."

Jonah's mouth dropped open. "Eric killed her?"

"Yeah."

"But what about Robert Heath's blood? How did that get there?"

I didn't answer, just looked away and shook my head.

"Petra?" He stared at me. "Did you put it there?"

I pulled at my hair, ruining the job the hair person had done. Then Jonah grabbed me and shook me. I was stunned. Jonah had never touched me like that before. His eyes were furious. "Did you put Heath's blood there?"

"I thought he was guilty!" I said. "He confessed, remember? We were both so sure he killed Livvy!" *But when Heath said "I can still see her body lying there on the floor," he must have meant seeing those crime scene photos on the internet.*

Jonah let go of me, roughly. "For God's sake, Petra, how could you do that?"

"I was framing a guilty man!"

"Only he wasn't guilty!"

"What do you want me to do?"

"How could you put me in this position? You made me a participant in your—your crime!"

"I'm sorry! I was trying to do the right thing!"

"You lied to me. Again! And all because you're so desperate about your stupid fucking career!"

"That's not true—"

"All you care about is you!"

"I thought he killed Livvy! What do you want me to do, Jonah?"

"You tell me, Petra. I have no fucking idea!"

I blurted out, "Robert Heath is dead anyway, what does it matter?"

"Because Eric Anderson needs to be in prison!"

"It was a crime of passion. He'll never do anything like that again!"

"Come on, you don't know that."

He was right, I didn't know. Eric had sex with his fourteen-year-old sister. Then he killed her in a drunken rage. He was clearly pathological.

But . . .

"Eric wouldn't go to prison anyway, even if I did say something. There's no evidence against him!"

"Sure there is—there's DNA."

"But the chain of custody is total shit. No judge would ever allow that in court. If I tell the truth, I'll get arrested! For obstructing justice, tampering with evidence—do you want me to go to prison?"

"Jesus fucking Christ."

"It won't help Livvy any, and I'll get fired from here and no newspaper will ever hire me again!"

Jonah's eyes filled with such distaste, my heart broke. He stood up. "Just do whatever you want, Petra."

"Jonah—"

"Goodbye. Lie to somebody else from now on."

He walked out.

Elaine entered, passing him, and bustled toward me. "Honey, it's time to be amazing." She eyed me in alarm. "What have you done to your hair?"

She took me to the set, fixing my waves along the way. I walked slowly, in some altered state where I was unable to hear her chatter.

A couple of producer types walked up, spoke in encouraging tones, and sent me out onto the stage, where bright lights assaulted me. Joel Caldwell came up and shook my hand. He said words to me but it was just sounds without meaning. I knew I was supposed to smile, so I did. I was supposed to look out at the audience, so I did that too.

With the lights shining into my eyes, it was hard to see people. But I knew Mama was there, and Detective O'Keefe. And maybe Jonah, unless he had gone.

The audience rose and applauded for my first day as an anchorperson. And for my glorious success at solving the murder of the century. I stood there listening to their applause and forgot what I was supposed to do.

Oh yes. Smile.

But I didn't seem able to. There was something else I was supposed to do too. If only I could think what it was . . .

Then my eyes adjusted enough so I could see that sea of purple. All those girls. All those pictures of Livvy on their chests.

The audience was still clapping, waiting for me to acknowledge them. But I just stared at all the Livvys.

Justice for Livvy. Nobody can ever give that to her but me.

I raised my eyes toward Mama. She waved to me, looking so ecstatic in her bright new yellow dress. If I told the truth, Mama would be hurt so bad.

Next to her, Detective O'Keefe actually smiled. But if I revealed the truth, what would O'Keefe do to me then? Would she arrest me?

And all the girls with their Livvy T-shirts and everyone else in the audience, applauding for me. Would the whole world turn on me if they found out how I'd lied to them, deceived them, over and over?

I looked at Joel Caldwell, standing on the stage nearby, so full of goodwill. How long would it take him to get rid of me?

I was taking too long to speak. Joel stepped toward me, a question in his eyes, asking if I was ready to say something or did I want him to take over.

Justice for Livvy.

My career will be fucking done.

You're a reporter. The truth will set you free.

I opened my mouth to speak. I wasn't sure what I would say.

"Hello, everybody," I said. My voice felt rusty, but the audience didn't notice. They applauded even louder. I was bathed in their love. It felt so good.

I looked down once more at all the Livvys. Then I raised my arms, asking for the audience to quiet down. Eventually they did.

I cleared my throat. "Tonight's show will be a little different from what you expected," I said. "There's a story I need to tell you."

And then I told it.

EPILOGUE

"AFTER A FEW weeks hanging out at the park after school," the young woman, Jasmine, read aloud to the group, *"me and Ace hooked up. I became an Important person and people respected me. Or at least they pretended to. I don't really care, cause all I know is for the first time in my life, I had a lot of money around me and I could buy whatever I liked. I didn't have a license, but Ace gave me the keys to one of his cars and I could drive it all I wanted. He gave me new boots and new clothes, a ring, some cash to take around, and a couple cell phones. He even bought me an Apple Watch to help me exercise more. He liked me being fit and in shape. So, I went to the gym every day and worked out a lot."*

As Jasmine read, my mind wandered a little. There were eleven women here in the chapel, not including me. That was good—five more than last week. I was planning to edit a collection of their stories and get Mateo to put it out on the internet. In a way this was another form of journalism, and I loved doing it.

Prison was much easier than I had feared. When Detective O'Keefe went gonzo on me, arresting me not only for obstruction and evidence tampering but five related offenses, I was terrified. I ended up with an eighteen-month sentence—or twelve months, with good behavior—at Massachusetts Correctional in Framingham. I thought it would be like *Orange Is the New Black.*

But it wasn't so bad, except for the food and the boredom. I felt oddly peaceful in here, more at ease than I'd been in years. No striving, no fear of getting laid off again. Even Mama had noticed, when she came to visit, how relaxed I seemed.

Mateo had visited too, twice. But Jonah never did. I hadn't seen him since that night at *Dead to Rights,* and I expected I never would. My chest ached when I thought about Jonah and his soft eyes and curly hair, gone forever.

But I knew if anyone deserved to be broken up with, it was me. I had screwed up too many times. Now I'd just have to pick up the pieces and move on.

"When my parents found out I was hanging out with Ace's gang," Jasmine read aloud, *"my dad slapped me. My mom cried and they kicked me out of the house. They were much more worried about the cops coming looking for me and finding them, and deporting them back to Mexico, than they were about anything else. So I moved in with Ace and became his bitch. Making money for him. Whatever he wanted, I would do. I didn't have any place to go back to. I was only sixteen but I couldn't go to the police or child services or anything—they would have deported my parents."*

I thought, *This is the kind of story I want to tell, as a journalist. I'll find some way to do it even if I don't make money at it.*

Because stories mattered. Even my investigation of Livvy's murder, flawed and messy though it was, had made a difference.

In the end, I did get justice for Livvy.

It didn't look like that would happen at first. As I'd told Jonah, the screwy chain of custody for Livvy's shoes made the DNA useless. There was no other solid evidence against Eric, so even though the whole world now believed he was guilty, there was nothing the police could do.

But Eric's own feelings of guilt became his undoing. After I revealed on *Dead to Rights* that he had killed Livvy—*"Blood doesn't lie,"* I'd said, and that became a meme—Eric began drinking even more heavily, and acting more erratically. On New Year's Eve he reeled into an Alcoholics Anonymous meeting in Brooklyn dead drunk and proceeded to share with everybody there that he had killed his sister. The other alcoholics were stunned, but one of them had the presence of mind to turn on her recording app. She caught Eric slurring weepily, "I didn't mean to do it. But she cut me and I grabbed that stupid piece of shit lamp and swung it and she just fell down. I didn't mean to . . ."

Recording conversations without the other person's consent was legal in New York. So that recording made its way to the Brooklyn Police, and from there to Detective O'Keefe in Boston, who had put off her much-desired retirement to try and nail the one big fish that got away. She promptly arrested Eric.

His drunken confession might not have been enough to convict him. But Eric couldn't take hiding from the truth anymore. As he put it in court when he allocuted, "I knew unless I confessed for real, I'd probably try to kill myself again, and next time I'd do it right." So in the end, Eric pled guilty to manslaughter and was sentenced to ten to fifteen years in prison.

As for the others . . .

Viktor went back to Sweden without ever speaking to the media, so I had no idea how he was doing. I always wondered if he had suspected his stepson of the incest and murder. My guess was yes, and that was why Eric acted so mixed about Viktor when I first met him at the Parting Glass.

Danny Madsen wasn't talking to reporters either; hopefully his reputation was permanently destroyed and he was miserable.

But Brandon Allen got drafted in the third round, as the experts predicted, by the New England Patriots. Sarah Fain was doing well too. She was teaching and coaching crew at a small private school in Maine for kids with behavioral problems.

As I looked around the chapel at my fellow inmates, I wondered if Eric was handling prison as well as I was.

I had mixed feelings about him. He was a bad guy who had done some truly horrible things. But he knew it, and he felt guilty. He didn't *want* to be a bad guy. I wondered if prison, and getting older, might change Eric.

I hoped so. And I imagined Livvy, the sweet girl who wanted to save wounded creatures, would probably hope so too.

"Then things started to go bad with Ace," Jasmine read. *"He was just not into me anymore. Some of the other guys started to harass me. They touched me a few times. When Ace didn't stop them, they touched me more. Ace had a lot of guns and I knew where he kept them. So one night..."*

Jasmine looked up shyly. "That's as far as I got. I'm gonna try to finish it tomorrow."

"You're doing a great job," I said. "I can't wait to hear what happens next."

"Yeah, this shit is better than Stephen King," Charysse said. She was a middle-aged woman with a big scar on her chin.

"Let's all give Jasmine a big round of applause."

The other inmates and I clapped and slapped Jasmine five. Then I asked, "Who wants to go next?"

A blonde girl named Lauren raised her hand.

"Cool, let's hear it," I said.

As Lauren stood up and started to read, I thought about how I'd weave all these women's stories into a feature-length piece.

Then I thought about how I used to sit at the kitchen table with Tata, reading the newspaper together and talking about all the different stories.

I smiled. I was home at last.

AUTHOR'S NOTE

I began writing this novel because I'm a huge fan of crime podcasts like *Serial* and *Accused* and crime documentaries like *Making a Murderer* and *Jinx*. At the same time, I'm a skeptic of these shows. I'm intrigued by how reporters sometimes omit key details or distort the truth in order to tell a better story. In this ultra-competitive era, getting clicks and followers can be more important than getting the truth.

Another inspiration for *Killer Story* is all the men and women I know in their twenties who are fiercely dedicated to going into journalism despite the huge obstacles they face. Journalism is such a rapidly changing field, with newspapers dying, internet news sites unable to find workable economic models, and decent paying jobs increasingly hard to get. These aspiring young journalists have a sense of mission that I admire. Their passion refuses to be denied.

I also found inspiration in my own life. All TV writers get fired at least once in their careers, or to use the industry parlance, they "don't get their contracts renewed"; and that has happened to me as well. There are many reasons TV writers don't get renewed—often it's as simple as, there's a new head writer who wants to hire people they've worked with before. But whatever the reason, losing your job is painful.

And it happens all the time in the newspaper industry. Will Doolittle, a reporter for the *Glens Falls Post-Star*, told me that when he started out twenty years ago, they had fifty reporters; now they're down to eight. All over the country, newspapers are laying people off or going under.

So I created a main character in *Killer Story*, Petra Kovach, who is about to get laid off from yet another journalism job. She obsesses about all the things that just about everyone I know who's ever lost their job, including myself, stresses about: Did I choose the right path in life? Is what happened somehow my fault? Will I ever get a job in the industry again?

But Petra gets back up off the mat and keeps on fighting.

As I've indicated, Petra is based partly on me; I identify with her feelings and forgive all her flaws. She's a young woman who's trying to make it in a very difficult business. Petra is also inspired by a brilliant young woman I know who, like Petra, is a first-generation immigrant with big dreams from an economically disadvantaged family. She's working her way through law school now.

Olivia is inspired by the alt-right media figure Tomi Lahren. While I'm not a fan of Olivia's politics, I found it intriguing to speculate about all the pressures that might have transformed this sweet, caring young girl into somebody who is, on the surface at least, a pretty unlikeable person.

Writing *Killer Story* gave me a renewed, healthy skepticism of the news media, along with a new appreciation for journalists like Petra who overcome all kinds of obstacles to bring us the truth about the world. I hope you are as captivated by Petra as I am, and that you didn't guess the killer until the very end!

BOOK CLUB DISCUSSION QUESTIONS

1. Do you feel journalists have an obligation to tell the truth as they observe it, even at the expense of other people? For instance, was Petra right to out the gay football player and release a young woman's juvenile criminal record in order to catch the murderer?

2. Sometimes, when Petra's boss tells her to do something questionable, she does it despite her reservations. Do you think you would have had the courage to fight back harder against the boss?

3. Petra has been repeatedly laid off, and all of her actions at the job are affected by that. Have you or a loved one ever gotten laid off? Did that change your point of view about Petra?

4. From your perspective, how did Petra's childhood and upbringing affect her actions on the job?

5. In the end, Petra catches the killer and gets justice for the victim. In your opinion, does this redeem her ruthless tactics?

6. Jonah sees things in black and white, while Petra sees things in shades of gray. Is one way better than the other?

7. Are you glad that Jonah broke up with Petra? Why or why not?

8. Did you guess the killer? Who did you think did it?

9. Success in journalism now is often measured by how many clicks a story gets. How do you think this affects journalists?

10. After catching the killer, Petra gets sentenced to a year and a half in prison—one year with good behavior. Do you think she deserves a year in prison?

11. Does *Killer Story* make you question the veracity of what you read in the newspaper, see on TV, or hear in podcasts? How do you try and figure out the truth about things you read about?

PUBLISHER'S NOTE

We hope that you enjoyed *KILLER STORY* and want to suggest that you read Matt Witten's prior novel, *THE NECKLACE*, a chilling psychological thriller—if you have not already.

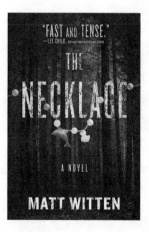

THE NECKLACE

Small-town, down-and-out waitress Susan Lentigo is determined to make her way from her Upstate New York home to North Dakota. The driving force: to witness the execution of the man who murdered her daughter twenty years ago. But what she finds along the way makes her trip a heart-pounding race against the clock.

"This is as fast and tense as a great thriller should be, but it's full of warmth and humanity too—one small-town woman's quest for the most poignant kind of justice you could imagine. Buy it today and read it tonight!"
—LEE CHILD,
New York Times best-selling author

"*The Necklace* is an addictively readable story of a mother's quest for justice. Surprising, propulsive, and poignant. I inhaled this novel."

—MEG GARDINER,
Edgar Award–winning author

We hope that you will enjoy reading *THE NECKLACE* and that you will look forward to more of Matt Witten's novels to come.

If you liked *KILLER STORY*, we would be very appreciative if you would consider leaving a review. As you probably already know, book reviews are important to authors and they are very grateful when a reader makes the special effort to write a review, however brief.

For more information, please visit Matt Witten's website:
www.matwittenwriter.com

Happy Reading,
Oceanview Publishing
Your Home for Mystery, Thriller, and Suspense